Crime, Australian history, and international politics are all passionate interests of author Greg Barron. He has lived in North America, New South Wales and in and around Katherine, Northern Territory. He once crossed Arnhem Land on foot and has a passion for outback landscapes. Published by HarperCollins Australia and Stories of Oz Publishing, Greg's books are gutsy page-turners that have won a wide readership and critical acclaim.

gjbarron@outlook.com
Facebook.com/storiesofoz
Facebook.com/gregbarronauthor
gregbarron.com.au

ALL BOOKS AVAILABLE AT OZBOOKSTORE.COM, libraries, and good bookshops.

SCAN to visit ozbookstore.com

Also by Greg Barron

HarperCollins Publishers Australia
Rotten Gods
Savage Tide
Lethal Sky
Voodoo Dawn (short fiction)

Stories of Oz Publishing
The Hammer of Ramenskoye (short fiction)
Camp Leichhardt
Galloping Jones and Other True Stories from Australia's History
Red Jack and the Ragged Thirteen
Outlaw: The Story of Joe Flick
The Time of Thunder
The Last Days of Dom Sebastian
Beyond the Big Bend
Will Jones and the Dead Man's Letter
Will Jones and the Blue Dog
The Pedestrian
Wild Dog River

For junior readers:

High Country Caper
Gulf Country Adventure

WHISTLER'S BONES

Greg Barron

Stories of Oz acknowledges the traditional custodians of Country throughout Australia and their connections to the landscapes on which we live and work. We pay our respects to elders past and present and extend that respect to all Aboriginal people. We pay tribute to tens of thousands of years of storytelling, and artistic tradition.

First published 2018 by Stories of Oz Publishing
This edition 2025 by Stories of Oz Publishing
PO Box K57
Haymarket NSW 1240
ABN: 0920230558
facebook.com/storiesofoz
ozbookstore.com
admin@ozbookstore.com

The right of Greg Barron to be identified as the author of this work has been asserted by him in accordance with the Copyright Amendment (Moral Rights) Act 2000

 A catalogue record for this book is available from the National Library of Australia

ISBN: 9780648062745

Cover Design: Pixelstudio
Interior screen prints by Catriona Martin

Dedicated to the men and women of Australia's history, from the Dreamtime to today, whose stories still need to be told.

Author's Note

This is a work of fiction blended with fact. The story is based on the life of drover, stockman, and adventurer Charlie Gaunt, who, as an old man in the 1930s, wrote of his experiences in the Northern Standard Newspaper. Yet, there were many gaps. He rarely mentioned his feelings or anything of his personal life. In this novel I have attempted to build him into a complete person, with flaws, desires, relationships and regrets.

I have presented this world of the late 1800s, including the often brutal frontier, in the way Charlie saw and experienced it. The book therefore contains words, scenes and descriptions that readers may find confronting. Indigenous people, particularly those with links to Northern Australia, should read with care.

Excerpts from Charlie's articles at the beginning of chapters are his own words as originally written; only minor punctuation has been changed. In some places in the novel, usually dialogue, I've used a line or two verbatim from Charlie's articles, as altering them seemed pointless.

I am indebted to many people who helped with the research and production of this novel. Lesley Steabler, Steve Russell, Rob and Claudia West, Lyn and (the late) Stewart Dundas, the welcoming crew at Broadmere Station, Brian Cook, Bob Barron, my wife Catriona, sons Daly and James and all my friends and family.

Thanks to my inspiring writer mates, like Peter Watt, Nicole Alexander, Lily Malone, Jenn McLeod, Desley Polmear and many others. But thanks most of all, to the loyal readers who make the long hours of research and writing such a pleasure.

Greg Barron

Eungai Creek, 2025

PROLOGUE

I take no sides with the black or the white. I know them both, and as
Mark Twain says: 'The more I see of men, the better I like dogs.'

January 3, 1933

I know what that cunning bastard is up to. A born thief, old Bismarck
has lately taken to wandering about, out here on the Two-mile. I see him
amble past with his opium-crazed eyes and tangled mess of black hair.
Known for his nimble fingers in and around Pine Creek, I suspect that
he sees an old pensioner like me as easy pickings.

The Two-mile Creek winds its way out of dry slopes in a shallow
channel, with a few ratty pandanus palms and some salmon gums. Dry
for most of its length, the only decent hole in the creek lies just below
the shack I built from cypress poles and corrugated iron. I have a bed in
one corner, a serviceable kitchen bench, and a table I made from rough-
sawn planks. On top sits a Royal typewriter I've been learning to use.
Fred Thompson from the Northern Territory Standard newspaper has
kindly loaned it to me for the purpose of writing down my adventures.
For three weeks I have stared at that infernally clever device and found
myself unable to start. I typed up ten pages from one of the dime Western
novels that sit in a stack beside my bed, just to get the feel of the keys.

The brothers rode into town with their six-guns loose in their
holsters. Judge Hall was about to learn that you don't cross a Robinson.

But it's no use, I'm distracted by that thieving wretch Bismarck.
That's his whitefeller name, anyhow. He calls himself Koonbianjo, and
lives in the blacks' camp near the railway line. Like most of them he is
addicted to opium, thinking of nothing but lifting an honest man's

possessions, trading them for another pipe of dope.

It's only a matter of time before he comes again. After an hour wasted staring at the typewriter, I see through the windows his tall dark figure leave the road and walk sidelong past, casing the joint. His opium pipe sits between his lips, avarice glittering in his eyes.

I switch my gaze to the Lee-Enfield carbine that sits on wooden pegs above the door. I don't want to use it. Many years have passed since I fired a shot in anger. Yet, there is enough of the old Charlie in me to act.

I rise from the table, grab the rifle and open the bolt to check the spring-loaded brass cartridges below, closing it again to drive one into the chamber. I saunter out the door, holding the weapon at my hip. I'm a bony old bastard but I can hold a gun steady.

'Keep walking boy,' I say. 'And don't come back, or I'll put a hole in you.'

The insolent stare makes my blood boil. I know that he is biding his time.

Two days later, when my pension cheque falls due, I prepare for my walk into Pine Creek. Leaving a pumpkin pie cooling in my camp oven, I take more than my usual care with securing the hut. The windows are hinged shutters, corrugated tin, and I lash them down with greenhide rope. The door bolt padlocks shut, and I drop the key in my top pocket.

The walk into town takes an hour, and I call first at the post office, where I collect my cheque. I cash it at Ah Toy's store – that fat, smiling Chinaman standing behind the counter. Seventeen shillings and sixpence buys a man very little. I get a bag of rice, some tea, and a mean little bar of home-made soap. I wander over to the butcher's shop for bacon bones. As usual I have enough money left for a tumbler of rum at Playfords Hotel, but even that luxury tastes sour on my tongue. The thieving mongrel Bismarck fills my thoughts. It's a strange thing. Apart from aiming a rifle at him I have not lifted a finger, but all the old feelings are already damming up inside.

When I get home, my worst fears are realised. The shutter on the northern side hangs, broken, from its hinges. The lashings have been cut with a sharp blade, nails levered out, and iron sheets disarranged. Inside, the place has been ransacked.

My tobacco box is open, and empty. The shelves bare. Even my pumpkin pie has been scraped from the camp oven and eaten.

I take one of the pages that sit piled up ready for use in the typewriter and make a list of all the missing things. One pie. One tin of Capstan, a couple of old tobacco plugs and a pipe. One small sack of flour. One of sugar. Four pumpkins. This last infuriates me the most. I grew them myself, painstakingly watered with buckets carried up from the hole in the creek.

I lock up as best I can, walk out to the roadway and start towards town, but the schoolteacher comes along in his Model T Ford and pulls over. He's a tall, gangling bastard, all brains and no common sense, but with family money behind him.

'Hey Charlie, you alright?'

'That mongrel Bismarck, he's robbed me.'

'Damn it all,' he says. 'Jump in.'

At Pine Creek, I get myself dropped outside the Police Station. Constable Ronnie Pryor is the boss, half asleep on the verandah with his hat brim over his eyes. I'd heard that there was trouble at the pub last night and more than likely he's had little sleep.

Together with Constable Greville and a black tracker we drive back out to the Two-mile in the police truck. The three of them walk around my room, surveying the ransacked shelves, clicking their tongues and talking in low voices.

Most of their interest centres on a broad, bare footprint outside, underneath the window. No white man's footprint that. Pryor sets his tracker on the spoor, then sticks a monocle in his eye and starts peering into every corner of my hut. It's all a waste of time, for the thief has left nothing apart from that footprint and a mess.

'There's no need for the Sherlock an' Watson routine,' I say. 'It was that bloody Bismarck, who done it. The bastard's been casing the place for days.'

Pryor ignores me, the surly bastard, waiting until the tracker gives up and we all pile in the truck again.

I'm seething when we reach the blacks' camp, and there's the thief, squatting by the fire. I see from his eyes that he is rotten from the pipe. There are three lubras there, each as starved-looking as the next. One has a piccaninny clamped to her hips as she stands. Another has a sore on her arm that looks like leprosy to me, and you better believe that I've seen it plenty. The weekly truck must have missed her, for these camp blacks hide the disease so as not to be taken away.

'Hey boy,' says Pryor to Bismarck. 'Me-feller goin' search yer wurlie, orright?'

The thief stands up, complaining, and the policeman puts a hand on his chest and pushes him gently backwards. 'Now just get your lubras out of the way and we'll make it quick.'

I watch as Pryor's black tracker goes through that mean little wurlie. He's a Queensland boy originally and he hates these local blacks: takes delight in rummaging through Bismarck's rubbish. The smell of smoke and rotten old meat scraps and piccaninny shit fills my nostrils. The search takes no time at all, and of course he finds a handkerchief I hadn't missed but I know is mine, along with a small calico bag and a straight-stem tobacco pipe.

I snatch the things back, and that old anger comes like a wave. 'Now arrest him,' I demand, pointing at Bismarck.

'All in good time, Charlie.'

'Bugger you Pryor, do yer fucking job.'

'I need to talk to him first.'

I reach out, take a pinch of Bismarck's ear and twist. 'Own up, you ragamuffin.'

Now that thieving old wretch puts on an act fit for the stage. His knees buckle, and he wails. 'Not me, owww, never done it. Galloping Paddy and Short Nipper done it. I seen 'em.'

'Leave him Charlie,' Pryor says to me. 'Let me deal with it.' Then, to the thief; 'Now Bismarck, you're in a pile of trouble, so answer truly, did you really see Galloping Paddy and Short Nipper rob Mister Gaunt's hut?'

'Yeh boss. I seen 'em.'

'Then where did you get that pipe an' handkerchief from?'

'I been find 'em other side of the creek near Gaunt's place, close up alonga small-fella fire.'

'Can you show me this fire?'

'Yeh boss.'

Now we have this charade while the lying mongrel takes us all down the creek until he finds some old campfire and he points and says. 'That's where I been find them things.' And then he shows us where he was supposedly standing when he saw Galloping Paddy and Short Nipper rob my hut. Of course it was four hundred yards away and through the scrub there's no way he could have seen a thing.

Finally, when we get back to my hut, my mate Jack is waiting there. Like me, Jack also lives on the Two-mile, a little further along. He's an old rascal, with whiskers at all angles and a battered old felt hat.

'I heard you had a break-in, Charlie.'

I point at Bismarck, who is still with us, probably hoping for a lift back to his camp now that he has muddied the waters of his crime. 'Yep, I reckon this mongrel Bismarck done it.'

'Well, that's a funny thing,' Jack says. 'Bismarck turned up at my hut earlier today and sold me two plugs of tobacco and a tin o' Capstan.' He lifts a tin from his pocket. 'Look familiar?'

Pryor screws up his eyes suspiciously. 'What time was this?'

'Ar, about eleven.' Jack waves a hand at the poor looking nag he'd fixed to a verandah post. 'I was shoein' the horse when he came.'

I make a face at Pryor. 'So now go and do your duty.'

'Alright gents, I'll arrest him. Selling stolen goods is good enough for me.'

But Bismarck is no fool, he's followed every word and now he takes off into the bush like a dingo. For all his age he's fleet, dodging and zigzagging in case one of the policemen sends a bullet after him.

'Aren't ya going to chase the bastard?' I shout at Pryor. His mate, Greville, is even more useless, lounging back and smiling.

'Nah, he'll be back at the camp in the morning,' Pryor says. 'I'll arrest him then.'

That night, I light my kerosene lamp and sit at the table before the typewriter. I can't even muster the energy to type the words from page eleven of the dime Western I've been trying to copy. Maybe I can't see the point of writing other men's words.

I stare at a blank page and try to force the words to come. I have told and retold the stories of my youth and middle age so many times, with my knees under so many different tables that I can almost recite them by heart. But still my fingers won't move on the keys.

I hear the door slam. I know straight away that Bismarck has come back from the bush to finish me off for fingering him. He's a vindictive bastard, and as cunning as a snake.

He walks so softly that I can scarcely hear him coming. He smells like the bush; campfire smoke and gamey old meat.

I start to turn, but too slow. He whips a garrotte around my neck, and the hard cord bites deep. My eyes stare upward, rolling back so I can see his black face. Blood runs down over my bony chest. I begin to feel weak from lack of breath. My mind flashes back to when I was a stripling; a boy with fire in his eyes, and a thirst for new horizons. I understand what I have to write. From the beginning. Everything. The truth. I want to write it all. Every breath of my life. Every stream I crossed and every kiss; every mile I walked or rode.

As Bismarck's cord bites deeper into my neck I begin to fight. There is a story to be told, and I must live to tell it.

CHAPTER ONE

As I write these lines, an old age pensioner, existing on a mere pittance
… a picture like a cinema picture passes before my eyes.

Sandhurst (Bendigo) 1880

Hooves thundered on the hard-packed dirt as I urged my mare, Constance, across the arena, holding her at a canter with a touch of the spurs. My breath burned in my nostrils, and my fifteen-year-old muscles ached from hard riding.

The catcalls and yells of my mates who lined the rails like sparrows on a wire were pitched to carry over the thump of machinery, for we were down at the showgrounds off Barnard Street, across the road from the Royal Hustler's Mine. A light winter rain had only recently stopped falling, leaving a wet sheen on the mullock heaps and poppet heads.

I was absorbed in a game we called feather-and-flag. The method was to start in a backwards position, turn and gather speed, take a sharp bend around a barrel, then lean down from the saddle, attempting to scoop up a goose feather stuck quill-first in a pail filled with sand. There were six barrels in all, and six feathers. All six had to be dumped into a bucket at the end of the course to finish. Even one misplaced feather meant disqualification.

Having failed twice to get Constance running straight enough to reach the last feather, I reined in and started backing her up to the starting mark. I blocked out the shouted advice of my mates, the unceasing machinery and the sound of someone hammering nearby. I fancied my chances at winning the game. I was a capable horseman, even then. I lived to ride, and thought of little else from dawn to dusk.

A feeble but welcome sun burst out from the clouds, and I appreciated the better light as I settled Constance with her rear hoof just behind the mark. At that moment I saw a young lady of my acquaintance, Margaret Anne Croxton, hurrying down Park Street, towards the arena, in a yellow dress. I took a moment to appreciate her trim waist, slim neck and full bust. Not only that, but she had blonde hair down to her waist, and a face alive with cheeky good looks.

Margaret Anne was the niece and ward of the Reverend Croxton, the Church of England minister. The Reverend stood six-foot-tall in his black leather boots, and had a voice like thunder. He had ears so big they were almost see-through, with red veins that glowed like river deltas, and nose hairs that curled out to meet his stiff moustaches.

'Pleasure,' he would shout from the pulpit, 'is God's warning bell for sin!'

Horse and feather forgotten for a moment, I stared across at Margaret Anne.

'Charlie,' she called out. I waved back, confused at the serious tone of her voice. I guessed that something momentous had occurred. But I wanted to ignore it, at least for long enough to show the girl my horsemanship.

'Geddup,' I called, jagging Constance's flank with my left spur and twitching the reins to the right so she turned on her hindquarters, now facing the barrels. My eyes moved from Margaret Anne's face and body, to the task at hand. My weight shifted forward, and my backside touched the saddle but lightly as my mare straightened and sprang into the gallop off her hindquarters. The reins moved in my hand without conscious direction, and I did not heed the cup-sized dollops of wet earth that flew from my mare's hooves.

Constance came smoothly around the first barrel, her strides shortening and rhythm changing to keep her turn narrow. I plucked this first feather easily, for the feathers get lower each time, on decreasingly high stands, so that the last pail stood on the ground itself, making it difficult to grab from saddle-height. The second feather came into my hand with perfect timing.

I rode in tune with my horse, guiding her with foot and rein without conscious thought. The first five feathers were soon bunched in my fist. All but the last. I focussed, as if that feather alone was my life's goal, then straightened, urging Constance on.

This was the key moment, lining her up perfectly for the next stage, my vision on the feather only – this final test of the relationship I had nurtured with my horse. At the perfect time I transferred the reins to my left hand, swung my body down, close to those dancing hooves with their shoes of steel. Then, my arm at the limit, I realised that I would miss grabbing the feather by a whisker.

I felt the saddle start to slip, wishing that I had checked and tightened the girth one more time. Seconds away from hurtling to the ground, I heard a warning shout from one of my mates on the rails. Yet the slip of the saddle gave me those few inches I needed.

With my thumb and forefinger quivering I snatched the goose feather. But I was not out of trouble yet. Getting back up, with the rail looming, was now the problem. Constance whinnied in fear, the saddle continuing to slide, my unbalanced weight upsetting her.

My only hope was my left foot, still hooked around the cantle. I used the spring-tight muscles of my abdomen, coiling up, swinging with the momentum, already starting to turn Constance before I was fully back in my seat. At the last moment I paused to drop all six feathers into the waiting bucket.

With a deft change to my seat and light pressure on the reins I pulled up just a few yards from Margaret Anne, raising my hat high in victory while the spectators applauded. I grinned at the young woman, separated only by the post and rail fence.

'Charlie,' she called again. 'I've been sent to fetch you. It's your da … he's … passed away.'

I dismounted, taking a grip on Constance's bridle with my right hand, and looking down at the ground, rearranged the words she had just said in my mind.

'Of course your ma wants you home right now,' she went on.

'Yeah, sorry. Just give me a minute, I'll come 'round through the gate.'

Leading Constance, I followed Margaret Anne dumbly. I didn't know what to think or feel. My father – John Gaunt by name – had been sick for years, his body bloated with dropsy, and his liver riddled with cirrhosis. As he shuffled down the street children would follow and taunt him. Old Fatty Gaunt, with a chin that hung like dewlaps on a bull over his collar, arms like sausages.

Once one of the State of Victoria's brightest young magistrates, years of boozing had seen my father struck off the roll. His final government appointment was here to Sandhurst, to perform the duties of Paymaster and Receiver. It was his last chance, and we all knew it.

We'd settled into a house rented from the Parish, on Rowan Street, within walking distance of the offices where Da worked, and the Masonic Hall he attended weekly. In the afternoons Da would spread out on the lounge with the Argus or Advertiser, reeking of vomit and whisky, reading aloud of the chase for Ned Kelly and his gang around Benalla.

Ma was ashamed of him, but in public she was unfailingly loyal – at church, on the street, and when a clerk arrived to see why he was not at his desk.

'I've come to fetch Mister Gaunt,' the clerk would call from the gate.

'He's poorly,' Ma would say, standing behind the half-open front door, hair parted down the middle, barley curls around her ears.

'Again, Missus Gaunt? There's five hundred men will be lining up for their pay packets this afternoon. What in blazes can I tell them?'

'In t'name of sweet baby Jesus, can you just let him alone for a day or two so the poor man can mend?'

My elder brother William, my sister Marion and I all attended the Church of England school, run by the Reverend Croxton next to the All Saints Parish church. Nellie was still too young for school. William was a scholar, while I stared out the windows, looking out over Pall Mall and the business district, through a goldfields haze of fog, smoke and dust. My imagination roamed over distant horizons, rays of sunshine touching golden plains of waving grass and far oceans. In my room, by candlelight, I devoured books by Ryder Haggard, Daniel Defoe, and the work of

19

Australian poets like Adam Lindsay Gordon.

My heroes were drovers wearing dusty felt or cabbage-tree hats, drinking beer from frosted glasses outside the Metropolitan Hotel. Those restless souls filled my heart with longing for wide spaces where no white man had trod, for wild rivers that flowed like galloping horses, and mountains glowing red hot in a late afternoon sun.

Meanwhile, his dropsy worsening, and entering the final stages of alcoholism, Da was dismissed from government service for 'gross neglect of duty.' At around the same time, my grandfather back in Yorkshire died – he had been an alderman in Leeds – and we expected a decent inheritance.

Da coped with his disgrace and worsening health with gallons of single malt whisky. And now he was dead.

Nudging my mare with an elbow or shoulder occasionally when she tried to cut in front of me, we reached our little house in Rowan Street. Margaret Anne went to join her uncle, who was consoling Ma, while I dismounted and led Constance into the yard. I unsaddled my horse and gave her a pail of chaff before heading inside.

A small crowd had gathered in the sitting room. I wished William was there. I wasn't ready to be the man of the house. Ma hugged me so tight I thought my ribs would crack.

'Oh, Charlie,' she said. 'It's a blessing for him really.'

Yet, it was no blessing for us. It turned out that Da had not troubled himself to pay rent. The Church Wardens gave us seven days to vacate the premises.

'There are debts,' Ma said, 'and we won't be able to use Da's bank account for weeks, maybe months. I'm sorry, but we have t'sell everything.'

Like any young bloke my thoughts were mostly on myself.

'Even Constance?'

Ma squeezed my hand. 'Yes … I'm sorry.'

'What will happen to us?'

'I've sent word t'your Aunt Charlotte and Uncle Henry in Ballarat.

We'll go there for a short time, until we find our feet.'

I said nothing, hating the thought of living on the charity of my aunt and uncle. But it was selling Constance that upset me the most.

On the day of Da's funeral the four of us set off down Rowan Street and around the corner to church. Ma was dressed all in black, hand in hand with Nellie and I. Marion walked alongside. Ma looked grimly proud, refusing to let the world see her ruin. The broad streets were busy with carriages, drunks sleeping under trees and in alleyways. The old widows who haunted the church like grey ghosts were gathering for the service in the courtyard, shepherded by the tall and severe figure of Reverend Croxton.

I dreaded the interior of that squat and unimaginative church of yellow stone, weighed down with the Saints and their tears, the candles and windows not enough to beat back the gloom. My eyes roamed the pews and found them almost empty. My father had become a pariah, a laughing stock, and few of his old colleagues had come.

When I had settled into the front pew, half-listening to the service and holding my mother's hand, I tried to understand what I felt for the man in the coffin.

Home had for years been a place where we walked on eggshells. If Da was sober he was likely to be brittle and hungover, and a careless shout would earn a clout under the ear. If he was drunk things could be much worse.

'What did you say to y'mother, Charles?' Da would demand, in the Yorkshire accent he had never lost. 'Damned if I'll hear a whelp a'mine show disrespect to his ma.'

'Settle down John, the boy didn't mean anything.'

'Get away from him, dammit Aggie, I won't take insolence from a brat ... my father was a gentleman and if he were here he'd thrash the boy senseless.'

When Da's tempers were bad, and I was dim-witted enough to get caught, he belted me with his hand, a lump of wood, or a broom handle. He never hit my mother, however, just bombarded her with sarcasm; the dried-out carcass of his sense of humour. I learned to spend as few hours at home as possible.

The beatings grew worse, and for the first time, at the age of fourteen and a half, I tried to fight back. It started when I came home late one evening, sitting down with filthy hands, to the supper table.

'Look at the state of yer,' Da shouted. 'You wretch, I've a good mind to …'

No one at the table dared breathe. That's what it was like at our house. Knowing what was coming, I walked out to the back yard, slamming the door. Da cornered me between the water tank and the wall, slapping me twice around the head with a huge, open hand.

'You think life's a game,' he accused. 'Yer've responsibilities and duties and you think you can just shirk it all and do whatever you like. Treat yer Ma and Da like goats. It's time you were learned a proper lesson.'

Almost unconsciously, blinking back tears of pain, I raised my fists, more to protect my face from the coming flurry of punches than anything. My stance came naturally; turning sideways with my left foot forward, chin down just like I was sparring in the gymnasium after school.

He chuckled, deep in the back of his throat. 'You want to fight your own Da, you stripling? Let's see then.'

I'd done enough boxing by then for instinct to take over. My left jab flew, aimed for Da's heart, but his body was so heavy that it seemed to absorb my hand and the energy behind it. Before I could follow up with another jab to the chin he threw an open-palm swing that collided with the side of my head. I fell sideways to the ground. Thank God there was grass or I might have dented my skull.

I scampered to my feet and tried to run for the door, back to Ma and the others. He grabbed me by the back of the neck and lifted me off the ground. Even then he was a powerful man.

'You never run away from a fight,' he screamed, spittle flying from his lips.

'Yes, Pa.'

'And don't ever stop until they know who's boss. Don't be cowed, boy, for once you be so marked you're no better than a cur. Now get inside and eat your supper.'

Now, looking for distractions during that dour funeral, I picked Margaret Anne out of the choir. She looked the image of a minister's niece. Her hair was braided close to the back of her head, its glory hidden. She wore a white robe with purple-dyed edges, with a white peony pinned to her breast. Yet, her body shifted constantly, irked by sitting still, and her eyes wandered while her uncle delivered his sermon.

While I enjoyed looking at her, my mind roamed on to thoughts of my utter despair at having to sell my beautiful horse. She was truly mine, for Ma insisted that each of us children be given our portion of the inheritance money that came from our grandfather. She made sure that this was done before Da squandered the lot on booze, a process that took him only a few months.

My older brother William used the funds to get out – setting off for England to study medicine. Surgery was a family calling on Ma's side. The girls set their money aside for dowries and spent hours at department stores trying on fashionable clothes. I was different. I was keenly aware that I had been born an Australian. Her rivers were my blood, her red deserts my heart. Wanderlust was in my veins. I longed to know the outback, to see the core of this land where I had been born. That I felt such an affinity for.

Like any self-respecting colonial boy, I spent my inheritance on a horse. Constance was three and half years old when I first slipped the bridle over her soft ears. She had come from a travelling horse breaker, who told me that she had thoroughbred and Arab bloodlines with a dash of Cape or Timor pony. Her coat was a light shade of chestnut known as sorrel, but with three white socks and a blaze on her nose. She was long in the legs but strongly built, with a deep chest and wide nostrils.

There was enough money left over for a saddle, riding boots and concertina leggings to go with them. I thought myself the flashest young bloke in town, and spent every spare moment at the showgrounds with like-minded friends, learning new skills, and pushing our mounts to the limit. I loved her, and now I had to sell her. Unless …

I was a pall bearer, and the weight of my father's bloated body was a strain on my young shoulders. My face was stony. No tears. At the wake in the school hall adjoining the church I soon grew bored with adult conversations and relatives offering their condolences: Grandma Fuller, Uncle George; Aunt Charlotte and Uncle Henry from Ballarat, these last with whom we were going to live.

I sat down on a chair. My stiff Sunday shirt had been pinching at my neck and I unbuttoned the top collar, feeling a flood of relief that the blood could flow again. I caught Margaret Anne's eye. She was standing dutifully next to her uncle. Looking at me once, then twice, she came over and took a seat one chair away.

'Hello,' she said. 'You were staring at me, in church.' Her voice was perfectly correct; flowing like running water.

I shrugged. 'No law against looking, is there?'

'At school they taught us to lower our eyes if a boy looks at us.'

'You didn't lower your eyes.'

'No … I didn't.'

Gosh she was pretty. Skin clear as cream. Eyes like crystal chandeliers. I wanted to take the initiative, grasp her hand, but didn't know how to start.

I groped for something to say. 'Is it fun being in the choir?'

'It passes the time, and besides, I like singing.'

'You must have your own special way to get in and out of the church, because I was watching for you outside.'

'There's a little corridor that leads to a small room where we keep the robes. A door takes you out to the back of the church. Do you want to see?'

I did want to see.

Margaret Ann took me out of the hall, through a side door, down a corridor past the Reverend Croxton's office, and into the church itself. Even then, in the middle of the afternoon it was dark, and somehow

24

forbidding.

I paused before one of the columns. On each was carved one of the Twelve Commandments. This one read, in Latin and English, *Thou Shalt Not Kill.* I don't know why, but I stopped to look at it. Margaret Ann skipped back to see what was keeping me.

'My uncle says that all the other commandments can be forgiven, but not this one. You'd never kill anyone, would you, Charlie?'

I said nothing. I didn't think so.

'I know you wouldn't, Charlie. You have a good heart.'

We went on, past the altar, past the rows where the choir sat. In between was a narrow aisle, panelled with oak on either side, leading me into a dark room.

'I'll light a candle,' she said.

'No!' I took her wrist and spun her like a dancer into my arms. I kissed the soft skin below her ear.

'Charlie, you mustn't.'

My hand moved to cover her left breast, her right pressing into my wrist. Then I kissed her on the mouth. She responded for a moment then broke away.

'Charlie, there's no use, your family's going to Ballarat.'

'I'm not going with them,' I said. It was the first time I had put this thought into words.

'You're staying here?'

My hand crept up to the seam at the top of her dress and slid below. She grabbed my wrist and tugged at it hard.

'No Charlie. Stop. There were other girls … at boarding school. Who would creep out and meet with boys, and do things with them, but I'm not like that.'

I didn't move my hand any further, but I didn't retreat, either. It was the first time I had touched a girl and I liked it very much. After a few moments she stopped struggling and let my hand stay.

'Now tell me,' she said. 'Are you just teasing me, are you really going to stay here in Sandhurst?'

I moved my hand from the front of her dress along the curve of her

25

neck. I know she liked it because she shivered and pressed against me like a cat.

'You know that your uncle wouldn't let me near you, even if I stayed.' I rubbed her ear lobe between my thumb and forefinger, so softly I could feel the downy hairs.

'Oh no! He says that you're one of the brightest students …'

It wasn't about being bright or dull, and we both knew it. Our family had been given a chance, but Da ruined it. The widow Gaunt and her brood were so far down the totem pole from the Reverend Croxton and family we were almost underground.

I moved so I was in front of her, half sitting on a banister so that our faces were at the same height. 'Don't tell anyone, but I'm leaving tonight,' I said. 'So kiss me goodbye.'

This time she kissed back. Her mouth was hot and beautiful, and all the more attractive now that I had made the decision to leave.

There were precious few things I needed – blankets, knife, warm clothes, and a hunk of bread from the kitchen. On my way out I walked past the girls' room, then looked in on my sleeping mother. I felt tears prick my eyes. In my heart I knew that it would be a long time before I saw her again.

Unfastening the latch, I went outside, past the packing cases in which all our worldly goods were being stowed. On the back porch I sat on the stump and slipped on my boots. It was raining as I walked to the stable.

Constance was in her stall, suspicious of this night excursion, and I comforted her with soft clicks of my tongue. I was careful to avoid any jingle of harness as I dropped the saddle on her back and tightened the girth. I packed my belongings into the saddle bags that hung on either side. My blanket roll, protected with canvas, I tied behind the cantle as I had seen drovers do.

I was out of town on the Shepparton Road, passing dark farmhouses and barking dogs, before the guilt hit me. I was taking a horse that would have sold for a good fifteen pounds, enough for Ma and the girls to live on for some time. Not only that but I should have at least left a note for Ma, told her not to worry. I thought of turning back to write one, but Constance, already miserable at being forced up and out on the road in this weather, would stamp and snort no matter where I left her, and my wet oilskins were an issue.

While the excuses piled up, so did the miles pass, and soon it was too late. Besides, wearing my hat, oilskins and boots, high above the ground on horseback, I felt like a man who could achieve anything. With the benefit of the passing years I'd like to clout that selfish fifteen-year-old over the head and send him home, yet how could I deny myself the adventures that awaited?

As I rode on through that sodden night I looked back over my shoulder, now and then. I will never forget my sadness at abandoning Ma and my sisters, yet also the excitement deep in my gut. The world was a place of untold promise. Ahead was the long and unwinding road to forever.

CHAPTER TWO

That's your humble servant when prosperity smiled on me. King Wanderlust grabbed me by the back of the neck and said, 'Hike,' and I hiked.

I MADE MY WAY north and east, camping outside one pub towns, working here and there for a week or two. I wandered up through the goldfields around Yackandandah; tried panning for gold but I was too impatient. Looking for warmer climes I crossed the Murray at Albury, where I waited a week for a stone bruise on Constance's front near-side frog to heal, then rode on into New South Wales.

I learned a little of the dangers of travelling alone as I walked my horse through the Narraburra Hills past Temora early one morning. It had rained the day before, but then cleared at dusk, leaving the grass wet but the air cold, with a steaming ground mist. Constance, for her part, did not like these forested hills, choosing each footfall carefully, looking back at me now and then as if to impress on me her displeasure.

Through the gloom ahead I saw two men standing, watching me. My body tensed, and the hackles rose on my neck. The men were bare-headed, wearing dungarees and shirts. One was white and freckled, the other dark, with slanty eyes.

I understood the danger, and told Constance with my heels that it was time to run. She was happy to oblige, but the man on our right hurried forward to intercept us. He took a firm grip on Constance's bridle, stopping her cold.

'Whoa there young'un,' said the man. 'What for such an 'urry at this time of day?'

I had no weapon save for a pocketknife in a leather pouch on my belt. I thought of trying to draw it, but realised that these hard men would laugh at such a tiny blade.

'Let go my bleeding horse,' I said, talking as tough as I dared.

'Haha, the little Lord wants me to let go of 'is 'orse.'

'What do you want?'

The white man lifted his chin so I could see his face under the shadow of his hat. It was a pinched and awful visage, scarred across both cheeks. 'The Chinky and I 'as a fire just yonder. P'raps you might come sit for a spell. If there's any tucker in them saddle bags of yours I'd count meself blessed if you'd be moved to share it.'

Looking down I saw how the hem of his shirt caught on the wooden handle of a pistol.

There were, at that time, bushrangers at large, and I had wondered many times, since leaving Bendigo, what it would be like to meet them. Captain Moonlite and his gang had only recently been caught, and I was not so far from Jerilderie, where Ned and Dan Kelly, along with Joe Byrne and the others had held up the entire town.

These men, I decided, were not of such high reputation. The white man was not long out of the gutter, and the Celestial had all the hallmarks of a Tong assassin or similar, including a jagged scar on his neck.

I was up the creek, paddling in shit and no mistake. Deciding to change tack, I fought to keep my voice steady. 'Well then, that's a fine offer, and I have a little bacon and some bread, enough for the three of us. Lead the way.'

The man let go the bridle but walked close enough to grab it again at a moment's notice. His mate led the way down a spur to where a fire was smoking away.

Constance must have felt the trembling through my legs and thighs for she was thoroughly spooked, her ears erect, twitching like dragonfly wings. Much as she had disliked that cold foggy trail, the company of these two wild men was even less to her taste.

I saw that there were no horses tethered at this little camp, and that the men had no swags. A night in the open at least partially explained the bedraggled state of these two. I wondered why anyone would roam the bush without their plant. I tied Constance up to a tree branch near the fire, with my usual quick-release knot. Every muscle in my body I kept tensed, waiting for a chance to run. The white man was clever, though, he kept himself close to my horse, even when I rummaged in the saddlebags for the food I had promised.

As I squatted down at the fire my hosts did the same, watching hungrily as I prepared some tucker. The two men had no cooking gear, and the frying pan I slipped onto the fire to heat was my own. Then, without any fuss, I unclasped my pouch and took out my knife. It was small, four inches of blade, but honed so it would shave hair, with a wood and bone handle.

I locked eyes with the white man, as if to ask him permission to use the knife. He nodded in reply. I sliced the bacon and dropped it in the pan. The smell of the frying meat had the two men salivating, grinning to themselves, and when I cut the bread they did not wait for the meat, but ate it wholesale, stuffing it into their mouths.

When all the food was gone they asked me for tea, but I didn't carry any.

'I suppose it ain't no use asking for tobacker either?'

I shook my head.

The white man rubbed his hand in a circular motion on his belly. 'I guessed as much. And there's only one thing I'd appreciate more than a pipe right now. A pint a' grog would be a fine gut warmer.'

We made small talk about the weather for a few minutes then, without making any move to stand, I said, 'Well I suppose I'd best get back on the track then.'

'I'm terribly sorry,' the white man said, 'you seem like a good young cove an' all, but I'm afraid I'm going to 'ave to take that 'orse.'

'An' the boots,' added his mate, showing a mouthful of broken, yellow teeth. 'I want the boots. 'E looks about my size.'

'That's all I own,' I said. 'If you take my horse and boots I'll have nothing left in the world.'

'Look on it as charity, boy. As your elders we've 'ad our turn and more at walking barefoot through this freezing bloody winter.'

'And what if I refuse?'

The pistol I had seen earlier appeared in the white man's hand without me seeing him grab it. 'Simple. I blow a big 'ole in your guts an' leave you as a treat for the crows. Then we take the fucking 'orse and boots without regard fer your feelings on the matter.'

Now that he was holding the revolver up, his long baggy sleeves fell down enough that I could see an iron manacle still on his wrist, attached to one broken link of chain. 'You're escaped prisoners?'

'Thirteen days out of Goulburn Gaol with the traps scratching their 'eads at every turn. Filthy fucking 'ole that it is, like the bowels of hell only more shit. Now take off your boots, and them clothes, and walk away, back down that track from whence you came.'

'That's not fair,' I said, being too young and stupid to know when to keep my trap shut. 'I'll freeze to death.'

The man with the gun shrugged. 'Someone will come along, as the sun gets up. They'll take pity on an 'andsome young fellow like you.'

I glanced at Constance. She was a good ten paces away. She turned her head and looked back at me with one deep brown but nervous eye. The gun was the key. I moved my head so I could examine it.

I was, at the time, interested in all kinds of firearms. This was an older kind of weapon called a firelock. It had a big hammer that carried a flint on it. When the trigger was pulled and the hammer fell, it struck steel, making a spark that then ignited a pan filled with powder. This flaring pan set off the main charge that had been tamped down in the barrel. This process was not instant, and misfires were common, more likely after a night in the damp. I also recalled that with a barrel only a few inches long these things were not very accurate beyond twenty or thirty paces.

On the other hand, such pistols fired a heavy ball that dealt fearful damage. If he did manage to strike me, the crows would not have long to wait. I folded my knife and placed it in its sheath, then picked up the frying pan.

'I suppose you want this too,' I said.

'Now that you mention it lad, yes I—'

He was cut off as I pegged the frying pan full at his face. I heard a shout of surprise and pain but I was already on my feet and running full tilt for my horse. Untying the reins took only a moment. I grabbed Constance's mane without trying for the stirrup and vaulted aboard. Scarcely had my rump hit the pigskin when I gave her my spurs and shouted, 'Gee up.'

Constance started to run.

A moment later the very air seemed to explode with the retort of the pistol. I reeled in shock, for I had all but convinced myself that it would misfire. The effect on Constance was more dramatic. She reared up, confused, slowing my getaway. 'Shhh … shhh …' I cooed, bringing her back under control, but as she finally responded to my heels I turned to see the half-breed running after us.

'Get him,' his mate called.

I was trying to coax my horse into a canter when the runner caught up with a last desperate leap and grasped Constance's tail. She slowed, whinnied, and no matter how much I dug my spurs in, or whipped her with the reins, she would not speed up, but nor would she stop.

We blundered under some trees, and finally Constance must have realised that her only way out of this confusing, painful situation was to run. Her natural instinct for flight overcame all else.

At the gallop within a few strides, the China-man could no longer hold her tail. We broke free and had travelled some hundreds of yards away, almost back on the path, when I had an odd feeling.

My father's voice rang in my ears, 'You never run away from a fight … and don't ever stop until they know who's boss.'

I pulled Constance up, clicked my tongue and turned her. Again I set her to the gallop, back towards the two villains who would have robbed me.

The half-breed was standing with his back turned to us as we came. His head whipped around and he tried to run, but I steered Constance into him. We did not hit him squarely, he was too fast for that, but her shoulder connected and sent him flying.

The white man was still reloading, and I'll never forget his panicked, cold fingers fumbling as Constance trampled him down. I heard his yelp of pain and felt her hooves connect with him. Twenty or more yards on, I stopped and turned my mare. I saw him trying to get up. I put my heels into Constance, and mowed him down for a second time. This time, as I looked back over my shoulder, he did not move at all. I reined in and waited, and before a minute had passed the sound of a pitiful wailing came from that bloodied lump on the earth.

Satisfied that I had not killed him, I urged Constance on, and we were soon back on the road, my racing heartbeat returning to its usual pace.

I journeyed on with my spine tingling at the thought of the turns my life might take in this wide-open world. Over many weeks I rode the bullocky tracks up to Forbes, then camped a night on the Macquarie River as it wound through Dubbo.

In the town itself the streets were abuzz with talk of Ned Kelly and his gang having taken control of a pub in Glenrowan, Victoria, and that a train full of police were on the way to confront them. I'd say that nine out of ten people I talked to wished the bushrangers well, the others were mainly what you might call 'pillars of society' who could not be heard to sympathise with an outlaw.

Riding on to the North and West I wondered about Ned Kelly a lot. To many he epitomised the spirit of this brand-new country. From what I'd heard Ned was as true a friend as a man could ever wish for, and had been ill-treated and persecuted into turning on the police. Yet you could not doubt the criminal side of his character.

I also wondered about the black people of this land. In out of the way places on my travels I had seen remnants of what I can only describe as villages. Burned out wurlies scattered in clearings. Some had been substantial, built of poles and clad with bark or thatch. The people were no longer there, but were camped on the fringes of the towns.

Like me, and Ned Kelly for that matter, they were native-born, and must have counted their generations in the thousands. What about their spirit? At that stage I had talked to only a few of these wild people, and

33

I was warned everywhere I went to be careful of thievery and worse. Still, I wondered and worried at their fate – not knowing that later I would play such a part in that terrible human drama.

I had moved on to Gunnedah before I heard the outcome of the Siege of Glenrowan. Dan Kelly and Joe Byrne had been shot. Ned himself was taken prisoner. It was a big moment and people talked of little else but the trial and hanging over the following months.

Heading north and west, my first experiences of those open outback plains raised the gooseflesh on my arms. Big skies and pink dusks, red stone and orange dirt.

In later years I would stand at the quarterdeck of a four masted barque, sailing on a broad reach as if she were riding the wind itself. I've seen the Rocky Mountains up Alaska way, the Kilauea volcano towering over the Hawaiian seas, and the wide Missouri River. They are beautiful, sure, but nothing can compare, for me, with the journey into inland Australia, most particularly for the first time.

Ever so slowly the green disappears, then the trees grow smaller and more stunted. Mulga, saltbush, bluebush and spinifex appear, and the earth deepens into shades of red, white and orange.

It was a harsh journey, to be sure. As the months passed and the weather warmed, the skin of my face and arms burned to a deep brown and my hat faded with the sun. The white blaze on Constance's nose was prone to sunburn, the pink skin beneath growing angry red and peeling until I purchased an ointment of zinc oxide from a travelling apothecary west of Burke. As he promised, a thin coating each morning protected her from this affliction. Horse and boy, we endured the heat together – dry days with scarcely a bucketful to drink between us became all too common.

Through North-western New South Wales and into Queensland, we crossed the Darling, the Warrego and the Bulloo. I fell in love with those inland rivers, some little more than gutters of brown, others yet to feel the hoof marks of sheep and cattle. Running sluggish through twisted clumps of sunken trees, the banks were stained almost white with the dried clay of past floods, cracked into shapes like the jigsaw puzzles my sister Marion had been so fond of back home. Cockatoos and crows marked the start of day, while Constance's hobble chains tinkled nearby.

My first stop was to see my uncle – Da's brother – in Western Queensland. He had a mail run between Charleville and outlying towns. I found him in a yard on the fringes of Adavale, living under a bough shed in a plot filled with wagon parts, draught horses and weeds.

I had met Uncle James only a few times, but according to family legend he had played a small part in the Eureka Stockade, and was never shy of a challenge. The news that Da had died hit him hard, for I had ridden ahead of any written communication. He was happy to see me, though, and happier still to put me to work. For two weeks I stayed, learning to drive a four-in-hand, handle horses and equipment like a man.

Like my Da, Uncle James was everyone's mate in public, but he was also a hopeless drunk. His melancholy night binges wore me down. I had work, sure, but it was adventure I wanted, not another version of my father, and I moved on.

I followed the channel country into a horizon lost in heat-haze. My finances dwindled until I existed on hand outs from station kitchens, heading ever north or west. Everywhere I went there was always somewhere even further out.

My brief experience in mail carrying for my uncle came in handy. When a bush contractor called Atkins broke his neck in a fall from his horse, an acquaintance from the road convinced me that we should take on the role.

In hindsight neither of us had the skills for such a journey. We started out at Rocklands, Queensland, on a five-hundred mile journey to the Northern Territory. My mate talked me into attempting a short cut, then together we rode in a two-week-long circle, utterly lost and near dying of thirst. Embarrassingly, we ended up twenty miles behind where we started.

Humiliated, we were both sacked, and the mail run was handed over to an experienced Aboriginal bushman, Harry 'Tambo' Taylor. The insults and criticisms raining down on me after this aborted mail run included, 'You can't send boys to do a man's work,' and 'wet behind the ears, both of them.'

My salvation came in the stony hill country outside the town of Cloncurry. I spied three men standing on the side of the road. It was obvious they were drovers, from the numbers of horses, and the mob of brown and white cattle pouring through the gaps in the hills. Two or three more riders could be seen, galloping to and fro in a cloud of their own dust, keeping the stock moving.

At first, I stopped just for the pleasure of watching them, but whether consciously or nor I walked Constance nearer to the group of men. She was a sociable animal, and was likewise interested in their stock horses, big in the hindquarters with deep chests and broad foreheads.

The men looked up as I dismounted and led Constance up with the reins looped in my right hand.

'Hi there,' I said. 'Where're you heading with that mob?'

One of the three stepped forward. 'Up to the Territory, young fellow. I'm Nat Buchanan.'

I was so green I hadn't heard of the outback's greatest drover. 'Are you the boss?'

'I sure am.'

'I think he's after a job, Bluey,' one of the other men said.

'You'd better sign him up quick, the poor bastard.'

Blowed if I know, to this day, why they called Nat Buchanan Bluey. He was no redhead, just a brown-haired Irishman. Nothing special, you would think, but he had more ticker than ten ordinary men.

He looked me up and down like I was a horse. 'Ye're a skinny bastard,' he said. 'How old are ye?'

'Fifteen.'

'Ye reckon ye can hack life on the road fer six to eight hard months?'

'Yes sir. I reckon I can.'

'Can you ride?'

It seemed like a stupid question, since I was leading a horse by the reins, and he had surely seen me dismount. 'Oh yeah, 'course I can,' I said finally. 'I can ride as well as anyone.'

'Orright then,' Bluey said, pointing at a big roan gelding feeding near the road. 'Ride that one.'

My eyes narrowed, guessing I was being set up. Still, I had ridden some rough station stock on my travels. I placed Constance's reins on her withers and reached for the girth so I could tack the gelding up with my gear. One of the older men touched my arm. 'No saddle mate. We want to see if you can ride. Go on, I'll hold your mare.'

Thankfully the gelding had been hobbled, so at least I didn't have to exhaust myself trying to catch him. I came up at him on the near side, spent a moment stroking his neck, then removed the hobbles. I had one last look at my potential employers, who were laughing amongst themselves, watching me.

Determined to show them up I gripped the horse's mane, swung my right leg and landed on his back. So far so good. I looked back at Bluey Buchanan and his mates as if to say, *I got up here, now what can be so bad?*

I clipped my heels in lightly and the horse moved off. I felt in control. What did my three spectators want to see? A controlled canter with some sharp turns and maybe a jump or two?

I was just thinking these thoughts when my mount started to reef, front then back, finally pig-rooting like a bastard. I bounced like a rag doll in the jaws of a dog. For about ten terrifying seconds I managed to hang on, legs locked around his flank, and my hands gripped tight on his mane.

I'd been thrown before, but this was different. The gelding was an expert. He dropped his head, then kicked high with both rear legs, using his hindquarters like a spring to eject me from his back. I flew through the air, landing on my arse in the dust. My hat detached itself from my head and fell on the ground beside me.

The three men watching from the road were laughing fit to bust, and when I limped across and joined them, Bluey Buchanan threw an arm around my shoulders. 'Ye can ride sonny, don't doubt that. And ye're game too. Not many men can stick to that bastard for as long as that. Ye want a job? It's yours. I'll pay tucker and what I think you're worth when we get on the track.'

CHAPTER THREE

Buchanan had the gift of bushmanship and location. He was a fine, genial comrade to have; you only had to look at Nat Buchanan to see in his physique, actions and general appearance, a thorough, typical bushman with the face showing dogged determination and strong will power; one who would stand by you in time of need until the 'bells of eternity rang.'

This was the job I'd hungered for, and no wannabe drover ever got a better start. At the tender age of fifteen, I was one of seventy or so men hired by Nat Buchanan to move twenty thousand breeding cattle, in ten separate mobs, to Glencoe Station in the Northern Territory.

The first leg of the trip, from Richmond Downs Station between St George and Roma, far to the South, had already been completed. Horses and cattle from all over the state had now swollen the numbers. We waited near Cloncurry while fresh provisions and camp necessities like pack saddles were purchased from the local Harris and Goldings store, or ordered from Townsville.

As we struck out for the Gulf, Bluey gave me time to learn the ropes, and the mistakes I made were not too serious. A serious mistake meant a smash – dead stock – a disaster, for a drover was paid for live animals on arrival. I kept myself together, alone with the mob on night watch. I never talked of home, nor shed a tear for Ma so far away, and no one asked.

Bluey and the crew taught me how to front-leg and tail-throw a beast. They taught me how to wheel the leaders when a night rush happened, how to shoe my own horse, and the importance of standing up to any man in the camps or along the track. Once or twice, I was bullied into proving my ability with my fists. Win, lose, or draw, I did not once run away from a fight.

The droving team I joined was run by a bloke called Tommy Cahill, just five foot two in height, but fierce and organised. His brother Paddy, also on the drive, would later become a well-known bushman and buffalo hunter in the Territory.

For the young hands like me, there were rites of passage: being given all the shit jobs, for example. I was often the butt of practical jokes. I learned that the drovers' track is not always easy, and that extremes of temperature are to be weathered without complaint. In those days, flashness was not tolerated. A man could be the best whip cracker, or the best rider, but could never say so. Neither did you piss in any man's pocket.

The routine was tightly controlled and varied only a little from day to day. Long before dawn, Tommy, last on watch, would wake the cook and horse-tailer, at which time me and the other stockmen buried ourselves deep in our swags, snatching another forty winks before it was time to get up.

'Awwlright you bastards,' Tommy would sing out, as he prowled the camp. 'Roll those swags up. You can smell the Johnny-cakes, don't tell me you can't.'

Up straight away, no excuses, dilly dallying in your swag was to invite a boot in the side. Up for a piss away from the camp, then damper and tea, while the cattle lowed softly, and night bells clunked as the horse-tailer brought in the day horses and tacked them up. The tailer would know each horse, which ones were due to be rested or ridden, and the preferences of the stockmen, who were often picky bastards.

Each man used up to three 'day' horses, allowing for each to be ridden hard one day, then rested for two. There were also ten or a dozen 'night' horses, handpicked for their night vision, willingness to work in the dark, and tractability around cattle.

By first light we were in the saddle, with the sun slanting gold through the mitchell and kangaroo grass. The cows, at that stage, would be lumbering to their feet, hungry for feed.

Those first hours of the day I helped bring the mob onto grass, forming them along a broad front so they all found fresh pasture, making a plodding progress forward, heads down, necks sloping forty-five degrees from the shoulders. At this stage we rode our horses behind, not rushing, talking and skylarking as the day warmed.

Finally, with the cattle's bellies tight with grass, it was time to get some miles down. Working in concert, we'd move the cattle off, bunching them into a mob and taking our positions on the rear, wings and lead.

At times small groups of livestock would resist, stopping with their progeny under trees, and we'd ride in, stock whips cracking, baulking at them, calling 'Yah, yah,' waving hats or throwing stones at them and any other tricks we could dream up. Day after day, the same animals would misbehave, and we'd give them nicknames that stuck – simple descriptive names like Blackhead, Whitey, Shit-for-brains or One-horn.

Late in the morning, if all went well, we'd take the cattle into dinner camp. Most times Tommy Cahill or one of the black boys would have scouted out a good waterhole, but if the hole was small or treacherous we would cut out small mobs and supervise them before bringing in the next lot.

Then, while whoever's turn it was to watch the cattle did so, the rest of us ate cold lunches we'd packed that morning, usually corned beef and Johnny cakes. We also wolfed down mugs of tea. Time for washing, shaving, even a quick nap, hat tilted low over the eyes, often just yarning while the cattle chewed their cuds and rested.

An hour or two later the mob would be walked off again for a couple of hours before reaching a designated night camp. The cook and horse-tailer would be waiting there with a good campfire and tucker.

Before dusk, the cattle were pushed into a roughly circular camp the size of a football field – not too tight – with the animals having room enough to lie down if they wished to.

At precisely sunset Tommy set his pouch clock for drovers' time – six pm – for there was no way of determining the actual time. The night watches began at that point, shared at two-and-a-half-hour intervals. The watchman guarded the herd, riding around them; reciting poems, voicing his thoughts or singing softly to let them know his location and to keep them settled. Always he stayed alert for signs of a rush. This happened when something spooked the herd: a twig breaking under a hoof – a cook dropping a pot – sometimes we never knew. Two thousand cows, bulls and calves on the run could do fearful damage which was why a blazing fire burned all night between camp and the cattle. If the stock ran in the direction of the camp the fire would split them, and prevent sleeping drovers from being trampled. The camp was made squarely on the trail on which we had arrived – a common direction of a rush – with lanterns hanging on the wagonette to further deter them.

If a rush started the night watchman would call for help, and we'd race from our swags, grab a horse tied ready at a tree just behind us and hurry to help. The night watchman would then gallop for the leaders of the rush, and cut in on them, attempting to 'ring' them back on themselves. This is where the term 'ringer' originally came from. I was new to cattle work, but I learned quickly as we pushed the mobs down the Flinders River and into the Gulf. The Wet Season let loose its fury, with all the associated problems of bogged stock, lack of provisions, heat and humidity.

We pushed the cattle along ridges to avoid the waterlogged ground between the channels, but this was a hard time to be on the road. Rations, obtained at Normanton, and heading towards the drive by bullock dray, were delayed for weeks.

Hungry and exhausted, the drovers staged a strike, and many deserted. Stayers like me had our workloads increased to cope with the shortfall of manpower.

Across the 'Plains of Promise', from Floraville onwards, conditions improved, and the big drive hit Burketown. The men were more than ready for a spree. By chance, a Burns, Philp and Company Steamer arrived at the same time. Seamen and drovers combined into a rowdy mob, crowding the pubs and keeping the local police busy.

I was school educated and smart. I was a good talker, full of fun and mischief. At that stage, I was too young to drink, but I joined in the high-jinks and fights that characterised those days in that wild Gulf town. Uncontrollables were chained to a log overnight while they sobered up.

Penetrating on towards the Calvert River, the men of the wild Gulf nations did not allow our herds and men to pass unmolested. Horses were constantly speared and stolen. Armed warriors lined the cliffs above the river, clattering spear on shield and jeering, voicing their displeasure at the incursion.

I owned no weapon, at that stage, but the older hands responded with gunfire. I recall how one stockman's revolver jammed, and later when he tried to clean it, he accidentally shot himself in the leg. For weeks he had to be carried on a dray. He walked with a limp for the rest of his days.

Strung out over a hundred miles of wilderness, the drive pressed on. Nat Buchanan had rules about not letting wild blacks into the camp, mostly intended to prevent the men from abducting women and forcing them to their swags. This prevented a lot of trouble, as did his preference for giving the cattle 'the old gooseberry' – driving them on at speed.

Good leadership trickling down from the top, as well as the sheer size of the drive, helped prevent serious trouble. Tommy Cahill was smart enough to kill a bullock or two, leaving beef for the tribes as we went through.

Once the drive reached the Roper River, the western extreme of the Gulf Track, we found better feed, and freshwater creeks for the men to bogie and relax. Plentiful stores of quinine kept the fever toll to a minimum, though at least one white man I know of died on that trip.

I learned so much, droving with Nat Buchanan. I learned that things happen on the frontier that a man doesn't talk about. Especially not when you get back to the world of picket fences and newspapers. I was lucky enough to see the Northern Territory before it changed: the waving, golden grasslands still the domain of the kangaroo, and emu: where the black man was proud and free, terrifying in ochre and bone adornments.

One night, camped on the Elsey, the sky flickered with light, and soon after we heard a tremendous explosion in the distance. The cattle rushed, and the night horses, tied ready behind our camp, strained at their halters until we caught and calmed them, riding out to turn that rush before we lost dozens, maybe hundreds of head.

'God's hooks!' Bluey swore. 'It's August, shouldn't be a thunderstorm within cooey of us.'

We learned at the Telegraph Station a few days later, that an island volcano had exploded some eight hundred miles to the north. A place called Krakatoa.

In the months and years that followed, as smoke and dust from that eruption filtered the sunsets into red and yellow glory, men would say that it was heaven and hell meeting up in the sky. I was young enough to believe them.

CHAPTER FOUR

I was preparing my dinner in the camp when up rode a white man and two black boys, with packs and spare horses, and fastened to their stirrup irons with handcuffs were four young lubras ranging, as far as I could judge, from twelve to sixteen years of age. I asked the white man to stop and have some dinner and he and the boys forthwith unpacked their horses, hobbled them out, and with a light chain fastened the lubras up to a tree.

Ten months of hard work and few rations left me raw boned and thin as a mongrel dog. After discharging the cattle, and collecting a cheque from Bluey Buchanan, three of us rode back from the Territory through the Barkly Tablelands into Queensland. My mates insisted that we decamp at the first grog shanty we came to, at Fort Constantine.

Wearing out our welcome we moved on to the Drover's Rest in Cloncurry, but my pocketbook was getting thin. Counter meals, ginger beer and hotel rooms were, I decided, unnecessary expenses. After buying myself a second-hand revolver I had little money left at all.

Eager for work, I visited an agent in the 'Curry, and signed up as a shepherd on Sandy Creek Station, north of Boulia, Far Western Queensland. It was the beginning of January, 1883, and I rode two hundred miles from Cloncurry in the summer heat. I was just seventeen years old, but already I looked like a man: five-feet-nine and a half inches tall, lean as a whippet but sinewy from hard yakka on the track. A quart pot and canvas waterbag hung from my saddle Ds, and the rest of my gear was carried by a packhorse trailing from a long rope.

The job meant taking six hundred sheep twelve miles up the creek, setting up camp with two sheepdogs and my horses. The sheep were poor from a long journey overland, and after a few miles it was obvious that they weren't ready for more travel. Some quit walking and refused to move, even when the dogs barked, bit at their heels, or stood on them. I was forced to carry a near-perishing ewe across my saddle and press on. Once we were settled on the creek my job was to keep the sheep moving onto grass, bring in strays and stragglers, and take pot-shots at the dingoes that slunk out of the blue bush and gidgee.

There were some pretty spots along the creek, but all in all this place was far from what I had been dreaming of when I rode off from home. There was something mean about it. Some country is like that. There was little in the way of wildlife apart from the odd gang of laughable emus and those mongrel dingoes. I had one or two books, including some poetry by the likes of Adam Gordon to while away the time, and I soon settled into the quiet life of a shepherd.

Once a week the rations carrier, a rough old prospector called Billy McLeod trundled up in his wagonette, dirty white canvas spread over iron hoops to shade the load and protect it from dust. I was always excited at the prospect of company, and stacked in the back of the cart were bags of flour, and salted meat wrapped in damp cloth, tea, sugar – not all for me – there were dozens of shepherds on Billy McLeod's 'run.' The dogs were not forgotten, with fresh bones and offal.

I scarcely had time to get bored with the shepherd's life, however, before I got myself sacked, through no fault of my own.

One day, around noon, three horsemen rode up; a white man and two black boys. The former was a ringer from another Collins property – Mount Merlin Station – some thirty miles away on the Burke River. Between them they had four black girls cuffed to their stirrups, miserable and crying as they tried to keep pace with the horses.

Being lonely I asked the riders to stop for a cuppa and a bite to eat. They dismounted and secured the lubras while we shared a hurried pot of tea and some Johnny-cakes, but they were soon on horseback again, hurrying on like the hounds of hell were after them.

That wasn't, it turned out, so far from the truth. The Kalkadoons were on their trail: almost certainly the menfolk of the women they had

45

stolen. Kalkadoon land ranged from Cloncurry down towards Boulia, and the men had proved that they weren't afraid to take on whites with guns. In general they were tall, strongly muscled in their arms, shoulders and chest. They wore full beards, their hair plastered down with dried clay. They lived in huts of bark and sapling poles built on impregnable crags in formidable cliffs.

It was a practice of this tribe that, when wronged, they did not feel they had to apprehend one particular white man. Another one would do, and it was unfortunate that a man called George Britcher, brother of my Uncle James's business partner from Adavale, happened to choose a crossing on that creek to camp for a night. The next morning, while moving my sheep up along the creek for new feed, I saw carrion birds – kites and crows – wheeling around a well-known stopping place on the mail track. I'd been uneasy since the visit from the ringer and his stolen girls. I walked across to the camp, heart thumping in my chest. There I found a disturbing sight, Britcher lying at the base of a tree. His shirt was off, his skull partially crushed, and his body pierced by multiple wounds.

I had met the man before, which made the encounter with his mutilated cadaver all the more harrowing.

George was in his early forties, originally from South Australia. He had good reason to be wary of Aboriginal attacks. In a tragic coincidence, his own father, also called George Britcher, had been speared to death at Mount Dispersion on the Murray River some thirty-five years earlier.

A marking on the tree read: G. Bri … the unfinished signature telling the story of the traveller's last moments. A line of sap dripped from the letters to the base of the tree. I backed away, aware that Britcher's killers could be anywhere in the scrub around me. I whistled for the dogs, left the sheep feeding, and walked back to where I had left my horse. At any moment I expected a fatal strike to come from the trees surrounding the creek. I was still only seventeen years old then, alone in a hostile environment. Having just seen the aftermath of the violent death of a man I knew, I was shaking with fright as I mounted Constance. The station homestead seemed like a very distant sanctuary.

I cantered off in that direction, the wind whistling in my ears, and my revolver gripped tightly along with the reins. I did not call back at my camp for my swag and other possessions. The two dogs ran alongside me on that twelve-mile journey.

When I reached my destination, the manager was out at the yards, standing with his hands on his hips, surprised and annoyed to see me ride in alone.

'What in damnation are ye doing here?' he called out.

Exhausted from the ride, I dismounted and blurted out the news of the mutilated dead body.

'What's become of the mob of sheep then?'

'Left them,' said I.

'Ye damned scum,' cried Fraser and before I could dodge, he grabbed me by the throat, trying to throttle me there in the dust of the yards. I fought back, kicking him in the stomach so he grunted.

Fraser was no pushover, gripping my foot and pushing backwards so I lost balance and fell to the dust on my back.

'Get back out there and find the sheep before I run ye off the place,' he said.

I went out with McLeod, the rations carrier, to fetch the body and find the sheep. The body was the easy part, even after the crows and kites had taken their share. Unfortunately the sheep had been driven off, and we lost their tracks in stony country.

When I returned to the station without my ewes, I was sacked on the spot and told never to set foot on the place again.

That was the only time I ever worked with sheep.

CHAPTER FIVE

At last Jerry Durack said, 'Do you want a job, kid?'
'What?' I asked.
'Going back to the Territory with a mob of cattle to stock new country
in the Kimberleys,' he answered. 'Two pounds per week and about a
two years trip. Take it on?'
'Alright,' I said, 'I'm game.'
Forthwith I became one of the Durack's Clan to hit the Trail of '84
to the far off Kimberleys.

AFTER MY dismissal from Big Sandy, I rode alone down to the Channel Country, exploring and fishing, living on wild duck, yellowbelly perch and handouts from stations. I had vague thoughts of heading home to see my mother and sisters, but it was a long ride, and I had no inclination to hurry.

One night while walking down to fill my pannikin from a hole I was bit on the leg by a deaf adder. I spent the next three days swollen and in agony, convinced that I was going to die alone out there, shivering and weeping. I was soon back in the saddle, but half-starved as I was, full recovery took weeks.

Near Windorah I camped on a broad waterhole on the westernmost channel of Cooper's Creek. It was a grand camp site, with water the colour of milky tea; gently flowing, river red gums leaning together, almost touching, forming a natural arch. Corellas squawked and carried on in the branches and wobble billed storks cruised upstream, catching small fish in the shallows.

I'd hoped to catch a yellowbelly overnight on a set line, but my bait, a fat grub, had been taken without a hook-up. Disappointed, I stowed the line, rolled my swag and saddled up. Constance was flat from work, and still coming back into condition, but she bore my wasted frame easily.

I hadn't travelled more than a mile or two before I heard the beat of hooves, and topped a rise to see a mob of several hundred breeders, all round-boned beef cattle, carrying the brand 7PD. It was good country; mitchell grass plains all the way to some distant sand hills.

A rider came my way, a black stockman with a talent for the saddle. He wore a red shirt, dungarees, and a wide-brimmed cabbage tree hat on his head.

'Is there a station hereabouts?' I asked.

'Sure thing, boss. Follow alla same creek upla big-feller waterhole. You see the homestead there. Them-feller all eat breakfast now. Jerry the boss-man.'

I liked the rider straight off. He was a fine looking man, with high cheekbones above a wiry mess of a beard the same deep black as his hair, only not as tightly curled. I found out later that he was a local Bunthamara man – one of the original people of the Kyabra Creek waterholes – a member of the 'carpet snake' people.

'What's your name?' I asked.

'Dick.'

'I'm Charlie. Nice looking herd,' I ventured. 'Who owns that brand?'

'Them all Durack cattle. You see 7PD brand all same round these parts, you know.'

'Good-oh.' I said. 'See you later.'

I rode on, seeing more mobs of cattle out on the plain behind the creek. A nicely-laid-out homestead came into view, the track that led up to it broadening into a dusty square, bordered by gardens, stables, and a dairy. Cattle runs, then and now, are judged not only on their stock, but on their fixtures, so even the meanest cocky likes to build something substantial to live in once he's begun to earn a crust. This one was better than most, with slab walls, wide verandahs, and a roof thatched with cane grass.

Judging from the cattle I'd seen on the way in, and the numbers of horses, both yarded and tied to the house posts, this outfit was about to move a sizeable herd. Men spilled out of the kitchen and onto the verandah, eyeing me off as I approached. Barging in on a meal was poor form so I dismounted and held Constance's reins loosely, stroking her neck. She was around six years old by then, and we knew each other like a married couple. After a while three children – two boys and a girl – wandered out and stood watching me. The tallest, a grubby-faced mite of about six years, gripped her smaller sister's hand and pattered determinedly towards me.

'What's your name?' she asked in a tiny voice.

That cheerful spirit made me smile. 'Charlie. What's yours?'

'Bridget. Have you come here to work?'

'Can't say that I have. My thing right now is to ask the missus for some tucker and be on my way.'

A man in his thirties, with a neat moustache and hair parted down the middle walked out from the house. 'Hey you littlies, run along now and leave the gentleman alone. Looks like he's had a hard road and he don't need an inquisition from the likes of you.'

The man, their father, I assumed, stuck out a hand. 'Well met, young fellow, I'm Jerry Durack.'

Jerry was as pleasant a cove as I'd ever met, with a powerful figure, and blue eyes filled with mischief. I shook his hand. 'Pleased to meet you. I'm Charlie Gaunt. You probably know my uncle, James Gaunt, over in Adavale?'

'Oh yes, the mailman. I do indeed know him, and a fine man he is too.'

Jerry shooed the children, gesturing with his hands until they ran back into the house. 'Sincerest apologies for the humbug from the ankle-biters. Find a place to tie up and come join us for breakfast.'

'Thanks Mister Durack. You won't need to ask me twice. Are these your children?'

'To be sure they are.' I couldn't mistake the pride in his voice. I tied Constance to the rail within reach of a water trough, gave the pump handle a few hefty blows, then rejoined my host.

'So you're the boss here?'

'In partnership with my brothers.' Those blue eyes looked me up and down. 'Gaunt by name, gaunt by nature, you look fair weared out. Not on the run from justice are ye?'

'Not me, sir. I've been droving, up the Northern Territory with Bluey Buchanan. Feed was scarce on the way back for man and horse alike.' I didn't mention my time at Big Sandy.

Jerry raised his eyebrows, impressed. 'So where to now then, young Charlie?'

'Not sure yet. Right now I'm having a look around the country, planning my next move.'

'Well, this is indeed a lucky arrival. Ye'd better come inside. We'll get some tucker into ye and pick yer brains. We're heading off on the track that way ourselves.'

'I figured something like that.'

The kitchen was decorated with icons of the Virgin Mary. Rosary beads hung from convenient hooks next to hand-made representations of the Holy Cross. A girl, dressed in a clean white apron, served lumpy porridge with molasses, followed by fried fresh eggs, the like of which I'd not tasted since I left Sandhurst. To wash it down there were strong cups of tea with a dash of fresh, creamy milk. The meal was supervised by Jerry's wife Fanny, with her head of long red hair and a spark of Irish wit and good-humour.

'Charlie Gaunt eh?' she said, thin arms on her hips, and reddish curls all the way down her back. 'You've come to the right place to get some meat on those bones.'

Gathered there in the kitchen was a crew of station hands and horsemen, yet with not a trace of flashness about them. All except Jerry wore standard cattleman's clobber of elastic sided boots, concertina leggings, dungarees held up with belts or rope, and shirts or singlets. Felt or cabbage tree hats and rifles or revolvers were close to hand. Jerry Durack, being a gentleman and owner, wore fine black trousers and a white cotton shirt.

'My brothers and cousins and I are taking seven thousand head of cattle from here to the Kimberley,' Jerry explained. 'Split into four mobs.'

I whistled. 'That's a tall order.'

'You've been to the Territory. Tell us what it's like.'

They waited silently while I chose my words. None of these men had any experience of the Gulf Track and beyond. 'The Territory is a hard place, but you've never seen pasture like it; and all for the taking by men who are strong and willing.'

The questions came thick and fast. Will there be dry stages? How hostile are the blacks? How do you get cattle through gorge country?

Patsy Moore, Jerry's second in charge for the drive, was another fine looking man of Irish stock, who shook my hand warmly. Patsy was a relative of the Duracks, born at Blackney's Creek, New South Wales.

Then there was Billy Higgins, who saw himself as the senior hand, and had done a fair bit of droving through the backblocks of Queensland. He had dead-straight black hair to his shoulders, and a beard the same colour, kept short with scissors. Billy looked me up and down in Jerry Durack's kitchen and did not like what he saw. I suppose my talk must have made me seem flash to him.

'A whelp like you has been to the Territory and back with Nat Buchanan?' he growled. 'You're barely off the tit.'

I shrugged. 'I'm young, but I'm game.'

'Prove you know Buchanan. What do men call him, up the track?' The kitchen went silent then. This man was all but calling me a liar. We were just a whisker from stepping outside to discuss things with our fists, and in my condition right then I wouldn't have stood a chance.

'Well, up the bush his mates call him Bluey,' I said. 'But to be honest, I still don't know why. The blacks have another name for him: "Old Paraway," but blowed if I know where that came from either.'

Billy Higgins sniffed aloud, and went on. 'So tell me how he rides, this bloke you say you know.'

I took a forkful of egg and bacon smeared with relish, a flavour made sublime by years of bland food and want. When I'd finished chewing I said, 'Nat rides with long stirrups for a man not especially tall. He has as fair a skin as you'll ever see, and he rides with his hat pulled down and cotton scarves affixed to the sides. His skin burns something awful if he

52

lets the sun get to it.' Billy must have known I had him cold. He picked something from the side of one nostril and flicked it on the floor before he turned back to me. 'What else?'

'Bluey sings as he rides, old Irish songs, and he never sings the same song twice. Not only that, but when rations are low, every morning he fills his pockets with dried apple, and eats on the run. He reckons that dried apple, followed by a swig of water, swells up and makes a man feel full all day.'

Higgins wiped his plate with his bread and made for the door, spurs jangling. He carried a Colt revolver in a holster at his belt. One of my dreams of wealth was to buy a brand-new revolver like that one.

Gun or no gun, when Higgins had gone the atmosphere relaxed. 'How many head in your mob?' I asked.

'Twelve-hundred breeding cattle.' Jerry Durack enthused. 'How many do ye reckon will ever eat grass on the Kimberley?'

I shook my head. 'It's a blasted long way. Blacks, crocodiles and drought will all take their share. If you get half of them through you should be thankful.'

'That's about what we reckoned on.'

Jerry Durack had been looking at me seriously. 'We're shorthanded, and as you know, breeders are the devil's own battle to drove. What say you join us on the track, two pound a week and all found?'

I was thinking furiously. Most stockmen would rather wear stinging nettles for underwear than drove cows and calves. Cows are nervous at night, and prone to rush. Newborn calves have to be collected from under the noses of protective mothers, and either killed or slung in hammocks under a wagon until they can walk. Yet, there are pleasures in the cycle of birth, the sight of mothers nurturing, those great rasping tongues wetting down and smoothing.

'All the way to the Kimberley?' I asked.

Jerry grinned, 'That's it. Make no mistake, we're banking on two years on the road. After that ye can stay on for stock work or light out. Up to you.'

'I'm game. Sign me up.' All thoughts of heading home were

forgotten in that burst of camaraderie and excitement. And for the next three years my fortunes would be bound with this family of battlers turned squatters.

The Duracks were a clan of Irish settlers, from County Galway. They had originally settled near Goulburn, and when the patriarch, Michael, was killed by an out-of-control dray, his son Patsy stepped up, becoming the head of the family.

Heading down to the Victorian goldfields, he made £1000 in eighteen months of hard work, and returned to the farm. A few acres near Goulburn, however, was never going to be enough for him. He dreamed of wide grasslands and never-ending horizons, all with Durack cattle grazing and multiplying.

The move came in 1867, and after selecting some of Western Queensland's best pasture, along Kyabra Creek, Patsy set about forming new stations for relatives and sponsoring their move into this harsh, but productive land. Life in such a remote reach of the outback was hard on all the family, but Patsy was determined to make it work.

The ties to Goulburn endured, however, and generations of male Duracks were sent to Saint Patrick's College, high on a hill at the west side of the town, for their education. They spoke of the cold halls and severe rules with a mixture of awe and hatred. Their greatest reverence was reserved for the head of college, a strict disciplinarian, Doctor John Gallagher, later Bishop of the Goulburn diocese.

By the early 1880s, when the combined Durack herds numbered in the tens of thousands, Patsy heard of the potential of the unsettled Kimberley region, and he stumped up the cash for an expedition to explore it first-hand.

This exploratory trip cost thousands of pounds, with Patsy's brother Michael leading experienced bushmen Tom Kilfoyle, James Josey and Tom Horan. Travelling by ship, they stopped at Darwin for more stores and also recruited two Larrakeyah boys who they nicknamed Pintpot and Pannikin. Landing near the site of present-day Wyndham, they followed maps sketched by explorer Alexander Forrest. They penetrated coastal swamps and 'gator-infested rivers before following the Ord River south, viewing the legendary Kimberley grasslands for themselves.

The great Kimberley drive was on! The planning was exhaustive, the substantial costs all but emptying the family coffers. Complicated partnerships bound up ownership of the destination selections, most of which were counted in the thousands of square miles.

As we set about last minute tasks, I wondered how they would have managed with one man less. Jerry and Patsy Moore were both handy cattleman. Billy Higgins, for all his arrogance, was too. Mick Skeahan, Jerry's nephew by marriage, was a likeable young cove who had all the skills, but lacked confidence and seemed unable to make decisions for himself.

Camp cooks were generally known as babblers – rhyming slang for cook – babbling brook. Ours was a middle-aged chap called Alfred, with a mouthful of rotten teeth and a hide like old wrinkled leather. Our first task after breakfast was helping him load the wagonette with heavy cast iron camp ovens, drums of flour, sugar, oil, mustard, and a dozen other items.

This vehicle was set high off the ground, with fifty-two inch back wheels and forty-two inch versions on the front. It was drawn by two horses and driven from a bench seat. A frame in the rear supported a canvas cover with sides that could be rolled or unrolled to provide shade, dust protection and to keep out pests. Pots and pans hung from a rack spread between the two rear-most hoops.

'Jesus,' I said, 'I reckon that lot will make a clatter down the track.'

Like most cooks Alfred was a touchy bastard, whose hooded eyes told of a troubled past. No last name was given or asked for. He glared at me, 'I reckon maybe you should keep your opinions to yourself, love, especially if you want to get fucking fed. Jesus, you're like a scarecrow as it is.'

'His name's Gaunt,' Patsy Moore said.

At that Alfred the cook threw back his head and laughed. Then, addressing me, 'You bloody look like it too, love. Had a hard road have we?'

I raised my eyebrows and kept loading. 'That's not really any of your business, is it? So bugger off.' I knew not to take attitude from anyone, especially not from a bleeding cook. I glared at Alfred until he dropped his eyes.

When we'd finished Jerry strode across and said to me, 'So what about horses? I see ye've got your own mare. Ye can take her if you like or if you want to, leave her here. I promise she'll be looked after. We've got plenty of horses for the trip.'

'No, I'll take her, best horse in the world, she is.'

'She's a nice looking girl, no doubt about that, and you sit well on her. Just take her round to the yards. George Rae the tailer is up there now. He seems to have a fine touch with the plant.' I was relieved, I couldn't ride Constance all the time, and it was best for her to be managed with the rest.

Walking out to the yards, leading Constance by the reins, I soon ran into George. We'd met at breakfast, but spent a few minutes chatting about this and that before getting down to business.

'I'm wondering what to do with my mare,' I said.

George smiled and fronted her, running his hands down the side of her head and scratching below her ear.

'Oo's a gorgeous girl then?' he cooed.

Constance was a friendly soul once she got to know you, but I'd never seen her take to someone straight off like this, nuzzling at the horse tailer's armpits.

'I'll just run 'er wif the others, if you like,' said George.

'You won't let anyone else ride her?'

George grinned, 'To be 'onest she's too light for anyone but you or Mick. But the answer's no. She's your mare, no one else rides 'er. Are you fixin' to use 'er as yer number one day 'orse?'

'Not really, I don't want her worn out. But she's a good night horse too.'

'I'm not surprised, look at the size of 'er eyes. Like deep pools, they are. You want me to brush 'er meself, or will you take care of 'er?'

'No, I'll find time. Where'd you learn horses?'

'Me old dad was a canal man back in the Old Country. My job was to steer the 'orse and set the locks. I learned 'orses the 'ard way. After that I ran away to sea, but 'orses is in me blood.'

We had three hard but pleasant weeks at Galway Downs in all, before we set off. Fanny cooked around the clock, vowing to fatten me up for the road, heaping my plate at every opportunity with home-grown spuds and fatty cuts of beef. I had always been able to hold my own with a plate but never been given the opportunity to eat like this.

The oldest girl, Bridget, who I'd met on the first day, was apparently named after her grandmother. Every time she said something Jerry and Fanny would nod and say. 'T'ere she goes again, just like auld Bridie.'

In all, she was a happy little slip of a thing who took a shine to me, following me around until her da chased her off.

'One day,' she told me, 'when I'm growed up, you might ride back and marry me, Charlie.'

'Well I might,' I told her, 'for I'll not be in a hurry to get hitched.'

'Why not?' she asked, eyes wide with innocence.

I kneeled down so my face was level with hers. 'Oh I don't know, but it seems to me that the world's a big place, and I want to see as much of it as I can before tying myself down.'

'You'll change your mind,' she said, with a knowing air. 'You'll see.'

CHAPTER SIX

After a few weeks all the mobs were mustered, and we hit the trail.

ON JUNE the fourteenth, 1883, I rode out with a mob of one thousand, two hundred and seventy head of mixed breeding cattle, most carrying the 7PD brand.

The horse-tailer had control of a string of around forty horses. Many of the station crew rode beside us for the first few miles, saying how much they wished they could come along, and that they might live a hundred lifetimes without such adventure. Even the children followed along as far as the end of the brown station waterhole, riding two to a horse, their unshod feet and skinny legs hanging while they laughed and called out. 'Remember Charlie,' young Bridget called, 'You have to come back and marry me.'

'Never doubt it,' I called back. It seemed like a safe bet to me, for it was a big country, and I wasn't sure I'd ever call at Galway Downs again. Bridget's brother and sisters fell into hysterical laughter at her childish crush, and she hid her blushing face behind her hands.

'Looks like you're on a promise,' Mick Skeahan ribbed me, but I was feeling good. A couple of weeks on station tucker and the feeling that I was (mostly) amongst friends as we set off on a ground-breaking journey was too good to resist.

Mick was a good mate to me in those days. He was the product of one of the least successful branches of the Durack family tree. His mother was yet another Mary, (how the Irish love that name!) sister of the patriarch Patsy. She had chosen to marry a likeable but hopeless drinker called Dinny Skeahan, who preferred gold panning to steady work, and soon became known as the family ne'er do well. No matter how many times Patsy tried to help, Dinny always managed to ruin his family's prospects all over again.

In any case, being on the open track with a mob of cattle was thrill enough for Mick, and me also. Those first heady days as we settled into our roles with the herd; the rhythms of gully and plain; the curves and moods of Cooper's Creek as we followed her northwards.

We had two minor rushes in the first week. The cattle were restless, unhappy, looking longingly back towards home, and never really settled in at the night camps. Both times Patsy Moore was on night watch, and both times he did well, turning the herd singlehandedly, and only losing a couple of head.

After that we started to think that we had the herd where we wanted them. That was a mistake, of course, but we didn't know it then.

I would have enjoyed those first weeks more thoroughly if Billy Higgins hadn't taken such a confounded dislike to me. It all seemed to stem from our first meeting, when he thought I was being flash, big-noting myself about my association with Nat Buchanan.

'You there,' Billy would shout if he saw me at the fire talking too long as we broke camp. 'You aren't being paid to stand around exercisin' your jaw.'

'I haven't been paid yet at all,' I retorted.

'Well, you won't be, if you'd rather yarn than work.'

I folded my arms over my chest. 'You're not the boss.'

'I'm the boss of you. Jerry himself said I was, being a senior man and all.'

Our mutual dislike was made worse by the close conditions that we worked and travelled under. Our swags, every night, were laid out in a line, protected by the fire at the front and a tree behind, where the night horses were tied. We ate together, and could hardly avoid each other. If Billy had anything to do with it, I always found myself with the dog-watch, in the middle of the night. If blame was to be handed out, it was always me on the receiving end.

'Took you a while to bring in them stragglers,' Patsy Moore accused one evening as we rode late into camp after an exhausting ride after a cunning old angus cow called Specklehead and her gang. 'You left us shorthanded bringing the herd into camp.'

'Sorry Patsy,' Billy said. 'Would have been back an hour ago but Gaunt here lost two weaners and I had to go looking for them.'

'That's a damned lie,' I said.

'Like hell it is.'

I was not afraid of Billy. He was heavier than me, but I was fast, and more solid after three weeks of homestead feeds. I threw up my fists. Jerry, however, would not have it.

'No fighting in the camp, or I'll write ye a cheque and ye can fook off right now.'

I lowered my hands, and turned away.

As we worked our way north through Galway Downs I saw that the Duracks had chosen their land well. This was superb pasture, knee high most of the way. Through the midst of it all wound the channels of Cooper's Creek, some having cut deep gutters, others just shallow depressions. Here and there were yellow-brown waterholes, often narrow, but deep.

The cattle were homesick, and soon grew restless. We left the plains and entered mulga country, with the cattle feeding not on the ground but above it; chewing leaves until, after the herd had passed through, virtually every tree was cropped to nothing below about five feet in height, the limit at which most animals could reach.

We horsemen were happiest in the open range, where the sky was huge, day and night, and there were few trees, just grass, salt bush and blue bush. For days at a stretch, however, the mulga grew so thick that a man could scarcely see a cow that stood ten paces away from him. Trying to control a herd was nigh impossible.

Not only that, but the horses hated getting scratched and spiked, and hearing noises of other beasts and men through the scrub. It was always with relief that we left such country; the swearing and cursing would stop, and the men would smile again.

We loved the Western Queensland plains of pale-yellow mitchell grass best of all, with the heat-haze disconnecting distant ridges of dark red stone from the horizon so they appeared to be islands floating on a blue ocean. There were also dunes in rows with deep orange sand part-covered by patchy spinifex grasses, the cattle sinking hock-deep near the crests. Or gibber country coated with millions of tiny, dark-purple pebbles of iron pyrites, or sometimes larger stones. In either case the cattle grew footsore and bruised, complaining bitterly as we pushed them onwards.

Yet what a privilege I felt to see the dusk sky livid bloody red with the clouds stacked up like the rib bones of a 'killer' after we'd stripped away the hide. To rise at dawn, with the ground just as dry as when you hit your swag, for the air lacks enough moisture out here for dew. To camp by a waterhole, with spoonbills, avocets and storks stately out on the muddy bars, and stands of long-dead river red gums bristling like protective quills along the edges. What a feeling to be tucked up tight in warm blankets with the sound of water birds out in the night, never quite knowing what beauties and hazards, or even what type of country the next day would bring.

Three of the Durack mobs joined up just south of the township of Jundah, where the Barcoo and Thomson Rivers join to form Cooper's Creek. Two rivers joining to form a creek! Only in this wild nonsensical country of ours.

From Jundah we moved on in tandem, north along the Thomson. There we had a visit from Big Johnnie Durack, who was overall boss of the drive. Big Johnnie was six feet tall with broad shoulders and slow-moving ways.

His head was wide and set on a bull's neck, though unusually for a big man, his beard grew sparsely; the whiskers on his cheeks sprouting every which way. He struck me as thoughtful, and was naturally cautious.

I shook his hand, impressed by his sheer size and quiet air of competence in equal parts. 'Pleased to meet you, Mister Durack, I'm Charlie Gaunt.'

'Good to meet ye too, Charlie. Is this yer first drive?'

'No sir, I droved with Nat Buchanan to the Territory.'

61

'So you did, now I remember Jerry telling me about you. More than glad to have a man with experience along with us.'

'Thank you. I'm enjoying the work so far.'

Big Johnnie turned his attention to the rest of the team. 'Well met, every one of ye. We're all part of a history-making drive, and I'll see that you share in the good things that will come at the other end. Whether that be jobs or assistance in claiming some land of yer own only time will tell.'

I clearly remember the day Gracie Oswald came into my life, for an emu stalked me all the morning, stop-start running in great arcs, hiding behind bushes like a constable stalking a thief. Then, bursting from cover it would sashay back with, it seemed, the heavy body moving first and then the legs clawing at the air trying to catch up.

Every time I reckoned it was gone, I'd see it again, sprinting after me when it thought I wasn't looking, then stopping dead still apart from the swaying of its brainless head. The whole affair made Constance nervous, for these emus stood as tall as a man.

'Why don't you shoot the beggar?' Mick asked. 'It gives me the blessed creeps.'

'Oh, it's kind of funny,' I said in reply, but I was already distracted, watching a line of rising dust appearing in the distance. The arrival of a heavy wagon drawn by four grey clumpers made us pause from trailing the herd and watch.

'Who the hell is that?' Mick asked as the wagon creaked to a halt in a cloud of its own making. A swarthy, bearded giant, with thick, overdeveloped forearms, stepped down to meet Big Johnnie Durack, who had ridden up towards him.

'I reckon that's the blacksmith,' I said. Up until that point we had been without a blacksmith or farrier. Though most of us could turn a hand to shoeing and minor repairs when necessary, there was already a backlog of smithy work in all the camps, everything from broken spurs to wagonettes in need of repair.

Our interest surged when Patsy Moore rode over.

'It's a blacksmith orright,' he said. 'Big Johnny met him in Jundah and hired him for a few weeks. Walter Oswald is his name if I remember correctly. I hear he has his daughter with him, a lass of some sixteen years. Oswald's wife died years ago, and he growed the girl up himself. Most of her time, she spends at the Ladies College in Toowoomba, right now she's on holidays.'

We rode as close as we dared to have a look, earning a scowl from the blacksmith as he stepped down from the wagon. Behind him appeared a girl with long, straight dark hair, and flashing eyes, as different to Margaret Anne, back in Bendigo, as it was possible to get. 'Oi, you, Gracie,' Oswald called. 'Get back in the wagon this instant!'

Only when she was out of sight did the blacksmith and Big Johnnie Durack shake hands. 'Pleased to meet ye, God knows there's a mountain of work waiting.'

'Work is what I'm here for, so I'm glad to hear it.'

'One other thing,' Big Johnnie said, 'we're pleased as Punch to have you along with us, but aren't too sure about you bringing a woman into the camp.'

The blacksmith scowled, 'What the hell do you mean? She's no woman, just a little girl, barely sixteen she is, and in three weeks she'll be heading back to school.'

'We just don't want trouble with the men on her account.'

Walter Oswald's face turned beetroot red and he glared around at the spectators. Even the Duracks took a step back.

'Any man,' he growled, 'who dares to touch my girl – nay, any man who dares to even look at her ...' He drew his revolver and raised it high. 'I'll shoot him right between the fucking eyes. You all understand?'

'Put that thing away,' Big Johnnie said, but then glared back at us. 'There'll be no need for any shooting. You have my solemn word that the men will keep away from your daughter, but I suggest that you keep your camp separate from the rest of us.'

'That I will do, Mister Durack. You can bet on it.'

When I rode back to the mob I had a strange feeling. That glimpse of the blacksmith's daughter had set loose something warm in my chest.

I must have betrayed something of my thoughts, because Billy Higgins snarled at me. 'Get that look off your face, never seen a lubra before?'

I glared at him. 'That girl isn't a lubra.'

'I reckon she is. Look how brown her skin is, and that makes her a lubra in my book, no matter how dolled up she be.' He hitched up his trousers, and made a show of scratching his balls. 'Mind you I'll do her myself if I get a chance: nothing wrong with black velvet when there's no better around.'

'You ever call her a lubra again and I'll punch your face in,' I said.

Billy Higgins grinned, pleased that he'd annoyed me, and rode back to his position on the wing.

Big Johnnie's promise didn't stop me from riding close to the blacksmith's wagon in the hope of glimpsing young Gracie Oswald. I wasn't the only one energised by the presence of a girl in the camp. Reports were whispered from man to man, far from the ears of our bosses.

'Today she's wearing a yellow dress,' Mick Skeahan said breathlessly one morning. 'I seen her myself, not an hour ago, walking around near her old man's wagon.'

'I guess she's the kind of girl who likes a morning walk.'

'Dunno about that,' Mick said, with a superior air befitting the man who had made the sighting in the first place. 'She seemed more purposeful than that.'

'Maybe she was looking for her horse,' I suggested. 'I heard that she rides every day.' There were murmurs of agreement.

'Bit late for horse hunting,' said George Rae, who had been listening in.

The truth of it was, that none of us knew. Walter Oswald's daughter was a mystery, but tantalisingly real.

We kept our eyes peeled for her, but the blacksmith kept a closer eye still. Most of the time he left for the next night's camp with the cooks and horse tailers, so our only chance was in the afternoon. Alfred became a good source of information, for, being the camp babbler, he saw a lot more of her than we did.

'Her name's Gracie Elizabeth Oswald, my dears,' he told us one night. 'Her eyes, up close, are light blue, almost grey. A very pleasant young lady. Spirited, I can tell you, why just today ...' If our necks had craned any closer they might have snapped, but Jerry came back from washing himself down the creek and Alfred shut his gob. We had to wait an hour before he could tell us the story of how a brown snake had slithered out from a patch of rocks beside the wagon.

'It were a big bastard too,' he told us, 'six feet long if it were an inch, spittin' angry, and full of poison having just been hibernated. But young Gracie picked up a huge rock, and dropped it on the bastard's head, then dusted her hands off as if nothing had happened. It were a sight an' all, I call tell you.'

'Blimey,' Mick said at last. 'You're right, she has got spirit.'

A few days later we were crossing some lightly wooded country that had been burned out recently, just long enough ago that the green pick was coming up and the cattle moved along contentedly, grazing as they went. Half asleep on the saddle I heard hoof beats behind me.

Slow on the uptake, I screwed up my eyes, confused. What kind of stockman was this? With dark pigtails hanging on either side of a felt hat, riding a chestnut thoroughbred. Up closer, her gender became plain. I realised that it had to be Gracie Oswald. I turned to the front so fast my neck cracked.

If her old man was somewhere nearby with his Colt I didn't want to be seen looking at her. With Constance poking along at her own pace without any input from me I expected the girl to keep riding past, but to my horror she came alongside. I turned to look at her, my insides all messed up. She was stunning to look at, her face all perfect lines and rosebud lips. At some stage she must have passed through or under a wattle branch, for her hair and left shoulder were smudged with the yellow blooms.

'Hi there,' she said. 'What's your name?'

'Charlie. But us blokes aren't s'posed to talk to you?'

'I'm not scared of my dad.'

Alfred was right – her eyes were grey as light summer rain clouds. I felt a surge of righteous pleasure. Of course she was white! Yes, her skin was deep olive, but whoever heard of a lubra with eyes like that? Billy Higgins was a fool.

I started angling away from her, my guts buzzing like a hive of bees. Part fear, part embarrassment, part attraction. The feeling only got worse as she casually idled after me, her horse's long legs moving smoothly as it stretched out its neck to sniff Constance, who wasn't fond of overly friendly strangers. My mare started a little, hurried a yard or two then settled.

'Sorry about that,' Gracie said, keeping her distance now.

'Tulip's a bit fresh with new horses sometimes.'

I scratched Constance on that velvety skin on the side of her neck with the pads of my fingers. 'My girl is just a bit wary, that's all.'

'I hate boarding school,' Gracie said, out of the blue. 'I have to go back in a couple of weeks. At the end of the year I'm quitting for good, no matter what Pa says.'

I was trying to think of a reply when she dug her heels in and took off. I watched her go at a trot, posting rhythmically. Her buttocks were tight and hard looking, and she knew how to ride. I took off my hat and wiped my brow with the back of my forearm.

The trouble started one afternoon. The waterhole we were planning to camp on was trampled and low. Alfred had his fire going, and the Johnny-cakes almost ready. Jerry Durack was ropeable when he saw the camp, making the babbler put out his fire and pack up his gear.

'You'd think a bloke with half a brain would know that we can't bring the cattle into that pox-ridden mud puddle.'

'You told us to,' Alfred roared back.

'But I hadn't exactly seen the bally thing and how little water was in the bastard. You should have pushed on!'

The argument was short lived, because we had limited time to drive the cattle two miles to the next water. This turned out to be a series of small holes near some clay pans, spread over an area of twenty acres or so.

There was water enough near several of the pans, but little feed. The cattle didn't settle quickly, and when we fell into camp, exhausted and frustrated, Mick Skeahan was given night watch first up.

No one noticed that Alfred didn't bother to build the fire up before he climbed under his blankets. It was also good practice in this country for the cook to pile a bunch of dead branches from the low acacia bushes that grew in abundance, ready to throw on the fire to provide instant leaping flames. For reasons of either laziness, or bloody-minded ignorance, he did not do so on this night.

I was deep in sleep when I felt an arm on my shoulder. It was Mick.

I slowly blinked awake. 'What's going on?'

'The cattle are spooked, will you help me?'

'Yeah, just give us a moment.' I pulled on my boots. I would have taken George Rae, the horse-tailer, with us, but he was fast asleep, so I let him be. If there was one thing George could do it was sleep.

With Mick silent beside me I walked to the tree behind the camp where the spare night horses waited, ready, saddled up as always in case of need.

Mick chatted nervously as we rode away from camp and around the herd, still boxed in tight. 'I just dunno what to do, they've been rushing in small mobs, trying me out. Something's got them more wound up than usual.'

'Blacks maybe,' I said. 'Or native dogs.'

'Maybe.'

Mick prattled on as we rode. 'I've been working on a few verses,' he said, 'just in my head as I ride.'

'That's a fine thing to pass the hours away,' I said, though I wasn't partial to the general mania for thinking up poems myself. To me there are enough real things to worry over without inventing new ones.

'The problem is,' Mick went on, 'I can't think of a single blasted word to rhyme with 'journey' and it's driving me bonkers.'

I ignored him, trying to get the mood of the cattle. They had not really settled at night camp, not since day one, so it was hard to judge if this night was somehow worse. 'The cattle are pressed close in,' I said. 'Maybe if we let them stand a bit looser they'll relax.'

'Worth a try, I guess ... you got any ideas for words that rhyme with journey? I thought of Tourney but it don't fit.'

'What about Guernsey – you know – a dairy cow?'

Mick scratched his head. 'Not sure if I can make that fit, neither.'

I stopped my mare, watching, for we had come up to the core of the herd. Every mob has its leaders. One of ours was Brutus. He was a big bastard, with horns of creamy yellow, the left one snapped off clean near the tip from some long-ago fight. He was tireless, stronger than any two of his mates, and would walk from dawn to dusk without fuss. He was a real asset on a journey like this.

To me he was the key, and he seemed to be settled. 'They're alright, I think,' I said. 'I might as well get some more rest.'

'Sorry for getting you up.'

'That's fine mate, any time. Better to have an extra bloke on hand than to wish you did.'

I turned away from him, heading back towards the night horse tree, but I didn't hurry. I knew what Mick meant. The cattle were on edge, but not enough to wake the camp.

I was almost back when I felt the start of the rush in the ground, transmitted through the horse I rode. The bereaved mothers started running first. The bulls and calves joined or were crushed underfoot. The unstoppable run of cattle that the Americans called a stampede had no beginning. It just was.

'Get up you bastards,' I screamed, so loud that I thought my throat would tear. 'The cattle are rushing.'

I tried to turn them, riding as fast as I could for the leaders, but I had no time or space to save our camp. 1200 adults, averaging 1000 pounds in weight, turned for home. In their direct path was our camp, with sleeping men in their swags, and the wagonette.

The fire that would normally have split the herd had died low and was instantly scattered. I saw sparks fly; broken sticks tumbling end over end in the night.

Saplings fell before the onslaught, slammed to the earth and trampled into woodchips.

Patsy, Billy and Dick had time to mount their horses, joining me in that mad ride for the front of the herd. It was already a disaster, we knew that, but the scale was only just dawning on us. I saw Jerry standing on the wagonette with his rifle, firing vainly in the air in an attempt to stop them. The press of cattle was so strong they were forced into colliding with that vehicle.

I saw it start to move, then rise up, carried along like flotsam in a flooded river. Jerry himself was lost to view.

I saw Alfred, the babbler, scrambling into the lower limbs of the night horse tree.

George Rae had reached a horse, and was attempting to climb on, bareback, but the horse was shying in fear, trying to run from the rampaging herd. I shouted George's name, but then he was down. I felt something terrible in my chest. Yet turning the herd was still first in my thoughts.

Jerry had somehow got clear of the wagon and found a horse, so it was he, myself, Billy, Patsy, and Dick, all galloping like mad things in that surging tide. Before we knew it we were far past the camp or what remained of it.

'Ring them,' Patsy shouted, and I saw that at last we were up with the leaders. The four of us moved in. I was the only one with a stock whip at hand and I cracked it over my head. The maddened beasts ignored me, their hooves like thunder and their bellows ringing from horizon to horizon.

Patsy had his revolver out and fired it, not in the air, but close over their heads, over and over, until all six chambers were empty. Now, at last, they started to turn, but were still far from spent. We circled them on each other for what seemed like another mad hour before they finally ran out of puff, standing, blown with exhaustion, twin jets of steam puffing from their nostrils.

Jerry whistled us in, and we rode to him, exhausted and wide eyed at what we had seen, worried about what fearful damage we might find back at the camp. By then Mick, too, had joined us, pale as the moonlight itself, voice shaking with terror at what he had seen that night. 'Jesus I'm sorry, Jerry. I didn't know——'

'No one knows what a big rush is like until they've seen it for themselves,' Jerry said gently. 'It wasn't yer fault. Now, Dick, Patsy and Mick stay here and contain the herd. Bring them in when they're ready. Charlie and me'll ride back and see how the others have fared.'

It was a good three miles to camp, but we rode that pathway of increasing devastation in an hour. Over the last mile or so, when the cattle had been concentrated the closest, only the largest trees still stood. Everything else was flattened.

The way was littered with dead and dying cattle, not only calves, but grown bulls and cows. Jerry stopped to put a bullet in the heads of the unfortunates who were alive but suffering there on the ground with their broken limbs. He ran out of shells long before we got back to camp.

The wagonette was matchwood: even the wheels splintered and broken. The cook's utensils had been crushed to nothing. Alfred himself, sitting at a fire fed by the remains of the wagonette, appeared unhurt. He looked up from his seat at Jerry, with deep hollows in his eyes. 'What kind of tin pot crew is this where the stockmen can't control their damned herd?'

'A man should get up off his knees and help rather than just complaining.'

'You can get yourself a new cook,' Alfred said. 'Damned if I'll stay in this cursed outfit another day.' He looked at me and spat.

I broke a long silence with, 'Where's George?'

The cook shook his head, 'How the fuck am I s'posed to know?'

I felt like kicking the darned babbler in the face, but was too worried about George to waste time. What if he was lying dead somewhere? I rode off in the direction of the place where I thought I had last seen him, no certainty in the dust and the confusion of running cattle.

Since there had been little enough grass to begin with, and the rest was either grazed or trampled flat, the earth everywhere was imprinted with hooves. Seeing a drag mark and partial footprints I followed, down towards the nearest water.

I found George there on the edge of a brown-stained puddle, clothes ripped, one leg out at an odd angle, swollen as hell. One side of his face was badly grazed.

I dismounted, relieved to see him alive but aware that the injury was serious.

'Jesus,' I cried. 'Thank God I found you.'

'I'll be alright.'

'Like hell you will.'

'How're the other blokes?'

I kneeled and examined the leg. I was no doctor, but it looked ugly. 'I think the cook just quit, but apart from that it looks like you're the worst. Lucky no one was killed.'

'Don't worry about your mare,' George said. 'Constance is fine. I saw her just before.'

'That's good news. Thanks, I'll find her when I get a chance.' I'd been a little worried about her, but not much. In the evenings George would generally hobble and bell the plant. They'd wander off from the camp and feed and sleep. They rarely came to any harm save for the occasional unlucky nag that managed to get a leg tangled in the hobbles in a waterhole and drown.

I rose slowly. 'Sit tight. I'll come back with some help.'

George forced a grin, 'Well it's not likely I was planning on wandering off.'

I walked back to camp, where Jerry was gathering bits and pieces of equipment. 'I found George,' I announced. 'His leg is broken.'

Jerry turned on Alfred, who was still hanging around waiting for a cheque. 'You left an injured man out there while you sat here and felt sorry for yourself?' The normally laughing blue eyes were now as cold as iron. 'You're not quitting, you're sacked.'

'I didn't even know he was out there,' Alfred complained.

'It didn't occur to you to look?'

Alfred said something, but Jerry was already walking with me to where I had left George. Between the two of us we splinted his leg and used a panel from the wagon to lay him down while we snigged him back to camp.

Jerry said, 'If he can sit on a horse I'll take him back to that station we passed yesterday. Won't be more than a couple of hours' ride.'

'I'll do it if you like,' I said.

'No lad. I will. Never let it be said that Jerry Durack doesn't look after his men.' He glared at Alfred, then wrote out a cheque, tearing it out angrily and throwing it at the ground. 'And as for you … don't ever ask my family for work again.'

Long after Jerry and George had gone, and Alfred had rolled his swag and walked off to the east, we had a visit from Big Johnnie Durack. The boss drover clicked his tongue at the destruction and helped me finish off the rest of the injured cattle. My ears rang from the gunshots, my heart sick at the blood and death that day.

Big Johnnie stopped for a cuppa before heading back to his own mob, and was still there when Mick, Patsy and Billy rode into camp and dismounted. Dick stayed with the cattle.

Billy walked up and poured a mug of tea for himself. 'Hi there Johnnie. A sorry business this is.'

'No mistake about that,' agreed the boss. 'I've seen at least a hundred dead animals, how many more do'ye reckon are still missing?'

'We've been finding stragglers all day. But another hundred maybe.' Billy turned and growled at me. 'I bet your famous Nat Buchanan would have loved to see your handiwork last night.'

I near choked on the air I breathed. 'That rush wasn't my fault.'

Billy turned on Mick. 'A couple of real stockmen would have stopped the rush before it got out of hand.'

I noticed that he was careful with Mick. Inexperienced as he was, Mick was a Durack, and thus important. I, however, was just another mongrel in the mix, and Billy did not like me.

Big Johnnie tipped the dregs of his tea into the fire. 'That's enough,

Billy, but look boys, Jerry's lost a couple of hundred head killed, and many more in the scrub that ye'll need to try to find for him. Ye've lost a cook, and young George Rae's down with a broken leg. Not to mention a wrecked wagonette. Have you learned why it happened?'

It was funny, I could front-leg a bull without flinching, but an accusation of being derelict in my job had me close to tears, a feeling I fought desperately. 'Because the cattle were nervous,' I said. 'And we pushed them on from where they thought they could settle.'

'Yes, but why were they so nervous?'

I shrugged.

Big Johnnie stood up, and walked out from the remains of the camp in his boots. 'Now just be quiet and listen to me walk.' Given that he clumped along excessively hard, it was impossible not to notice the thumping hollow sound that his footfalls

made on the earth.

'You made a mistake. You camped here because there's water, but this area floods. The top gets crusty dry, but water lurks underneath until it dries out. So the ground sounds hollow, and that always spooks the cattle. You, and Jerry too, made an error, boys, and a costly one.'

I felt like shit. We should have known that. I'd heard of rushes being started by a beast rubbing up against a dead tree, and cracking it in the night, but this was my first experience with hollow ground. Never in all my years as a cattleman did I again camp on ground such as that.

Only young Mick saw a silver lining to that terrible event. 'At least I'm pleased that Alfred's gone,' he said when we were alone with Dick and Pasty that evening. 'That's one good thing to come out of all this.'

I looked at him. 'Yes, he was a bastard, but now we've got no bloody cook.'

In those next few days, the pall of disaster hung heavily over us. Jerry returned after leaving George in the safe hands of a station missus, but he was in a terrible mood, particularly when he heard Johnnie's verdict about the hollow ground.

'Well, he's my cousin,' Jerry said darkly, 'but I'd rather have a warning like that beforehand than afterwards.'

We mustered as many of the lost cattle as we could and set off after the other herds. Without a wagonette we were forced to use pack horses to carry our remaining tucker, mostly handouts from the other teams.

This was a pain in the arse, as pack horses have to be carefully loaded each day, with an eye to balancing the weights on each side. Not only that, but the straps almost always galled, and the horses needed tending-to every night: a good brushing, and salve rubbed on the chafed areas. We also had no cook, so we stockmen were forced to take it in turns. Not only was this job seen as beneath us, but some, like Mick Skeahan, had no idea how to boil a tater. I was a little better off, as Ma had forced me to learn some skills, and as a small lad I had enjoyed helping her bake.

To make matters worse, though, we also had no horse tailer. Having to contend with our usual duties as well as cooking, then catching and tacking up horses was getting bothersome fast.

CHAPTER SEVEN

Then came Hangfire Mick Durack ('Hangfire Mick,' or 'Stuttering Mick') with twelve hundred Thylungras. This comprised the whole outfit that was to form and establish the properties now known as Argyle, Rosewood, Lissadale and the Denham Stations.

THE FINAL MOB, from Mount Marlow, joined the drive a few days after the rush. This party, led by Michael Durack, brought the biggest herd thus far, managed by eleven men, sixty horses, a two-in-hand wagonette and a heavy wagon.

There were now, officially, 7520 cattle overall. Big Johnnie Durack worked like a dog to control it all, riding between the teams, ironing out problems, planning the route and making sure the wagonettes were stocked with supplies.

A new cook, responding to a message sent with a rider heading south, arrived within a week. He was a welcome sight. Not so welcome once he opened his mouth with bad tidings from home. Jerry Durack's smallest daughter Janie was gravely ill and not expected to live.

Jerry readied himself to leave within an hour, handing over the boss's role to Patsy Moore, with Billy as his second-in charge, leaving us even more short-handed. He rode off with all speed, scarcely turning his head at our shouted goodbyes.

As well as my sadness at the illness of that pretty little sprat, I was browned off at having to work under the mean-spirited Billy Higgins. In those days I suffered under his tongue mercilessly. My best strategy, I found, was to spend as little time in his company as possible.

Even so, he needled me like a mosquito. If I was on watch before him, he would stay in his swag, no matter how many times I went to wake him. I was usually exhausted and freezing, and he'd take pleasure in keeping me waiting. If I mentioned it to Patsy, Billy disputed the time, for the only clock we had was that time piece in Patsy's keeping, wound each day and set each sunset for six pm. Drovers' time.

'Just do your bloody share and shut your mouth,' Billy hissed at me as soon as we were out of earshot.

The new babbler was an Englishman who had been abroad for some years, with time in South Africa's diamond fields, and also New Zealand. His name was Kendall Newton, with fine sandy hair to his shoulders, always neatly combed.

He had a pair of round spectacles made with very fine wire, that he kept in a leather case, retrieving them only for reading or writing. Like Mick, he wrote poetry in his idle moments, often claiming a waterside log as his own, scrawling and crossing out and swearing to himself.

From our point of view, Kendall kept a neat camp, and made food that wasn't too hard to digest. For breakfast he served Johnny-cakes with molasses, honey or sugar and canned milk. Supper involved beef of some kind, and often fritters for dessert. He also helped with the horse tailing and was a wizard at weighing and balancing the packhorse loads.

I listened to his stories of his travels across the globe, night after night. In later years I was able to verify the details of many of these yarns, though the others scoffed at the time.

'You spin a good yarn,' Billy told him. 'But there ain't a grain of truth there that I can see.'

Kendall just shrugged, 'I don't give a damn if you believe me or not.'

'I believe you,' I said.

'That's good news, young fellow. Where do you hail from? You sound like you've had some schooling?'

I hadn't told a soul about the circumstances in which I left home, but strangely, I poured it all out one night to Kendall: my father's death, my fling with Margaret Anne, and my silent exit from Sandhurst.

'You left without a word lad?'

'Yeah.'

'That's a low and rotten thing to do to your mother.'

I looked down. 'Yeah I know.'

'Of course, you've written to her, told her you're safe?'

I know my face went red from guilt because I could feel it burn. 'No, I haven't.'

'Shame on you boy. Write and let her know that you're fit and well. She's your mother, for God's sake. Write her a sodding letter, and post it off as soon as you can. We'll be at Winton soon, I hear.'

So seriously did he take this assignment that he lent me a pencil and some paper.

'What should I say?' I asked.

'Just whatever flows out of your heart. Tell her what you're doing. Tell her that you're sorry you rode off without saying goodbye.'

I grumbled to myself at first. Not knowing what to write, I was annoyed to be forced to try. Funnily enough, though, when I sat down that night, the paper resting on my saddle, the words came in a rush. I'd always had a knack for writing. I composed the first few sentences that night, then a little more every day until I had to ask Kendall for more paper. Strangely, I hadn't even sent it, but I already felt better about myself.

We reached the town of Forest Grove, a teamster's stop with good waterholes on Ernestina Creek and the Thomson River. It was a bustling little place, with supplies of goods and services in demand by drovers. E.W. Cohen's chemist shop also offered dentistry, and some of the men took the opportunity to get troublesome teeth pulled.

John Coleman's mud-brick Club Hotel was a welcome diversion, the attached store supplying the Durack wagons with fresh produce. John's wife Catherine was working hard behind the bar or store counter, doing the books and smoothing over staff problems.

I bought from Catherine Coleman a brand-new volume written by an Englishman called RL Stephenson. She promised me a tale of pirates, adventure and treasure – right up my alley – and we passed an agreeable hour or two discussing our favourite books. I left her, mightily impressed. I was sad, a few years later, to hear of her husband's early death.

The Duracks were a devout lot, with deep Irish Catholic roots, and an old coot from Tom Kilfoyle's team called Jim Minogue ran a church service around dawn every Sunday morning. Jim was no priest or anything, just a lay preacher with a passion for bringing religion to the waybacks.

Even though Jim was a practised and entertaining talker, most of the stockmen preferred to ride out in the morning sun and get the herds moving than stand, hats in hand, under a tree. Team bosses were duty-bound to go in, and I guess this served a purpose, for afterwards the leaders would drink tea and discuss the progress of the drive.

When word got around the camp, however, that not only the blacksmith Walter Oswald, but his daughter as well, were attending these Sunday services, the number of men requiring religion swelled. Many a pair of clean moleskins and best cotton shirts were dug from the bottom of kitbags. Most of the younger men on the drive fronted up for the service the following Sunday.

Jim Minogue had selected an airy hillock, swept by a chill wind, and gridded by the shadows of a couple of spindly trees. He stood with his hands clasped around his Bible, and started off by reminding us that he was not an ordained priest, but that he loved God as much as any man, and that God approved of good men in the wilderness standing up to ensure that His word was being observed.

The blacksmith's daughter, Gracie, wearing a white dress, stood beside her father in the front rank of worshippers. I couldn't keep my eyes off her. Love struck me a solid clout over the head and kept on hitting.

'Let us pray,' cried Jim Minogue, raising his free hand in the air. We then mumbled a psalm that I remembered vaguely, though of course I had been raised in the Church of England tradition rather than the Catholic one. Their Bible, it seemed, was pretty much the same as ours.

'It don't fall upon me,' Jim offered when the psalm was over, 'for us to offer the consecrated body and blood of the saviour like we might a' done in a church with real clergy an' stained glass windas an' such. But we can see Him in the beauty of the new lands He has given us with his bountiful love, as we move north to claim it from the wild creatures, an' accept the harshness as part of the burden with which He tests each living one of us.' At that moment, as if to demonstrate the beauty he was talking about the sun broke free of the hilltop, and directed golden rays down upon us. It was a beautiful sight.

As Jim continued his observations from the high ground, a chorus of giggles broke out. It seemed that with the sun behind her, a couple of the best placed men could see the shape of Gracie Oswald's legs through her dress.

They started out whispering behind their hands. Then one of the younger lads, unable to contain himself, spluttered out, 'Jesus Christ!'

This stopped Jim Minogue cold, and every man there turned around and stared at the speaker. Gracie's father, the blacksmith, was a sight. His face was terrible, his lips jagged as the tears in a half open tin can.

Jim Minogue beetled his dark brows at the culprit. 'I'll take that outburst as your love for the Heavenly Saviour overflowin' beyond your humanly control. If that is not correct, then I suggest you leave.'

No one dared move, and after trawling his eyes down along the lines from man to man, old Jim started on with his homily; that old saw about a man and his calf. I didn't really get the point of the story, but it seemed fitting, out there on the track.

Then, just when everyone had settled again, young Gracie, I swear, turned around and winked at her admirers, with a special (I so thought) glance reserved for me before she turned around again. With the wisdom of my years, I can now say that the wink was not really meant to be an encouragement. It was a wink of a shared sense of fun. To the young, whatever their gender or location, provoking outrage in their elders and betters is always a good lark.

This time the giggles couldn't be contained, and that was way too much for the blacksmith, who must have known what was going on. He marched across, picked out the main giggler, a scrawny bloke a bit older than me called Thomas Barnes, took hold of his neck in a pincer grip, squeezing until he howled like a dog.

'You think it's fun to ogle my daughter and disrespect God?'

'No, no, I didn't mean nothing ... I swear!'

The blacksmith marched the offender a good distance away and followed it up with a boot to the arse. 'Now fuck off out of it, you clown.' This done, Oswald walked back, tipped his hat to Jim Minogue. 'Beg pardon for the interruption, Mister Minogue. Please carry on.'

There were no more giggles, and no more winks, for that matter, but as the party broke up I swore I caught another glance from Gracie. It was just one look, but I saw something there. I collected Constance from the tree where I had tethered her, and rode away, feeling a little warmer inside.

Bypassing the site of the town that would one day be Longreach, then just a waterhole on the Thomson, we followed the Darr River, then the Western River, to Vindex Station, the pride and joy of Churnside, Riley and Company. Vindex was one of the first operations in the area to really work on their water supply. By the time we came through it boasted twenty-two tanks and dams, all but drought-proofing the property.

The Mitchell grass plains that had stretched from horizon to horizon, were interrupted by the first of many flat-topped hills near Vindex. Some were deep red, others grassed over, and some could be climbed on horseback.

This dramatic scenery helped pass the time as we closed on Winton. We were looking forward to the promised new wagonette, and thus the end to the packhorse droving experience that none of us were enjoying. Being cart-less, we had also lost our ability to keep at least some of the breeding herd's progeny, born on the journey, alive, and our route was littered with cairns where we had buried dead calves.

The men were also excited at the prospect of a blow-out at Winton's two hotels. Apart from the obvious lure of beer, we were all keen for a change in diet – a meal of pork or mutton and vegetables. Not a man from that camp would order beef; we were sick of it. Mick Skeahan penned a verse that was oft repeated around the campfire:

We 'ave a wondrous diet, with tucker of every kind,
Liver for bleeding breakfast, and stew for bleeding tea,
Corned tongue at the noon-time, and jerky when we ride,
And if a calf should chance to fall, it's staggering Bob besides.

The other reason for stronger than usual interest in the town of Winton was that the newest watering hole, the North Gregory, apparently boasted a barmaid by the name of Polly, whose cleavage and general good looks had pulled whole droving teams hundreds of miles from their intended route, halting the show in the dry dust of that Western Queensland town for the chance of a glimpse of white skin and a chat over the bar.

Men from all the Durack teams had been talking about Polly for days before our approach, gaining intelligence from travellers on her height, bust size, complexion and eye colour. One dusty wanderer confided that she was five-foot-six in her bare feet, soft and fair. Another reported that she was taller than any woman he had ever seen, and definitely beautiful, but that she thought herself too good for one and all. 'Carried herself like a queen,' he added, 'and turned up her nose every time I said a word. Got no time for her now, I can tell ya.'

One rumour suggested that beer was threepence a glass for most, but if Polly liked the look of a man tuppence was enough. Others suggested that for a greater investment a man could purchase time upstairs with the famous barmaid. Others said that this rumour was false, and that she was a woman of virtue.

For my own part, the town didn't interest me a great deal. As I've said before, I was not a drinker, in my younger days, and my thoughts were busy with Gracie and how the shape of her legs had revealed themselves at the church service, so I didn't share the general anticipation for our arrival at Winton.

It was entertaining, however, to listen to the lads as they talked of what they'd like to do to Polly. They all had a plan with which they might win her heart. Mick Skeahan had a nugget of pure gold as big as a fingernail that he had found on one of his father's prospecting expeditions. Kendall trusted his good looks, and had a brand-new suit neatly packed in his luggage.

'It's all in the presentation,' he whispered. 'You're offering a woman not just one night, but a future. You have to show her that you take yourself seriously.'

We camped some two miles southeast of Winton, a grassy spot on a billabong known as Policeman's Waterhole. Of course, we couldn't leave the cattle alone and all split off to town. Lots were drawn, as to which evening we could attend. I know the system was rigged, for Mick and Patsy, the Durack relatives, along with Billy, went the first night, leaving Ken, Dick and I in camp.

The trio came back well before midnight, so drunk they could scarcely ride. Mick fell off his horse and took his place at the fire, smiling crazily to himself.

'So what happened?' Ken asked.

Patsy built up the blaze and swayed before it, turning this way and that. 'I'm a married man, lads, I didn't so much as look at her.'

Billy Higgins snarled. 'The man who pegged her as a haughty type told the truth,' he said. 'Hardly gave me the time of day.'

'What about your gold nugget, Mick?' I asked.

The poor lad had a lost expression in his eyes, clearly lovelorn. 'She said it were real pretty, and that it made her day.' He pointed to his cheek. 'She kissed me, right there. If you look closely you can see where her lipstick came off on me skin.'

We examined Mick's cheek in the firelight, and there was indeed a rosebud shaped red mark. This was an exciting discovery, and Mick puffed out his chest.

Billy Higgins shook his head. 'Give it up you stupid lad. You just threw away a nugget worth twenty quid for a kiss on the cheek.'

'Better than what you got,' I said.

'And you mind your tongue … just because I'm not stupid enough to give away valuables to barmaids … I paid my money and got a skinful of whisky and that's all I wanted in town. I don't go chasing after barmaids who think they're too good for everybody.'

I would have reminded him that he'd been singing a different tune before he rode into Winton, but I knew that the time wasn't yet ripe to push him too far.

CHAPTER EIGHT

At that time thousands of cattle were following this trail en route for the Kimberleys and other country. The boom was on and mob after mob were being rushed to the north.

DICK, KEN, AND I took our turn late the following afternoon to ride into town. I'm not sure why Dick wanted to go in, most of the black boys stayed at camp, but he was a curious fellow, and very loyal. We started riding off at a walk, but at the last minute I said, 'Hang on you fellers, I forgot something. I'll catch you up.'

I cantered back and dug into my swag for the letter I'd been writing to Ma and the girls. I buttoned it into my top pocket. Thus prepared, I hurried back so as not to be left behind.

The town was some five miles away, but it wasn't long before we found ourselves following a beaten road, with other droving camps here and there, hermits in shanties and a couple of China-men. Their faces were invisible under their wide, cone shaped hats, weeding their vegetable plots in the poor soil, using water raised from a narrow billabong called Pelican Hole.

Before long, however, we entered Winton, a frontier town of jangling spurs, bright-painted stores and dusty bullockies. The main strip boasted a chemist, newsagent, a Bank of New South Wales branch office, police barracks, boarding houses, blacksmiths, saddlers, and best of all — four pubs — the Royal Mail, the Western, the Cosmopolitan and the North Gregory.

Washed and wearing our best clobber, we whooped with delight as we tramped into Elderslie Street, singing ditties popular at the time, the favourite being Billy the Brink.

There once was a shearer by the name of Bill Brink,
A devil for work and a devil for drink,
He'd shear his two hundred a day without fear,
And he'd drink without stopping two gallons of beer.
When the pub opened up he was very first in,
Roaring for whisky and howling for gin.

We visited a fine store belonging to town pioneers, Corfield and Fitzmaurice, with everything on sale from boots to tobacco. Tomato sauce was a popular purchase, for it was the closest thing to fresh fruit available on the trail and helped keep scurvy – Barcoo rot as we called it – at bay.

I found the post office next to the bank, and there bought an envelope and stamps. The postmistress offered to address it for me, but I laughed and did it myself with a quill and ink on the bench. My Uncle Henry's place in Ballarat had been familiar to me since childhood and I knew the address by heart. I sent my letter off, and with a lighter heart met the others outside.

Across the other side of the road, I saw a well-dressed young woman stepping into a coach, and behind her was the blacksmith himself, Walter Oswald. I realised that it was Gracie getting in, and feeling bold, I rode up to the side of the cab.

'Back to school?' I asked.

Gracie's face lit up when she saw me. 'Yes, one more term, and then I'll be done with it.'

The blacksmith came around the back of the coach. 'Oi lad, I'll thank you not to talk to my daughter. Unnerstand?'

'Just being polite, sir. Wishing her my best.' I tipped my hat and smiled at Gracie. She smiled back.

'Not my place to say anything,' Kendall said as we rode away, 'but you're playing with fire there. That damn blacksmith is a maniac. He'll kill you if you touch her.'

'She's beautiful,' I said.

'Indeed she is.'

'I just hope she comes back,' I said.

'I saw the way she looked at you. For the sake of your health, I hope she doesn't.'

The North Gregory Hotel was an improvement on the basic pubs we'd seen along the way. It was a ground-level building, with a steeply pitched roof, extending low to shade the verandah that ran the full length. White posts were spaced every few yards.

Stockmen, travellers, and local businessmen spilled out from inside; drinking, laughing, yarning and arguing about cricket, horses or politics. Although it was still spring the evening was warm, and beer glasses emptied quickly.

We tethered the horses to a public hitching post, and removed our saddles, prepared to take them inside like most of the others had done, but Dick said, 'I just sit down alonga saddle and horse.'

Kendall was by then preoccupied with brushing dust and horse hair from his suit, but I was a little saddened that after having ridden with us, Dick wouldn't come inside the bar.

'Don't do that,' I said. 'Come inside for a feed and I'll buy you a drink.' Few white men would break the rule of not providing alcohol to blacks, but there were always cordials and brewed soft drinks.

Dick pointed a callused forefinger up at the verandah. 'Hey boss, how many blackfellow you see alonga pub?'

I looked. 'None.'

'True. I alla same jes' stay alonga plant. Plenty 'a wild horse duffers inna place like 'dis.'

'As you like mate. I'll bring you out a feed and try not to let him—' I nodded my head at Kendall, 'stay too long.'

The drinkers, sitting or leaning on the rail, stared as we crossed the verandah. I entered the pub first, through floor to ceiling swinging doors, designed, I guess, to keep the flies out. Inside was the image of a frontier watering hole, with a bar that occupied the centre, so that drinkers could order from any side of the room.

There were perhaps fifty dusty men inside. A yarn at every table and stained hats resting beside jugs of whisky and pots of beer. Most wore revolvers in their gun belts. It was warm, as I have said, and the smell was ripe, of beer as well as male sweat.

In the centre of all this was Polly herself. I knew it was her straight away. Not as tall as legend suggested, nor as buxom, but she was a well put together young lady. She was thin in build, with blonde hair tied in a bun behind her head, and wearing a dress and apron. Her impressive bosom was, artfully, on partial display.

The hubbub stopped as we walked in, and I felt every eye in that place on us. Kendall was one of the few men wearing a suit, for a start, and he looked like he'd just stepped out of the Sandhurst Club back home. We tried to behave as if no one was watching, straight to the bar. Polly herself came over to serve us.

'Evening gents, what will it be? I've got beer by the barrel straight from Brisbane, plenty of whisky and rum. Not only that but we make our own refreshing ginger beer, and we've been selling it by the gallon, if you'd like to start with that.'

'My dear lady,' Kendall said, 'My name is Ken, and this is my young friend Charlie.'

'A pleasure to meet you, gentlemen. What'll you have?' She peered at me. 'How old are you?'

'It doesn't matter. Ginger beer for me,' I said.

'Do you have champagne?' Kendall inquired of the barmaid.

A crease of amusement crossed her lips. 'I think there's a bottle or two in the cellar.'

'That would be magnificent.' But as she turned again to leave, he stopped her. 'Now before you go, please tell me, mademoiselle, I'm thinking about your accent. Which part of Paris do you hail from?'

'Of all the ... stone the crows, I've heard some sweet talkers before, but you take the cake. If I was from Paris I'd be speaking French, wouldn't I?' She had her hands on her hips, and her lips made a pout, but even I, relatively inexperienced with the fairer sex as I was, could see that her eyes were lit up like gas mantles, and that she seemed to be dancing on those previously tired feet.

'Not necessarily,' said Kendall. 'In my experience, all the noted Paris beauties speak English as well. The French value education for their women, which of course we should too.'

Polly rolled her eyes. 'I'll get that champagne.'

While we waited Ken winked at me. 'Maybe you'd better leave me to it, lad. I work best alone if you know what I mean.' He didn't need to ask me twice. I was keen to mix with the men rather than just watch what I expected to be a boots-and-all but futile attempt on the fair barmaid's honour. Drovers from the other mobs made up a good proportion of the crowd in the bar that night, and I'd noticed some 'famous' faces. Two more Duracks, along with Tom Kilfoyle and the giant Scot, Duncan McCaully, known universally as the 'Scrub Bull', to name but a few.

I picked up my glass and headed away from the bar. As I passed by a table one of the drinkers stood up and introduced himself.

'Hi there young fellow, I've seen you around the camps. Me name's Black Pat Durack.'

I could see how he'd earned the nickname: his skin was tanned deep brown. Even his eyes were like twin pebbles of coal. 'Hello. My name's Charlie Gaunt, I'm working with Mister Jerry's mob.'

'To be sure you are. I hear that you're a first-rate horseman.'

I couldn't help but smile. That was pretty much the biggest accolade a man could get in this world. 'Thank you.'

He looked around the table. 'Some introductions are in order, then a dram or two to seal new friendships.'

I'd seen most of the men at that table on the drive, but now I had the opportunity to shake their callused brown hands and learn their names. We commented on the state of the country; (dry as the plains of hell). We talked about the town (friendly), the pub (crowded), and before long the yarns started.

In between meeting new friends, I kept half an eye on our cook, as he worked on Polly the barmaid. He talked to her every time she took a pause. He asked her questions about herself, complimented everything about her from the silver brooch she wore to the 'uncanny blue' of her eyes.

I was listening to Black Pat opine on the degradation of the Australian stock horse (twenty year ago was the peak, lads,) when a man's voice cut through the general clamour in the room, loud enough that all conversation stopped, and eyes turned to identify the speaker.

'For fuck's sake—' the voice shouted.

I had, as soon as we walked in, noticed a table of ringers in from one of the local stations, eight or nine of them, drinking steadily. The relationship between drovers and station folk was strained all along our route. After all, we lobbed in from far-flung districts, camped on the best waterholes, and fed our stock on pasture they regarded as their own.

One member of this crowd was a true loudmouth, about my age, tall and wiry, and obviously a firm believer in his own wit.

'Why do we have to put up with this? There're more of these grass thieves and cattle duffers in here tonight than I've seen in a whole month.'

Punches would have been thrown, but a couple of the man's companions managed to get him to sit down. An older man in the party apologised for his mate. 'Sorry fellers, young Eddie here had a hard day in the sun and has drunk himself a skinful tonight. He weren't intending to mean anything by it.'

The apology would have carried more weight, but for the troublemaker loudly struggling, and shouting gems like. 'Too right I meant it,' and 'let me up and I'll fight every one of the bally grass-thieving bastards.'

They eventually settled him down, and the conversation at our table was now being led by a man called Scrutton, the half-caste son of a British Army Officer and a high-born Indian woman. He too had served in the army, pacifying his own countrymen, before deserting and taking ship to Australia.

I wanted stories of cavalry charges and frontal assaults, and said so. Scrutton merely scratched his whiskers. 'War is not like you think. Well, not in my experience.'

I tried to hide the hero worship from my face. 'Sounds bloody exciting,' I said, 'charging with bayonets fixed and all that.'

Scrutton gave a sad smile. 'You ever killed a man?'

'Not yet.'

One of the other men piped up. 'You droved to the Territory and back and never had cause to shoot a blackfellow? I hear they're thick as crows up there.'

'Nat Buchanan doesn't fight them. He travels fast, and single-minded. We saw them, and lost a few horses and bullocks, but Nat don't bother with them much. Shots were fired by others, but I never went near to killing one.'

Scrutton patted me on my shoulder. 'Don't hurry to that milestone, lad. Only a psychopath thinks it feels good to take a man's life.' He stood up, belched loudly and patted his belly. 'I'm off to the bog, save my seat and watch my drink, will you, boy?'

After Scrutton wandered off I found myself no longer part of the various discussions going on around me. Quickly bored, I turned my attention back to Kendall, who now had Polly the barmaid leaning over the bar towards him. He had prevailed on her to join him in a glass of champagne, and she sipped daintily from what appeared to be a crystal glass.

'I have composed a verse in your honour,' Kendall was saying loudly, removing a folded sheet of notepaper from inside his coat.

The look in Polly's eyes was of pure captivation, and I was slowly revising my assessment of my friend's chances.

'Oh, have you?' she cooed. 'Before you even met me?'

'Indeed I did, shall I read it?'

Kendall not only read that verse, but did so like a born actor, in a voice loud enough to shake the rafters with his ringing tones. The room went quiet, for this was a performance worthy of a San Francisco oratory hall, such as I had the pleasure to visit later in life.

Of course, I knew for a fact that Kendall had not composed that sweet poem of love, but had copied it with steel pen and ink onto paper, from a published volume of poems. The true author was an Englishman called William Wordsworth, and Ken had guessed correctly that a Winton barmaid would not know that he had ripped off those lines off a real poet.

Still, the performance was glorious to watch. Kendall finished on his knees, looking up at her with eyes that, I'm sure, shone with love. His voice rang out one last time. 'My lady, would you do me the honour of taking a stroll about town with me tomorrow?'

Every man listening, along with Polly herself, knew that the hooves of countless cattle and sheep had turned the already drought-stricken town of Winton into a dust bowl. The invitation to stroll, issued in Ken's Oxford accent like a gentleman might have invited his lady to walk down Leicester Square, provoked howls of laughter.

The loud local stockman, escaping from the restraining hands of his fellows, stood up from his chair. 'Oh la-di-dah. You bally toff. Never heard such a heap of steaming bullock turd in my life.' His mates tried to grab him again, but he escaped by leaping athletically over their restraining arms.

He climbed on a table, facing Kendall. 'Why don't you,' he said, 'fuck off back to wherever you come from with your grass-thieving mates.'

I was into the spirit of the night by this stage, and knew that Ken would have little choice but to fight this larrikin, which might ruin his chances with the lady. I was also the loudmouth's own age, and thus a logical choice to champion the honour of my mate. Accordingly, I dropped my drink with a clunk to the table and stood up.

'Hey mate!' I shouted, to get his attention. 'Where are you from?'

The local wit screwed up his eyes, not sure if I was making fun of him or not. 'What's it to you?'

'I'm just trying to work out where they breed mongrel dogs as ugly and loud as you.'

The Durack crowd roared with delight, then an expectant silence took hold as all eyes fell on me, asking the same question. I'd uttered strong words, was I man enough to follow through with my fists?

Well, I'd learned that lesson at the hands of my own father. You'd not find me backing away from a barney. Not then. Not ever.

Every soul in that bar, apart from Kendall and Polly, followed us outside, carrying their drinks to watch us fight. I took off my shirt and handed it to Duncan McCaully, the Scrub Bull, effectively making him my second. Apart from his size, a revolver hung from Duncan's gun belt. There would be no dirty tricks from the opposition.

The loudmouth also took off his shirt, and he was a specimen worthy of respect, fortified with tight corded muscle from top to toe. He was also taller than me, with long sinuous arms. On the plus side, I had prepared for the fight with three glasses of Winton's finest ginger beer, whereas he had ripened on the real thing. I could smell the vomity rankness on his breath as we faced each other on the dusty street.

Michael Durack, the most senior of the Duracks in the pub that night, took our wrists in a grip of iron. His nickname was 'Hangfire Mick,' because of the stuttering, but he was also a tall bastard, and as wide across the shoulders as a door. 'R-r-right gents, we've got Charles G-gaunt here at say one hunnerd and twenty-five p-pounds, and ... what's yer name, sonny?'

'Eddie Oakes.'

'Here we have Eddie Oakes, say one hunnerd and thirty-five. M-m-make it a clean fight boys, p-prize-ring rules. D-don't be in too much of a hurry, let the boys get their bets on before you start.'

I spat on my hands and bunched them into fists. I had learned to box at school, and while droving with Nat Buchanan I'd extended my skills with a few dirty little scraps, usually with men much older than me.

We shaped up and started to move. Eddie Oakes was a dancer, light on his feet, eyes locked on mine. I sized him up quickly, deciding that this was not a fight I could win at long range – he would tear me apart with his superior reach.

He tested me out with a left jab that I deflected away with my right fist, forcing him to keep his weight committed to the punch so I could counter with a short jab into his sternum. He grunted like a dog, and his eyes narrowed.

I heard voices, money changing hands, comments on our physical condition, and loud advice, yet it all seemed very distant. I wanted respect in this open air world of mine, peopled by hard characters. I knew I would be judged for a long time on how I handled myself here. It focussed me, brought everything in to a bright speck of light.

Backwards and forwards we went, with a mist of dust rising in the yellow glow of the gas lamp. I saw Dick in that ring of men, cheering me on like the others. His face was black, but he was like any other stockman inside, for I never had cause to doubt him in all the years we rode together.

In that early period of sparring, I fancied that I had the measure of my opponent. Left jab. Block. Hook. Sometimes I allowed him to lead then tore in close, punching into his body, then his lip. On my second attempt this combination brought a streak of blood trickling down over his chin.

The blood gave me confidence, but then instead of standing back and punching straight he did something I didn't expect. He advanced on me, throwing wide swinging hooks with both hands. These were dangerous punches, launched outside the area in which I was able to focus my vision.

The crowd roared and backed out of the way as the energy of that charge pushed me backwards. I fended as much as I could with my forearms, elbows protecting my ribs, but one good blow landed on my ear like a cracking whip, and started to burn. It took a big effort for me to stop my retreat cold, crouch low and punch short and deep into his gut. He staggered, grunted, but was setting himself for another swing when I pivoted again, slipped outside the range of his left and chopped into his kidney.

He bent over, and Hangfire Mick came out and started to count, his stiff moustaches twitching with the excitement of the moment. Right there on the street my adversary spewed up hours of beer and whatever he'd been eating.

The crowd howled with delight. 'Bring it up mate! Aw fuck, sausages.'

I thought that was it, and so did Hangfire Mick, for he gripped my wrist in preparation to lift my arm high as the winner. Eddie Oakes, however, was made of sterner stuff than this.

He wiped his lips with his forearm and came at me. I was expecting more wild swings but he took me by surprise with a combination of jabs: body, then face, smacking me hard on the nose.

The bloke wouldn't give up, and hurting him enough to stop his punches seemed to be impossible. Blood from my nostrils ran into my mouth and I could taste the salty tang of it. Still, I gave back as good as I was getting.

Our punches meant business, and as we tired, we stopped blocking and weaving so that we both started to land more blows. I got his left eye twice until it swelled red, and he swotted my nose again.

We fought until blood spattered our arms and chests, and our breathing came hard. Still that bloke could not put me down, and I could not put him down, try as I might. He stung me on the ear again, snapping my head sideways with a vicious left hook. He knew he had got me a good one, but hadn't the strength to follow up. I found myself staggering drunkenly back a pace or two. For the first time in that fight I felt the fire of rage in my blood. I wanted to show him who was boss. I wanted to grind his face into the dust with my boot.

I raised my fist and headed back in. I guess I didn't know how spent I was, for I had hardly made a pace or two before Hangfire Mick grabbed my right forearm and stopped me cold, also gripping my opponent in the same way. In a loud voice he asked the crowd if they'd accept a draw, in the interests of two fine young lads not causing permanent damage to each other.

I stood back, groggy, the world reeling. A few punters complained, wanting more blood, but the rest of them agreed.

'Right fellers, well done on a fair fight, now shake hands.'

All the aggression left me. Eddie and me shook hands, then hugged like brothers. Someone came out with buckets of water and sluiced the blood from our faces and bodies as the others went inside. Eddie and I sat on the front steps, swore an oath to be mates until death, and talked as honestly as old friends.

'If you want to come a-droving with us,' I told him, 'I bet Hangfire Mick will hire you.'

'Dunno. Me little brother and sister are at Roma and I'm saving enough to take up a selection back that way as soon as I can.'

'Well good luck with it.' I sighed. 'I'm done for the night. Gonna head back in and see if I can drag my mate away.'

We both went inside. But no one was going to let me light out just then. They all wanted to clap me on the shoulder. I could have drunk beer for free for the rest of the night, but the soft stuff was enough for me. In any case, before ten minutes had passed, Kendall left Polly to help cope with the rush of post-fight drink orders.

'Let's go back to camp,' he said.

'Suits me. Any luck? Is she going to walk the fine streets of Winton with you?'

He gave me a look. 'Of course she is. I must say that by getting into a fight and taking most of the bar outside you did me a great boon, lad.'

'Do you think she'll um, go all the way?'

'Now that depends on a number of factors beyond my control, partly that I have very little time in which to work. Polly is a strong-minded woman, and I respect her for that. Overall, I must say, I'm mightily impressed with her.'

We collected Dick and our gear and as we rode back to camp other men called out on the track as we passed. 'Good stoush mate, well done. You had the bastard's measure, a few more minutes and you'd have laid him low.'

Scrutton, the half-caste Indian I had so admired, rode up, and was overtaking us on the track with a couple of his mates when he must have recognised me in the moonlight. 'Hey, young Charlie. Well done there tonight.' Then, to Kendall. 'I must say, old chap, that was as fine a reading of Wordsworth as I've heard in many a year.'

There was silence for a moment, before Kendall said, 'Thanks a million. Glad you were a good sport and didn't spill the beans.'

Scrutton laughed. 'Just because I can't have something meself won't cause me to ruin another man's chances. Good luck, you've got a smooth way with you and that always goes down well with the ladies.

An older stockman, a hard-bitten native Queenslander called Bob Perry introduced himself and rode beside me for a bit. 'You did well, son, you proved you can box, but you need to learn how to finish a fight. If you get a spare hour one afternoon ride on over to see me at Hangfire Mick's camp and I'll give you some tips.'

Kendall listened to this exchange, then said, 'I take it that you are a fighter of some note.'

'Oh, I've had a bout or two in me day.'

I ignored my mate and addressed my would-be instructor.

'I'll do that, thanks Mr Perry.'

'Bob, that is. Call me Bob.'

CHAPTER NINE

The country was now dry and parched, and grass and water were scarce.

For the next two days, while we rested the cattle, Kendall stayed almost all the time back in Winton. This didn't go down well with the men. Not only was our dough-roaster failing to provide the quality of tucker we expected, but a fog of jealousy filled the camp, as if we didn't need any more problems. Billy Higgins referred to Kendall only as that 'sopping ladies' man.'

When we finally moved on, Kendall drove his horses glumly, up high on the box of our brand new wagonette, purchased in Winton.

I tried to cheer him up several times on that first day, walking Constance beside him for a bit. 'Snap out of it,' I said. 'You're dragging everyone down.'

'I can't. I love Polly, and she loves me, but with every chap who lands in Winton vying for her, sooner or later she's going to hook up with someone else.'

'There are other women, in other places,' I said, though I knew for a fact that the number of Englishwomen between here and the journey's end would most likely be counted on one hand.

We turned southwest, following the twisting, multiple pathways of the Diamantina River. At first this was a flat landscape smeared with clay pans, upstaged by the handsome Macartney Ranges that appeared on the horizon and grew bigger every day. These hills led us all the way to the Diamantina Gates, a narrow section with a very welcome waterhole. Tough times were ahead as drought tightened its grip on Western Queensland.

To make matters worse, some of the stockmen had learned in Winton that the going rates of pay for drovers in this part of the world were almost double those being earned in the Durack party. The whispering started, and discontent spread quickly.

'Hey Charlie?' drawled a man who appeared on my flank and trotted up so he was riding alongside.

'Yes?'

'Now much are you being paid?'

'Two pounds – forty shillings – a week.'

'Well, that's better than most of us. But we should be getting sixty shillings at least. Those tight-arsed Duracks are ripping us off, and we're going to do something about it. Are you in?'

I was too smart to let myself get labelled as a 'scab' on a long droving trip. 'You bet your arse, mate. More money will suit me fine.'

Nothing happened just yet, but the word spread, and a couple of the older hands came to be seen as the ringleaders.

'Soon,' they said, 'we're going to do something about it.'

I should have known something was up when Kendall suddenly turned bright and chatty – quite his normal self. Pitching camp early, he prepared a tasty beef stew, chased down with fresh Johnny-cakes dipped in the gravy. There were pots of tea, and on full stomachs the spirits of the men of our crew lifted. Even Billy Higgins seemed happier.

At sunrise, when we took our quart pots over for breakfast the fire was cold, and Kendall's swag and horse were gone. Back to his lady love at Winton. Later I heard that they rode to Brisbane and were married.

'Damn that man,' Billy Higgins spat. 'I had him pegged as a rascal from the moment I laid eyes on him.'

Now we had a new wagonette, but no man free to drive it. Unwilling to lose it to another team, however, we took turns to take it ahead of the mob and get some tucker on. Taking pity on us, Hangfire Mick lent us an extra man, a sharp horseman by the name of Jack Sherringham. He fitted in straight off.

Yet we remained desperate for a new cook, and when we passed a hairy old swagman on the track, Patsy Moore leaned down from his horse.

'D'y know how to cook and drive a wagon, old man?'

'Yairs, I reckon so.'

'D'y feel like driving one all the way to the Kimberley for tucker and a good cheque at the end?'

The old man shrugged, 'Where in fuck's name is the Kimberley?'

Patsy pointed to the north-west, a hazy horizon of dust and salt bush. 'That way a thousand miles or so.'

'I guess I will then.'

We sighed with relief in unison. We'd hated taking turns driving the wagonette. It was cursed boring work, and every now and then a wheel would get stuck, or fall off, setting off hours of aggravation. We all preferred to be riding with the cattle. The new cook took to his role without enthusiasm, but managed to keep us fed and do his job. His main vice was sleeping, and several times we found the wagonette wandering into the bush, the horses trailing off wherever they felt like it, with the old swaggie fast asleep at the reins.

Heading west to the Hamilton River we encountered an area of upwelling waters called Parker Springs. Bubbling pools, fed by aquifers deep below the surface provided a welcome indulgence.

At this oasis, we crossed paths with Australia's longest-ever sheep drive, heading from Rich Avon Station in Victoria to the Barkly Tablelands. Men from both drives mingled at the springs and around campfires. We looked down on the sheep-men – called them ewe-shaggers and joked that they stank like wool – but they were mostly good types, and it was fun to swap a yarn or two.

This short break on the drive brought the festering sore of industrial action to the surface. A deputation of the organisers fronted Big Johnnie. 'Now listen here, Mr Durack. Fair's fair, but we're not going to work for half wages. Anyone can see with this drought that tough times are ahead, and even these sheep drovers are earning twice what we get.'

Big Johnnie had no desire to double his wages bill. Red faced and blustering, he refused point blank. 'Damn ye all to hell, and we'll bring new stockmen out from Ireland to replace ye.'

'You've got twenty-four hours to agree,' said the organiser. 'Then every one of us walks away and you can take your cattle on alone.'

The enforced rest was invigorating. Some of the pools were too hot for swimming, but the larger ones were no warmer than a bath. We took the opportunity for the first real bogie in many weeks, and even now, at the remove of more than fifty years I can remember just how those waters restored us in body and mind.

It was long after sunset when I came off the mob, handing over to Dick, who was on watch. The old cook, along with Mick and I, wandered up to the springs. The water surface was black and steaming, and it seemed underworld-like to me. But still, we stripped naked, shy about our white bodies with their stockman's tans, and stepped into the water, laughing with delight as the warm waters claimed our skin. We had each brought bundles of filthy clothes, and for an hour we washed every thread we owned.

It had taken me a while to get to know Mick Skeahan, but he was as honest as a judge, and good company. He also owned a lump of carbolic soap that we shared between us. With our newly-washed clothes hanging off branches of the surrounding trees we skylarked for a while, splashing and carrying on like kids in a creek.

Mick and I were just youngsters, and there'd been little time for play on the track. Even with games like mumble-the-peg or riding stunts there was always an element of having to prove yourself, to be better than the next man. That night, in the steaming water, we had a bit of fun, laughed until our throats hurt, and let ourselves be boys for a while.

Finally, the old cook and Mick declared themselves waterlogged and wandered back to camp, but I could not bring myself to leave. I laid myself back, firmly planted on an underwater rock, and closed my eyes. I thought about Ma, Marion and Nellie. Then I started thinking about Kendall and Polly, and how they were getting on together.

Eventually, of course, my mind touched on Gracie, back at boarding school, in some fancy uniform. I guessed she'd be asleep by now, and I imagined her in some great four-poster bed, with gossamer curtains, lying on her side under silken sheets, beautiful dark hair on a soft white pillow.

It wasn't long before I undressed her in my mind. I pictured her, slim and naked with the sheets thrown back. Images of Gracie's face, her lips brushing mine, filled my head.

I heard footsteps, then Billy Higgins appeared on the other side of the pool. 'When you've finished laying around like Lady bloody Muck in that hot water you can help Dick with some bogged cattle.'

He turned on his heel. I wanted to ask him why he couldn't help Dick with the bogged cattle himself. It was always me. I wondered if he hated me because he knew deep down that I was already better than him at just about everything. I stood up from the water, goose bumps breaking out in the cool air after the hot water, and dressed in moleskins and shirt. They were sodden wet, but would soon dry on horseback.

The cattle grazed happily for a few days, while we all bogied and rested. Johnny Durack finally agreed to the new terms and the mobs moved on.

CHAPTER TEN

We had now been three months on the road and the wet season being close at hand, and the country dry ahead, we decided to make a fixed camp ... finding a suitable camp on The Georgina, at a big permanent water hole known as Parapitcheri. This water is ten miles long, good stock water, but brackish and sweet tasted. We made a grave mistake camping there as we found out afterwards.

DESPERATE FOR PERMANENT WATER, we followed the Hamilton River westwards. After weeks of dry stages and desperate scouting parties riding ahead, local blacks, communicating with Dick in some old trade language, told us of a reliable waterhole on the Georgina they called Parapitcheri. We had no choice but to drive the herds that way. Drought was tightening its grip, and three days without water would finish the drive before it was so much as halfway to the Kimberley.

On the fringes of the Simpson Desert, the Parapitcheri was deep and long, but there were no big river red gums throwing shade, nor a broad channel. It was more of a gutter than a hole, marked by twisted melaleucas and stunted gidgee trees. The northern bank was crowned with a spiny marsh grass.

Despite the black soil plains on either side, the pasture was pale grey and poor. None of us liked the place; it had an eerie feel about it. There was no decent firewood, either, just brittle dry acacia branches that burned hot but fast.

Like most advances into good water after a long dry stage the cattle smelled the hole from miles off. We were forced to cut them out into smaller herds to prevent a portion being trampled to death or drowned in the shallows.

There was still some feed on the plains above, and Big Johnnie

Durack sent Bob Perry around to tell us that we'd be making a long-term camp here to wait out the drought. After all, seven thousand head of cattle was a sizable asset, and a few months of stockmen's wages was little enough in comparison.

'Hey all you blokes,' Bob called out as he rode up. 'Big Johnnie says we're stopping here. He wants temporary horse yards and good clean camps.'

Before he left, he said to me. 'The offer of the boxing lessons is still open. Looks like we're going to have time on our hands here.'

'Thanks Bob, I'll be in that, for sure.'

There was work to be done first. We all claimed a little space of our own on the banks, with the boys vying to make a decent home for themselves out of sticks, rocks and the natural lay of the land. Furniture took on all weird and wonderful forms; chairs, tables, shelves cobbled together with twine, greenhide and wire twitches.

Our camp centred on a rock bar at the halfway point of the waterhole. It was a good fishing spot, and we caught big, red-clawed crayfish by tying a lump of beef on the end of some string, waiting until the creature grabbed it, then slowly pulling it closer to the bank until it could be scooped up with a makeshift net.

There were blacks camped on the upstream end of the waterhole. Dick and Johnnie went to see them as soon as we arrived and reported back that they were mainly the local Pitta-pitta tribe, with some Kalkadoons from further north mixed in. When a couple of old men brought us some large yellowbelly perch and some crayfish they had speared, Big Johnnie took the opportunity to hire five or six of the youngest and fittest to help look after the cattle in return for rations of flour, tea and beef. It was a clever move, made with the aim of preventing the spearing of cattle and horses, through creating goodwill between our groups.

It was also good management, for the cattle mingled into just one big mob, and ate the grass out from the immediate vicinity, meaning that they had to move longer distances each day to find grazing. At night they would walk back to the Parapitcheri for water. Our black helpers assisted in directing the mobs to grass, on the vast plains that surrounded Parapitcheri.

I was curious about this local tribe, and spent some pleasant hours talking to them about their customs. The complicated social systems they lived under staggered me, for you would never have guessed by looking at them. For example, a man of one particular caste was forbidden to eat goannas, certain species of ducks, dingoes or small yellow fish. Men of another caste could not eat plains turkeys, brown snakes, black dingoes or white ducks.

All, it seemed, could and would eat beef and Johnny-cakes.

The help from the Pitta-pitta tribesmen took the heat off the stockmen, and we soon settled down to a variety of activities designed to fill in time. Gambling games with cards and flash riding were all popular, and I set myself up with a two-up school on Sunday afternoons, which soon attracted a number of punters.

Mumble-the-peg, however, was the main diversion. The basics of the game were to throw an opened pen-knife in various ways so it stuck into the ground: flicked from the palm, from the back of the hand, with the blade-tip held between thumb and forefinger. Other throws called for it to be chucked over the shoulder, around the waist or between the legs.

Another pen knife was hammered into the ground, one blow for each failure of the blade to stick. The loser then had to remove, or 'mumble' this from the ground with his teeth, copping heaps from his mates as he did so.

Crafty types set about making stock whips, not just for their own use, but to sell to other stockmen, either here or along the way. They shot kangaroos, and skinned them for the greenhide.

Handles were carved from hardwood. I saw some fine whips made on the Parapitcheri.

Big Johnnie Durack issued orders that men with nothing else to do were to make rope. I tried my hand at this. It involved cutting a circle of greenhide, trimming it into a long thin strip, plaiting it, then combining it with two other strands, wound the other way. It was fiddly work and I hated it, putting in a turn when I had to, but preferring to ride tracks, fish or hunt.

Lively campfires were in big demand, and there was always a good crowd when Jack Sherringham had his concertina out. He could also sing a fair tune, and we passed many an evening with the cattle lowing softly as a backdrop to Jack's melodies.

Bob Perry, the pug who had offered me boxing lessons was in the same crew as Jack before we 'borrowed' him. After the first flurry of work from our arrival had settled down, and boredom had started to set in, I went to see him one afternoon.

We chased a couple of brolgas from a dried out mudflat on the waterhole. There he set me up on a ring of earth, swept clean of sticks and leaves.

When he took off his shirt, I saw that despite his age he was still in good condition; a little soft in the belly, but big and toned in the arms, chest and shoulders.

'Where did you learn to fight, Charlie?' he asked me.

'School sports, mainly.'

'I thought as much. They teach you all the fancy stuff. Things you'll get points for in a competition with your ma and pa sitting on chairs drinking lemonade and watching. You don't want to be that kind of fighter, not out here. There's no points. Just winning and losing.'

A couple of men wandered down to watch, then a few more. Even Hangfire Mick Durack stopped what he was doing and came for a look.

'Now Charlie,' Bob began. 'There are three ways to put a man down, and the most important way is a punch to the chin. You can use a right cross or an uppercut.' He pointed to the hinge of his own jaw. 'There's a nerve back in there, and it connects to a man's brain. When you hit the jaw hard that connection gets broken for a bit, and the whole body shuts down. If you do it right your man will hit the deck like a sack of potatoes.'

He shaped up to me, swinging a massive right cross, but in slow motion, landing it on the side of my jaw. It was done just as a demonstration, but I could feel the power in that raw-boned fist.

'Now you try it. I won't block just so's you get the idea, but later I'll show you the best way to counter these punches.'

I tried to do it just as he had shown me.

'Not bad, Charlie, but listen, you've got good biceps and shoulders but you're relying on them too much.' He patted his flanks down to his thighs. 'A hard right cross comes all the way from down there.'

I tried again. 'Is that better?'

'Yes, better. Now once more with a bit more guts in it.'

By then other blokes were stripping off their shirts and trying the punch out on each other. Bob drilled me without pause, until our feet were sinking in the mud and water seeping through, culminating with some sparring where he never stopped instructing me.

'Now, for the uppercut. Wait until the other bastard throws a hard left jab, go right so you're outside the punch. Pivot and shoot for the chin. Have your left ready in case you need it, but nine times out of ten, if you deliver the punch properly, it'll put him down.'

He showed me a bunch of exercises that would improve what he called my core strength, and the shadows were growing longer when he clapped me on the back. 'That's enough for one day. Come back tomorrow arvo and I'll teach you about the liver punch.'

As I walked back up towards the bank, buttoning my shirt as I went, Hangfire Mick Durack said to me, 'Y-you know B-bbob won the unofficial welterweight title for Queensland a few years b-back.'

My admiration for the man, already sky-high, rose still higher. 'That doesn't surprise me.'

Needless to say, Bob Perry's boxing school became one of the most popular diversions on the Parapitcheri, and it was exciting to see ten or a dozen lads all squared up and practising their moves, or doing push ups on the sand.

One man, who had doubled as a saddle-maker back at the Durack station Thylungra, used his needle and tanned calf hide to make us a punching bag, and some gloves, stuffed with horsehair. These allowed us to spar without hurting each other, though more than a drop or two of blood was spilled on the Parapitcheri mud.

News from Jerry Durack filtered back into the camp. The story went that Jerry had ridden south as fast as three good horses would take him: seventy, eighty miles a day until he reached Galway Downs.

Three-year-old Janie had held on to see her beloved daddy, for her eyes widened in recognition on her deathbed and he held her frame of skin and bones as tight as he dared. That little girl passed away, the morning after his arrival.

They had scarcely interred her in a tiny garden plot when their eldest girl, Bridget, also complained of fever and aching pains all over.

'I'll be damned if I'll bury another one of my girls,' cried Jerry. 'Pack up, we're heading for civilisation.'

They loaded a cart with their belongings and headed east to Ipswich, where Jerry bought a farm called Moorlands.

Yet, even with a doctor in visiting distance, young Bridget failed to recover, and when news reached us on the Parapitcheri she was not expected to live.

There was something of the fighter in her blood, however, for she hung on for two and a half more years, dying on the sixth of May, 1886. My promise to ride back and marry her, would forever remain unfulfilled.

I received the news of Bridget's illness and Janie's passing with deep sadness. There was little enough of the softer aspects of life in my world. The young Durack girls had touched my heart. Lying awake that night I tried to put myself in Jerry's place.

I felt a cold shiver as I pictured Janie's tiny coffin being lowered into the earth, adorned with roses and chrysanthemums. I tried to fathom how her mother felt, after bearing, raising, hoping for, caring for, loving, then nursing the child through dark days until death. My lips moved with the prayers I imagined Fanny Durack must have uttered.

When I finally slept, I dreamed that Bridget sat beside me, the skin of her face as white as chalk, hands cold as ice. Waking in a sweat I went down to the dark waters of the Parapitcheri to wash my face.

Many of the men were becoming ill and disconnected. One problem was a condition we called Barcoo rot, though it was properly called scurvy. Years later, I would see half the crew of a windjammer torn down by this affliction. The first sign was often scabby sores and bleeding gums, and for most of us, that was the extent of it.

But there was something else going on. The cattle were sickly and listless, and eventually too tired to walk out to feed.

Some of the men were badly affected, and a general malaise took over the camp. Our boxing training fell away to once or twice a week. The Duracks warned us of the dangers of inactivity and started dreaming up penning and roping competitions to keep us on the go. When the first man died, it became clear that we had a medical emergency on our hands.

Theories raged through the camps. That we were being stricken with plague, that the local Pitta-pitta warriors had acted against us. A meeting was held up behind Big Johnnie Durack's camp.

'Those black mongrels have poisoned the waterhole,' Billy Higgins said.

Big Johnnie dropped his eyes. 'I'm inclined to agree with ye. There's no other reason for this dashed illness.'

Billy pressed his advantage. 'I say we round every damn one up in the morning and drive them off.'

I could not bring myself to agree with Billy. 'That's not going to help if they've already poisoned the water.'

Hangfire Mick said, 'I agree w-w-with the boy. N-no point shutting the g-g-gate after the stallion's b-b-bolted.'

'If it's true,' Big Johnnie said, 'I wouldn't want to see the perpetrators go unpunished.'

'What a load of bally rot,' scoffed a man called John Urquhart. A member of Big Johnnie's party, he was known as an amateur veterinarian. 'This waterhole runs for miles. You'd need ten wagon loads of poison.'

'Maybe,' said Big Johnnie. 'But if I find out they had anything to do with it—'

I looked from one man to the other. There seemed to be no answer to the problem. Like the others I too had lost my usual energy and enthusiasm, though I was fitter than most.

Collectively we were at a loss as to how to solve this cri sis. We could not push the mob onwards because drought had tightened its grip, wiped

108

bare the grasslands, and sucked up all the smaller waterholes.

One morning, Dick rode off early, turning up again as I was still eating breakfast. I pointed to the billy, and offered him a cuppa, but he waved it away.

'Hey there Charlie. Couple of blackfulla wanna talk to you.'

I narrowed my eyes. 'What kind of blackfella do you mean?'

'Blackfulla who belong this country.'

Even though Big Johnnie had signed on a couple of these local blacks to help look after the cattle, I was still suspicious, I wouldn't be the first drover to be lured away from camp and speared. Not by Dick, I trusted him, but these local Pitta-pitta men were still three parts wild.

'Blackfulla won' hurt you, Charlie. They got help for you.'

I mounted one of the horses standing ready and rode off with Dick. We skirted the waterhole and rode upstream about five miles past the muddy end of Parapitcheri. Finally, I saw smoke rising ahead, and some rough bark humpies, black urchins running for the shelter of their parent's legs. Men, women and children alike wore decorations made of fur and feathers. Some wore items of white men's clothes; dungarees and shirts, and bits of jackets. One old bloke was naked apart from a faded old hat on his head – surely some cast-off picked up beside a lonely track somewhere.

When we dismounted, two of the blacks came across, but didn't approach us directly. They stopped half way and looked around the place. It was up to us to tie the horses to a tree and walk over to them. One was not much older than me, the other's beard was 'flour bag,' – as white as snow. I recognised the men as the ones who had been telling me about their culture some weeks earlier, which is, I imagine, why they singled me out.

As usual, Dick translated for me. 'This blackfulla say that waterhole is bad water. 'That why 'dose fulla dying and others alla same sick.'

'What?' I gasped out. 'We've been drinking that water for two blasted months.'

Dick translated, then again as one of the Pitta-pitta men spoke. 'That water go bad only when the water low like now. He show you where blackfulla get good water.'

I shrugged, 'I guess it can't hurt.'

Dick and I walked our horses, and the two black men loped alongside, leading us down into the main dry river channel above the waterhole, dark mud shaped by floods that seemed unimaginable then in the grip of that drought. Our guides fetched a couple of sticks, and began digging on a sharp bend. For want of something to do I was soon on my hands and knees beside them.

The sun was hot, but slowly we delved deeper. We were disappearing head and shoulders into the hole before I noticed that it was growing progressively wetter. Our efforts slowed as the size of the gravel mixed with mud and sand increased, and we were forced to work harder.

Soon, however, water was filling the hole faster than we could dig, and one of the local men waved at us to stop. He made a pantomime of dipping his hand, raising it to his lips and drinking deeply.

'Good water,' he said in halting English. 'Sweet water.'

Within the hour I was in conference with Big Johnnie, Black Pat, and Hangfire Mick. By the afternoon every water bag in the camp had been emptied, and refilled from that well, a five-mile haul from the closest of the camps. We used the wagonettes, drawn by horses or bullocks, to haul barrels that were emptied into troughs made of split hollow logs sealed with tin and beeswax at the ends.

'I've been wondering for weeks if the billabong water becomes caustic when the level drops,' John Urquhart said. 'But I had no way of testing it.'

The effect of the clean water was hard to believe. Within days men were whistling and singing again, the sounds of galloping horses and arguments over games of mumble-the-peg resumed.

With good water also improving their condition, the cattle wandered further out for grass. Occasionally a mob would stumble on a new source of surface water many miles away, and not return with the others. Most often this water would be little more than a soak and shallow puddle, but the cattle would not leave it.

Mick Skeahan, Dick, and I set off after one of these mobs one dawn, when Patsy noticed that at least three hundred head with the 7PD brand were missing. We located them finally in rough country some thirty miles from Parapitcheri and drove them back all night, finally reaching camp after more than twenty-four unbroken hours in the saddle.

We collapsed onto log-chairs around the fire, devouring the Johnny-cakes laid out for us, and drinking tea.

I had just settled when Billy Higgins called out to me. 'Hey boy, fill this bucket for me.'

I looked up at him. He was technically of higher rank in the drive to me, but I was being bullied. The others knew it. They looked at me.

'Maybe you should go and fill it yourself,' I said.

'Are you disobeying me boy?'

'You're being unreasonable,' I said, then stood up and walked over to him, hands clenched at my sides. 'If you want me to fill that bucket, you'll have to make me.'

I looked across at where Patsy Moore was sitting. He did not intervene, and I think he knew it was time we had this out.

I was a smidgin taller than Billy, but he was heavier in the shoulders and trunk. He had been as sick as any of us, and we were both out of condition. Neither of us were fit for a long fight.

For a minute or two I danced and ducked, throwing jabs and waiting. Billy was strong, but I had the advantage of recent practice, and of having studied the science of dropping a man to the ground.

My chance came when he swung a wild haymaker. I ducked and went clockwise, pivoted from my hips, putting everything into a right hook, just as Bob Perry had taught me. It took him clean on the chin and dropped him like an ox. It took him five minutes to wake up, and he sat, shaking his head, a little dribble of blood trickling from the corner of his mouth.

'You,' he spat. 'Get out of this camp, and don't come back. If we cross paths again I'll shoot you like a dog.'

111

For a moment he had me rattled. I hesitated. But then again, he had no right to sack me. I could almost see my father watching me. *Don't ever walk away from a fight, and don't stop until they know who's boss.*

I felt my lips press together, my face ugly I ran in as if I were bowling a cricket ball at school. I kicked him hard in the side of the face, snapping his head sideways with my boot.

'Don't threaten me,' I said. 'I'm happy to join another gang, but you and me will have to work together again on this drive, sure as hell. Next time you see me you can dip your hat. I've earned it, right?'

There was not a sound in that camp, but all eyes were on me. I could sense the respect. Billy Higgins was not well liked, and I knew I'd have little trouble signing on with another team. I walked over to Patsy Moore, who had still not said a word or tried to stop us.

'Go with my blessing,' he said, 'but tell Big Johnnie I'll need another man, at least when we start up again ... if the cursed rain ever falls in this place.'

'I'll do that,' I said, and shook his hand warmly. Patsy was a good man, and he had taught me a lot.

I saw the look in young Mick Skeahan's face. He'd come to rely on me for backup. 'Don't fret Mick. I'll just be down the river a way. You can visit for a yarn anytime.'

I rolled my bluey and walked away towards the makeshift yards, where Constance would be waiting. When I looked back, I saw Billy Higgins half sitting up, staring after me with all the poison of a brown snake in his eyes.

CHAPTER ELEVEN

After a weary wait, at last the rains came, and with it pigweed and
scurvy grass and we used to gather these herbs and, mixing them with
vinegar, give them to the scurvy stricken men, they eating the mess raw.
It soon cured them all. It was not long before they were about again.

AS I'D SUSPECTED, all the other team bosses were on the lookout for
hands. Everyone had lost men, and I could take my pick. I'd liked a man
called Tom Kilfoyle from our first meeting. He was a stern looking bloke:
hard but fair with strict standards of horsemanship and behaviour. His
gang was famous – Tom Hayes, Mick Brogan, Steve Brogan, Jack Frayne
– and the big Scotsman Duncan McCaully; the Scrub Bull, who I'd met
at the Winton pub.

They were a tight, very professional team and I knew I'd have to
prove myself all over again. In those first few days I threw myself into
my work, and was scarcely out of the saddle, doing needless things like
checking on cattle when we knew full well where they were. I was with
every water party, and if a new bog had to be dug I was first to grab hold
of a shovel handle.

After a week of this Tom Kilfoyle clapped me on the shoulder.
'You've proved your point, that you're a worker, but maybe just relax a
bit now, eh? Everyone in this team does their share, but they won't like
it if you show them up.'

I looked back at Tom. He was about my height but with a sturdier
build, and a long face that was handsome but a little fierce. His whiskers
and hair were very dark, almost black.

'I understand,' said I. 'It was just that I wanted to show that I'm no
shirker.'

'You've shown that, now just take it back a peg or two.'

'No worries, Tom, that I will.'

With time on my hands, and tired of beef, I took it upon myself to help vary the diet of my new gang. So far I had shot a couple of scrawny ducks, but set my sights on a fish. One or two of the other lads had managed to haul good sized yellowbelly perch out of the waterhole and I wanted one for myself.

Choosing to take a hands-on approach rather than a set-line, I used a carefully bent and barbed nail for a hook, baited with a fat white bardi grub, and catgut line wound on a bottle.

At the end of a rock bar there was a narrow bridge of boulders jutting into deep water. I made myself comfortable, line held between my fingers. I tried different times of day – when the sky was like a burst of falling yellow flower petals before sunrise – in the warm sun of midday and even after dark, but apart from losing my bait, nothing had happened.

A couple of weeks after joining Tom Kilfoyle's gang I was on my rock in the late afternoon, hat low over my eyes and half asleep. At first, being naturally energetic, I had found myself impatient with the long periods of waiting necessary for fishing. Strangely, however, I found that there's a kind of energy in holding that line, like a connection to the water and the earth that appealed to me.

I heard the sound of hoof beats, raised my hat, and stood up to see who was coming, still holding my line. My heart started to thump in my chest. I knew that figure; that face.

I waved my hat like a crazy thing. Words flowed from my lips, 'Gracie, you're back!' I felt like an idiot, but she smiled when she saw me. If anything, she was prettier than I remembered. Her hair had grown longer, and her face had filled out a little. Her lips had more colour, or was it lipstick? I didn't know. Didn't care.

Just as I watched her dismount, and tie her horse to a tree, an immense jerk on my line pulled my hand downwards, almost causing me to overbalance and fall into the yellow-brown waters of the Parapitcheri.

Gracie crossed the bank, and stepped lightly onto the stone bridge. 'What on earth are you doing?'

'I'm fishing, of course. Don't just stand there, come and help me land this bastard.'

Laughing, she walked out along the stones, both hands waving in the air for balance. 'What do you want me to do?'

'Hold me so I don't bloody well fall in the water.'

I swore as the line burned through my hand, but I was intensely aware of those slim hands linked on the muscle of my abdomen, and two small but firm lumps pressing into my upper back. The fish was tiring quickly and I saw it for the first time, golden-flanked, with a high back sweeping to a smallish head.

It was a good seven or eight pounds in weight and I dragged it from the water with the line until I could grip it by the gills. I struggled to carry it up over the stones to the bank, Gracie skipping along ahead of me.

'What a beautiful fish,' she declared.

I slipped my knife from my belt and unfolded it one handed, using the blade to kill and bleed the fish. With blood pouring over my hand, I looked up at her, grinning. 'It's good to see you, Gracie. I never thought you'd come back.' I ran the point of my knife into the fish's anus and eased the sharp blade along the gut.

'Me neither. Dad was only supposed to stay with the camp for a month or two, but the work keeps piling up. The Duracks commissioned him to build two more wagonettes and so now I'm here.'

I pulled out the innards and threw them into the water with a plop. After months of rough men and coarse speech, Gracie's voice was a melody in my ears. I looked up into her eyes. 'I'm glad it worked out that way.'

Her cheeks flushed with pale rose. 'School's done for the year, and I'm done for good. Got my certificate and all. Not only that but I'm a certified lady. La-di-dah!'

I grinned. 'How did you get here?'

'Coach to Fort William, then dad rode in with a spare horse and got me. He reckons just a couple of months more and we'll be on our way.'

She flashed her white teeth in the sun. 'Soon as he finishes the new wagons. I think it'll be a while.'

I said a silent prayer that the work required of the blacksmith would keep on coming, but I knew we had already crossed the line with this little rendezvous.

'You'd better get out of here,' I said, 'before your father sees you with me.'

'Why? Are you afraid of him? I didn't think you were, that day in Winton.'

'I'm just worried about you copping it from him,' I said.

'Oh don't worry about that. He'd never hurt me.' She looked frankly into my eyes. 'He would hurt you though.' We held each other's gaze for a bit, and she was the first to look away, staring down at my hands, slimed with fish guts. 'So how come you're not in Galway Jerry's team any more?'

'Because I had a fight with Billy Higgins. I beat his stupid face in. It felt good too. Wish you could have seen it, he had blood all over by the time I was finished with him.'

Gracie made a face. 'Why would I want to see you hurt someone?'

'Dunno. Cos he's a loudmouth bully, I suppose, and he got what was coming to him.'

'Anyway, I've got some work of my own.'

'Really?'

'Yes, horse tailing for Hangfire Mick's team. Just until they find a man to do it permanently.'

'Your dad agreed?'

'Yes, as long as I sleep back in the wagon and not in the camp. He said that the money will help us get out of here quicker. I start tomorrow. Joe Larence has been showing me the ropes today and then he's going over to work with Patsy Moore, your old crew.'

'That's good news, on all counts,' I said, hefting the fish and standing up. With Gracie on the loose I would no doubt see her much more regularly.

It became a joke around the other camps that Hangfire Mick had a girl for a horse tailer, but they treated her well. And of course it turned out that she was good at her job. Up at four thirty, she'd ride over, catching the horses and saddling up three or four for the limited day work required during that long camp. Then she'd groom and hobble the night horses, stow the gear and ride back to her father's camp.

In the late afternoon she did the opposite, always without fuss. While pulling my weight with Tom Kilfoyle's outfit, I spent as much time with Gracie as I could.

One of her jobs as horse tailer was to keep all the harnesses oiled. This not only kept them supple, but helped prevent galling. Saddle blankets, made of heavy felt, had to be washed regularly and dried. A build-up of sweat or dirt in any part of a horse's tack could cause galling or sores, and Gracie was more dedicated than most.

So, we'd sit on our stumps, running oily cloths over leather, talking and carrying on. I had a store of yarns and jokes, built up over three years of campfires, and I loved to make her laugh.

There was also time to empty out our hearts. I told her about Da's tempers and drinking, and about how his huge body looked on his death bed; eyes closed and mouth open as if to gulp down one last whisky.

'I've never had a friend before now,' Gracie told me, with a downcast look and a strange smile.

'Never?' I was incredulous. 'What about at school?'

'They … I guess they were mostly the daughters of squatters and bankers. I never did fit in with them.

I grabbed her hand and gripped it hard. 'We're mates for life, you and me,' I said.

Christmas 1884 came and went, then my eighteenth birthday. Despite the novelty and distraction of seeing Gracie regularly, I was sick of that waterhole, and anxious to be on the track. Supplies were running low, and the constant company of the same men palled. The older bushmen watched for signs of rain and talked excitedly about ants building nests higher in the trees, the number of stars in a ring around the moon, or the direction of those dry afternoon breezes.

A half caste stockman, one of the best riders I ever saw, Harry 'Tambo' Taylor came to camp with us for a few days. I had first met him after my failed mail run back in '80, and he remembered my embarrassment with a smile. That boy was long gone and we both knew it. He told yarns that spanned the continent, for he had worked right across the North of Australia, and he was welcome at our fire.

Then, four months after we first sighted the yellow water of Parapitcheri, four months under a blazing, pitiless sun, we saw clouds spin down from the north, big black thunderheads, accompanied by a breeze so sweet that Big Johnnie Durack declared that it was like the breath of God himself. Bosses, stockmen, cattle and horses all came alive, and the sounds of whooping carried across the water.

Rain started to fall. It was such a sight – raindrops landing on the dust – turning to tiny balls, dimpling onto the surface of the waterhole. Yet, those first drops of rain had scarcely had time to fall when a pair of riders galloped in, whooping and yelling, down from a station to the north. They carried not just the news of big rains upriver, but a shouted warning.

'Get out of here, you mad bastards, the Georgina's up and flooded, and she's coming down fast. Get out of the way or every man and beast will be drowned.'

This local rain, apparently, was just a roving band of the monsoon coming down from the Gulf Country, where it had poured down rain for a week.

Only Dick wasn't surprised. He'd been telling us for days that a flood was coming, and it was true that the local camp of blacks had pulled up and disappeared, including those we had been paying.

Our camp went into a frenzy of movement that I've rarely seen repeated.

CHAPTER TWELVE

The horses and cattle soon began to pick up and we began to muster and put the stock together and then the fun and excitement began. Seven thousand head of cattle had to be separated into four mobs again. Watching them at night, we held them until all was collected and then the cutting out began. That cutting out by separate owners on that Parapitcheri cattle camp remained in my memory for years afterwards.

MONTHS OF BEING STATIONARY meant that our gear was spread all over the place. The cooks had constructed shelves and bread ovens. Rough shelters had become temporary tack rooms, with saddles and other harness hung on pegs or draped over poles. Some of the men seemed determined to get everything stowed correctly, even folding the tarps that had been strung between poles to create shade. Others, with experience of this part of the country shouted, 'Leave it. There's no need for a scrap a' canvas when you're bleeding well drowned.' With the whole crew mounted up, and the wagonettes trundling off to some low hills a mile or so to the north, we stockmen had our work cut out trying to bring in the cattle. Tom Kilfoyle, Hangfire Mick and the other Duracks tried desperately to control what was, effectively, a hurried muster. The cattle straggled out of the gullies, lowing madly, whips cracking at their tails, many with mud to the stifles.

We formed the herd around a mob of tame 7PD branded bullocks, who acted as coachers as we brought the mob in, driving them away from the river onto higher ground. With the stock and plant safe, I joined Duncan, Big Johnnie and Tom Hayes on a last minute check to see if anything or anyone had been left behind. As we crossed the dry ground above the waterhole, from the safety of my saddle, I had the pleasure of seeing the first tongues of foamy brown water probe their way down, stopping each time they hit a depression, filling it, then rolling on. This was a march that could not be stopped by any force on earth, all the way until it reached the fabled Lake Eyre, far away in South Australia.

Water that was at one moment barely covering our horses' hooves, was soon rising to their knees. We were forced to canter away to the rest of our party on the high ground as the real flood started to churn down that ancient channel – tumbling water driving the debris of years ahead of it, throwing white water as it struck old dead trees and roots.

Back at our camp on the high ground, I cast my eyes anxiously around until I sighted Gracie under cover of her father's awning. If she was safe, nothing else mattered. Not to me, anyway.

The rain set in, and we shivered around smoky fires. Yet the camp hummed with excitement, for we knew that as soon as conditions allowed, we were on our way.

For five more days we camped, until the rains lifted and the sun rose on a steaming land, complete with a welcome goose picking of grass. It was time to hit the trail!

Yet, leaving the Parapitcheri after so many months was an event in itself. The herds, over our time on the waterhole, had mingled into a mob of some seven thousand mixed cattle – Galway Jerry's handpicked breeders, Patsy Durack's young bulls from Comeongin, bullocks and steers all mixed up with hundreds of cleanskins, either acquired by the herds along the way, or calves born on the trip.

A period of sorting and cutting out ensued. The branded cattle were easier, and we spread out over the sodden plains, rebuilding our respective herds.

My new outfit, with Tom Kilfoyle at its head, were expert cattlemen, and we made a game out of cutting our branded cattle out from the main herd. The real fun, though, was with the cleanskins, for it had been decided that they were fair game. Of course, this set the teams on a collision course, and the fights soon started.

With the sun burning down on the dank plains the humidity rose to a near unbearable level. Words were hurled like stones, horses barging into one another, then out-thrust palms on chests. Fist fights degenerated into swinging stirrup irons: fearsome weapons that dented many a skull.

When a fight started the rest of us would drop what we were doing and crowd around to watch, for these were not mere skirmishes but savage, wholehearted affairs born of months of living on top of one another, of desperation to get away, and just plain old competitive pride.

The highlight was a battle of giants. When Duncan McCaully struck Big Johnnie Durack with his stirrup iron, bringing a trickle of blood down over his left ear, the pair, roaring with rage, dismounted to fight with their fists. The whole muster came to a standstill, and we gathered like crows to watch.

'A zac on the Scrub Bull,' I shouted.

Of course, the men from Big Johnnie's team were happy to oblige, pulling unused coins from hidden folds of their clothes and untied from handkerchiefs.

The two big men put up their guard, circled warily for half a minute, then flew at each other. Fists shot out like pile drivers. I remember how Duncan struck his opponent fair on the opposite side of his head to the stirrup iron injury, and blood spattered into the air. But Big Johnnie was as tough an Irishman as you'd ever see, keeping his feet and giving the Scot a hammer blow in the sternum in reply.

The fight went on until both faces were bloody, and Hangfire Mick stepped in, stuttering out a compliment on both their fighting skills. He made them shake hands, to a burst of scattered applause.

'Now there's no b-b-blinking winner, so k-keep your moneys. Ye all c-c-can get back to work and let's finish, and get on that track north.'

Bob Perry had been standing next to me, and he shook his head in disappointment. 'He likes to call every fight a draw, that bastard. Can't he just let it run its course?'

That may have been true, but the heavyweight bout seemed to have cleared the air. It was the last of the serious fights.

When we finally moved north, we heard talk of war against the

Kalkadoons: a fight that started with the killing of George Britcher on the Great Sandy, and escalated when a copper called Beresford and his men took sixty Kalkadoons prisoner and penned them in a ravine. The captives rose up during the night, killing Beresford and six of his troopers.

The police swore vengeance, mustered a small army in Cloncurry, and set off to wreak havoc on the Kalkadoons.

CHAPTER THIRTEEN

At every point they ran to they were met with a withering fire from rifles and revolvers and the black troopers were amongst them slaying with revolver and tomahawk – they were in their glory. Vengeance was satisfied for the killing of the Sub Inspector and his black troopers, also the innocent man, George Britcher. The Kalkadoons had gotten a clean receipt for the murder of those men.

HIDDEN SEED SPROUTED from below ground, unfurling green shoots that climbed for the life-giving sun.

Within a few days those once dry plains were a sight to behold. Countless millions of seeds germinated, tiny stalks straightened like soldiers, and the march of green went on forever. Splashes of yellow daisies livened the red slopes of sand dunes, while purple and white wildflowers raced the grass out of a rejuvenated earth.

Getting back on the trail was a grand thrill, though we struggled with bogged bullocks, and grass fever. Sprayed mud coated us from boots to waist, and sweat ran down from forehead to eye, stinging like turpentine.

We moved on at the drovers' pace, six or so miles each day, north of Boulia along the Burke River. A chain of muddy pools in dry periods, the Burke was now a fully-fledged river, with milky tea-coloured water churning past coolabah trees alive with corellas, and pelicans steaming past against the current as the water flowed on to where it met the Georgina, far downstream.

Often, Gracie found an excuse not to travel ahead with her father's wagon, but rode with her plant up behind Hangfire Mick's mob. Learning my general whereabouts, now and then she could ride up for a quick hello. The weeks were passing and while her father still talked of heading off, the work kept piling up.

We talked of so many things that it's hard to remember them all. She told me that her hair was naturally curly, but was forced to be straight through the weekly application of a device called straightening tongs, two hinged plates of metal. These were apparently heated and drawn through her hair until it was straight. I asked her why and she did not answer, just shrugged her shoulders.

One day I was telling her the old story, that every stockman knew, about the head stockman stealing kisses with the station cook, who then served particular recipes depending on what nocturnal activities she was in the mood for that night. Strawberries meant kisses. Cabbage meant ...

Gracie's eyes widened, but she was smiling. 'You're very bold, telling me that,' she said. 'I bet you've never even kissed a girl, you being out here on the track like this.'

'Well I have, actually.'

She coloured. 'Not one of those ones you pay—'

'No,' I said, and I think I must have blushed too. 'I've never even met one of those kinds of girls.'

'Have you thought about kissing me?' I remember her eyes and how they shone like deep pools, with currents, ripples and deep structure underneath.

Our horses must have conspired together, for they slowed down and walked side by side. We leaned close on our saddles for a long kiss that left me gasping.

'There,' she said. 'Now we're even. We've both had a kiss.'

One particular cow had stopped to watch us with tilted head, as if trying to figure out what we were up to. Gracie laughed and pointed, 'That silly old cow doesn't know what she's missing out on.'

'I hope your father never takes you away,' I blurted.

Our horses started moving again, without instruction, reading our minds. Gracie looked away. 'He will. Sooner or later.'

Those days became a game of snatched moments; engineering a meeting, swivelling my head to look for prying eyes so often that I seemed to have a permanently sore neck. Those minutes with Gracie made up for everything: all the hardship, the lack of sleep, and the endless riding after cattle.

Within a few days we were doing more than kissing. One morning along a side gully of the river we slipped down from our respective saddles and pressed close together in the privacy of some gnarled old melaleucas. My hand dug down the front of her shirt and under the tight undergarments. I swear the ground moved under my feet as I felt that silken skin for the first time. I heard her breathing change, but she gripped my wrist and dragged my hand away.

'Not now. I saw Billy Higgins riding on the wings not ten minutes ago … I think he's suspicious.'

I stopped cold. Billy must not be allowed to catch us out.

'When can we be together?' I whispered urgently.

'Soon, I promise.' I watched her buttocks move in her moleskins as she hurried to her horse, off to collect the rest of her plant.

We passed a column of mounted men, some half a dozen police troopers and the same number of armed blacks: the feared Native Police. They rode along with us for company and when we went into dinner camp we had time for a fire and billy of tea. The leader was a surly Englishman in his twenties called Frederick Urquhart, no relation to the man of the same surname in our party.

Sub-inspector Urquhart was, he told us proudly, responsible for a vast area, all the way to the Gulf of Carpentaria. 'You want justice around here? I'm it,' he declared.

Urquhart and his men were on the trail of a party of Kalkadoons, a mopping up operation from the war that started with the killing of George Britcher. I told Urquhart and his men of my part in that tragedy, and my opinion that the Mount Merlin stockman who stole those girls had blood on his hands.

Urquhart told us how he reached the place where Beresford and his men had been hacked to pieces. The grisly task of burying the dismembered bodies followed. He told us how he and his men had pursued a large mob of the killers up the Cloncurry River. The weak and old were left behind by the Kalkadoon party as they fled.

'We put the old men and lubras down as we went,' Urquhart said. 'We were in no mood for prisoners.'

Finally, in the headwaters of the Leichhardt River they found the main camp of blacks. At dawn they attacked, and the slaughter was terrible. Very few escaped. 'Those rascals we killed,' he said, 'were almost certainly the ones who had killed Britcher, and stole your sheep. The bones and hides of sheep were very much in evidence.

'That day was not the end for them,' the policeman went on. 'Not yet. The last fighting men of the tribe rallied sixty miles north of Cloncurry, now called Battle Hill. It was their last stand, and we broke them.'

His moustache quivered with excitement as he told us how two hundred mounted men – police, trackers, stockmen and farmers – had charged that rocky knoll, while around the same number of Kalkadoon fighters on the top pelted them with spears, rocks and lumps of ant hill. Urquhart told us how it ended with his party reaching the summit. He told us of the massacre that followed and how the leader of the Kalkadoons, a warrior called Mahoni, wore a headdress of white, and strings of possum fur around his waist and neck.

Urquhart's story, I have to say, was much more favourable to himself than other versions I later heard. He spoke with trembling voice of his own bravery, and the persistence of his men in the face of fierce resistance.

He did not mention the story, doing the rounds in later years, that Urquhart himself had been knocked out by a lump of ant hill dirt, thrown down from above, and missed most of the battle.

He went on: 'Now we're just mopping up the remnants. You see any blacks down around Boulia? I heard that some of the killers ran off down there and are hiding themselves with the local tribes.'

I thought of the Parapitcheri camp, and the natives who had helped us find water. I was pretty sure there were some Kalkadoons amongst them.

'Only a few old men,' I said, catching the eyes of my mates. 'None worth troubling over.'

The blacksmith's habit was to break camp at four or five in the morning, ahead of the cooks and horse tailers, and head for the next day's camp at a spot predetermined by Big Johnnie and the other bosses, each selecting an area for their particular mob.

Oswald, with the cooks not far behind, would arrive at the location by mid-morning, travelling much faster than the herds. Within an hour he would have his coals hot and be hard at work on the forge, and Gracie would join him when all her work was done.

One morning Tom Kilfoyle and I came upon our cook and his wagonette stuck in a deep channel beside a creek. We pulled it clear with a horse team, but a shaft coupler was broken.

Tom Kilfoyle sent me on ahead to the blacksmith. 'An' no dillydallying, mind,' he warned me. 'Tell him it's an emergency, for if we don't get the damn babbler on his way there'll be no tucker in camp tonight.'

I rode off without delay. It was fun to be away from the herd, and I scarcely came off the trot except to drink from my water bag.

Smoke hanging in the sky guided me along the last mile or two, and I came onto the scattered wagons of the advance camp. Walter Oswald's wagon was something out of the ordinary and I headed straight for it.

That vehicle was heavily built, with a chassis of iron. On the front was affixed the strangest thing: a pair of glass lenses with oil lamps behind them. The cunningly cut glass refracted the light, setting aglow the landscape for a goodly distance in front of the wagon even in full darkness. This device allowed the blacksmith to get up and running well before dawn. The lamps were, he reckoned, the invention of a mate of his down in Toowoomba, a glass maker who had asked Walter to take a prototype for an extended test.

Apart from the lamps the entire wagon was fitted with unusual modifications: hooks, even an iron ram at the rear. The downside of all this, of course, was that the vehicle was unusually heavy, prone to bogging, and a bastard to remove from the mud when that happened. Oswald, as I approached, was busy hammering away at his anvil, and I saw that Gracie was there, walking across to meet me as I reined in. I untied the broken wagon part from the saddle, and she stopped short, watching as I secured my horse and approached on foot.

Her father was by now glaring at me, tongs and hammer in hand, dousing a lump of glowing hot metal in water with an expression like disgust in his eyes. He threw down his gloves.

'Hey there Grace,' he roared. 'Get back to yer needlework.'

'Yes Pa,' she said, but made no move to leave.

'Now lad, what's the problem?'

Gracie leaned on the wagon side. 'Maybe there's nothing wrong at all, Pa. Maybe Charlie only wanted to see me.'

My heart did a somersault and I glared at her. The blacksmith's eyebrows knitted furiously together. 'I told you to get out of it. Now do what I tell you.'

My racing pulse slowed. 'A broken shaft coupler, Mister Oswald. Tom Kilfoyle said to tell you that it's an emergency.'

'It always is on this cursed drive,' the blacksmith spat. 'I've got a fucking wagon full of emergencies.'

'Can you mend it?'

'Yes I can, and since you've ridden all this way I'll do it now, but tell Mister Kilfoyle he's a pain in the arse.' He pointed to a spot where presumably he could watch to make sure I kept away from Gracie. 'Stand right there.'

I did as I was told, watching as he bent to the bellows and gave them ten or twenty puffs. Even from where I stood, I could feel the heat. Using the tongs he pushed the two broken ends of the iron coupling into the coals and went again at the bellows.

While he was working, Gracie came around the corner of the wagon and smiled at me, round eyed, lifting her forefinger to her lips. I tried to tell her with my eyes to stop the game, but it was almost impossible without her father seeing me.

The girl I loved made a rosebud with her lips, pressed them to her hand and blew me a kiss.

I must have let something slip at that point, because Walter, tongs in hand, stopped, made narrow little wedges of his eyes, and then whipped his head around to where Gracie had been just a moment earlier. Of course she'd skipped behind the corner of the wagon and out of sight.

For a moment I thought he was going to call her and see what was going on, but he plucked the two lumps of molten iron from the fire and placed them on the anvil. Even while he hammered them together, with a tool that would have taken most men an effort to lift, he turned occasionally to glare at me, the hammer head still landing precisely where he aimed it.

I had no doubt that those hammer blows were meant for me, a warning of what would happen if I touched his daughter. When the shaft coupler had been cooled in water, with a hissing burst of steam that rose to the sky like a demon, the blacksmith called me over.

While I was thanking him, Gracie appeared again. 'I think Charlie likes me,' she said innocently. I wanted to sink into the ground.

'Well if he does, then let this be fair warning,' said Walter Oswald. 'If he touches my little girl I'll feed him to the dingoes.' Fear, however, could not dampen the fires that Gracie Oswald had stoked in my heart. Fanned with the bellows of real liking and admiration, I believe that nothing could have kept us apart from that point.

The middle watch, from half past midnight to three in the morning, was a lonely task. A mob that had been on the road for as long as ours was generally quiet, bunched up into a tight group, sleeping and ruminating. That night the moon was near full, and the plains were painted ghostly white. It was a time when a mind could wander, when the moon and earth touched. The grasslands appeared to extend forever.

Once, feeling thirsty, I walked my night horse back into the camp to drink from the water bag hanging from the wagon. I was heading back out, just having mounted up, when a slight figure came out of the scrub at the edge of a gully.

'Who's that?' I whispered. But I already knew who it was.

'Just me, Gracie.'

'Go back to bed.'

'I can't sleep, and I need to be at Hangfire Mick's camp in an hour anyway.'

'Where's your horse?'

She pointed further along the gully. 'Back that way, you can give me a ride if you want.'

The gelding I was riding was a big fellow, a type of heavy stock horse called a clumper. There was no question that the weight would trouble him, but still I hesitated. Before I knew what was happening, however, she had clutched my leg, inserted her foot over my ankle and swung herself up in front of me onto the pommel. Her sweet breath was on my face as she turned and said, 'Don't take me to my horse yet, show me the herd first.'

When we were away from the camp I hissed at her. 'What the hell was that, at your father's wagon today? Are you trying to get me killed?'

She rubbed the side of my knee. 'I'm sorry Charlie, I was just having fun.'

'Having fun? I thought I was going to cop a hammer in the face for a moment there.'

Her hand moved back from my knee and over my thigh, continuing to rub gently. 'I'll make it up to you, I promise.'

We rode in uneasy silence for a short while, the gelding surefooted with the extra load. We rode a circuit of the camped cattle, locating a couple of strays that had wandered over to the river bed. We hunted them back, then I aimed the night horse past the mob, through a small patch of scrub.

We came out of the trees and onto the grassy slopes, bathed in moonlight with tall grasses, curved with the weight of their seed heads. My left hand was resting lightly on her waist, my right holding the reins low so that my forearm touched her thigh. Her hair was in my face and I could smell the mingling of carbolic soap and healthy sweat.

'Imagine what the other coves would think if they saw us like this,'

I said.

'It could be worse,' she said. 'It's not like we're actually doing anything.'

In the silence that followed I fancied that I could hear her breathing change. I knew that something had altered between us. I moved my hands so they encircled her waist, touching her flat stomach with the tips of my fingers.

She did not protest, but covered my hands with her own. Encouraged, I leaned forward and kissed the side of her neck, nuzzled into her while my weightless body seemed to leave the earth. She turned around so she was facing me, thighs spreading over the knee pads. The gelding protested with a sharp jerk. Both of us laughed softly. Our lips met.

With both hands she gripped my swelling groin. I dropped the reins so my hands were free to unfasten the buttons of her shirt, one after the other. So well trained was the night horse that he kept padding slowly around the cattle in the moonlight. How that moon shone on Gracie's white body, on her breasts as I ran my hands over them. Somehow, she managed to raise herself from the saddle, drawing down her breeches, and then unbuttoning mine. Artfully she wrapped herself around me, and the hot moistness enveloped not only my organ, but filled my vision, my world; my soul. My nostrils flared with the smell of her. Her tongue was in my mouth.

Years later, I would make love to Columbian princesses, innocent Indian women from the Yukon and genteel American wives. But nothing ever compared to that night with Gracie. It was my first, and hers too. I guess I tried to recapture it over and over, always falling short. It seemed that at the age of eighteen I found a perfection few people ever know.

Silent with wonderment, spent, and utterly self-absorbed, neither of us saw the horseman from a neighbouring mob pull his mount up and watch across a moonlit plain, nor the jealous, hungry stare in his eyes.

CHAPTER FOURTEEN

The (Snider rifles) were single shot, and a heavy gun. The cartridge had a bullet, hollow with a thin partition in the centre. The fore part of it was hollow, filled with a sort of clay, and as big as a man's thumb. At the back of this formidable piece of lead was a charge of black powder sufficient for a big gun. They used to kick like a mule if not held properly, and when those guns spit lead, you got your meat no matter what part you hit. The bullet made a big hole on entering, mushrooming as it tore everything out before it.

AT CLONCURRY, Black Pat Durack re-joined us from a sojourn in Brisbane with a string of fresh horses, more than thirty in number, bred for stock work by some of the best stud farms in the business. They were lean from the track, but Pat was known for his husbandry, and he had kept them in fine condition.

The Drover's Rest Hotel was a welcome stop, and once again we visited in relays, anxiously awaiting our turn. Not just for the grog, of course, which I still had not sampled, but for a counter meal of roast meat, pastry, taters, green vegetables and gravy. The first wave of visitors came back with news of the menu.

'Have the pork,' Tom Kilfoyle told me in grave tones as he wrote me a cheque for more than twenty pounds. 'You'll get crackling so crisp it'd break a dog's teeth, and apple sauce.'

We salivated at the feast to come. We talked of pork and lamb and what they would taste like.

The first men were already returning, many smuggling jugs of rum and whisky into camp. There were some raucous and illicit parties – fights and high jinks, until Big Johnnie rode from camp to camp and poured every drop of grog he could find into the dirt.

Finally, my turn came, in company with Duncan, the 'Scrub Bull' and Jack Sherringham. I rode tall in the saddle, delighted to ride with such men. The landscape here appealed to me – iron red hillocks of hard stone, that seemed to gather heat and light and hum with power through the night.

At the Post Office I found a thick envelope postmarked Ballarat, Victoria, waiting for me. I was burning to read it, but would not open it in public. At the bank I had fifteen pounds converted to a draft made out to Mrs Augusta Gaunt, and mailed it off with a short note I composed on the spot.

Then, passing the police station, we saw a sad procession coming down along the road – the police party we had run into out along the track – Frederick Urquhart and his men. On foot were two black men in chains, so bony that their ribs showed like rowboat timbers under the black of their skin. Their hair was wild, caked with mud and blood.

We were almost up with them when I recognised two of the natives I had met at the Parapitcheri camp. I know they recognised me too for their eyes stabbed out at me across that street. 'No, Charlie, don't get involved,' Jack Sherringham urged me. 'Let's go eat.'

The policeman drew up his horse and started addressing a swiftly gathering crowd. 'Justice has a long reach,' he began. 'These murdering bastards have nowhere to hide. The law has patience, and endless resources. They kill one of us, and two more arrive to take his place.'

He reached into his pocket and removed a sheet of paper. A crowd gathered around as Urquhart began to read a poem, apparently of his own authorship. A verse tale of black men who murdered a white woman, and a policeman, obviously himself, out avenging her death. The final stanza left the crowd speechless for a moment, before a scattered applause rang out, along with a few muttered, 'Here, heres.'

> *'I have heard a lot of playin'*
> *On piannys and organs too;*
> *But the music of them there rifles*

As the crowd dispersed and the police party made to disassemble I urged my horse forward.

'No,' Jack hissed. 'Leave it.'

I ignored him, riding close up to Urquhart. The policeman screwed up his eyes. 'I remember you ... I should run you in. You lied about having seen these little beauties down Boulia way, now isn't that true?'

I looked into his black-marble eyes, and the stiff moustache, the spread of whiskers on his cheeks. 'I thought they were Pitta-pitta.'

'The others were. These two were hiding with them. One had a pocket watch that belonged to Britcher, rather damning evidence don't you think?'

'What will happen to them?'

'These ones'll be charged with murder, front the local court tomorrow, and by week's end be hanging from a rope. Fast is good in these cases, I believe it cruel to keep a native behind bars for too long. Have you a problem with that?'

'I feel for them, is all.'

'Don't waste your sympathy. You saw with your own eyes what happened to George Britcher, and he had never raised a finger to them. Don't forget how they raped and killed a white woman. Slaughtered those policemen in their sleep. Think, Charlie Gaunt, before you give away your sympathy.'

I stared at him, but slowly gave Constance my heels. I was moving on at a good clip, intent on re-joining Duncan and Jack when the Sub-Inspector called out again.

'Wait!'

This time, while the crowd hushed, Urquhart rode towards Jack Sherringham, addressing him directly. 'Haven't I see you before somewhere?'

'No sir, I don't think so.'

'Perhaps your likeness in the Police Gazette?'

'I reckon not, sir.'

Urquhart clicked his fingers. 'I have it. Your name is Jack Sherringham, correct?'

Deadpan, Jack answered, 'No sir, my name is Joseph Brown.'

The policeman turned on me. 'Is that his name?'

'Yes,' I said. I had no idea what was going on, but if Jack felt the need to lie then I would back him up. 'His name is Joe Brown, alright.'

'Well, I happen to know that a special detective has been sent up from Brisbane to track down a Jack Sherringham, and you look a lot like him. I'll be making more inquiries about you.'

As we rode off, I cut Jack a glance. 'What in blazes was that all about? Are you wanted for something?'

'I'll tell you later,' Jack said. 'I'm lighting off back to camp.' We dawdled to a halt outside the Drover's Rest, and Jack pulled a few shillings from his pocket. 'Can you bring me some dinner?'

'Of course.'

'Pork and taters, if you don't mind.'

With a fearful glance down the road towards the police station he wheeled his horse and cantered off. I turned to Duncan McCaully who had said scarcely a word since we reached town.

'Did you know Jack was wanted for something?'

The big Scotsman shook his head. 'I dinnae ken, but I've waited five hard months for a pub feed and dram a' whisky. The longer we sit oot here blathering the longer I'll suffer the lack.'

'True,' I smiled, and swung down from Constance, making her reins fast to the long horizontal rail that ran along the outside of the pub. Already some of the drinkers on the verandah were looking at us, cold glasses in their hands. The smell of food made me swoon, and I was ready to eat. Anything but beef.

Inside we fronted the bar, and a middle aged barman in a white apron peered through his eyeglasses at us. 'What'll you have, gentlemen?'

Duncan scowled. He was a man who disliked beating around the bush, and said whatever he thought in the broadest Scots accent I'd ever heard. 'How the fuck can I answer that when I dinnae ken what you have?'

'Perkins from Toowoomba: ale, bitter or dark according to what takes your fancy. All ice cold and shipped by the barrel.'

'What aboot whisky?'

The barman turned to look at a shelf lined with bottles. 'With all the Irish in here we've had a run on the Jameson's of course, but you being a Scotsman I can offer you an aged Glenlivet or Walker's Old Highland.'

After providing the Scrub Bull with a glass of ale and a 'shot 'a whisky to chase it down,' the barman turned to me. 'What'll you have, young fellow?'

'Have you got ginger beer?' I asked.

That wiry cove folded his arms across his chest. 'Yes, but there's something even better. Have you ever tasted cream soda?'

'Can't say that I have. What is it?'

'An ice cold bubbling cordial flavoured with vanilla and fruit. A recipe straight from heaven, made by Wards Cordial Works in Gladstone, and shipped west, bottle by precious bottle.'

Duncan rolled his eyes at me, as if to indicate that I was being given a sales pitch.

'How is it so cold?' I asked.

'Because we are the first hotel in the west to have a fully-functioning ice machine on the premises. It works through the compression of ether, and the ice itself is produced in zinc moulds. See the frosting on your friend's glass? That beer is truly cold.'

Duncan, who had tackled the whisky first, took a sip of the beer. He nodded slowly. 'Aye lad it is cold.'

'I'll give the cold cream soda a try,' I agreed.

When my drink arrived, poured into a tall glass, laden with ice, Duncan raised his glass and touched mine. 'Here's tae us, who's like us? Damn the few and they're all dead!'

I'll never forget how good that cream soda tasted, sweet and so frothy it tickled my nose. I laughed at the sensation. The sugary fluid flowed into my veins, knocking on the door of every organ as it passed by. Full of sugar and good cheer, I ordered my pork roast, while Duncan's eyes roamed the room, falling upon the only woman there.

'Guid-looking hen,' Duncan commented, 'but just a tad long in the tooth fer yours truly.'

I followed his gaze – there were no flash young barmaids here. This was a woman of more senior years, doing the rounds of the tables, tucking cash money into her cleavage and showing off everything she had. By the shouts and laughter as she moved around, she was very popular.

A heaped plate of pork, vegetables and gravy appeared on the bar in front of me. Only a bushman could imagine what it was like to eat such a meal after months of beef and Johnnycakes made from weevil-ruined flour. I started with the beans, lathered with gravy, then alternated between the spuds and the pork, cutting small slices and drawing circles in the apple sauce. I did not talk. I did not look around again. Nothing could distract me until that heaped plate was safely in my gut, washed down with another bottle of cream soda.

A young Englishman was in the bar that night, undoubtedly the best dressed man for five hundred miles. He wore high heeled riding boots, moleskins, gleaming leather chaps, and a fur felt hat that looked so bright he must surely have purchased it that day.

I had just finished one full plate and was waiting for the barman to walk closer so I could order another when the Englishman approached.

'Excuse me,' he said. 'My name is Henry Sharp, can you please direct me to the boss of this outfit, I'm looking for work.'

'Well in this outfit,' I said, 'boss means a Durack, and I can't say there's one in here right now. Isn't that right Duncan?'

The big Scotsman had already started on his second meal. 'Mick Durack will be here presently. I'll point him oot to you when he walks in the door.'

'Do you mind if I sit with you? My treat for a round of drinks of course.'

I was about to answer positively, for I was a little in awe of this young gentleman. He seemed to sweat confidence and had obvious high breeding. I wondered how he came to be in Western Queensland looking for stock work.

Duncan, however, glared. 'Ye've got a big fat mouth haven't ye? I've ridden a thousand hard miles to get here, and I won't blather with a jumped up sassenach with more money than sense.'

'Well I say, that's unfair.'

'That may be, laddie, but be content that I'll give you a whistle when Hangfire Mick comes. In the meantime, park yer hurdies somewhere else.' With that declaration, Duncan picked up his whisky glass, looking tiny in his massive hand, drained it and banged it down on the table.

The Englishman opened his mouth to say something else, closed it again, then wandered back down the bar to a table of local business types with whom he was obviously already acquainted.

'He be a right scunner, he is,' Duncan muttered into his whisky.

Later, when we rode back into camp, Duncan shaking his head sadly at the lack of eligible 'hens,' Jack was waiting for us, pacing the camp, a frown making gullies across his forehead. I unwrapped his dinner, soggy in the napkins in which I had made a parcel of it, but he took to that meal like a crow to a carcass.

'Did I miss any fun at the pub?'

'Not much, but Hangfire Mick signed up two new men. One of them is the toffest cove you've ever met ... so fresh off the boat you can smell the seagull turds. Still he reckons he can ride, and knows a thing or two about cattle.'

Jack was so busy eating he barely grunted in reply. It was like I was seeing him for the first time. The bony arms, twined with veins, and the heaviness of his jaw standing out from his scrawny neck. I had never seen the fear in him before, but now it was plain. The deep eye sockets. The hunted look. He finished the last of the meal, then licked his fingers clean.

'You didn't see that cursed walloper again, did you?' he asked.

'No.'

I wanted to ask him what he had done, but as I've said, there was a code in the stock camps. You don't ask. Not unless information is freely offered. I knew that his crime must be serious, for they don't send special detectives up from Brisbane to chase poddy dodgers. Jack was a likeable bloke, he played the concertina better than most, and could carry a tune with his hearty baritone too. I wouldn't have suspected him of hurting anybody.

Jack stopped cold, eyes as wide as those of a possum as we heard the sound of hoof beats carry through the night. We heard a man dismount, leading his horse into the camp on foot, finally captured by the light of the fire.

On his feet in a moment, Jack was now wild with fright. The horse, we saw as it entered the firelight, was a thoroughbred stallion, almost as tall at the shoulder as the man leading him. That man was none other than the colonial experience Englishman from the Drover's Rest, Henry Sharp.

'Why hello again,' Henry said. 'I'm wondering if one of you chaps would be good enough to direct me to Michael Durack's camp? It seems that I am now in his employ.'

Duncan McCaully looked up miserably and pointed to the north. 'Ride that way, yew'll see the fire beside yon creek bed.'

'Thanks awfully much.' He made to ride off, and then stopped. 'I say you fellows, I'm looking forward to working with you.'

Duncan stood up slowly, addressing the Englishman. 'Before yew ride on, a word in yer ear.'

The thoroughbred started nervously as the big Scot approached, but Henry Sharp calmed him with a soothing hand on his neck. 'Of course, advice is always welcome.'

'Oot here,' Duncan said, 'things are different. No man gives a fuck who yer mother and father are, or how many confounded quid a year you have. Class an' breeding here is fer horses, not men. The lads will care that yew do yer work well, and that you don't rate yeself too high and be flash. Them fancy trewsers ye're wearing, makes you stand oot like a red dick on a white 'orse. Do what I tell you, laddie, ride that fancy cuddy a' yours into Cloncurry tomorra, gi' every stitch to the nearest swaggie. Present yewself to the store and ask for good, practical clobber like the rest of us wear.'

Henry Sharp's eyes widened. 'Well, I do thank you for the ... ahem

139

… advice, but I'll be doing nothing of the sort. My clothing was purchased from Brisbane's finest stock and station outfitter, and will outlast your gear by a long shot, I'll warrant.'

Duncan shrugged, 'I'm telling it to yew straight. If yew dinna fash with it that's up to you. But at least tone down that toffy sassenach blather.'

'Why that's just plain rude,' said Henry Sharp, as he dug in his heels and rode away. After he was lost to view amongst the dark trees we dissolved into fits of helpless laughter. Only Jack remained stony-faced, staring into the fire, hardly moving.

The next day, the cattle safely in dinner camp after a long morning in the saddle, I turned my attention to the letter from my mother. I didn't care to read it where anyone might be able to see me, and I rode off a good distance from camp before I sat with my back against the smooth bark of a gum tree and unfolded the papers.

Dearest Charles,

My hands are shaking as I write this. I cannot express the joy with which your sisters and I received your letter, along with an address with which we could write back. I understand why you left us, and although it was sad, you are my son and I do love you dearly.

Please look kindly upon my plea for you to come home, even if just for a visit, as soon as it is possible for you to do so. You can expect only love from us. We have moved back to the suburb of Saint Kilda that you will remember fondly. Our current address is enclosed.

Then followed news of William, now over in England, studying to become a doctor. Nellie had just turned eleven and Marion fourteen, both at school in St Kilda, where we had lived in my younger days.

There was a short letter from Nellie enclosed, telling of how she won the girls' hundred yards dash at a recent sports day, along with some other news. There was nothing from Marion. I guessed that she was angry at me for leaving them. I wasn't sure, but she had always been highly protective of Ma, and a great one for nursing a grudge.

At that moment I would have happily turned my back on the drive and ridden two thousand miles home. I wanted the embrace of my family more than anything in the world.

I knew that they needed me and that was a weight on my shoulders. Sitting with my head on my knees, I admit that tears flowed, but I kept my composure. I could not leave men who had shared so much hardship with me. I could not look Tom Kilfoyle in the eye and say that I wanted my mother and sisters so badly that I would let down the team that had taken me in, taught me so much, acknowledged me as a man among men.

Neither of course, could I leave Gracie. That thought caused a wave of pain.

I folded the papers, returned them to the envelope and secreted it in my saddle bags for later re-reading. I mounted Constance without spirit, and I know that her heart was in concert with mine as she carried me back to camp.

The only other interesting occurrence while we camped at Cloncurry was the news that Black Pat Durack had purchased not only horses in Brisbane, but ten or so Snider rifles. This was a big talking point, for we had few decent weapons between us at that point. The Duracks and some others had long-arms, and just about everyone owned a revolver, but few of us stockmen had heavy-calibre rifles.

'We're heading into a land where the blacks hold sway,' Big Johnnie told us, delivering two of these new rifles to our team. 'By all accounts they're getting more and more stirred up with every droving party that comes through.'

The Snider rifles were breech loading, with self-contained brass cartridges, and a rifled barrel. They fired a .577 calibre shell that travelled accurately for up to five hundred yards. The projectile spread on impact, causing, I was to find by experience, devastating injuries in man or beast.

All the men, of course, wanted to carry one of the new rifles, but with only two for each of the teams that wasn't possible. Tom Kilfoyle already had a Snider of his own, but Tom Hayes didn't, and he took one of the two new weapons.

The rest of us agreed that a shooting contest was the fairest way of deciding who would get the remaining new rifle. Big Duncan McCaully was probably the keenest shot in the party, but refused to compete like 'a wee squirt' over a toy. Besides, he already had a German breech loading rifle called a Dreyse, which he regarded as the best weapon ever made. That left me, Mick and Steve Brogan, and Jim Minogue. Jack, while he hung around our camp a lot of the time, was rightfully in Hangfire Mick's crew, and was off working.

We used a knife to mark out a target on the smooth bark of a gum tree, then paced out one hundred yards, locating a natural berm of higher ground where we laid down a couple of saddle blankets so we could shoot prone.

'Let's shoot in order of age, oldest first,' Mick Brogan declared. 'Five rounds each, and the closest wins. Fair enough?'

Mick Brogan laid himself down, the rifle stock snug against his shoulder, legs spread wide. I could see from the start that he would not offer much competition, the barrel was wandering all over the place, and he managed to clean miss the tree on all but two shots. After each man had fired, we all walked downrange to inspect, and marked each impact with an X so we didn't get mixed up. Mick's brother Steve was a little better, and Jim Minogue landed all his rounds into the outer and inner rings. We marked them carefully and I took the Snider rifle in my hands for the first time.

For such a deadly weapon it was compact – this was the carbine version, perfect for men on horseback. Yet it was solidly made, with a heavy walnut stock, and a bore so big a man could stick his little finger inside.

To load the Snider you pulled the big hammer back to half-cock, then pressed a catch on the side of the action, at which time a hinged section would lift. The big cartridge was then slid home and the block pushed down.

I pulled the hammer back all the way then settled into the prone position, with the butt hard to my shoulder. I lined the pip foresight up in the middle of the vee and held my breath, squeezed the trigger and braced myself. The carbine went off with a thump like a kicking horse into my shoulder. My ears started ringing and didn't stop for eight hours. My next four rounds made me wonder how a man could stand to fight a war with such things. I felt weak-kneed and dizzy, but when we walked down to inspect my shooting the result was much like Jim's, except for one thing, a hole right in the dead centre of the target.

Jim shook his head, disappointed. 'Damn it all, you lucky pup.'

Tom Kilfoyle couldn't hide a smile. He was becoming quite the father figure to me, and I know he took pride in my work. 'It's yours, lad, but if I see a speck of rust, or the barrel pointed in the wrong direction I'll take it off you. Got it?'

'Got it, thanks.'

CHAPTER FIFTEEN

The grass and water was now good and plentiful and all our stock fattened. Passing Cloncurry we headed for the Gregory River crossing.

BACK ON THE TRACK, we were overjoyed to find ourselves on the northward flowing catchments, so close to the Gulf of Carpentaria we could almost smell it. On the eastern bank of the Cloncurry River, we searched in vain for a crossing place. Dick and the other black boys were sent up to rove five to ten miles ahead of the leading mob, and they finally identified a passable ford.

There was a gathering of sorts while we studied the chosen spot, a gravelled sweep on the tail-end of a bend. There were some fifteen of us altogether, along with the new recruits, including the flash young Englishman I had met in Cloncurry. Now, in daylight, I saw him in all his flash get-up. He greeted me with a nod, and I returned it.

Now, deep river crossings with cattle can be problematic. The best way is to get some of the stronger animals across to act as coachers. The others will usually follow, with a couple of riders on the wings and in front, keeping the herd swimming straight all the way to the other side.

The preparations began. It was important for the men to strip down to undershorts and carry their clobber in their saddle bags, for if something happens and they are forced to swim, stockman's gear makes keeping afloat difficult.

We sorted some of the strongest bulls and hunted them into the shallows, with a couple of mounted men leading the way into deeper water, not faltering as the horses lost their depth and were forced to swim. Others flanked the eight-deep line of cattle. On the other side these coachers were allowed to rest and feed in plain view of the herd.

'Now get 'em moving boys,' called Big Johnnie Durack. We needed no further urging, and there was a chorus of confused lowing as we committed the first mob to the crossing.

I was riding Constance, who had no fear of water. I sensed the moment when her hooves stopped touching the bottom and she swam free. A swimming horse isn't steered with reins or feet, but by using your hands to splash its head on the opposite side to that which you wish to go. My mare was used to this, though I noticed some of the other stock horses getting frightened at the depth.

At the half way point all was going well, but then the first line of cattle got scared. It might have started with one of them brushing a submerged branch, or simply deciding the far bank was too far away. First one cow, then another, tried to turn back. This was the start of a mill – when the leaders attempt to turn back, front hooves churning the surface to froth as they meet the rest of the mob midwater. Panicked beasts try to climb atop one another, pushing others under, potentially drowning hundreds. A 'smash' like that is what we drovers work day and night to prevent.

The worst course of action is to scare the cattle further, or pressure more individuals into entering the water. Much better to let those panicking cattle swim back to shore, and reorganise for another push.

Henry Sharp, our colonial experience man had, at every opportunity, been brandishing an out-size stock whip, made in Brisbane by a firm that made their living outfitting men fresh off the boat. Henry had spent a goodly amount of time learning to crack it.

Seeing his opportunity to make a name for himself, he swung that wild bit of gear and started cracking over the heads of the swimming mob. The fetlocks of Duncan McCaully's horse cleaved through the water as he rushed the fool, taking the Englishman's arm in an iron grip and throwing the whip to the ground. Meantime we did our best to stop the mayhem resulting from this foolish act.

Already the leaders were drowning, crushed under the weight of the panicking beasts coming from behind, desperate to escape the whip. There was nothing for it now, but to push the herd across, despite the losses, which we reckoned at some thirty head.

On the other side, Hangfire Mick was in a towering rage. 'Yy-you in the bloody fancy duds. Get over here.'

The colonial experience man placed his hands on his hips and flapped his elbows like bird's wings. 'That's the way we do things in the Midlands.'

'This is not bleeding England. You just killed those cattle as surely as if you held a gun to their heads.'

From an oilskin in his saddlebags Mick Durack pulled out a chequebook, ink and quill, scribbled furiously and tore it from the book. 'This is how we do things here. Take this and don't let me ever see your bally face again.'

'You're dismissing me?' The man was disbelieving.

'No, I'm t-t-telling you to get the fook out of my c-camp before I kick your arse all the way back to Blighty.'

The colonial experience man put on a show worthy of the stage. He drew himself up and huffed like a steam engine. 'Well, I've never been spoken to like that in my life, and by a man who pretends to be a gentleman.'

'You're g-going to g-get spoken to like that some more if you don't light out like I told you. Just be glad Big Johnnie's not over here yet, he'd be laying into you by now.'

The bloke just wouldn't let it go. 'Are you serious? I'm sacked.'

'I don't know how to make it any plainer without using my fists. G-get out of here.'

The colonial experience chap turned bright red, then stalked across to the paperbark tree where his horse was tethered. He booted a tree root hard with his right foot, and swore loudly. Every man watching started to laugh. It was cruel, of course, but the man's arrogance had just cost a packet in dead stock.

We watched him swim that thoroughbred stallion back across the creek, dismount to find his whip, then ride away at a textbook trot.

'Blowed if he wasn't the most useless bastard I've ever hired,' Hangfire Mick said. 'And now you b-bastards, get back to work.'

Getting the wagonettes over the river was the next issue. We couldn't swim them across with horses in harness, not without risking drowning the lot of them, but used long ropes with a team on the other side to haul them across. The blacksmith's wagon was the hardest work of all, for as I've said, it was a beast of a thing, with six-foot wheels and more iron than timber in its construction.

It was also filled with heavy equipment, and the only real bonus was that Gracie was there to help, smiling coyly at me at every opportunity, touching hands as she pointed out something else to be carried.

Only the truly heavy items, the anvils mainly, stayed in the wagon while we dragged it across, a task involving horses, ropes, and swearing, straining men. By the middle of the river it was lost to view, heavy wheels trundling along the bed. By the time it reached the other side, the sky was dark, and many lanterns burned, creating a festive atmosphere, like Christmas Eve or a town show.

Gracie and I managed ten fumbling minutes up against a fine old paperbark tree upstream. So pleasurable was our lovemaking for both of us, by then, that I worried someone would hear her cries of pleasure even over the lowing of cattle and sounds of camp life.

Her thighs were wrapped around me, her tongue moving from my neck to my lips to my ear. We both knew it was borrowed time, her father expecting her in camp, most likely watchful because of the nature of this crossing-day camp. So we hurried, straining and thrusting.

When we were done, I was breathing like I'd just climbed a steep hill. I sat on a buttress root to watch her dress and when she was ready I kissed her on the stomach, between two buttons, our mingled scents filling my nostrils.

'Thank you,' I said.

Gracie smiled in the darkness. 'All part of the service,' she said.

As was our practice she left first, heading straight back to the horses at Hangfire Mick's camp, and I followed a few minutes later. I was almost back at Tom Kilfoyle's fire when I saw another man on horseback a couple of hundred yards from a mob of cattle. He moved onto a converging course with me.

There wasn't much of a moon, but I fancied that I recognised Billy Higgins from his round-shouldered seat on the saddle, staring at me. I made no effort to pull up, just continued on my way past him, with a sick feeling in my guts that the man who hated me most knew my secret.

Yet, over the coming days, nothing happened, and I reckoned that I must have been mistaken. Not a word was said to Gracie nor I, so my nervousness subsided, and I soon put the man on horseback who had watched me ride back from our tryst out of my mind.

We got back into the rhythm of the range, with the rising and setting sun, the phases of the moon and the gentle circuit of the stars, until I could almost feel my blood ebbing and rising like the tides, my destiny interlocked with the natural cycle. Around lively night campfires, our long-moustached Chinese babbler told stories of pirate junks in the South China Sea, of emperors and boom and bust on the goldfields, his low voice soft and timeless in the night.

Along with my work with horses and cattle, I devoted myself to self-improvement. The Snider rifle took much of my attention. I oiled it every few days whether I had fired it or not. There was little enough ammunition for target practice, with only fifty cartridges in my saddle bags, but every now and then I would waste one or two rounds on a termite mound or tree trunk, levering the big hammer back with my thumb and firing from the saddle so that Constance or whatever camp nag I was riding got used to the sound.

Gracie and I made love as often as possible, not every day, but whenever opportunity offered itself. We did it in creek beds, on saddle blankets spread on the grass, with the smell of horse sweat thick in my nostrils as my face fell into her hair and her thighs locked around my lower back. It was important to her that I became adept at something she called *coitus interruptus*, which meant using self-control to remove myself from the warmest, wettest, most comfortable place on this earth and spill my seed on her thigh or flat muscled stomach, or sometimes on the earth itself.

She made no other demands on me, and I none on her. Our world was temporary, every day a new camp, new horizons, and so talk of the future seemed ridiculous.

CHAPTER SIXTEEN

Ahead of us was a long stretch of fever stricken, black infested, sour and poor country with plenty of water, but a country of scrub and poor grass.

STILL OBSERVING the strict drovers' routine, day in, day out, it was July 1884 when the drive reached Normanton. By then we had been travelling for more than a year. A drover from Hangfire Mick's mob succumbed to the conditions, dying of fever and exhaustion.

Apart from a blow-out at the pub, most of the men looked forward to mail from home, as we had at towns along the way. I posted a long letter to Ma and my sisters, and within a few days we were off again, now on the Gulf Track.

It was Nat Buchanan who first told me of how this ancient trade route went back far earlier than the early cattle pioneers. This was a trading path of the northern tribes – the goods being basalt spear heads from the Kalkadoons, yellow-red schist from Arnhem Land and ochre from Central Desert tribes – all bartered across a network established through custom and tradition over thousands of years.

The track was used by Ludwig Leichhardt, then occasional prospectors and Nat himself. The needs of a route for drovers were the same as they had been for the blacks – regular water, shallow fords over the many rivers, and plentiful grass for stock – or in the case of Aborigines, game. Before white settlement this path may have been four feet wide, kept clear with fire and foot traffic. Now, with our six thousand cattle, and countless other mobs coming before and after, the track became a swathe of trampled shrubs and eaten-out grass.

We crossed the Flinders River without incident, and with plenty of water now, it seemed that the drive might run smoothly for a while. One problem, however, was that cattle stations were springing up along the stock routes and it was not always easy to keep up with the changes.

The law of the land demanded that drovers had to notify properties that they were intending to pass through, at least twenty-four hours before their arrival. The station would charge a stockman with the task of meeting the drovers at the boundary, then riding nearby to watch their progress.

This allowed the station to make sure that none of their cattle joined the travelling mobs, that no 'killers' were taken by the travelling stockmen, and that the drover didn't hang around – moving on at the minimum legal pace – five miles per day.

This was not always possible, and one afternoon, forced to halt, looking for some three hundred head of cattle, lost through the incompetence of another recently hired hand, we prepared to camp on a good waterhole on Cabbage Tree Creek. It was a top camp, with sweet water fringed by a carpet of water hyacinths, and acres of grass on good hard ground. We supervised the mob while they drank, then boxed them in for a night on the flat.

'Duncan, you stay on them 'til sunset,' Tom ordered, 'and it's Jim's turn for first watch. The rest of you can stand down.'

The cook had set himself up during the day, and the smell of roasting Johnny-cakes met us as we rode in, the tailer taking our mounts and removing saddles and bridles, fussing over the horses, inquiring after their spirit and gait. The current tailer was a regular stockman called Jack Frayne. He worked like a dog, loved the horses, but was as hard a man as you'd ever meet, and would not step aside for anyone.

We were settling down around a good blaze for the evening when two riders came up, both strangers to us. We expected a friendly introduction, but instead they stayed on their horses. One of the two was older than the other, wearing a new felt hat, complete with feather, over a ruddy red face.

'You blokes've got a hide, just rolling up whenever you feel like it. I'm the station manager here – Clonna Station.'

While most of us looked blankly at each other, Tom Kilfoyle said, peaceably enough, 'Must be a new station, for we've never heard of it.'

'Better mark it on your fucking maps real fast. Then you can get out of here.'

Jack Frayne, quickly riled, crossed his arms. 'If you don't want us here you can get down off that horse and show how game you are.'

The horsemen loosened their feet in their stirrups but stayed mounted. 'I don't have to fight to get your bloody herds off our land. You ride in here like you own the place, and take every blade of grass. Now I've wasted enough time with the hired help. Who's the boss?'

Tom stepped diplomatically between Jack and our visitors. 'I'm Tom Kilfoyle, and this crew is mine. The Durack brothers are in charge overall, and if you're after a fight don't choose big Johnnie Durack.'

'We don't want a fight, we just want you off our land.'

Jack Frayne couldn't let it go. 'I said it before, and I'll say it again. You want me to leave, get down off that bloody nag. I'll make a meat pie out of yer face, and see how bad-mannered you are then.'

The men on horseback glared back, and the stockman seemed about to take up Jack's invitation. The manager, however, kept him in check with a sharp word and the two of them wheeled their horses and took off for home.

Tom levelled his eyes on Jack. 'I don't reckon that was the smartest way to approach those blokes. I can see why they're angry at us.'

'Well, I guess I could have dropped my drawers and let them take me up the arse,' Jack Frayne declared, and the men laughed so loud that a mob of corellas took off from the trees along the creek.

Even Tom cracked a smile. 'I guess you would have enjoyed that, Jack.'

Frayne muttered darkly. 'Fucking squatters, they think they own the whole country.'

'Even so, butting heads with them is a bad idea.'

Later, when Hangfire Mick came over for a visit, he listened gravely. 'The d-damned problem is that l-l-last year this were open range and now someone's got a b-b-bloody title to it. R-right in the middle of the stock route, too. We'll move on in the morning, early.'

Three days later, however, a pair of policemen caught us up, and served a writ on Jack Frayne and Tom Kilfoyle, charging them with trespass and threatening bodily harm. It was a beat-up, of course, and as soon as the two wallopers had gone, Frayne ran for a horse.

'Now where are you going?' Tom yelled.

'Back to find those piss-weak bastards and beat the daylights out of them. Who's with me?'

'You'll get down off that horse and shut the hell up. You got us into this mess and I'm not going to let you dig us any deeper.'

'No damn it, they need to be taught a lesson.'

'If you go, don't bother coming back. I won't have a man who can't control his temper.'

For a moment I thought Jack might defy Tom, but he slowly dismounted, and stood, shuffling his weight. 'I just hate seeing squatter mongrels like them get away with a stunt like that.'

Tom must have known the effort backing down had cost Jack Frayne, for he declared. 'I know it. Me too. Now I just remembered that I have a small bottle of Jameson's in my saddlebags. Let's have a dram all round and drink to their stinking souls.'

Days and weeks passed, and we crossed one river system after another. We were passing to the north of Lawn Hill Station when Black Pat Durack organised a party to take a wagonette down to the store there for supplies. Jack Sherringham and I got the nod. The station store had apparently been doing a good trade in supplying drovers like us, heading west for the Territory.

The manager at Lawn Hill Station was a man called Jack Watson, a well-known bushman with the nickname, 'The Gulf Hero.' I was a little in awe of his reputation.

He must have heard us coming and was there to meet us outside the homestead, which was situated on a hill with cliffs that faced the creek, bounded on the other three sides by stables, sheds, and further out a set of cattle yards. When I say homestead, it was a basic affair, with walls of timber rounds, and roofed with sheets of paperbark. It had a solid kitchen table and a fireplace oven made of crushed and shaped termite mound.

'It ain't much, but it's home,' he told us. 'Come in and wash the dust from your throat.' By that he meant cups of hot tea, prepared by a skeletal teenage lubra whose eyes remained fixed on the ground. Never once looking at us, she bustled around and brought us chipped mugs to drink from.

It'd been a while since we tasted milk, and sugar had been low, so we topped our mugs up and sighed contentedly, watching out through the rifle slits in the walls of that hut. A sign of things to come was a set of forty dried black ears nailed to one wall. It took me a moment to understand what they were.

'Dead niggers,' Watson said, seeing me staring. 'We've cleared the mongrels off most of the run. We see one – we shoot – it works a treat.'

'It was funny,' I said. 'When I droved with Nat Buchanan we didn't have much trouble with them. Now the way everybody talks it's like there's a fuckin' war going on.'

Jack Watson shook his head. 'You can't live with them, and believe me, I've tried. It starts out fine, but next thing they start spearing horses and cattle and stealing stuff, and killing people. They're savages. Best to thin 'em out and drive 'em off.' He patted his lubra on the rump as she moved past him. 'Except for the women, of course. They make fine domestics if you know what I mean.'

I pondered this discussion on the trip home. When I had passed through with Nat Buchanan, I reasoned, the blacks were still not quite sure what to make of us. It was the same with the men who built the telegraph line running all the way from Adelaide through the wild heart of this country to Darwin – they never lost a single man or had a serious confrontation.

In those first encounters we must have seemed to them like apparitions, riding in from distant horizons, some with huge herds of cattle, all weighing half a ton or more. We carried guns that burst with light and sound, but those initial contacts were fleeting, mostly flavoured with curiosity. Perhaps just as importantly, Nat Buchanan had a strict rule: the men who worked for him did not touch the women. The telegraph men had apparently worked under the same strictures.

The white men who came next came to stay. The vanguard of a new civilisation, they shot to kill. They didn't just camp on the waterholes but built homesteads, fences and had something tangible to protect with their guns.

Those early settlers were lonely, and took women by force. That's when the real conflict started. They killed angry husbands. The blacks retaliated. Those ears nailed to a wall became a symbol to me – that ahead was a frontier war.

Before leaving we rode a few miles south to view one of the grandest sandstone gorges I had yet seen. We came through the trees, and then the world fell away as if it had been riven in by a cold chisel, leaving gouges in the plains, slabbed with stone. Such was the grandeur of that canyon that we stopped the horses and stood on the edge, air rising up to our faces from far below where a silver line of water made its way downstream. We turned away with goosebumps dusting our arms.

On the last hour of the ride home to the drive we passed by a small rocky creek and I left the others to investigate. It was secluded, with pools of effervescent water tipping down tiny cascades from pool to pool. I took Constance in for a drink, lifting her legs high, her shoes clopping on stones dark with oxides and smooth as skin.

I tucked away the location in my mind as we rode on, and as soon as I got back to camp I sought out Gracie. I found her bringing her precious night horses back from some decent feed she'd scouted out for them.

I tipped my hat as I rode up. 'Hi there stranger.'

She grinned at me. 'I was wondering who that fine figure of a man was.'

'Just good old me.'

There were others around, so I didn't linger, just rode in close so Connie's shoulder bumped her gelding. 'If you went for a walk around moonrise you might well find a bloke on horseback lurking around your

155

camp.'

'I don't know, Charlie. I'm not sure if I can get out that early without Dad hearing me.'

'You can do it. I found a little swimming place; a nice pool. We can bathe, and I've even borrowed some soap.'

'Tempting ... though I do have my own soap, you duffer.'

'Well you don't need it. I've got a whole cake. I ... need you Gracie.' My voice was as soft as a whisper, but I felt the passion grow between us.

'I'll meet you,' she said. Then, 'Now get out of here before someone sees you.'

CHAPTER SEVENTEEN

Once, when we were looking for new country, we came on to a very big blacks' camp and with them was a very old horse. He travelled with them from camp to camp following them like one of their own dogs.

I SERVED MY night watch duty, then woke Duncan for his turn. I lay on my swag until he had ridden off. At that point I got up and worked my way back through the camp to where I had left Constance, saddled and ready, tied to a black wattle tree.

I waited half an hour for her, but never worried. Gracie took her word seriously, and if she said she was coming, then she would be there.

Finally, I heard her approach through the trees. Without a word we rode back downrange, where 20 000 hooves had ripped their way through the grassland. We soon reached the creek I had seen during the day, illuminated by a waning half moon and stars. We stopped beside that channel of running water.

'Is the water deep?' she asked.

'Not very, so don't dive in.'

I watched her undress. She was thinner than she had been, with exposed ribs below her breasts, and sharp bone at her hips. I took off my own clothes, and produced my cake of yellow soap.

The water was cold and made us shiver as we slowly submerged, and in the moonlight I saw how her nipples changed, darkened and hardened long before the water touched them. I paused with my head still out of the water, arms crossed around my body. Gracie was braver, dunking her whole body.

I went straight to her, but she shrugged me away. 'Not yet, buster, not until I've scrubbed every square inch of skin. Where's that soap?'

While she washed, I lay back in the water, watching her attend to her arm pits, neck, arms and feet. Never having been too interested in cleanliness, I was amazed that someone could wash themselves so thoroughly, and enjoy the process. Gracie started a low, contented humming. Her hair she washed twice, throwing her head back to squeeze it dry between coats. It was fun to see her lose herself in my presence.

It was the first time, I think, that I saw her as the young woman she must have been at the Ladies College in Toowoomba. The lady she could be. Finally, she moved closer, holding out the soap. 'Now it's your turn.'

I reached for her again, surprised to be pushed away with a firm hand.

'No,' she purred. 'Not until you've washed.'

Our passionate meetings were usually so hurried that she had no objections to skipping the preamble. Now the delay irked me. I ran the soap down my arms and legs, dabbled at my armpits and neck, then declared myself done. 'There,' I said.

Gracie laughed. 'You call that a wash? No wonder you men are always so dirty. I can do better than that out of a pannikin. Here, let me help you.' Her hand wrestled with mine, removing the slippery cake of soap. She reached for one of my arms. With strong but gentle strokes, learned, I imagined, from hundreds of hours of grooming horses, she rubbed my arm clean.

It was a sensual and warm feeling. Like I was the centre of her universe. She washed my neck, my chest and belly before working her way slowly down my legs.

Finally, she washed my most intimate parts, twining her hands around me so that she both washed and pleasured me at the same time. I found myself swooning, dropping into an abyss of pleasure. I ran my hand down along her thighs, then pulled her closer, attempting to manoeuvre her legs on either side of me, but found her strangely resistant. 'What's wrong?'

'Slow down a bit, you always want to make love to me straight away. Can I show you something?'

'I guess.'

I let her take my hand in hers, guiding my middle finger down between her legs. Slowly she ran it over her hot and open lips, into the opening, then up a little until it nestled against the place where the petals of her sex joined. From there she manoeuvred it upwards, then increased the pressure until I felt a hard little button no bigger than a match head. She hissed in her breath suddenly. 'There,' she said, 'can you feel it?'

I could indeed.

'Now rub it gently.'

It took me a few moments to get it right, but as she moaned and started to rock gently I felt a sense of power, and strangely my own pleasure increased with hers. Her eyes lolled back, her mouth opened, and she uttered shrill and regular cries.

Then, every muscle in her body tensed, as hard as iron, then racked powerfully with a series of contractions. She cried into my ear as if only I could rescue her. I could stand it no more. I pulled her onto me. I had no will to remove myself at the crucial moment this time. Deep inside her I delivered, over and over again, convulsing with each spasm as if I were dying.

I was on my way back to camp, a quarter hour after Gracie, when I saw a horseman emerge from the trees, cantering out to meet me. As soon as I saw that it was Billy Higgins I felt a warning twitch in my gut.

'Hey, Gaunt,' he called. 'I want to talk to you.'

I leaned back on the saddle and Constance came to a stop. 'Now what would you and me talk about, Billy? You're as interesting as cow shit.'

'You can cut the superior talk, Gaunt.' Higgins walked his horse until he was close enough that Constance shook her head irritably at the close contact. 'Where did you get to, these last few hours?'

'Couldn't sleep, thought I'd track ride the camp.' I watched his face as I spoke, and the explanation seemed, at first glance, to satisfy him – track riding the camp was a common morning chore – looking for the marks of stock that might have strayed in the night. 'What's your excuse for wandering around accosting people?'

'I wanted to talk to you about a couple of coincidences.'

'What might that be?'

'Well a month or two ago I were on night watch and I had cause to chase a couple of poddies that had wandered. It were a good white moon and as I brought them back I happened to look over towards the Kilfoyle herd, and I seen the strangest thing. Not one, but two people riding a horse. Very close-up and friendly like. Unusual, wouldn't you think?'

I said nothing, but my heart felt like it was being squeezed in a vice. 'I guess so.'

'Well it were night, as I said, and a good distance away, but I'm pretty sure that it was you. I even managed to check with Tom that you were on middle watch that particular night. Not long afterwards, young Gracie turned up to see to the horses. Early. Now who ever heard of a horse tailer getting up any earlier than they have to, especially a lubra?'

I gritted my teeth. 'Don't call her that.'

'Anyway, so I started to keep an eye out. It seemed to me that something'd been happening right under our noses. Like that night when we crossed the river. You and Grace disappear all of a sudden. Then half an hour later she turns up, and you a few minutes after. I suspect,' he sneered, showing his teeth in the moonlight, 'that right now daddy's little girl is rinsing out her drawers. Am I right?'

Well technically, since we'd been in the water anyway, that wasn't true, but I didn't deny it. 'So what are you going to do? Run off and whisper in the blacksmith's ear? Dob me in like some snot-nosed kid?'

He lifted his chin. 'You don't know what I'm going to do. But I've got you cold, you upstart, be assured of that.'

I went quiet. 'What do you want?'

'All in good time, Charlie Fucking Gaunt. All in good time.'

I nudged Constance with my heels and rode away, full of a frustrated anger that had no outlet.

All the next day I felt like someone was following me with a cricket bat, and was about to crack me on the head with it at any moment.

Yet, by the time we put the cattle into night camp, nothing had happened. All day I had expected to see the blacksmith riding pell mell across the range towards me, murder in his heart, with Billy Higgins beside him pointing an accusing finger.

I spent hours in the saddle composing and rejecting the excuses that I would use. But we got the cattle boxed in quickly, and with the horse tailer out on watch I started washing my clothes in one of the cook's iron tubs, by way of keeping my hands and mind busy.

I had just finished when I saw someone leading a horse at the other side of the waterhole. It took me only a moment to realise that it was Gracie, and that she was looking searchingly in my direction. Nothing like this had ever happened: she was offering what amounted to a summons, close to her father's camp. I stood up, and shook the suds from my hands. Carrying my wet washing as if I was taking it from the camp to hang it up, I slapped it in a ball onto a bough and hurried to where Gracie had now disappeared into a grove of she-oaks, skirting the muddy waterhole.

There was something wrong. I could see from the dampness of her cheeks and puffy eyes that she had been crying. She came into my arms, holding me tight with those strong arms of hers.

'What's wrong?' I asked into her ear.

She pulled back. 'Lots. Billy Higgins knows about us.'

I breathed out so loud it came as a sigh. 'I know that. He saw me coming back this morning when we … you know. Did he say something to you?'

She started to cry then, and her words came between great gasps for air. 'I'll say he did. He got me alone after I took the night horses out for grass this morning. He told me that he knows everything. He … told me that he wants some of what you're getting, and if he doesn't get it, he'll tell Pa all about us.'

'Fuck!' I spat. My hands curled into fists; my breath was like fire. 'Did he touch you?'

'No. He said he'll give me a couple of days to think about it. God, Charlie, what are we going to do?'

'I'll beat the living shit out of him, that's what.'

She jutted her face towards me, chin so tight a dimple formed on the point. 'No Charlie. That is the stupidest thing you could possibly do.'

'If he touches you, I'll do it, God help me. I won't be able to stop myself.'

'No. Pa says he's only got a few more weeks of work, then he and I are heading up to Burketown – you can meet me after the drive is finished. That might be the best thing now anyway. Think about it. I have to get back. Don't do anything silly, please.'

'I won't, unless he touches you. If he does—'

'We'd better keep away from each other … for a few days at least,' she said.

We pressed our lips together, kissed hard as if it were for the last time, then she swung onto her saddle and rode away.

It turned out that an emergency with the cattle forced a delay to any resolution of the Billy Higgins problem. In fact, for the next couple of weeks I scarcely had time to think about Gracie at all.

It all started the morning after Gracie's revelation. Unable to sleep, I woke when Tom called out for the cook and horse tailer, and went for a ride. Half wondering if Billy would appear and follow me, I rode slowly, checking in all directions as I went. I had just turned to take in the scene – a light ground mist – cattle all around, when I saw a cow standing alone, back arched and head extended, mucus dripping from her nostrils.

Up close I could hear her rapid breathing, followed by a percussive little cough, echoed by other animals out there in the range. I saw more cows on their knees. One lay on her side, breathing like a steam engine, a calf nudging her as if to say, 'Wake up.' I dismounted and pushed the poor old girl with my toe. I felt something like I had on the night of the cattle rush. That something terrible was happening that I had little power to stop.

I remounted and spurred my horse forward, heedless of the near dark and clusters of cattle, some down, many still seemingly healthy as I rode. Constance was much too clever a night horse for me to attempt to steer her in the dark, I just gave her a general direction and she made her own path, avoiding rocks, trees, bushes and cattle.

I smelled campfire smoke and saw the blue pall against the now brightening eastern sky. I saw orange flames, the shape of men nearby, and the cook bustling with his pots. I handed my reins to Jack Frayne, and walked up to where Tom was eating porridge from a tin bowl.

'Listen, I'm pretty sure there's pleuro, in the herd. I saw it once before, travelling on the Diamantina.'

Tom spat out his mouthful so it sat in a burning glob on the fire. 'Hey Mick, ride over to Big Johnnie's camp and tell him to get over here. It may be best if he brings John Urquhart.'

Within thirty minutes I was walking out around the mob with a party of five. When we reached the stock I had seen earlier, John Urquhart, who was, as I've said, a good amateur veterinarian, dismounted and examined the affected animal. 'Yes boys, it's pleuro, all right. Damn it to hell and back.'

'So what do we do?'

'First thing we do is try to quarantine this part of the herd, though God knows it's already too late.'

Hangfire Mick's face was as worried as that of any man I'd ever seen. 'So what d-d-does this mean in terms of losses?'

'If we do nothing, we'll lose half to two thirds of our cattle.'

'So, what can we do?'

Urquhart's nose twitched above his stiff little moustache. 'I don't want to blow my own trumpet or anything, but you can be thankful I came prepared for this.'

We sectioned the sick cattle off into a gully, but as the morning wore on it was more and more obvious that there were afflicted individuals throughout the mobs. All we could do was locate them and push them in with the rest, coughing and labouring at the forced effort.

Around noon, we were ordered to leave just a skeleton crew watching the cattle. Word passed from man to man.

'We're all to meet up at dinner time, ride in to the head of the gully. There'll be a meeting. Pass it on.'

'Why mate, what's up?'

'Big Johnnie Durack wants to talk to us.'

'What for?'

'Dunno mate, just pass it on.'

At the appointed time, with the sun burning down from directly overhead, Big Johnnie, Hangfire Mick and John Urquhart took station on a rocky outcrop, and we gathered around, some twenty-five blokes — those who could be spared from watching the cattle. I could see Gracie across the other side, standing well back from the men, and I got a flashing glance before the boss started talking.

If Big Johnnie Durack was worried he gave no sign of it, standing six feet tall, dark beard quivering as he talked. 'Now listen, you fellas, you know we've picked up pleuro, in the cattle. Many thanks to young Charlie for spotting it this morning.'

I shifted uncomfortably in my boots, no man liked being singled out like that.

'Anyhow,' he went on, 'John Urquhart here has come prepared. He's got some gear, and a plan about how, by the Grace of Almighty God, we might save the cattle. Listen good, because we're all going to have to pitch in.'

Urquhart was quietly spoken, but there was dead silence as he explained the process of inoculating the cattle. 'What we're looking for, boys, are survivors. Cattle who are but lightly affected by the pleuro and pull through easily. We put these animals down and take blood from them.' He lifted a clear glass bottle with rubber tube and sharp hollow needle attached. 'Once the needle goes into a vein, blood pressure will push the blood through.

'Then we'll use syringes to transfer blood to cattle that haven't been affected yet — and that's most of them. From my reckoning we only have about two hundred head badly sick at this stage.'

'So you mean,' called Jim Minogue, 'that we have to throw every single animal in the herd, one at a time, then stick a needle in them?'

'We've found some basic old yards left by some other drover. Me an' Tom Hayes are going to try to fix 'em up and make a cattle crush, but yep, most of them will have to be thrown. Any other questions?'

Young Mick Skeahan raised his hand shyly. 'Can us humans go catchin' this pleuro thing?'

'No, only cattle.'

'What aboot the poorly ones?' Duncan McCaully asked. 'Do we just let 'em stand around and die?'

'No, because they'll just keep spreading it around. Starting right now Hangfire Mick will be in charge of identifying stock too sick to survive. They will be shot, and we'll use bullocks to drag their carcasses together for burning.'

The theory was simple, to take fluids from lightly affected animals and inject it into the healthy stock. It was time consuming, thirsty, thankless hard work. Dick, Jack Frayne, Duncan, and many of the Western Queensland stockmen were adept at throwing. By the end of this caper I was as good as any of them. The stockman would ride pell mell for the bull or heifer, chase it for a bit until it was tired, ride alongside and grab its tail, then steer the horse sharply in, unbalancing the animal and sending it down in a tangled heap. Some men preferred to grab the tail, slip down from the saddle, then run forward so the animal would see them, at which point it would attempt to charge. With a mighty jerk on the tail the overbalanced animal would fall. As soon as they hit the dirt, hobble straps would be applied, thus preventing them from getting back up again.

Some bulls resisted throwing so fiercely that the favoured technique became roping them around the neck and tying them to the nearest tree, where they would be left for an hour or two, kicking and pawing until they were exhausted. At that point we could go in and pierce a vein.

It was hard, bloody, dangerous work. One man caught a hoof in the middle of the forehead, knocking him out and opening his scalp so it had to be stitched. Few of us escaped ugly bruises. But we all kept count, and around the fire those nights there were accusations of fudging numbers and witnesses called in from other camps.

We worked in teams of two, and I had been lucky enough to link with Duncan. He was a gun performer at this kind of work, and I was no slouch either. Most of the time he would tail and throw the bull, with his sheer strength a big advantage. I would dart in with the hobbles, then the inoculation flask. When the task was done we bangtailed the animal to show that it had been done.

By the end of the eighth day Duncan and I topped the tally sheets, and it was becoming harder to locate a beast that hadn't been marked. At noon we were one ahead of Frankie Cooper and Harry Barnes from Big Johnnie's crew, us on a score of two hundred and eighty-two head thrown and treated. Money had been changing hands all day, and we were desperate for the win. Friends and supporters of the two camps set off on scouting parties, searching for that elusive unmarked animal.

Johnnie Durack was all but ready to declare us the winners when Jim Minogue came riding in to say that Frankie and Harry had just located an old scrubber, a cleanskin apparently, probably lost or escaped from some previous droving party. Despite him being as cranky and wild as hell they had somehow got him down and the serum into him.

This gave Big Johnnie an idea, and he called us all together. 'If there's one scrubber out there, there'll be another. Let's get every man not needed to comb the bush hereabouts, and bring us in a beast. The first of the leading teams to throw the bastard, on foot, will be the winner.'

We all thought this was an enormous hoot, and I guess the Duracks knew that. We were ripe for a diversion after days of thankless work, and this one was perfect. But finding another scrub bull was the problem. Twenty-four hours passed before word filtered through the camps that Steve and Mick Brogan, also Tom Kilfoyle's men, had found a bull for us.

Hangfire Mick rode up to tell us the news. 'G-g-get yeselves ready, lads. They say he's the b-biggest, meanest bastard of a p-piker they've ever seen. Horns like spear-points, not far off a f-fucking ton!'

The parties gathered in a clearing, a plain of dust, and the betting started even before we saw the bull. Men rode in and out, on short shifts watching the herds so that everyone could take a turn at seeing the action. Duncan and I talked tactics, and I was pleased to have that big, broad shouldered Scot on my side.

They brought him in from ten miles out, where he'd been living a mean life between black men's spears and needle-sharp grass seeds. This one was no cleanskin, but carried a brand from some forgotten owner. Could it be, I wondered, an escapee from the mob I had taken through with Nat Buchanan, for those had been sourced from all over?

This scrub bull, or piker as we called them, was in his prime, five feet high and, though a long way from a full ton, had a heavy skull between wickedly sharp horns, covered by a short growth of curled white fur.

The Brogans had dogged him every yard of the way, and the mark of the stockwhip was on his back in shining red lines of blood. Head down, he charged everything that came within range, and a bunch of stockmen who had selected a fallen log as their vantage point were scattered like leaves by the bull's approach, the situation only helped by a couple of mounted men who drew the bull away. They left him in the middle of the clearing, stamping and snorting.

I looked at Duncan, and we both broke into nervous laughter. Big Johnnie tossed a sovereign and gave first go to Frankie Cooper and Harry Barnes. They were smart operators. Part of me wished them well, just for the sake of seeing this most extreme form of stock work well executed. Another part of me wanted my own turn at the bull. I wanted to prove myself; be better than the other men.

Frankie used his hat to get the bull's attention, while Harry placed himself in position. As the bigger of the two he would be the one to grab the tail.

There was no stamping, head shaking or snorting as the bull went for Frankie at top speed. After that there was so much dust raised that it was impossible to properly see what was happening. I saw Harry reach out at full stretch, and grasp the beast's tail, while Frankie took the risky option of grabbing the scrubber by the horns and trying to wrestle him around.

The dust swirled in, and I saw nothing more for a moment or two, but then came a blood-curdling cry of agony and a shout of dismay. Next thing I saw was Harry running backwards, and Frankie flat out on the ground. The bull chased Harry for a few yards, but then, dramatically, spun and went for the helpless figure of Frankie, pinning him to the ground, goring him until Big Johnnie rode in with the stockwhip and drove the thing away.

A crowd of us gathered around the injured man. He had a long bloody gash across his chest that would need stitching. The horns, however, had not penetrated the ribs, and he was soon on his feet.

'It's nothing, coupla licks of cat gut and she'll be right,' said Frankie.

Meanwhile the bull was getting boxed in by the men on horseback, which was entertaining enough. If we thought that bull was angry before, now he was like a thing from hell, charging the horses, sending them skittering out of the way. His eyes were red as fire, strings of mucus dripping from his nose.

Hangfire Mick rode over, his face running with sweat and worry in his eyes. 'You b-blokes want to pull out? I d-d-don't think there's any shame if we call this a d-draw.'

Duncan laughed contemptuously, 'Och, yew and yer bloody draws, Michael Durack. Nowt this time.' He grinned at me. 'Let's go.'

The plan we had developed, that I would draw the bull's attention and get it circling, seemed ridiculous as we walked closer.

'Hold yer nerve, laddie,' Duncan growled, 'that fucking animal is angry – but knackered.'

We stopped just out of his charging range, circled to find the best position, then steeled ourselves.

'Go!' shouted Duncan.

I ran forward, heart pounding, then scampered across the bull's line of vision. With a warning bellow he started forward. Duncan came from the side and grabbed that tail for all he was worth. The bull turned and went for him, forcing him to let go and retreat. The plan went out the window, and I loped in, looking for an opportunity.

The bull was fixed on Duncan. It charged towards him a few strides, but was confused by the big man's waving form. The bull stopped, trying to focus his rush. The Scotsman, meanwhile, never a slow thinker, grabbed a handful of dirt from the ground and threw it straight into the bull's eyes. Seeing my opportunity, I ran in and held the piker's tail, while Duncan got himself up close and to the side, where the bull must have got a glimpse and tried to charge.

Holding on with both hands I heaved with every reserve of sinew and muscle I had in me. This was the stockman's equivalent of the knock down punch that Bob Perry had taught me at the Parapitcheri, our one chance. With the shouts of the crowd in my ears, I gave it everything I had. For a moment it looked like the bull would straighten, but finally he overbalanced and fell with a thump I could feel in my boots.

My work wasn't over, for I removed one of the hobbles I had clinched to my waist and reached in through a hell of flying hooves, slipping the leather loops over the front hocks. Now, at last, Duncan and I had won, and I felt ten feet tall.

Young Mick Skeahan even composed a verse in our honour.

It started out something like:

> They brought that piker in from lancewood bush, thick as anteater quills,
> a-goading him with sticks and rocks, they drove him from those hills,
> they set him in a clearing and the boys all gathered 'round,
> First he gored Frank Cooper, an horned him on the ground,
> It were time to bring the experts – Charlie Gaunt and Duncan – down.

The strange thing was that within a few days our bull settled into Tom Kilfoyle's mob, and became one of the leaders on the rest of the drive, always pacing at the front of the herd. He didn't like us, but he respected us.

Duncan McCaully developed a soft spot for him, and would often be seen riding close by. We reckoned they were kindred spirits, and that the bull had met his match in human form.

CHAPTER EIGHTEEN

They thought the horse and rider was one, and under that impression well may they have been afraid.

THOSE NEXT FEW DAYS the wind came up from the south, gentle at first then building to a gale that darn near blew a man on a horse sideways. The cattle hated it, and continually turned northwards to escape it, making our lives difficult.

The wind unsettled me also, for I knew that as soon as the pleuro scare was over, things with Billy Higgins would come to a head. I just didn't know how. I couldn't watch Gracie all the time because of her father, not to mention that I had my own work to do.

When I had occasion to see Billy I glared at him, eyes driving into his like nails. The cocky bastard looked back at me and sneered. Meanwhile, Gracie and I dared not see each other alone. That was a torture I could scarcely bear, and it was his fault, I hated his smug grin, but his desire for Gracie even more.

In frustration I borrowed some paper on which to write a note, the only way I could think of to get to her.

My darling, I hope your work is going well and that you are finding some pleasant moments in your day. I miss you so much. Let me deal with that bastard so we can be together like we were. Love Charlie

I considered what I had written critically. It seemed brief and cold. I drew a love heart, wrote CG loves GO inside, then pierced it with an arrow.

By way of delivery I folded the note, sealed it with a drop of candle wax, and rode casually past her as she grazed her plant the next day. I waited until she was looking, then made a show of dropping the folded paper. I walked my horse on, only staying within sight to make sure she picked up the note, then rode away.

Gracie replied to my letter on scented yellow paper. I found it in my swag when I unrolled it that night, and of course it had been in the cook's wagonette all day. It would have been a simple matter for her to distract the babbler and place it there.

My dear Charlie,

It's alarming for both of us to know that someone has discovered our secret. Even so, the only thing that's happened is that he walked up to me yesterday and asked me if I was ready to fulfil my side of the bargain. I asked him for some more time. Pa says that we will be off to Burketown within a day or two. Otherwise, I don't know what will happen.

The next few pages were as precious a gift as I could have been given. Little anecdotes about her day, written in an entertaining style. Horses would often play the fool, or carry on with little feuds like sneaking up on each other and biting hind legs or backs. Gracie's words brought them to life. She finished with some sweet sentences about how she missed me too.

I was on horseback when I read it, but I might as well have been floating on air. At that moment I loved her so much my need was an ache in every muscle and bone, from brisket to brain.

I realised that day that there are parts of a man or woman's personality that only become plain in words on a page. It was like I was learning of another corner of her heart in those pages of near perfect copperplate. When I'd finished reading I replied straight away, sitting well back in the saddle and using the pig skin as backing.

Four days after leaving the pleuro camp, however, I was riding after the mob when Dick cantered towards me, then changed his angle so he came alongside.

'Hi there Dick, what's happening?'

Dick reined in. 'Mister Charlie, I seen a strange thing.' '

What was it?'

'I seen Miss Gracie's tracks, alla same wif' her horses.'

'Well, that's not unusual, you know she takes the night horses out to feed then moves them up to the night camp.'

'Yeah, but I seen Billy Higgins today, get hisself some fine rope, then he tell Patsy he get a belly ache and would ride slow. Maybe ten yard a' plaited greenhide, and I seen him tie a slip knot in the end. Strange t'ing, then I finds his tracks upla from the herd, and they followin' Miss Gracie tracks.'

My blood ran cold. 'Where? Take me there now!'

We rode like the wind, us two. Dick was a lighter man than me, and he could melt into the horse like a jockey. All horses worth their salt like a gallop, and there was a burning, steely anger in my eye as I allowed Dick to lead me the most direct route across to where he had seen Billy following Gracie.

We crossed a plain of dry, mostly flattened speargrass, and when the land rose into a low wooded hill, we saw Billy's horse with the reins tied to a tree. The animal stared at us, unconcerned, as we passed.

Dick lifted his forefinger to his lips, and motioned at me to stop and dismount. 'Close now,' he said. 'Shhh.'

We tied our horses to one of the many black wattle trees. I slipped the Snider from its scabbard, lifted the block, and pushed a cartridge in with fingers shaking. My breathing was shallow, my chest burning.

I held the rifle crosswise on my chest in both hands as I followed Dick on foot. He pointed out and interpreted Billy's tracks as we went.

'Billy chasin' her now,' he said. 'Fast running, see?'

Ahead was a line of trees that marked a dry creek. I heard Billy's voice before I saw him.

That mongrel was sitting on a log on the dry sand down below, and Gracie was in his lap. Thank God she still had her clothes on, but his filthy hand was under her shirt and glued to her breast, his face nuzzling at her neck. His other hand encircled her waist while she squirmed and struggled. Her eyes turned up to lock with mine. I saw fear in her face, and then relief.

A hank of rope sat on the log beside the two of them. Billy's gun belt was lying next to it, the polished butt of his revolver in plain sight.

Billy Higgins looked up at me and Dick on the bank. His face, I swear, turned white in an instant. I held the rifle at my hip, aimed in his general direction, though of course I had no intention of firing with Gracie so close.

'Let her go, you dog,' I called down. My voice was captured and concentrated by the venerable old-man paperbarks that lined the creek.

Billy removed his encircling arm, and a laugh issued from his throat. 'Come on, Charlie. Point the fucking gun somewhere else, will you? Can't blame me for wanting a bit of what you've been getting every night. We've all been through hell on this cursed trip, and you've been swanning around with Tom Fucking Kilfoyle and putting your prick into this hot little piece every night.'

Gracie got to her feet in a flash and stood back against the steep clay bank of the creek. I picked my way down, landing with both feet in the sand beside her. Continuing to grip the rifle in my right hand, I squeezed her around the shoulders with my left.

Then, leaving her, I walked closer to Billy, aiming the barrel of my rifle at his face. 'You know I can't miss,' I hissed. 'I'll kill you dead.' I saw the sweat burst forth from his skin as I thumbed the hammer. I was angry enough to pull the trigger. What was stopping me was a vague mess in my head that I could sum up with the word consequences.

If I killed Billy Higgins in front of Dick and Gracie I had no hope of riding back and acting as if it had never happened. Even if Gracie and Dick both covered for me, there would be search parties, and Dick's loyalties lay with the Duracks, not me.

'Don't shoot him, Charlie,' Gracie wailed. 'Don't make yourself a murderer.'

'She's right, Charlie,' said Billy. 'I didn't mean any harm, just wanted a kiss and a cuddle. Let's forget the whole thing and I won't say nothin'. I won't tell the blacksmith – we'll all just mind our own bleedin' business and get back to work. Is it a deal?'

I turned to Dick, who said. 'It wull be bad t'ing if you killim, boss.'

I gripped the rifle tight. 'Why? If we hadn't come along he would have raped my Gracie. The bastard deserves it.'

Billy piped up in his own defence. 'You know the Duracks, Charlie. They'll put you in chains and take you to the first policeman we come to. You'll hang, Charlie.'

At the word hang, Gracie started to weep miserably. I hissed in frustration. 'The bastard will go back and tell Gracie's father,' I said. 'I know he will. He hates me.'

'Wit' my people,' Dick said. 'When we doan wan' someone to talk we make it so him carn talk no more.'

I stopped dead, searched his eyes with my own. Dick was telling me what to do, offering a way forward, a wise compromise, and letting me know that he would help me. 'Tie his hands for me, Dick. Tight as you like.'

'No nigger's going to tie me up,' shouted Billy, and he started to rise. I stepped forwards and kicked him in the chest so he went over backwards. Dick was an expert roper, and could deal with bulls ten times Billy's size. Rolling him onto his belly in the sand, Dick gathered his wrists behind his back, and tied them together.

Still with the rifle barrel covering Billy I turned to Gracie. 'Dick will help you get the horses together and go with you back to the mob. I'll make my own way with Billy. We all say nothing of this. It never happened.'

Gracie looked pained. 'You're not going to kill him, are you?'

'No. I'm not going to kill him.'

I watched them go, then leaned down and grabbed Billy by the back of the shirt, half lifting him. 'Now you and me are walking back to our horses.'

He stood, spitting sand from his lips. 'I want my gun belt.' I fetched it from the log, emptying the revolver and belt loops of cartridges, placing them in my pocket. I buckled the belt tightly enough around his waist that it would not fall off.

With the belt on he seemed to regain more of his old swagger. 'You think you're going to ride me back in, hogtied like this? You think Patsy or Big Johnnie will even listen to your side of the story? I've been with them for years. You're a damned blow-in.'

'Just get moving. Walk in front of me.'

He staggered up out of that gully and across the plain, and when we reached the wooded hill, I did not give him a chance to run ahead and get to his grey. I circled around in front of him, untied the horse and ordered him to the front while I led the animal myself.

When we reached my horse, I saw that Dick had already taken his mount. I breathed a sigh of relief, at least he and Gracie were safely clear. Billy turned to look at me.

'So what now?'

I levelled the barrel at him and walked towards him. 'Lie down on the ground.'

The whining tone came back into his voice. 'You said you wouldn't kill me …'

'Just get down on the fucking ground, NOW!

He went to his knees, but unable to use his hands to help, he fell sideways.

'Face down,' I ordered.

When he had finally done what I asked I leaned the rifle against a tree. Casting around I picked up a rock a bit bigger than my hand, as jagged as broken glass. It hadn't taken me long to figure out Dick's meaning. Billy could not read or write. Talking was his only clear means of communication.

Falling to my knees I placed my free hand on Billy's shoulder and rolled him over.

His eyes widened at the sight of the rock, raised high in my right hand. For this to work I knew I had to do the damage in as few blows as possible. I brought that rock down right on target, with all the power of my arms and the weight of the rock striking him full in the mouth, breaking lips and teeth as it went. I'll never forget the noise that came from his throat as the rock struck him, and I felt a release of anger from my own heart. I raised the rock again and brought it down at the same time as he tried to move, so it struck an inch to the left, in the corner of

175

his mouth, smashing through incisors and molars alike, pulverising them. Later, John Urquhart would pull teeth from Billy's tongue with forceps.

My work done, I stood up, lips turned down at the corners. Let no man tell you that revenge is not sweet. My chest swelled with self-righteous pride as I threw the sticky-dark rock into the bush. Billy sat up to stop the blood from choking him, uttering an unearthly wail, for the pain must have been terrible.

I squatted before him, and grasped an ear in each hand, forcing him to look at me, his mouth a bloody cave of splintered teeth and fragments of lip. 'You won't be talking for a long time,' I said. 'But you ever cross me again, in any way, and I won't stop until you're dead. So help me God I promise you that.' I dropped my hands. 'Now get on your horse and go back. Your story, if ever you learn to talk again, is that you got kicked by a horse. If I find out otherwise, I'll come looking for you.'

His mouth dripped a trail of blood in the dust and up his horse's flanks as he mounted unsteadily. He did not so much as look at me as he rode away.

Bob Perry taught me how to knock a man down. I worked out for myself, with a little help from Dick, how to break his spirit, and I was still only eighteen years old.

Later, the story of how Billy Higgins rode into camp after copping a hoof to the face passed from man to man around the camp. Tom Kilfoyle rode across to Patsy Moore's camp that night to view the injury and came back clicking his tongue.

'I've never seen the like of it,' he said. 'His face is swollen up like a watermelon so's he can hardly breathe. I haven't ever took Billy Higgins as a fool, but how else would a man put his head in such a position for being kicked?'

'I heard that his cuddy picked up a jag in its hoof,' Duncan said, 'and he were tryin' tae pick it out.'

'I heard that too,' Jack Sherringham agreed. 'But of course the poor bastard can't talk.'

I was on tenterhooks for a day or two, but nothing was said. I heard that Billy caught an infection, and that he was bedded down in a wagonette for a couple of days while he fought it.

Within a week, however, he was back in the saddle, and I saw him one day from a distance. He was too far away to see clearly, but we both reined in and stared across that distance. He was the first to turn away, and there was none of the old belligerence in his gaze.

Bad news, however, was on its way. No matter what Billy Higgins had done, Walter Oswald was determined to get his daughter out of the camp.

Sending a note scrawled on the back of a jam label – I had used up the last of my paper – I arranged to meet Gracie. This was not to be a tryst, but a talk. I was worried about her state of mind, and also her reaction to the stories of his injury that were running like grassfires through the camp.

A black boy who had come back with us from Lawn Hill, however, was to take over Gracie's work as horse tailer for Hangfire Mick. When I found her, he was there, learning the names of the horses – which ones were easy or hard to catch – and the tricks they played.

I walked in openly, but had to wait until she sent him off riding on a little colt she was fond of.

'I broke that colt myself,' she said proudly.

I was impressed. 'I didn't know.'

'There's a lot about me you don't know, Charlie,' she said. 'We started out as friends, but all we ever do these days is … make love. We hardly even talk.'

I grasped her around the waist and squeezed her. 'I want to do everything with you. As soon as this damned drive is over.'

But she wasn't listening. 'You didn't have to do that to Billy Higgins.'

'Why the hell not? If I'd been five minutes later he would have raped you. Jesus, Gracie, what do you think that rope was for?'

'I don't know for sure, and neither do you.'

'I don't bloody understand you. I saved you Gracie.'

Something had changed, and now, fifty years later I can see exactly what it was. I've learned that every affair of the heart has a time and place

177

where it flourishes. You can sense when that magic moment has passed. When the colours of the sky go leaden grey, and the excitement fades.

'It doesn't matter, Charlie. Dad and I are going. He told me this morning – back to Burketown where we can catch a steamer to Queensland – or maybe Palmerston. Pa says that they're crying out for men with trades in the Territory.'

My mouth went dry. 'When are you leaving?'

'First thing tomorrow morning. I have to get back and help dad pack up.'

'When am I going to see you again?'

'I don't know.'

'Write to me at the Elsey, and tell me where you are. When the drive is over I'll come find you.'

Then, in a sudden change of mood, all the hostility left her. She threw her arms around me so tightly I felt like I would choke. Our lips met, salted with tears. She grabbed my chin between her palms and looked at me, misty eyed and so beautiful I felt like I'd turn to stone on the spot.

'I have to go,' she said.

'I'll find you. No matter what,' I promised. 'After the drive.'

Her eyes were brown and wide. 'I know you will.'

Watching her ride away around the mob. 'I'll find you,' I repeated under my breath, and closed my eyes so tight I saw stars in the blackness.

CHAPTER NINETEEN

The blacks now gave us trouble, killing our horses which they had acquired a taste for, burning the country ahead and behind, and stampeding our cattle when on camp. We pelted them with lead when opportunity offered, but that was not often. They were too cunning.

SO, DEAR READER of these memories. You might judge me as a poor excuse for a man, reading what I have done. Much worse, I'm ashamed to admit, is still to come. But this world – dear debutante with powdered nose, you schoolteacher with chalk on your fingers, or book keeper with your rows of neat figures in a ledger – is not your world. This land of open skies, horizon to horizon; air clean as a knife blade; the rich smell of horse-sweat and leather. This world of flies, snakes, and mosquitoes. Of taking a 'killer' out of the mob, dropping the beast with one head shot, elbow deep in blood, hatchet and knife moving with practiced strokes.

Days so hot the slightest breeze was like a rebirth. Hating and loving your life all at the same time, lying in your swag frightened shitless of the blacks out there with their stone-tipped spears and savage ways. We owned the daylight, but the black man owned the night.

This world echoed to the sounds of rough voices, words and phrases. Fist fights that ended with bloody faces and bloody handshakes. Laughing together, faces upturned to the wild sky. We were proud to be pioneers, and explorers. We loved naming creeks and hills, while Tom Kilfoyle or Big Johnnie marked them in their journals.

We took what we wanted, with horses, boots and guns, but hold back your judgement unless you have lived what I lived.

We made good time over the border and into the Territory, but I had sunk into a depressed state, and couldn't tell anyone why. Gracie had become not just part of my life, but my dreams of the future. Everything I could think of doing in ten years' time involved having that beautiful, hardworking, young woman at my side.

I was riding with John Urquhart a week or more after Gracie left, chasing a couple of brumbies we had spotted, up along a small waterway. We were always on the lookout for extra horses, and besides, getting after wild stock was a lot of fun. An effort had been made, a few years earlier, to breed remounts for the British army up here somewhere, and on my previous trip with Nat Buchanan we had caught at least a dozen fine horses.

They ran like the wind, manes flying and tails held high. Our energetic fillies made a game of the chase, following our quarry up from the creek into some dry hills where flinty stones flew from their hooves. Down gullies and dry valleys, those brumbies showed no signs of giving up. They had hearts as free as eagles. John and I both knew we'd soon have to give the game away, but our blood was up for the chase.

We pulled up, defeated at last, our horses blown, and walked them back down to the creek for water, talking companionably as we went. As usual we gossiped about men in the camp, their comings and goings.

'I miss that crazy blacksmith,' I said companionably. 'And Gracie too, she was a real young lady.'

To my surprise, John did not agree with me. He snorted. 'Not such a lady. Don't tell anyone I told you this, but she came to see me a day or two before they left. She asked me, seeing as I know a bit about animal medicine, whether I knew about a way for a girl to get rid of a baby if she happened to fall pregnant.'

I must have almost fallen off my horse because he said, 'Are you alright lad?'

'Yeah fine, are you saying that Gracie is … gonna have a baby?'

'Either that or she just thinks she is. Either way, she's been doing things she shouldn't have.' His eyes narrowed. 'Hey now, it was you, wasn't it?'

I didn't have the steel, right then, to deny it. 'Don't tell anyone for God's sake. Jesus, what should I do? I have to ride after her – they'd barely have reached Burketown by now.'

John spoke good sense, as usual. 'If she wanted you to know she would have told you. What do you think might happen if you go riding into Burketown and start shouting about marrying Grace because you got her in the family way?'

'Walter would shoot me?'

'Yes, he would. He's a madman. Besides, you can't just up and leave Tom Kilfoyle. He relies on you more than you know.'

'What should I do?'

'I'd say you've already played your part.'

'You won't tell anyone, will you?'

'No lad, I won't, but such things have a way of working themselves loose.'

That day I nearly rode off after Gracie a dozen times, but what could I give her? First off, a bitter fight with her old man, and he was as tough a man as I'd ever seen, misshapen with muscle, probably twice my weight, and he fought at the drop of a hat. Bob Perry's tricks wouldn't help me much against an opponent like that, and besides, Gracie loved her father. Provoking a fight with him, win, lose or draw, would hardly endear her to me.

The possibility that she might spill the beans on her own account also occurred to me, and all day I half expected to see Walter Oswald riding towards me in a lather, shouting my name, ready to shoot a hole in my guts.

In the end I neither rode off to Burketown, and neither did Walter Oswald appear. Yet my state of mind was now far worse, knowing that my baby was growing inside the body of the girl I loved. Most of all, I missed her. God how I missed her.

As we progressed into the Territory, we realised that wild blacks were watching us, by night and day. Rarely seen, but always there, they kept us all on edge.

These were hard men from a harsh land. They were warriors in every sense of the word, and if they got close, they might well kill you. Big Johnnie was adamant that we did not shoot unless we were directly threatened or if they were getting away with stock. 'We're passing through, we don't want a bleeding war on our hands. If they start something fair enough, otherwise, we leave 'em alone.'

They inhabited this area in large numbers, however, and were more visible and aggressive than they had been on my previous trip with Nat Buchanan.

One night I was roused from sleep by a shout from Duncan McCaully, who was on night watch. For myself and all the others it was a mad scramble for rifles, revolvers, and the night horses tethered to the night horse tree. We rode out in a group and smelled the smoke before we'd travelled a hundred yards. We looked down the slope and saw the orange flames of a grass fire, and dark figures running along with burning branches.

'Och,' Duncan growled. 'Devil take those black heathens, fa' they're trying to cook us all.'

The flames spread rapidly through the dry grass towards us. Tom Kilfoyle raised his rifle and I did the same. Yet it was difficult to see the iron sights properly in the dark, and our targets moved like shadows. Even so, I did my best to focus on one of those wraiths in the night. I squeezed the trigger and the butt kicked my shoulder.

I don't think that I hit anything, but the fusillade had the desired effect, for the firelighters melted away into the night.

Tom lowered his weapon. 'No point trying to fight that fire.' He turned to Steve Brogan. 'You ride for the other camps and warn them. They will have heard the gunshots so they'll be alert. Tell them to get the mobs moving.' Steve rode off, and Tom said. 'I don't need to tell the rest of you boys that if you see a black face, put a bullet in it – we didn't start this fight.'

All night we rode between the mobs in gangs, and the Snider rifle rested heavy in my arms. We geed each other up. We spoke of black sorcerers, and how it was impossible to see them until their mischief was done. Flames danced ahead and behind us as they lit more fires and we shot at silhouettes and figments of the imagination.

'There'll be naught in the way of peace,' Duncan McCaully said, 'until they all lie dead.'

But it was Jim Minogue, one of those men who have only one idea in their life, but hold fast to it for all they're worth, who painted the meanest picture of what we were doing here. 'God made men like us to lead all the birds and the animals and the savages of this entire earth. We have dominion over all things. If they try to fight us, we have no choice but to smite them down in His name.'

We reached the Calvert River where it loops down from the Barkly Tableland and drains a swathe of country into the Gulf of Carpentaria, the first major river on the Territory side of the border. Here, in addition to more night fires lit by the blacks and reports of war parties on the move, word reached us of the fatal spearing of a drover in a mob further ahead, a man called Frazer. Two or three of our horses were killed in cunningly concealed pit traps.

Of course they did not welcome us. We were part of an unprecedented migration of livestock. Dozens of drives had gone before, many crewed by men who shot first and asked questions later, or who saw kidnapping lubras as their right.

The blacks were watching the drive by night and day. Not often visible, but always there, they kept us on edge; a feeling that only the cold iron of a weapon could dispel.

When we did catch sight of them, they were frighteningly wild: either naked or with loin coverings of animal skins, bones through their noses and amulets of snakeskin or shell. They were often accompanied by their half wild dogs, yellow-orange brutes, low at the shoulder and slinking. Like warlocks and their wolves.

The dogs were often used to bring down cattle so a spearman could get close, a technique that infuriated us. We saw smoke signals on the hills as we advanced, and they always seemed to know we were coming, standing on clifftops and clattering their weapons, and even the wind seemed to say, 'Go away. Go away.'

On our third night along the Calvert, I was woken by a gunshot, then the thud of hooves as Duncan, the night watchman, rode in to camp.

'Get oop, you lads,' he called, 'them blasted blacks be stealing the horses. God himself only knows why they always strike when I'm on watch.'

My arse was one of the first to land on a saddle. I shoved my rifle into the scabbard and dug in my heels. 'Yah,' I cried, and wheeled to ride with Duncan. In a trice there were five of us mounted.

Tom Kilfoyle was never slow in a crisis, and he was already taking control. 'Steve and Mick, you watch the cattle. They'll be unsettled from all the noise. You men, Duncan and Charlie, have your weapons ready and we'll teach these thieving bastards a lesson.'

We thundered off at speed with the big Scot at the lead, wheeling around our plant, hobbled and belled, straggling around within cooee of the camp. The horses were as frightened as hell, whinnying and shying, and we could see at once that a number had been cut out. The moon was new, and while the starlight was enough to make out trees, cattle, horses and each other, there was no question of being able to track.

We slowed the horses and walked them along in silence for a while, spreading out and hoping to come across the thieves and our missing plant. Not wanting to destroy any spoor that might be visible in daylight, however, we soon returned to camp. We spent the rest of the night in front of the campfire, fingering our rifles and pistols.

CHAPTER TWENTY

We both wheeled and fired at a retreating buck. He staggered and fell.
We both had got him. One bullet cracked him in the neck and other
through the back.

AN HOUR AFTER DAWN, with skeleton crews watching the mobs, we scoured the hills and plains, looking for traces left by the horse thieves. No one had told us to shoot on sight, but it was understood that there could be no prisoners. I rode with Black Pat Durack and a boy called Jonas. Ten miles from camp we came upon the butchered carcass of a grey mare I had ridden many times, her bloodied ribs standing out like the frame of a ship. Chunks of meat were still roasting on the coals of a slow fire. Black Pat pointed out a line of trees lining a dry gully some three hundred paces away.

'Ye can stake your fortune that the murderous bastards are in there watching us.'

'I've no fortune to stake,' I told him. 'But I reckon you're probably right.'

My hands were tense on the rifle. There was something gut wrenching about the thought of a spear from an unseen enemy, spitting a man like a pig, that sharp stone barb tunnelling and tearing through flesh. Of course we were out of range right there, but that didn't stop fear climbing my spine like a demon on a ladder.

'So, what do you reckon we should do? We can't follow them in there, they'll pick us off from cover.'

'Has Scrutton been giving you lessons in tactics or something?'

'No, just common sense.'

'Well common sense tells me that you can't let *them* dictate terms.

These rifles are worth any ten savages.'

I screwed up my eyes, 'I'm game, but what's the plan?'

Black Pat pointed back the way we'd come. 'Jonas and I will ride down thataway, and then double back into the scrub along the creek. The blacks are afraid of the guns, so I'll fire off a few shots, chasing them back up through that gully there.'

He pointed to where a long ago fallen gum tree lay leafless and branchless on the earth. 'Meanwhile, set yeself up on that fallen tree with your rifle, and pick the bastards off when they come a-running out of cover. With a dead rest ye should be able to make good practice at that range.'

It seemed to me that I'd drawn the less risky of the two activities, but the idea of some sharpshooting with the rifle appealed to me, and it seemed like a reasonable enough plan.

'Worth a try,' I said.

So, while Black Pat and the boy thundered off the way we'd come I rode over to the fallen tree. Tying Constance up to a convenient branch, I set myself up, arranging spare ammunition near my right hand, and fetching a spare shirt from my saddlebags to rest the rifle stock on.

I had just settled myself, rifle butt to my shoulder, when I heard the first shots further down the gully, along with so much yelping and hollering a man would have thought it came from ten throats, not just two.

I squinted my right eye and settled the pip of the foresight into the notch of the rear. I aimed at the edge of the scrub, hardly daring to breathe, my forefinger filling the curve of the trigger. More yelling and shooting, but none of the wild black figures I expected to see. Minutes passed, then finally Black Pat rode out with his boy. He gave me a wave.

Part disappointed, part relieved, I slung the rifle, packed the ammunition and shirt back into my saddle bags and rode on over.

'No sign of them in there?' I asked.

'No, the mongrels have made themselves scarce.'

Pat was standing some fifty paces shy of the gully, with his back to it, and did not see what I saw. A tall warrior, black as coal and as strongly

187

built as a young bull, stepped out of the trees and let fly with a spear at the same moment. I will never forget how my heart froze as his body coiled and uncoiled into that stroke, using every muscle of his body.

I shouted a warning at Pat, giving him time to whirl and sidestep. The spear missed him by a whisker. The man who had fired the missile turned to run back into the scrub.

I unslung my rifle, and Pat was doing the same. I lined the would-be killer up with the sights, just like I had done so many times with targets, only this was no target, but a man. My Snider boomed, and Pat's shot came an instant later.

We rode up to view the body. The buck had fallen front down and Black Pat dismounted to roll him over. I can still see him as if it were yesterday. My bullet had passed through his back. Pat, also a good marksman, had struck him in the neck. Both slugs had torn bloody tunnels through his flesh.

As I said, the dead man was muscular, with amulets on his arms and ankles. His face was bearded, with young, vigorous growth. The middle of his nostril was pierced with bone, and he had an old scar above his right eye, as well as the usual disfiguring marks on his chest and upper arms.

Black Pat looked down at the dead man, 'He deserved death. There's no joy in it, but they have to learn that they can't go around thieving horses and starting fires.'

'Yes,' I agreed. 'We had to shoot.'

That was the first time I had killed a man. My throat was dry and my hands were shaky and weak. I did feel sorry for him, they only took the horses to eat, and they had not asked us to come here. I remembered, a lifetime ago, walking through the All Saints church in Bendigo with Margaret Anne, and those engraved letters staring at me: *Thou shalt not kill.* I felt a shiver of fear. *You wouldn't kill anyone, Charlie, would you?* the reverend's niece had asked me.

Defending one's land is as natural as breathing, but that dead man did not understand what was coming. This was not a matter of a few horsemen, and cattle, but of a civilisation, an irreversible change. If it was not us, it would have been the Spanish, or the Dutch. The white men, in one form or another, were coming, yet inevitability did not make the destruction of these people less of a tragedy.

I did not know it, back then, but the man we had killed was a warrior of the Garrwa people. He left one, maybe two wives and many children to grieve for him. He was part way through a process of learning the songs, and the knowledge, until one day it would have been he who passed it down to the next generation.

We thought they were simple, but years later I sat at the feet of a Yanyuwa elder while he explained the totem stories that had been passed down over thousands of years. The detail filled me with wonder. Each family had their own particular mosaic; part history mingled with landscape, part religion.

We thought they were primitive, but on the sandstone ledges I saw the dreaming pictures: Intricate fish, kangaroos. And back then they were fresh, touched up regularly by the artists. Even now, fifty years later, they are fading, and have lost the brilliance. Ah, what a sight, in the old days.

We thought they were no better than beasts, and if they crossed us we shot them down. God help me; we thought *Thou shalt not kill* did not apply to them. But even as the last echoes of our rifle shots died God was preparing His punishments for us.

I've lived long enough to see civilisation win through. I've lived to see the rise of the missions, those havens of protection where the bullets did not penetrate. I've seen the Chinaman bring his opium. I've seen syphilis and leprosy run through the camps of the north. I've seen the hollowed out eyes of the addict as if worms had crawled through his brain.

I've seen us kill them over and over, in so many ways, that the way of the bullet almost seems kind.

CHAPTER TWENTY-ONE

He loaded up a lot of provisions, not forgetting a big supply of whisky; square bottles, with green labels, named "Come Hither." Good God what havoc that terrible stuff did. It would make a jack rabbit fight a bulldog. A man that got a few shots of that stuff under his belt would charge hell with a bucket of water.

WE CROSSED THE WEARYAN RIVER in December, 1885. We had now been on the drive for near eighteen months. The herd was a little over half the size it had been when we started. Men had joined, men had died or left, and those of us who had been there since the start, felt an odd pride in the scars of the trail.

But now, after months of build-up, the wet season bared its claws. Lightning flickered on all points of the horizon, and sweat covered our bodies. Sudden downpours saw inches of rain bucket down in an hour, cutting us off from sight of the cattle and each other. Day and night, it was steaming hot, the air tainted with the heavy perfume of wild blooms on tree and ground foliage alike.

We came up to the McArthur River, where we made a temporary camp with good water, pasture and a succulent herb called milk-bush, that the cattle loved. As we settled in, however, a rider informed us that this was no longer open range, but a pastoral lease owned by the firm of Amos and Broad: railway contractors from Sydney.

We'd known that McArthur River Station had recently been set up in the area, but hadn't enquired too closely as to whether we were inside the boundaries. A group of us rode off to the homestead to plead for the right to camp where we were for a few days.

Tom Lynott, the manager, originally hailed from Melbourne. I'd heard around the traps that he owed his current position to the influence of his brother, Charles Lynott, a well-known cattle salesman in that city. Tom was a long, lean fellow with a nose too small for his face, but was well regarded by all of the crew who knew him.

'Nice looking homestead,' Big Johnnie said.

'Well, it might look that way,' Lynott said, 'if the blasted termites weren't finding it so much to their taste. We'd barely started nailing down the rafters when they were chewing on the floorboards.'

Big Johnnie had a suggestion. 'Have ye tried dousing the timbers with oil and kerosene?'

'Too right we have. It slows them down a little, but turns the bally house into a bomb. I daren't light a candle in the place lest it all goes up like London Town. Take my advice, you lot, when you get to building your housing, not to mention rails and yards, use cypress if you can find it. It's the only wood the damned termites won't eat.'

'That's good advice,' Johnnie said. 'Now on the matter of us, our plant and our cattle. It seems that we're camped on your place, and we need a week or two while we fetch provisions from downriver and get settled. We've had a hard time with pleuro, blacks, and the men are just plain sick of the track.'

'Everyone has those same troubles, and I sympathise with you blokes,' Lynott said, scratching his beard. 'But with our station cattle, your four mobs and another two heading into the area – one with Nat Buchanan, one with the McDonalds – there's not enough grass for everyone. You'll just have to move on. Sorry, but that's the way it is.'

'I understand that,' Johnnie said. 'Thanks for being straight with us.' His voice was civil, but he stood and poured the rest of his tea over the verandah rail. This done, he sat the mug back on the table. 'Alright lads, we've got work to do.'

Disappointed at having to press on, we were forced to find a ford over the McArthur, now rising into its wet season state; wide and brown, with debris floating in lines of froth, and the beaks of colossal alligators visible

191

here and there in the swirling currents.

Though these were, of course, crocodiles, we always called them alligators or just 'gators. Even now, fifty years later, Territory bushmen refuse to call salt water crocodiles anything but 'gators, though the freshwater variety will usually be called 'freshies.'

A Top End river in flood has a particular smell: of flattened grass, riverside blossoms, and also of rot; more fresh than dour. Later, when the water receded the scent would ripen, but for now it tantalised with promise and excitement.

The crossing was wide but shallow, with a firm gravel bed. We were able to drive the mobs across with water barely wetting their tails.

Then, while the rest of the drive carried on to a waterway called Rosie Creek, I found myself with Steve Brogan, Duncan, Big Johnnie, Jack Sherringham, John Mooney, and another of the Duracks called Stumpy Michael, back on the southern side of the McArthur, heading downstream towards a river landing that apparently boasted a store with provisions. It was a relief to get away from the mob for a day or two, but with every step closer to the sea, the air grew muggier and the heat seemed only more oppressive.

Mostly the riverbanks were open, easy going, but at times we entered paperbark swamps where the horses ploughed through water as deep as their chests and the wagonettes were forced to take long detours. There were dry forests also, thick with messmate trees, and ancient cycads that looked like soldiers from some supernatural world, watching as we passed.

The river we followed was soon, we decided, deep enough for large ships to navigate. We talked for hours about what this place might be like when civilisation came – what river ports and cities might sprout on the ridges. Meatworks and factories. At how fortunes would be made.

A mile from the landing, we sent Dick on ahead to scout the place out. He rode back an hour later at speed.

'Boss, that place busy. Lotsa white men. Bad white men.' Then his eyes turned on Jack. 'Jack, better piss off quick. There a policeman alonga landing – detective from Queensland – an' he ask if I seen you.'

Jack, always pale, now took on the colour of chalk. 'Oh Jesus. You sure he asked for me?'

'Yes. Mister Jack. He knowed your las' name – Sherringham.'

I saw the fear on Jack's face then. The look of a man afraid of the rope. 'Right then, you blokes, I'm off. I'll see you up at the Rosie.'

'Wait!' Big Johnnie's voice rang out. 'If ye're innocent then isn't it best to ride in like a man and set about clearing yer name rather than running off like a scared kid?'

Jack's horse sensed his nervousness, and shifted awkwardly while he stopped, reins in his hands. 'I wish it were so easy, Johnnie. I aren't exactly innocent.'

Big Johnnie shook his head sadly. We all liked Jack. 'You can't keep running. Consequences have a way of catching up to a man.'

Jack wheeled his horse and cantered off the way we had come, just as if he hadn't heard. I watched him go, knowing that no good would come of this. I had seen the fear on his face just before he turned away.

We rode on without Jack, up a rough trail that wound along the bank, with bog holes from wagonette traffic. Finally, we reached the McArthur River Landing where a shanty town had sprung up on the banks of the river, mostly north of Rocky Creek. The typical dwelling was a basic shack of poles clad with paperbark sheets or flattened kerosene tins. Packing cases had been put to good use for walls or furniture. Behind this basic little settlement ran the river McArthur itself.

The inhabitants of this place were as odd an assortment of fugitives and ne'er-do-wells as I'd ever seen. With no police station for two hundred miles, this wild Gulf region was already developing a reputation as a refuge for wanted men.

They weren't all criminals, by any means. There were also unemployed stockmen and brumby-catchers who made their living trapping wild horses lost by previous droving trips, and prospectors from the Palmer fields in Queensland, heading over to try their luck at Pine Creek.

Tired-looking horses searched for feed amongst the tussocks and stones. Men sat at their cooking fires or talked in sullen groups. Most had revolvers at their belts or a rifle slung on their backs, watching us with suspicion as we dismounted and walked in.

I got the shock of my life to find my old rations carrier from Big Sandy Station, Billy McLeod, in the process of setting up a store with two partners, O'Brien and Hunt. The store was one of only four or five substantial buildings on the landing. Doubling as a pub, it had a roofed verandah, floored with beaten earth, and furnished with rough tables. At those tables lounged a curious collection of lawless cut-throats and low-lifes.

Although these men were all new to me then, I learned their stories before long. Some I worked with in later years.

Among them was a thief and seller of stolen goods called Billy 'the Informer' Hynes, along with Jack 'The Orphan' Martin who had run a thriving trade on the Palmer River, North Queensland, as armed bodyguard for gangs of Chinese miners. 'The Orphan' had been forced to leave the area after he murdered one of the men he was supposed to protect, believing him to be carrying a large quantity of gold.

Harry 'Pigweed' Herbert was also in residence on the McArthur; a convicted horse thief from the Diamantina. Pigweed and I would later become great mates, but back then he was a stranger and as frightening a man as I'd met.

Even though Big Johnnie Durack, an uncommonly hefty man, led the way, and an even bigger man, Duncan McCaully, brought up the rear, our party was outnumbered and outgunned as we entered Billy McLeod's store. We crossed the verandah and moved on inside through an open doorway. The interior was shelved with raw poles and more slabs of paperbark. Two old men occupied a table, with mugs and a half empty bottle of whisky.

One was McLeod himself, and his face lit up when he saw me.

'Young Charlie, it's damn good to see you.'

'You too.' I'd come a long way since my time as a shepherd on Big Sandy, and we both knew it. Billy's beard was whiter, and his head shinier, but he looked little different otherwise. He pumped my hand and clapped my back.

'By God, Charlie. How you've grown up!'

'Are ye the proprietors of this here store?' Big Johnnie asked impatiently.

Billy adjusted his eyeglasses. 'That be the truth, and who might you be, good sir? A drover, I'm guessing, by the smell, begging your pardon – and casting no aspersions. None around here are exactly perfumed ... and besides, any mate of young Charlie here is a mate of mine.' His speech ended with a round of coughing that saw him doubled over like a snake over a rail.

'That sounds serious,' Johnnie commented.

'It be the infernal dust, part and parcel of the mining game. Once it gets in it takes years to cough back out again. Can I get you fellows a drink? Just whisky is all we've got.'

'We may have a tot directly, but mainly we're interested in stores; flour, tea, biscuits. It don't look like there's much on those shelves so I'm assuming ye've got those things stored out the back?'

The old man made something resembling an oyster with his lips. 'Not so much, I'm afraid.'

'Well, what's the problem?' Big Johnnie asked. 'This is a store, isn't that so?'

'It's a store all right, but we've run out of everything.' He raised his forefinger. 'Luckily ... it so happens that a schooner full of provisions is right now sailing up the McArthur and will be here at the landing tomorrow.'

Big Johnnie looked relieved. 'That's good news then.'

'All I can suggest to you is that you find yourself a patch of ground, park your wagons, and enjoy the hospitality.'

Big Johnnie turned sternly on us. 'One drink each, then we go find a camp and stay there, right?'

The old man hurried behind the bar to fill the orders. I waited at the back while the older men all ordered themselves a whisky. Of course, since the boss had allowed them only one, they made sure their glass was filled to the brim. When my turn came Billy McLeod looked me up and down.

'And what about you, young feller?'

The memory of a cold, smooth, sweet drink filled my mind. I guess my voice was a little too loud and shrill, for it carried to the ears of the gangs of miscreants drinking under the shade of the outside awning. 'You haven't got any cream soda, have you?' I asked.

The old men, the drinkers, and even Big Johnnie started to laugh. One local was so stricken with this condition that he rolled around on the floor.

Only in later years did I understand how funny this sounded. I had just crossed one of the world's harshest continents, with drought or rain and flies for company. I had endured under the midday sun, until my skin was burned deep brown. I had bashed in a man's face with a rock, and shot and killed at least one native in a kill-or-be-killed encounter.

After all that I walked into one of the toughest watering holes in the North. The men inside were well known fugitives and wild men. I walked into that shanty and asked for a cream soda. And I wondered why they all laughed their heads off at me.

Over the next twenty-four hours, waiting for the promised schooner to sail in, I had time to wander around this strange little settlement, watching men sitting around or doing chores – shoeing horses or improving their shelters.

Many of the inhabitants of the camp had their own lubras, some who had obviously had the pride knocked out of them. One in particular was a fine-looking woman: tall, and athletic. She was also an impressive horsewoman, bareback or saddled made no difference to her.

Tired of the tedium I went up to talk to her. 'Hey what's your name?'

'Virtue,' she told me, and never was a black woman named better.

'Are you from around this country?' I asked her.

'Yes, from this country. Yanyuwa people.'

I tried several times to say the name, and bade her repeat it before I managed it. 'What do your people call this place?'

The word she came out with was so strange on my ears I made her repeat it three times. The best I could manage was Borrowlooler or

Borralooler. Later, of course, the little town became known as Borroloola.

While Virtue talked to me her eyes stayed on the entrance to the humpy opposite, and sure enough when we'd been talking for a while, a man with a revolver strapped to his waist emerged. I recognised him from the day before, when he had called at the store for some salt, the only item still in stock. Jack Martin – the Orphan.

'Hey you,' he called. 'She's my property. Get away from her or I'll shoot you dead.'

There was something about his tone that impressed on me that he wasn't joking. I backed away. 'Settle down, I'm only talking to her.'

'Yeah, I know how things are – starts out talking then one thing leads to another. Good girl like Virtue don't know how to say no to anyone.'

I felt the heat rising in my cheeks. 'It wasn't like that.'

'I bet it weren't, sonny. Start walking, and keep walking.'

I wandered down to the riverbank, there to watch a game in which the local men took turns shooting at small barrels floated out onto the flooded river. Or, if they chanced to see an alligator, the game was abandoned while everyone tried their hand at killing the reptile.

After watching for a while, one of the marksman struck a barrel squarely, exploding it into shreds of timber and rapidly sinking iron hoops. There was a round of applause and then someone shouted, 'Sail Ho!'

Guns and barrels forgotten, we all ran to the point to watch the schooner *Good Intent* sail around the bend, tacking furiously to make the most of the wind. She was almost new, with fresh timbers and bright pitch in the joins. In fact, I could smell the fresh sawdust and tar stench of her as she hove to off the landing.

What appeared to be the full ship's complement, three men and a woman, furled their sails, and dropped the anchor, all accompanied by raucous shouts, yells and laughter. Even the wild inhabitants of Borroloola had gone quiet at the display.

We didn't have to wait long before the *Good Intent*'s crew launched a skiff and the captain came ashore. Tall and lean, with his hat perched at a rakish angle on his head, he looked every inch a pirate. At his side was a white woman and a huge black American called Harold Best. Later I met several other crew and passengers.

'My name's Jack Reid,' declared the captain. 'We're shorthanded,' he said, 'with a full cargo to unload. Some help would be appreciated.'

The locals, who had gathered to watch the schooner come in, had no intention of helping. Instead, they stared at their feet or started wandering off to their shanties.

'Of course,' Reid went on, hands in his pockets, and swinging his head from side to side to take in his audience like Reverend Croxton had once done, back in Sandhurst. 'We don't expect you to work for no return. There's a bottle of whisky for every man who puts in a decent turn with the cargo.'

The crowd of malingerers transformed into a gang of willing workers. There were drums of flour, sacks of sugar, and tinned goods – beans, peaches, apples and pears. It was enough to make a man salivate, and gave us plenty to think on as we sweated like bullocks, rowing out and back then humping heavy weights, stacking the goods on the store shelves while Reid issued orders like a king.

I soon learned that Reid was known as 'Black Jack' or 'Maori Jack' for his swarthy skin and New Zealand accent. His features were indeed reminiscent of a Maori from that country, though I guessed that he was from one half to three quarters white.

Now, half a century later, he is my neighbour at the Two-mile near Pine Creek, and I know all the stories – how he left New Zealand just ahead of the hangman, who strung up three of his shipmates for blackbirding and murder. He was a rogue of the highest order, but with the charm of Lucifer, and as handsome a smile as you'd ever see.

The white woman on board was called Henrietta. I don't think she could properly be described as Maori Jack's wife, but was most certainly his girlfriend. She was a tall lady, with a buck-toothed smile, reddish hair tied with a variety of clips and bows, and crimson lipstick in greater quantity than I had seen on all but the flashest barmaids.

Another male crew member was a half-starved boy of around sixteen years. Upon touching the shore for the first time, halfway through the unloading, he disappeared at speed down the track, sprinting like an athlete, with Maori Jack shouting threats as he went.

'Oh let him go, Jack,' Henrietta told him, waving her hand airily. 'He were a lazy little bastard in any case.'

The pair cannily left the most critical part of the cargo until last — crates of square bottles with green labels. As I've said, I did not drink liquor back then, and I am no expert on brands, but I have never before or since heard of 'Come Hither' whisky. When we'd emptied the holds, Reid had one crate of the stuff placed on the bar. 'Good work, mates,' he shouted. 'One bottle for each of you, just as I promised.'

I saw Big Johnnie's face, knowing that he would have liked to load the wagons and get us out of that place, but dragging the men away from rowdy company, and a free bottle of whisky would be like slapping mutiny in the face and not expecting it to slap back. Admitting defeat, Johnnie took his bottle to a far table and sat there with Stumpy Michael.

Henrietta installed herself behind the bar, filled a glass with whisky and downed it one go, finishing up clutching her bosom and smiling widely. 'Rightio gents,' she said. 'Consider this party started.'

When I pointed to one of the clay jugs of ginger beer that had arrived on the *Good Intent*, she didn't make fun of me like the men had, but talked kindly to me, like a sister. Apart from Gracie she was the first white woman I had met since Cloncurry, all those months earlier. Even the Duracks, I suppose, found it hard to take their eyes off her.

I downed that first ginger beer in a few sips, the bubbles tickling my nose and the sweetness hitting my stomach. 'That one didn't touch the sides,' she said. 'Have another.'

'Don't mind if I do.'

I smiled back at her, and we shared something then. I'm not sure what it was. Perhaps we had each reminded the other of something. Maybe a little whisper of home, wherever that was for her. Everyone I've met, even the toughest stockmen, have a tender little place inside, call it what you will: sentiment, longing, whatever. Suffice it to say that I had a tear in my eye when I turned away.

Maori Jack Reid bawled an order and she turned away. I took my mug and walked over to a table where Duncan and Steve Brogan were sitting.

'What's yer bother?' Duncan asked. 'You look like yer fucking dog just died.'

'Nothing,' I said. 'Just nothing.'

The drinking session that followed might more properly be called an orgy.

Henrietta opened a barrel of ale for the drinkers to guzzle between whiskies. Billy McLeod had a grill going out the back, and started bringing in plates of beef and also portions of fish from the river that we fell upon ravenously.

'Giant Palmer Perch,' he explained, 'but the black fellows who sell them to us call them barramundi. Best eating fish you'll ever encounter.'

I had partaken of them before, of course, on my previous trip, but after months of solid beef and little else it was much appreciated. Like the others I threw the bones outside the door where a pack of mongrel dogs, pets belonging to the shanty town's inhabitants, cleaned them up, snarling and fighting. Heavy rain started to fall, increasing the numbers inside the store. The smell of whisky and close-packed wet, unwashed men, hot and sweating despite the rain, will remain in my memory all my life.

The Come Hither whisky soon goaded the baser instincts of the men in that store. Captain Reid started a two-up school on the verandah, and Henrietta offered kisses for sixpence, which the men lined up for. One or two tried to grab her bosom or bottom but she was swift with her kicks and slaps, and Henry Best stood beside her with his arms crossed, that huge man a full head taller even than Duncan or Big Johnnie. A word or two and the over-amorous soon backed off.

The first fight of that day occurred just before the sun went down, while Henrietta hurried to light lanterns and keep the shanty bright. Two larrikins started arguing over the two-up game. One combatant was the

Orphan, who had earlier that day pulled a gun on me for talking to his lubra, Virtue. His opponent was called Big-eyed Billy.

The Orphan had been playing two-up for some time, and running out of cash, he put poor Virtue up as a prize. Yet, when Big-eyed Billy won, the Orphan found that he couldn't part with her, and refused to hand her over.

The fight that followed started inside, went through one wall, round one side, and down to the riverbank, with all the other drinkers standing around spilling whisky down their shirt fronts and shouting encouragement. Blood was drawn from noses and lips, though neither of the men, in my opinion, showed any real skill with his fists.

The lack of technique didn't matter much, for the fight reached its climax with The Orphan drawing his revolver and firing at Big-eyed Billy. His extreme drunkenness, however resulted in him not only missing the target, but accidentally placing his free hand in front of the muzzle at the moment of discharge, thereby blowing off his thumb and forefinger.

Some enthusiastic physicians on the scene completed the amputation with a knife, poured a dram or two of 'Come Hither' on the wound, bandaged up the hand, and the game of two-up resumed, apparently with no hard feelings on either side.

Later on in that same game, another of these exiles from society, Pigweed Harry, also put his woman up for a ten-pound stake and lost her. Since the last man who reneged on a similar wager had ended up with a bloody face and self-inflicted gunshot wound, he accepted the loss with better grace.

I also got to meet the detective who had come chasing Jack Sherringham. He was not a party to the unloading, but had ventured out on horseback looking for our droving party. He was forced, on his return, to stump up the cash for his own bottle of Come Hither. After a few quiet belts of this infamous stuff he too joined in the revelry. Later, after drinking most of a bottle, he fell in the river, and was taken by an enormous alligator in front of us all. Weapons were drawn, and we poured lead at the beast in furious fashion, spouts of water everywhere.

All this effort was to no avail. The monster slunk away under the

201

surface, presumably with the far-travelling lawman still in its jaws.

That, sadly, was not the only fatality of the night. A man called Dick Morris, blasted off his head on Come Hither, accepted a bet to cross the river on horseback. To a chorus of yells he rode his horse off into the river, drowning both his mount, and himself.

That cargo of Come Hither was a scourge that took three lives that I know of, for riders were coming in from Rosie Creek and taking back bottles of the stuff. No team boss liked grog in the camps but it was impossible to stop, and threats aimed at Maori Jack Reid fell on deaf ears. He was, as I've said, a scoundrel of the highest order.

Only one event, before I left that shanty on the McArthur, gave me any satisfaction. Early the next morning, after a night of sampling his own stocks of Come Hither, Reid was loudly boasting how he would never pay his first mate, Henry Best, any wages, but would simply give the man a bullet in the side of the head when he was finished with him.

Best, however, heard the whole thing and commenced to beat his captain to a bloody pulp. By all accounts a hurricane had nothing on what the first mate did to Reid and the grog shanty.

Shortly after we left town, word filtered through that that Reid and Henrietta were visited by a Government customs vessel and arrested on charges of failing to pay excise, later facing court in Palmerston. Henrietta, apparently, was allowed to keep an accordion she was fond of. Maori Jack later told me, with a laugh, that his girl had around £1000 in cash and cheques hidden inside, and they were able to buy their boat back, not long after their release.

Riding in to the Rosie Creek camp I saw a fresh grave and cairn. Tom Kilfoyle told me how John Mooney had ridden back from the landing and informed Jack Sherringham that the Queensland detective knew where he was and intended to ride out to arrest him the next day. This was, of course, before the policeman had himself been taken by a 'gator.

Sherringham was frightened out of his wits at the news. To make matters worse, Mooney had brought with him as many bottles of whisky as he could carry. Jack had eagerly reached for the solace offered by that fluid.

Later, while sleeping right next to Mooney, Sherringham aimed a Colt revolver at his own head and thereby blew his brains out.

I sank to my knees beside the grave, took off my hat and said a silent prayer. But there was little time to grieve. Men had died on this track before, and it would happen again. I was nearly nineteen years of age and I was growing up fast.

CHAPTER TWENTY-TWO

*The storms were now coming on and we had reached The Limmen
River between the McArthur and Roper which in the rainy season
would bog a turkey: It was ti-tree flats and swamps.*

WE CELEBRATED CHRISTMAS, if you could call it a celebration, on
Rosie Creek. A solemn church service was run by Jim Minogue. I've
never seen so many stockmen at a service, holding their hats to their
chests. Some even shed a few tears.

My thoughts roamed back to home, and our Yuletide feasts in
happier times, stockings hung on the mantle, and special toys that
delighted and amused us. Sometimes Ma would cry for Harriet, the little
girl she had lost along the way. Mostly, however, these were happy
thoughts, making me determined that I would find Gracie, make peace
with her father, and ride home to present my future wife to Ma.

When the service was almost over, our heads bowed in solemn
prayer, something heavenly and amazing happened. A boiling roll of grey
cloud came in from the sea, horizon to horizon, accompanied by a flurry
of wind and some rain drops. It was followed a few seconds later by
another, this one as dark as hell, seething with restrained power.

The hairs on our necks stood on end, and some men fell to their
knees.

'Surely,' Jim Minogue decreed, 'we have just seen the morning glory
of God.'

No one in that bush congregation dared to disagree.

We moved north-westwards through that sodden, steaming land. It
rained all through the afternoons and into the nights. After a day in the

saddle we were forced to sleep close up under a big tree. An oilskin coat spread over the blankets helped a little. Night watch duties were difficult. Clouds blotted out the stars and moon, making the land pitch black. It was necessary to rely on hearing and smell to locate the cattle and try to contain them in the dark. Keeping them away from water was a priority, for every tiny creek held 'gators that would tackle even the biggest bulls. Their presence kept the herds anxious. Blacks continued to drive off horses in the night, spearing others.

'This place is a horse's hair short a' hell,' Duncan said to me one night. 'Ah jest want tae go hame.' And to hear this most stoic of men losing heart did nothing for my own building despair. My mare Constance, my best friend, got a bad case of a condition known as the puffs. This is a devilish disease, in which the horse loses her ability to sweat. After the slightest exercise, even just walking, riderless, behind the mob, she would stand pitifully, chest expanding with each hard breath, nostrils flaring.

It broke my already aching heart to see her like that.

Because she couldn't shed her body heat by sweating, she would head for any surface water we neared, and immerse herself in it. Of course, due to the 'gators this was a great worry for me in those days. I still hoped for her full recovery, and had many panicked moments dragging her out of the haunts of these monsters by a rope.

I sought advice from that wonderful self-taught vet, John Urquhart, still the sole custodian of my secret affair with Gracie. Yet John, unfortunately, was hard hit with malaria and I have never seen a man so down.

'There's no cure for the puffs,' he said. 'Kindest thing you can do is put a bullet in her scone and stop the pain.'

'Not yet,' I said. 'I won't give up on her.'

Through the worry, fever, exhaustion and rain, despite my ache for Gracie and the thought that sooner or later she would bear my child, sometimes I felt a thrill that I could take the worst my country could throw at me and still ride high on the saddle. I was proud of my toughness; that I was surviving this hard land, that I loved.

North of the Rosie we happened on a wild black boy of about sixteen years. We knew where he was hiding out because the horses shied away. He was only one step from eternity: bony as a long-dead beast. He tried to stand and run as we rode up, and when Duncan swung a stirrup iron, preparatory to striking the lad on the head, Hangfire Mick, whose mob was running beside ours called out, 'No! Leave him. He's sick.'

Sure enough, a moment later, the boy fell. I dismounted and stood over the pathetic form. He stared back up at me with little fear. I imagined that he expected death from us, and was too fatigued to care.

'Don't hurt the p-p-poor b-bastard,' urged Hangfire Mick.

We sat him up, and poured water into his mouth. As soon as his lips parted, we could see that his two front teeth had been snapped off at the gum, very roughly – probably with a stick or a rock.

He was naked, and closer examination showed that his private parts were caked in a mess of bloody mud.

'A wound?' Duncan ventured.

The lad passed out, and we carried him back to camp. Between us we washed the mud away. The wound was on his penis. That organ had been split like a sausage to the core, obviously with a sharp stone knife.

There was a round of hilarity at this, but this was not the first time we had encountered the mutilation. Some members of the Pitta-pitta tribe who had helped us on the Parapitcheri waterhole in Queensland had similar disfigurements, and walked around naked, quite unconscious of their difference. The Duracks, of course, had quickly given them clothes to wear, thus covering their unusual members. The cutting of the penis to the central pipe was, I learned later, an extension of normal circumcision, called subincision.

Michael himself dressed this particular wound with iodine and bandaged it. We carried the boy in a wagonette for a couple of days while he burned up with fever. When he could finally sit up unassisted, he made no effort to run away, just stared out at the country passing him by. Of course, the cook wanted his space on the wagonette back, so was keen to evict the boy.

A couple of Yanyuwa bucks had signed on at the McArthur, and while the mutilated youth was a member of the next tribe north, the Mara, the dialects were similar and they could understand each other. Big Johnnie used the Yanyuwas as interpreters in order to question the boy. We waited in silence as the conversation went backwards and forwards. We were all, of course, interested in the cause of that terrible wound, as well as the removal of his front teeth.

The boy had, the interpreter explained, been readied for initiation with the other youths of the tribe, at which time a cord of human hair would be tied around their waists, and the elders would sing the necessary songs from night until dawn. Each man, they explained, had a particular country with which their family was associated. That country was also aligned with some animal or other, be it the water goanna or wedge-tailed eagle. When the time came for the final rites, the initiates then submit, not just to circumcision, but this greater mutilation they translated as whistlecocking.

You could have heard a pin drop as our interpreter described how a particular old man would use a sharp stone flake to cut the penis lengthways to the middle canal. He also explained that the word whistlecocking refers to how the penis can make a whistling sound when the afflicted man makes water.

'So why was this boy cast out?' Big Johnnie asked.

The interpreter talked to the boy again for a minute or two, then turned back. 'He doan know, boss.' He shrugged. 'Prob'ly just that he won't say. But he got sung big time by that old Yanyuwa clever man.'

'Tell him he can go home now,' Johnnie said.

Another bout of talking, then the interpreter again. 'He can't go home. He got no home.'

I shrugged, 'With so many men sick with malaria, we can use another boy. I'll teach the poor bugger to sit on a horse.' It was about time I had a black boy of my own.

'What are you going to call him?' Big Johnnie asked.

'Just Whistler will do,' I said, suggesting the first thing that came into my head.

And so, I began Whistler's training as soon as he had learned enough

English words to make it possible. He was a strange student, always working out whether an instruction suited him before obeying. Yet, he put his feet in the stirrups when I asked, had a good natural seat, heels down and weight balanced low. He learned quickly to guide the horse with his reins and feet, stop, and post on the trot. Within a week or two he could canter without fuss, and was out riding with the herd. At little expense, save a few rations to keep him nourished, Whistler made my life a little easier.

Perhaps because of his youth, Whistler was not quite as expert a tracker as most of the other blacks with our party, but he had very, very acute hearing, and we always knew if there were wild blacks in the vicinity because he would instantly become agitated. This explained why he did not fear us – he feared his own people more.

The heat did not worry him, nor did long hours and hard work. Many a night I called Whistler, and he would come padding out of the darkness, ready to saddle up, carry water, or any other task.

We rode on, pushing the cattle deeper on through that fevered wet season. We took what we wanted and we brushed aside the people that stood in our way.

Upon reaching the Limmen Bight River, we were told to stop and hold the cattle, while the Duracks caught up with their kinsman John Costello, whose Valley of Springs Station now encompassed most of this magnificent river valley. Costello's wife Mary and their six children were shortly to join him at the station, and some help knocking up a homestead must have been appreciated.

No one could fault the Limmen Valley for natural grandeur. Surely no Roman ruin could have left such perfect walls of loose fitted stone, white and yellow in the daylight and tinged with red at dusk and at dawn.

The country was fragrant, with deep orange bottle-brush blooms, ferny-leaf grevilleas, and so many different types of delicate wattle shrubs that I stopped trying to count them.

There was also a pool between two colliding giants of rock that was surely no less beautiful than the garden of Eden. Costello named it for the flocks of butterflies that lived in the dark crevices.

So while those bloodless Irishmen, the Duracks, frolicked in the Butterfly Spring and drank tea at the homestead, we waited with the cattle, downstream in the rain and mud, angry and hungry.

Our camp, one day, was looted by local tribesman. The raiders took everything: flour, meat and salt. From then on we had only beef to eat, baking liver on the ashes as a substitute for bread. Patsy Moore and Duncan saddled up and tracked the raiding party, but found only empty bags of salt and flour with spear holes in them.

A week later, riding out on the range alone, looking for a strayed horse, I heard distant wailing and crept up on a party of blacks in a clearing beside one of those magnificent Limmen River cliffs. The women were crying and beating their breasts, the men moaning with terrible grief.

Curious, I stopped dead still and watched. One of the group was obviously the tribe's witch doctor, for relics hung from his body on strings of human hair. His eyes were all but white with age yet his figure as thin and lithe as that of a much younger man.

A man's bones were lying on a platform of green sticks, with a smoky fire burning underneath. As I watched, the mourners, with great ceremony, took the bones down and consecrated them in the smoke.

I saw them wrap the man's bones in a sheet of paperbark, at which point the witchdoctor climbed high up on the cliff like a spider, secreting the package deep in a crack.

When he returned to the ground the ceremony was over. Leaving the remnants of the fire burning, the small group walked away, silent now but slumped of shoulder and with defeated eyes.

I never did find that horse.

Ahead of us by about a day, was a party of drovers led by Jimmy and Alf Randall, driving 1800 head of mixed cattle from Waverley Station, Queensland. The Randalls were heading for Blue Mud Bay, Arnhem Land, part of Florida Station, with a mob of M8M brand breeders.

Being so close we caught up regularly, swapping yarns around campfires. I struck up a friendship with the Randalls, particularly Jimmy.

'We need another good man,' Jimmy said. 'How about you leave Hayes and Kilfoyle to come with us?'

I was torn – keen for a change – but I also had a strong loyalty to my mates in Kilfoyle's crew, particularly Duncan and Tom Kilfoyle himself. Going with them would also delay other matters that were much more pressing.

'No,' I said, 'but after I finish the trip with Kilfoyle, on my way back I'll pick up your tracks at the Roper and follow you out to Florida.'

'Alright,' said Randall, 'we'll expect you.'

After I find Gracie, I said to myself. Only after I find Gracie.

Malaria had, by then, badly affected at least half of our men. Others were near blind from sandy blight, a contagious sickness of the eyes that spread easily from man to man. It was late January, and the wet season was at its height. We pushed on, but the rain came back with a vengeance. Staying put in camps swarming with mosquitoes and sand flies, waiting for rivers and creeks to recede, became a regular occurrence.

When we crossed the Hodgson I saw a giant 'gator try to take one of our cows with my own eyes. I was on my mount in waist deep water, getting a couple of the stragglers across, starting to relax in the saddle as my mates on the other side settled the herds ready to move out. I heard a terrible trumpeting sound ahead of me. One of our cows, almost reaching the other side, had paused to drink, at which time the 'gator had grabbed her by the head.

'Hey, no,' I shouted, and spurred my already tired horse, forcing him across the channel in a series of lunges that foamed the water to white. As I rode I saw how that beast from the depths dragged the poor old girl backwards towards deep water, bellowing and fighting. Yet she was still on her feet, blood staining the river all around, and spraying over her neck and flanks. Half the 'gator's body left the water as it writhed and twisted in an effort to throw that gallant animal over.

As I reached the scene I plucked the Snider from its leather scabbard, cocked it and fired at the 'gator, aiming back towards the tail where I would not hit the cow by accident. I must have struck it somewhere, for it let go of the cow and twisted in the air, rapidly slithering away.

The cow, covered in blood, bolted up the bank at speed, desperate for the safety land provided.

That plucky cow survived those wounds, hideously disfigured, and became affectionately known as the Alligator Cow. The only problem, from then on, was getting her to drink from any water more substantial than a puddle.

CHAPTER TWENTY-THREE

*The mobs ahead were also having trouble (with Aborigines) and one
and all we pumped lead into them.*

A FEW DAYS LATER we reached the final stop on the Gulf Track. The
Roper River was in flood at Leichhardt's Crossing, but a store was located
at a safe height, along with a grog shanty and a rag-tag of dwellings no
better than those at Borroloola.

The store, owned by William Hay, was known as the Hay and Co
store. It had recently been stocked by Maori Jack Reid's *Good Intent* so
had a good supply of provisions.

Matt Kirwan, the black sheep of a highly regarded Victorian family,
was running the grog shanty here. He had invented an innovative method
of selling grog. He kept open bottles of liquor on the bar and customers
could fill their glass as often as they wanted. When they were ready to
leave, they simply paid whatever they thought was a fair thing.

Kirwan was a bare-knuckle fist fighter of some repute, tough enough
to keep these frontier wild men in order. And the grog shanty's clientele
were almost as unruly as those back on the McArthur – misfits and
criminals moving into a lawless land, leaving behind the impediments of
law and society. Some had run off from droving crews or ships. Others
were adventurers; gold prospectors and hunters. The Malay crew from a
schooner down the river and some hard looking Chinese made up the
numbers.

Like their contemporaries at Borroloola the men of Roper Bar
carried revolvers or rifles and looked ready to use them, with a mug of
rum or whisky never far away. Day and night a serious poker game went
on at a table made from two wagon wheels, and I believe that an

earthquake might have struck without disturbing the game. They certainly didn't look up as we walked in.

'Help yourself,' Kirwan instructed from his hammock. 'No man ever goes thirsty at Matthew Kirwan's shanty.'

Black velvet, it seemed, was also in ready supply at the store: big strong Roper lubras who had come in for easy food or been snatched by force, I did not ask which. There was something in their eyes, however, that I had seen on the McArthur and I would see many times again. I think the women knew what was happening better than their menfolk. They knew how unstoppable we were. They knew already the white man's way. That if he sees something he wants, he takes it, and that nothing can stand in his way.

The most exciting news at that store, was a big supply of quality leather boots, both elastic sided and lace-ups. By then the boots we had left Queensland in were worn out. Big Johnnie announced that the Duracks would shout one pair for every man, and that was a cause for celebration.

The negative was that almost all of the men, making the trip to the store to choose their new footwear, also took the opportunity to stock up on liquor to take back to camp. Normally alcohol was forbidden in camp, but with travel necessarily halted by the Wet, and a previous relaxation of the rules at Borroloola, it was tacitly allowed.

There was a package of mail for various men on the drive, but nothing for me. In the next days the sight of a man sitting by a fire, wistfully rereading folded sheets from home, became common. Others, who could not read bade the more literate, me included, to decipher these missives from gentler places. Many a head turned away to hide a tear, especially after a rum or two. We took the cattle onwards seven miles to a place called McMinn's Bluff, but the rain was pouring and the creeks running a banker. The provisions purchased at the store, packed in the wagons, could not get to us over a creek that had become a river. Makeshift watercraft were fashioned from poles and tent canvas in order to get essential provisions across.

With feed everywhere, and the cattle too fat to bother moving far, the herds were easily contained with just a few men in the saddle at any time. Most of the men thus camped together, the different parties more or less combined.

These were some of the most miserable days I have ever known. Gracie had sent no letter. Half the men were drunk on rum brought in from the store, most had malaria and the rain and sticky heat never let up.

'We have to get out of here,' Big Johnnie said grimly one night. 'It's killing us all.' He turned to Dick. 'Watch that creek like a hawk. The second it falls low enough to cross you ride in here and tell me.'

But the days went on and rain continued. Night time brought hordes of midges, lavender beetles, brown snakes and dozens of other pests. I would lie awake in my swag, in a torture of sweat, crawling bugs and whining mosquitoes. For those stricken with fever it was ten times worse.

Finally Dick rode up one evening. 'Hey boss,' he called, 'I seen a crossing place, ten mile from here. Inna night time she drop enough to get us 'cross.'

Big Johnnie Durack smiled for the first time in weeks, and walked from camp to camp with orders to prepare for a move. Fatigued as we were, the news was like a lightning strike, energising us all.

'We leave at dawn,' Big Johnnie declared, 'and from the moment we get out of this place if I find a man with one drop of grog in his possession he gets a cheque and a kick in the arse.'

The result of this proclamation was an unexpected one, at least to Johnnie himself. Every man in possession of grog took it upon himself to finish his stocks that night, rather than pour it out and waste it. They drank into the small hours, and the camp was full of fever ridden, drunken men. Even the fights that broke out were laughable affairs, carried on by men too far gone to swing a decent punch.

At least, however, the mood of hopelessness had lifted. We were leaving this fever coast and heading inland. Or so we thought.

I woke the next morning, long before dawn, to find Whistler touching my shoulder with an insistent finger. It was his way of waking me silently. I opened my eyes and looked up into his face.

'What's happened?'

'Mob of blackfellas been here inna night time. Steal alla grub. One real big man lead them. Alla same like Duncan.'

'How do you know he's as big as that?'

'Seen him tracks, boss. Big-feller feet on him. Big toe anna little toes never touch groun'.'

I slipped on my new boots and followed. Whistler was right. The backs of the wagons were all but empty. It was infuriating, especially since much of what they took was useless or unknown to them, such as the flour bags they had opened, scattering the contents across the grass.

'The dishonest swine. Go get Big Johnnie.'

Within a few minutes the drive bosses were all there, swearing and cursing, finding cases of tea upended. Canned food bashed on rocks then left to spoil.

Big Johnnie took off his hat and threw it to the ground so hard it made a sound like a pistol shot. 'Finally, I thought we were leaving this cursed place behind. I thought those mongrel wild blacks had been taught a lesson.'

With Dick guiding us, we formed a hunting party, and left as soon as there was enough light to make out a trail. Sober volunteers had been thin on the ground, one of the reasons the marauders had managed to reach the heart of our camp so easily.

Dick found fresh tracks to the river, invisible to the rest of us, but at that point the 'Big Man' and his band had walked only along the shallows where the flooded river was over the banks. Even so, we continued to follow.

Occasional flattened stalks of grass were soon the only signs that anyone had travelled that route. I did not see them, of course, but Dick was right onto it, a picture of concentration. Black hunting black, each as artful as the other, and I'm sure the Bunthamara stockman enjoyed the contest.

It was Whistler's keen eyes that picked out the place where the marauders had swum the river and climbed up the steep bank on the other side. It was a brave swim in 'gator country, and ill-advised on horseback. We had no choice but to return empty-handed, and the 'Big Man' got away scot-free with most of our supplies.

While we waited for the wagons to return with fresh provisions the camp deteriorated further.

John Urquhart, that wonderful bushman who had saved so many of our cattle from pleuro was delirious with fever and had taken to the bottle. He did nothing but lie inside a canvas tent, muttering of hell on earth and God and prophets. Black Pat, who along with Hangfire Mick was in charge while Big Johnnie was away, met me as we rode in.

'Charlie, we're putting John on suicide watch.'

'You think he's gonna top himself?'

'He's muttering about ending it all. We can't take any chances, he's the closest thing we have to a veterinarian and he's a solid man besides. We have to get him through this.'

'I'll do what I can,' I said.

Still bitterly disappointed by our failure to track down the natives, I sat for the rest of the evening with John, cajoled him into games of cards that he played listlessly. He was so drunk on fever and rum that he fell into a kind of stupor, where he made occasional wild observations before lapsing again.

'The blasted heathens, they'll kill us all,' then, staring tearily at me. 'I just want to go home. I want my ma, Gawd how I want her.'

The next day, in record time, Big Johnnie returned with the wagons. He shook his head sadly when he heard how John Urquhart had deteriorated. 'He's too far gone to stay. We need to get him out of here.'

A government steamer called the *Palmerston* was apparently on its way upriver, and Big Johnnie's plan was to get the fever-ridden man aboard and thus transported to Darwin hospital. They placed him in a wagon and set off on in the night to get him there.

The next morning, however, word reached us that John Urquhart had died during the night. There were conflicting reports of what happened. The rider, Steve Brogan, swore that he had heard a gunshot in the early hours of the morning, but others hadn't heard a thing.

Myself and some of John's other mates set off on horseback for the crossing, there to find that fine bushman and veterinarian wrapped head to toe in his swag. Preparations for a hurried funeral were underway. I asked for details of his death but the Duracks closed ranks. The official line was that John had died of fever, and I had no real reason to disbelieve it, though rumours persisted that he had taken his own life.

We buried him near the crossing above the river. We marked the grave with a simple cross of cypress shaped with a broad-axe. I visited the marble headstone his family erected there, years later, a more fitting monument to a man of great wisdom and ability.

CHAPTER TWENTY-FOUR

On we went, passing the Red Lily, Bitter Springs and Abraham's Billabong (where Mataranka now stands).

Out of the thirty or so white men who had been employed at the beginning of the Durack cattle drive, at least five were dead by the time we left the Roper.

More had resigned or deserted along the road. New men had signed up – drovers were returning along the track after delivering cattle deep into the Territory, but much of the work load was being taken up by 'boys,' picked up along the way with the inducement of food and tobacco, purchased from other drovers, or simply taken as 'spoils of war.' Some were genuine and much-loved volunteers. Patsy Durack's Pumpkin was a good example, though Patsy only visited the drive a few times. Jerry Durack's Dick was another.

Some were not boys at all, but girls dressed as boys, sharing a drover's swag at night, and skilled riders and cattle workers by day. Either way, we were now operating with the support of Aboriginal labour. They worked long hours, took to the saddle like naturals – and were sometimes, not always – regarded as expendable.

It was a relief to head upstream on the Roper and out of that pestilential Gulf country, with its mud, fever, heat and humidity. As we trailed west one day, Whistler and I rode past a crow on a high branch, cawing loudly.

'Old crow sing that the rainy season have to end now,' Whistler said. 'He wake up the col' time to come along.'

I shook my head. 'How does a crow know that?'

'Crow feel that col' season wind before you an' me.'

Sure enough, within a few days the clouds were gone, and while it was still hot at midday, the heat was drier.

The air cooled at night, giving rise to light morning fogs, drifting off the river. Fog terrified poor Whistler, who cowered in his blanket, muttering that it was the work of some python-being his people believed in.

As we moved upstream, a stockman called Thomas Barnes stumbled on the skeleton of a stockman I'd known from my time with Nat Buchanan. His name was Louis Nash, and he had perished with a mate called Bayes. On Nash's body was a note from Bayes saying that he was too far gone to walk any further, and that Nash was pressing on to look for water. Nash's remains were found just five miles from the sweet fresh water of the Upper Roper River.

We also began to hear more about the 'Big Man' who had pilfered our wagons and escaped at McMinn's Bluff. He was, apparently, a Mungarrayi man called Charley, who had been at the top of the Territory's 'most wanted' list for some two years. His first crime had been to stave in the head of a white stockman called Duncan Campbell on the Strangways River.

'He's so hugely muscled, tall and powerful,' a rider told us, 'that the native police are shit-scared of him, and the local blacks too. Keeps no boundaries, but will put a spear through your back from Leichhardt's Bar to the Elsey.'

Charley and his warriors harried us relentlessly, stealing horses, and spearing cattle. Armed riders, despatched to retaliate, found themselves on a merry chase through stone country, waterless and harsh, until the spoor disappeared. The occasional lucky shot was treated as a triumph.

Something had to be done.

The closest of the cattle drives behind us belonged to Charlie and Willie MacDonald, who had lost their first herd in the drought up the Georgina, and were now, short-handed and lacking cash, bringing a smaller, second herd across. The poor bastards were famously dogged, and were carrying on with barely enough men and plant to do the job.

Behind the MacDonalds was a mob led by a man called Tom Spillisay, the so-called Bendigo Drover. I always listened for news of his progress as he hailed from the same area of Victoria as me. My old boss Nat Buchanan was on his way with another mob, headed for Wave Hill Station a couple of hundred miles to the west of us.

Along the Roper we had contact with these other droving teams, and they were all suffering from the depredations of Charley and his band. Vague plans were afoot for all the mobs to supply men to end the raids for good, and a messenger was sent ahead to the Elsey, requesting police support.

He came back with heartening news. 'Corporal Montagu and Constable Powell are right now organising a party of riflemen. Help is on its way. In the meantime, they said to keep our weapons handy.'

We were angry and tired. We were facing a dire enemy and knew it.

Red Lily Lagoon on the upper Roper must surely be as close to the Garden of Eden as can be seen on this earth. After a heavier than usual rainy season the banks were green and lush, the water like the face of a mirror. Hyacinth flowers bloomed in colours from flaming red to sky-blue, and reeds pointed to the sky in green soldierly ranks.

When we first rode in, we saw wild blacks on the lagoon in canoes made of bark, paddling dexterously, showing little fear until our bullets made geysers of spray around their flimsy craft, explosions as bullets struck the calm surface. This caused them to paddle ferociously for the other side, at which point they disembarked and ran, our laughter ringing across the water after them.

Big Johnnie declared a week's camp to regain health and allow one of the mobs that had been left behind to catch up. Our cattle were then free to spread out along the grasslands that surrounded the lagoon, lightly timbered country with numerous small holes and wallows still full from the now departed wet season. The air was drier, and the men suffering fever saw some improvement.

Best of all, to my mind, in the better conditions Constance began to thrive again. Her coat came good, and I started riding her. Of course, no matter what John Urquhart had said, she was not the first horse to recover from the puffs, but I took it as a sign of better things to come.

One afternoon, walking down to the lagoon to bathe, I noticed something unusual amongst the lilies there. The object was long – about twelve feet in length – and definitely boat shaped. I realised that I was looking at a canoe, left behind by the blacks who had run when we first arrived.

Whistler was quick to confirm this first impression. 'Bot, bot,' he said, flapping his arms excitedly. I nodded in reply then sank to my knees to examine our find.

The canoe, it seemed, was fashioned from a single sheet cut from a paperbark tree. Each end had been folded to a point and secured with a mixture of natural gums and plaited cord.

Whistler launched into an unnecessary explanation of what I could work out quite plainly for myself. The craft, I decided, was both primitive and ingenious at the same time.

'You-fella see 'im float?' Whistler asked me, his teeth resting on his lower lip so his missing front pair made a dark cave.

'Sure, why not?' The idea smacked of fun to me, and fun was something I'd lacked in my life for some time. Together we lifted and pushed the craft down into the water.

This was no easy task, for it was surprisingly weighty.

'We've got no paddles,' I said, but Whistler rattled his head, as if to reassure me that it didn't matter. We kneeled inside, with myself at the bow and he at the stern, and he proceeded to lean over and use his big hands to paddle us out through a narrow passage in the reeds.

The canoe was tippy, and when I tried to emulate him we nearly capsized, our weight shifting rapidly from one side to the other and back again. Once we had recovered, I turned and looked at Whistler. I was expecting him to be worried by the near disaster, but instead he was grinning maniacally. 'Haha, good fun alonga water, hey?'

By the time we were past the reeds, however, I had the hang of it. Hands were still a poor substitute for oars or paddles but they were enough. Out of the sheltered water by then, I found that there was a light chop that thumped against the bows as we paddled into the breeze.

In the open, we came in full view of our camp. Tom Kilfoyle was the first to see us. Next thing, he and Duncan were walking down to the bank, faces shaded by their broad hats.

I waved back for a moment, but then I saw something in my boss's face, even from a distance, that made me worry that perhaps he was not impressed. One thing that Tom Kilfoyle did not tolerate, and that was tomfoolery. It now occurred to me that taking this flimsy thing out on the lagoon might perhaps, in Tom's eyes, fall into that category.

I turned to look at Whistler, and pointed to the shore. 'We go back now.'

Whistler grinned back at me, and continued to forge up into the wind, a cross-wise path that would eventually see us reach the far bank.

I turned again, this time more urgently. 'Listen you bandy legged savage, I said we go back now.'

Again he ignored me. Damning him to hell under my breath I dug my right hand hard into the water in an attempt to effect a turn. Paddling at the front, though, had far less power than at the rear.

Whistler's face was twisted into that dopey smile of his. He was enjoying himself. I lost my temper, turning and trying to get to him with my hand. Of course he jumped backwards and the bark canoe tipped over, sending us both into the drink.

The water was warm, but deep, and I was no swimmer. Whistler himself was quite adept, making for the bank with an underwater crawling motion. I tried to emulate it, managing to keep my head above water, but soon panicked. My head went under, and I took a mouthful of water.

Up came my head. I took a breath of sweet air, and was relieved to see that whatever action I was using had taken me closer to the bank, just shy of the lilies. I felt sure that I could use them to pull myself to safety.

That idea proved academic, for someone had fetched a rope. Tom Kilfoyle threw it as if he were broncoing a bull. I grasped the rope and he pulled me ashore. I fell to my knees on the edge. He dropped the rope.

'Playing silly buggers almost got you drowned. I don't care for good men wasting time with infantile games.'

Tom Kilfoyle's disapproval hurt far worse than the burn of vomit in my throat. I turned to look down the bank to where Whistler had emerged from the water. He was standing there watching me warily.

My annoyance turned to violence, and while the other men on the bank shouted encouragement I went for the boy. He tried to run. Too late. I grabbed him by the hair, and with my right I pummelled him in the face three times very hard. His nose started bleeding straight away.

I dropped him like a gun, and turned away, shamed and still angry.

Just as we were preparing to hit the track again after a restful week at the lagoon, two policemen from the east rode in, along with nine armed, mounted Native Police.

They were on the trail of Big Charley, and brought alarming news – that a telegraph worker from the Elsey had been speared by the renegades, and two others wounded. Not only that, but Tom Spillisay, the 'Bendigo Drover' and one of his men had been shot, not, apparently by Charley and his warriors, but by a black boy working in the camp known as 'Hammer and Gads.' The culprit was arrested, but the killings had increased the level of outrage against the blacks in general.

The police contingent was led by a corporal called George Montagu. He wore the uniform of the South Australian police, for the Territory was then administered from Adelaide, as part of South Australia.

At the time, although I didn't know it, George Montagu was a powerful man. He led a small army of mounted constables, along with armed blacks. He could also call upon as many whites as wanted to ride with him – stockmen, prospectors, and wanderers, anyone wanting a taste of war or with a grudge against the blacks. In all these doings he was answerable only to the superintendent in Darwin.

He had an odd combination of blonde hair, and a dark moustache. The rest of his face was stubbled with the latter colour.

'Hi there young feller,' he said. 'My name's George Montagu.'

'Charlie Gaunt.'

We shook hands on horseback.

'Where you from?' he asked.

'Victoria originally, but I joined the drive on Cooper's Creek.'

'I s'pose you've been pestered by blacks the whole way?'

'Across the Gulf anyway.'

'There's not room for them and us. You can't trust the beggars.'

I looked at his face; the tiny eyes. 'The government of South Australia, do they know what we're doing here?'

'What do you mean?'

I cleared my throat uncomfortably. I did not want to admit to the blood already on my hands. It had been on my mind, in those dark midnight hours, what the civilized world and the law itself might think of what we were doing.

'The killing,' I said finally. 'Does the government know what we do to … them?'

'Why of course they do. I take my orders from Darwin, Inspector Paul Foelsche. He's a great man, harsh but fair. I'll tell you the order he issued, handed down straight from the Premier himself, Sir James Boucaut. "I cannot give you orders to shoot all natives you come across, but circumstances may occur for which I cannot provide definite instructions." Now what do you think that means, Charlie?'

'I guess it means that you can do whatever you want,' I said.

Montagu and his men did not catch Big Charley on that occasion, but just a few days later I met that renegade black man for myself, at heavy cost. I was out riding on my own, looking for missing stock, when I climbed a hillock into an eerie landscape of weathered sandstone hills.

One particular stone pillar rose from the surrounding plain like a stone temple into the sky, mired in red from the iron in the rock and the dying sun. Not just the bones of this land, but a bloody organ, exposed to the sky through aeons of wind and rain.

A huge black warrior appeared from between two rocks. I recall his noble bearing; the immense muscles of his chest and arms. I knew it had to be Charley himself. I had never seen the like of him.

His spear was notched into the thrower and before I could react his arm drove down on it like a stockman cracking a whip. I saw that spear fly through the air towards me. The barbed head struck Constance deep in her neck, and I felt her shudder as it tore through her throat and she seemed to stop mid stride, making a terrible gurgling sound.

Together we hit the earth and the wind was knocked out of me, an embedded stone striking my side so hard it was like a kick from a bull. I felt skin tear from my forearm, the side of my face, and my left hand. Constance was kicking; bleeding; dying. The hardwood shaft broke off in her struggles, yet the splintered end still protruded some eighteen inches from the wound, now bubbling frothy red with each breath from her shattered windpipe. I crawled close to her, using her body for shelter as I worked my rifle from the scabbard, tears running down my face as I did so.

I cradled her with my arms as her last struggles stilled.

I'm sorry, my darling girl. I should never have brought you ...

I lifted the rifle, using Constance's body as a dead rest, scanning around the rocks for the man I ached to kill with every breath in my body. I was trying to control the sobs that were building in my chest, threatening to throw my aim and spoil my purpose. I did not even compare the life of that wild black man with that of my beautiful mare. To me she was worth far more.

I saw something and jerked off a shot, partly because my pain was so strong I had to give expression to it. Stone chips flew as the shell scraped its way along the side of a boulder and my ears rang from the concussion of that gunshot, amplified by close echoes off rock slabs.

I reloaded, but now I could hear hoof beats, coming from a distance. Duncan McCaully and other members of the party had heard the shot. I didn't want them to come. I wanted to kill him myself.

I rose to a crouch, holding the butt of the rifle hard to my shoulder. My left hand was sticky on the rifle stock, red with the blood of the beautiful horse that my father's inheritance had bought me. The thought made me choke, but my steps, as I crept forward, were carefully taken, and I kept the barrel level in case Charley reappeared.

I heard a sound to the right and I swivelled, letting loose another round just as I saw a rock the size of a man's fist strike against a boulder, shattering in smaller stones that fell and rolled heavily to the earth. I turned with my back to the stone shelf, breathing like a madman, fumbling again to reload, realising that I was truly afraid.

The horsemen were closer now, calling my name. I stood up and rounded the stone wall. There was a clearing behind it.

It was empty. Charley had gone as if into thin air.

'You stinking, murdering, fucking savage!' I shouted, but there was nothing but the echoes to answer me.

We reached the Elsey in early May, and I grabbed the first chance I could to visit the telegraph station, which also acted as a post office. I was desperate for mail. The operator handed me an envelope. I recognised Mother's hand right away.

'Is there another one for me?' I asked, desperate for news from Gracie. 'From Palmerston maybe?'

'No sonny, that's the only one.'

'Well can you please look again?'

The surly bastard got a pained expression on his face, but he did what I asked, rummaging through the bundles of mail. 'No, sorry mate. Nothing else.'

A flurry of telegrams were sent and received during our stay at the Elsey. Much thought was given to one-sentence missives to reassure family and friends 'back south' that all was well. Big Johnny and Hangfire Mick Durack had the unpleasant task of composing a message for John Urquhart's widow. No contact was known for Jack Sherringham.

Being better schooled than most of the others, and good with words, some of the stockmen got me to assist with their messages home. Most were concerned with brevity: the maximum information with the smallest number of characters.

DEAR MUM STOP SAFELY IN THE TERRITORY STILL STRONG STOP LOVE TO ADAM AND MILLIE. JOE

As I was leaving I saw Billy Higgins, his mouth still out of shape from what I had done, sweating over a telegram with Jim Minogue's

226

assistance. As soon as Billy caught my eyes he looked away. Strangely, I felt nothing, no lingering hatred or pity. It was as if he had ceased to exist.

We camped at a hole in the river called Abraham's Billabong, and could not resist the steaming hot Bitter Springs nearby, fringed by green cabbage tree palms. All the stockmen availed themselves of these soothing crystal clear waters. We washed our bodies and clothes, and the health of the outfit was much improved.

While in the vicinity of the Elsey I kept a keen eye out for travellers from the north, desperate for any news from Gracie and the baby that she must have already borne. The lack of mail from her was puzzling, and doubt was eating me alive.

Mother's news was interesting. I was pleased to hear that she was enjoying life in St Kilda, and that the money I sent was a big help. Again she begged me to come home. The envelope also contained a letter from my brother William over in England, who was deeply involved in his medical studies. His world of cold corridors and examinations sounded so grey and formal, that I did not envy him one bit.

Even so, I folded the papers and put them in my pocket with a lump in my throat.

On the day before our departure, I was excited to find a party of surveyors heading south from Palmerston with responsibility for marking out the road east to the Roper. There were four horsemen, in all, with two wagon loads of equipment. They wore, to a man, trousers and collared shirts in varied shades of white. Most had substantial facial hair, moustaches or mutton chops, and scant evidence of the same on their heads.

They looked up as I strode across, and the man who was speaking shot me a glance before making a point of finishing whatever it was he had to say, something about the surveying trade that I didn't understand too well.

It was one of the others who piped up finally. 'Yes lad, what can we do for you? If it's a loan you want I make it a policy, as do my friends, to—'

'It's news I'm after,' I blurted. 'A mate of mine was heading for

227

Palmerston, a blacksmith by the name of Walter Oswald. I'm wondering if anyone has seen him up there.'

The man who had spoken started to shake his head, but another said, 'Douglas, wasn't your brother talking about a new man in town a couple of months ago?'

'That's right, he was, a powerful bloke with a bushy beard apparently.'

'That's him. Did he have his daughter with him?'

The man shrugged. 'I don't know, sorry lad. I never met the man, so I dunno who he lives with. Not sure whether he stayed or moved on, either.'

'Well thanks anyway,' I said. 'That gives me something to go on.'

I walked back across to where Whistler was waiting for me with the horses. A gang of blacks in uniform were standing across the roadway with their plant, and I recognised some from Montagu's gang of Native Police. They were well fed, glossy of skin and uniform, and wore pistols in their belts. No one seemed to give them a second glance.

'Just as soon as this fucking drive is over I'm going to Palmerston.' I told Whistler.

Whistler scratched his head. 'Palmerston?'

I pointed to the north. 'Bloody big white-man town up there. Lotsa people.'

'Blackfellas?'

'There would be, yes, but mainly whites.'

'I goin' alonga Palmerston too?'

'Dunno yet, we'll see. Depends if Tom wants to keep you on for his station.'

'Gracie's there?'

I had told Whistler about Gracie many times. Since he didn't seem to report back to anyone else what I said, I spoke freely about her to him. 'I hope so. Jesus I hope so.'

CHAPTER TWENTY-FIVE

Another strong point in the black is he can walk into your camp and stand alongside of you and if he wishes it you'll never know that he exists until he speaks.

THE DRY RIVER winds down out of the barren hills of Delamere and into a vast and waterless plain of grey woodland. Hard country for drovers and cattle alike, yet we were halfway across the Territory, with the scent of journey's end in our nostrils.

'Three months,' Big Johnnie told us airily. 'If all goes well we'll be dropping our swags on Durack land in the Kimberley ... and still have half the cattle we started with.' Given the trouble that was about to hit, I often wished he hadn't boasted so heartily on this score.

One of the few good things about this desiccated country was the relative lack of blacks. Whistler told me when we cut their tracks, but it wasn't often and most of the sign was old. He was also the first to alert me to sickness in the cattle.

'This cow all the same poor-fella,' he said, then got down on hands and knees, imitating the tired gait of most of the cattle. Of course, as soon as I looked I saw that he was right. The herd was lagging – nothing too serious yet – but enough to ring warning bells.

'I've noticed,' Big Johnnie grunted when I reported the condition. 'It looks like redwater fever. John Urquhart, God rest his soul, warned me that this might happen.'

'What causes it?' I asked.

Big Johnnie raised his eyebrows. 'No one knows for sure, but John had a theory. Have you noticed anything different in the last few days?'

I shrugged. 'Just the same, bushland and a few waterholes in the creeks that will be dry as a bone in a month.'

Careful not to spook the cattle, Johnnie walked up to the nearest small mob, a couple of cows eyeing him suspiciously, still chewing as he came. He reached out to one beast, and using the nails of his thumb and forefinger, plucked something from her back. 'Look here lad, a tick. John Urquhart reckoned that they came from Java with some of the first cattle ever to be shipped here over twenty odd year ago. They're rife in some areas and not others – just so happens to be the same areas as the red water. Bit of a coincidence, don't ye reckon?'

I eyed the still-living insect from up close, repulsed by its fat body and tiny legs. When Johnnie squeezed it, blood spattered over his fingers. It was the first time I'd ever seen a tick.

Joined by Black Pat Durack, we walked amongst the cattle, seeing more ticks on their hides, and signs of fever. We came upon one old girl, lying on her side and kicking her legs feebly. It took the three of us and a rope from Big Johnnie's horse to get her back on her feet.

'There's no way to inoculate the cattle like we did last time?' Black Pat asked.

'Nope, it's a different kind of illness.'

'What do we do then?'

'John's opinion was that the best thing was to get out of the area fast. So we push through until we're past the ticks.'

'Even the cattle that aren't sick are flat,' Black Pat complained. 'Pushing on might make it worse.'

The look Big Johnnie gave me said that we would beat the bastards through with sticks if we had to.

We took to the herds with swinging stockwhips, cracks like gunshots ringing through the bush. I understood what we were doing. Without the whips and riders, the mobs would have stayed still and died, one by one.

It was hard, thirsty work, the cattle reluctant, but we got them moving and kept them moving. We rode in relays, for as soon as we stopped pushing, they stopped walking. We left dead and seriously ill beasts on the trail behind us.

Two days of this punishing routine followed, before we noticed that the bloated ticks were dropping off and no new ones were replacing them. It seemed that we were in the clear.

Heading down the limestone country on the East Baines River, it was strange to ride past rounded grassy hills not unlike those I had seen on the Western Slopes of New South Wales. The river itself was green and lined with either sheer limestone walls, or mile after mile of near uninterrupted pandanus, so thick that a man had to run a gauntlet of spiky fronds to reach the water and fill a pint pot.

We heard reports from further east of stock losses in other droving camps from red water fever on the Dry River stretch. Big Johnnie despatched a boy to ride back with one simple piece of advice. 'Get out of there fast!'

At the junction of the Wickham River and the Victoria we camped while the cattle regained condition, and while there we had several visitors.

The first was Willie MacDonald, from the hard-working group behind us. He was near-starved: cheeks sucked in and eyes in hollows like caves. He parked his nag, who was in similar condition, and wandered in on foot. This silent approach was not the best idea, as he came close to catching a bullet from Hangfire Mick, who saw him coming through the shadows and assumed he was a marauding black. Instead, he had come to beg some provisions, and although our stores were meagre enough, we gave poor Willie all he could carry.

A day or two later, a drover called Edward Weldon, with his plant and two black boys, rode in from the west. Funnily enough it was the two Aboriginal horsemen, known as Pintpot and Pannikin, who earned the most attention. They had, apparently, accompanied some of the Duracks on their first, exploratory visit to the Kimberley a couple of years earlier, and were counted as old friends.

Pintpot and Pannikin wore dungarees and bright cotton shirts, each with a belt and knife, preening with the attention, happy to answer questions about what was yet to come.

I noticed that Whistler was squatting on his haunches, hissing at the newcomers. 'What's wrong with you?' I asked.

He shook his head and spat, a habit he had picked up from watching white men do the same thing. 'Them flash blackfullas, boss.'

Despite Whistler's misgivings, all three of the newcomers were persuaded to turn around the way they had come and guide us the rest of the way.

Now that we had extra help, Black Pat took Tom Hayes and headed for Palmerston, where they would stock up and take ship for the Cambridge Gulf, meeting the mobs on the other side with provisions for the new stations. Brave men those two; setting off on a five-hundred-mile land journey, then nearly as much again by sea without hesitation.

Heading towards the source of the Wickham we found ourselves penned in by the stone walls of a gorge so deep that the sun shone only at midday. The air was crackling dry, and the nights so cold that we shivered in our meagre blankets and lit three fires per camp, with us drovers throwing our swags down between them.

Also at night, we could see distant campfires on the ridges, and hear the sounds of clapsticks, singing, and didgeridoo. I hated these wooden tubes through which the blacks made a sound that crawled up a man's spine like something old and terrible coming up at him from beneath the earth.

Pintpot and Pannikin led the way, with Edward Weldon riding with the Duracks. His packhorses carried a supply of whisky bottles, with which he'd fill his silver hip flask at dawn, noon, and afternoon. Not that he ever seemed particularly drunk, just breathed fumes and muttered a mixture of bible passages and swear words.

The gorge sides hemmed the cattle in, and offered little in the way of grazing, but according to Pintpot and Pannikin it offered the quickest way through the razor stones of the red hills around us. The cattle hated walking on stone all day, and many grew lame or walked with caution. They shied at echoes off the gorge walls, and at night they would have rushed except we were careful to box them up, so they had nowhere to go.

At Mistake Creek, we turned north, close now to the end of what was then almost three years on the track. At least there was good grazing, and the cattle fattened along the route.

At the junction of the Ord and Negri Rivers the local blacks mustered in great force, ranks of them on the riverbank and still more in the trees. It was the most organised resistance we had seen. Their aim, it seemed, was to force us to turn back.

We did not turn back.

The excitement in Tom Kilfoyle's eyes was growing, for his Rosewood was the nearest of the enormous portions of this country the Duracks and their cousins had selected. Tom consulted his maps several times a day, and finally, while we pushed the mob north over as broad a grassland as I had seen on our travels, he came riding up, yelling, 'By God, boys, we've done it. This is Rosewood.'

We threw our hats in the air. Even those with the other mobs, who would be pushing on, north and west, joined in the celebrations. We had conquered one of the longest cattle drives in history, and with a fair portion of the herds still living.

We rode on a tide of elation, on land that had been decided by a stroke of a pen and the payment of a few pounds to the lands office, as the sole property of Tom Kilfoyle and his family.

Tom rode alongside me for a bit. 'Aren't this the grandest country you've ever seen?'

I studied the mitchell and kangaroo grass growing thick between the dramatic hills and could not disagree. 'It's grand all right. You'll make a fine station here.'

Yet already there was a hollowness in my belly. I had given three years of my life to make this man a cattle king, and the best I could hope for was a job as a ringer. The first year would be spent building – houses, sheds, yards, fences. Quite apart from my desire to locate Grace and be with her. Felling trees, squaring timber and digging holes just seemed like drudgery after life on the track.

Tom Kilfoyle was impatient, scarcely able to sit still in the saddle.

We pushed the cattle on, while he rode backwards and forwards searching for a homestead site.

The Kimberley was as scenic as we had been told to expect: foothills sloping at forty-five degrees to steep cliffs of cinnabar-red stone. Up close they reared so high that it strained a man's neck to look at them. Wedge-tailed eagles rode the clear skies, lords of the air.

On those plains of waving yellow I imagined future homesteads and yards, telling the world of the wealth of these men, who were no better than the rest of us, no better born, or smarter. Just with a vision, a self-belief that had allowed them to cross one of the largest and most difficult countries on earth, with the makings of an empire.

Tom Hayes had brought a wagonette down from Wyndham with fresh food, and a celebratory supply of rum that had the camps well and truly oiled up. That was the first alcohol that ever passed my lips, and I disliked the taste, smell, and the way it burned my lips. I did enjoy, however, the warm sense of camaraderie that saw me singing long into the night with the others, mostly sentimental Irish tunes that I had learned on the track.

Tom Kilfoyle and the others talked incessantly of plans – yard building here, wells here, sheds here. I had my own plans – to leave as soon as possible – taking loyal Whistler along with me.

'I'd love you to stay on,' Tom said as he tore off my cheque. 'You're young yet, but one day you'll make a great head stockman.'

'I'm not cut out to be too settled,' I told him. 'I'll see where the road takes me.' How could I stay? I was burning for Gracie, and to see my own baby. Nothing would keep me away.

Mick Skeahan was holding back tears when we said goodbye. 'I'll miss you Charlie. You've been like a brother to me.'

I shook his hand. 'You'll be fine, Mick. You're a man now, as good as anyone in this crew.'

My words were prophetic. Mick Skeahan became a cattleman par excellence. I know for a fact that he later managed a swathe of Queensland stations: Pinkilla, Ardock, Mount Margaret and Buckingham Downs.

Parting with big Duncan McCaully was no easier. 'Good luck to ye laddie,' he said. 'May ye keep hail an hearty an' haste ye back.'

'It's been grand to ride with you,' I said, clasping a hand as hard and weathered as stone.

The others made a fuss of me too – Jim Minogue, and Mick and Steve Brogan. We swore to be mates for life, and vowed never to let the fires of our friendship fade. Duncan rode with me for the first mile, and when we finally parted that hard-as-nails Scotsman had tears in his eyes.

CHAPTER TWENTY-SIX

*Big Johnnie Durack, a short time after the journey ended, was speared
by the blacks up the Benn River. Jerry Durack was shot dead by one
of his black boys at Denham Station.*

I RODE A HUNDRED MILES or so north to Wyndham. My mount
was a chestnut gelding, a gift from Tom Kilfoyle. I made the distance in
three days.

Leaving Whistler in the blacks' camp on the edge of town, I rode
on, the dramatic hills of the West Bastion ranges catching the afternoon
sun to the east of town. There must have been a land sale in progress, for
Anthon's Landing and the gazetted township area further on was neatly
divided into blocks, with rough tracks in grids. Hundreds, if not
thousands of plots were signposted with lot numbers, and brand new
houses were springing up. I made my entrance to the accompaniment of
hammers and saws.

Passing by a collection of shanties belonging to China-men and
hard-up locals, I stopped at the post office to collect my mail. I hoped
and prayed for something from Gracie but was disappointed again.

'Are you sure?' I pleaded as the postmaster pulled his eye-glasses
down low on his nose to get a good look at me.

'If you ask me that again I'll call for Constable Spencer and have you
removed.'

I slapped my open hand on the counter to vent my anger and glared
at him. 'Thanks for nothing,' I seethed, and walked out.

I cashed my cheque at the bank and rode down to the Landing,
where Mount Albany pushed close to the water, creating a deep-water
frontage. It was low tide, and to the north was an endless line of salt flats.

The waters themselves stretched out into the distance, with a shimmering line between sea, land on the other side, and the sky, so you could not be sure where they met. The smell of marsh gases met my nostrils, and midges went to work on my unprotected hands and face.

A clutch of sailing vessels lay at anchor out in the deep water, and there was a barque, half filled with water, lying on her side out in the mud. Twenty or so men, white and black, were busy with the construction of a pier, taking advantage of the low water to feverishly dig a hole and fix a new pile. A team of bullocks were bogged to the chests in black mud, and I could hear the crack of the whip and bellows from the animals.

I spied a man seated at a table, an umbrella shading him as he worked on a ledger. Striding across to him I said, 'Are you the boss of this port?'

'I am indeed, though it's not much to look at yet.' He smiled at me, and pointed back behind his head. 'One day, over there, we'll build an abattoir, and refrigerated ships will call daily to take frozen beef to the cities of the South. There will be mines in the interior, and the machinery of civilisation, the wealth of the nation will feed out into the world.'

I shook my head in wonder. 'Refrigerated ships?'

'The technology is there, it's only a matter of time. Now how can I help you?'

'I want passage to Palmerston. When's the next steamship coming along?'

'You missed the *Victoria* by a couple of days. Maybe a fortnight, to three weeks.'

'That's too long for me,' I said.

The master of that partially built port raised an eyebrow.

'Then I suggest you ride.'

I booked in at the Cable family's hotel, sharing a room with three other blokes, part of a prospecting syndicate. I ate in the bar, and drank a few beers afterwards. All the talk was of gold, with one fellow showing off a twelve ounce nugget he had found on some unnamed river, gathering quite the crowd of admirers around him.

Unused to strangers, but also impatient to outfit myself and be on the road to Palmerston, I retired to my room early. Kicking off my boots I lay on the cot, and opened my mail from home.

I read the letter twice more that night, and replied dutifully. Right then, however, I could hardly picture my family. It was images of Gracie that filled my mind, haunted me with longing. I wanted her more than air, food or water.

The next morning, I wandered down Wyndham's main street. From a dealer just out of town I acquired a pair of quiet packhorses. At Black Pat Durack's new store I bought leather packs, along with all the supplies I would need on the journey.

I was using scales supplied by the store to weigh my goods and pack them evenly, when a young lady of about my own age, in a long dress and carrying a parasol stopped beside me. 'I saw you ride in yesterday. Going again so quickly?'

'I reckon so.'

'That's a shame. There's not so many young men your age here. I could have showed you the sights – and there's a race meeting Sunday, out at the Three-mile.'

I looked at her face – skin unspoiled by the sun, and twinkling blue eyes like turning planets in the night sky. I had a feeling of being on the outside so strong that I could barely form the words, 'That would have been nice.'

'Oh, I'm Rose Byrne by the way, my father owns a store and butchering business here.'

I'd heard of her of course. The three Byrnes girls had been a hot topic of conversation in the stock camps since we crossed the border. Apart from the obvious attraction of three white sisters – Joe Byrne, their uncle or cousin, I can't remember which – had been a member of the Kelly gang, and died from blood loss after the siege of Glenrowan.

'I'm Charlie Gaunt. I'm riding to Palmerston.'

'How far is it?'

'About seven hundred miles in a roundabout way.'

'You look like you need a few square meals first.'

'I'll be right, I'm used to the bush life.'

238

'Is it a girl you'll be meeting up there?'

I nodded.

'I wish a man would ride seven hundred miles for me.'

'I'd say they will, Miss Byrne. I would, anyways.'

I left her blushing, and I realised that she was the first white girl I had spoken to since Henrietta in Borroloola. It was of great interest to me, a few years later, when I learned that Rose's sister Cattie had been wooed by my boss on the track, Tom Kilfoyle. The pair married in 1891, with Rose in attendance to the bride.

Not wanting to stay another night in Wyndham, I packed up and left town not long after lunch. I looked around but Rose Byrne was nowhere to be seen, and everyone else was too busy minding their own business to spare me a glance. I was feeling let down at having to ride – after years on horseback and my own two feet I had been looking forward to my first foray on a seagoing ship. Of course, I had plenty of practice at that later in life.

The company of townsfolk I did not care for. The bush had been my home for so long, that I felt my tense muscles relax as Wyndham dwindled behind me.

Whistler appeared from the blacks' camp and started after me. He didn't ask me where we were going, or how long it might take to get there, but he merely followed. I imagine that I was one of the few human beings, from our people or his, who had shown him any kindness. He gave me loyalty in return, and though I have known many a black to bite the hand of those who have been kind to them, I had no such fear with Whistler. On the track I ate the same food as he did, wore the same clothes. He had no cause to be jealous of me.

We camped some miles out beside a waterhole known as the Grotto, cut deep from the surrounding plain of smooth stone. The route back towards the Territory was a known track, and I shared the camp with a handful of travellers, mostly ringers trudging towards new jobs, or away from old ones.

After a discussion of Whistler's name, they wanted to see his prick, and the young black man happily unfastened his dungarees and showed off his disfigured manhood. The ringers gaped and laughed until the boy covered himself back up.

The trail was a lonely place, mostly, and days passed between each sighting of a white man. From Victoria River Downs to the north we endured long days in gorge country, and while neither Whistler nor myself were molested, every night we saw campfires on the ridges.

One night the sound of clapsticks and didgeridoo was so loud that Whistler grew increasingly distressed, wringing his hands, pursing and unpursing his lips, and cowering against the trunk of any handy tree beside our camp.

The native music had also been playing on my nerves, night after night. There was no stock camp full of men between me and them now. Just one lonely campfire. Even during the day we often heard movement behind us and, often, the call of a bird where I knew no bird to be.

Lying cold in a swag, not knowing when a spear would take me in the guts, gave rise to a kind of hysterical fear that I had little control over. When it all became too much I slipped on my boots, hefted my rifle, and walked through the night towards the sounds of those primitive musical instruments. At that moment it seemed to me that all my problems stemmed from these wild people and their noises in the night.

Before I had walked half a mile I saw a fire leaping high, with painted dancers like leaping shadows surrounding it. I did not know what ceremony this was. Later I learned a little of how their songs laid down stories of their world, of birth, acceptance into the clan, and death. Of food creatures battling across the sky. Of waking one mythical being and laying another to sleep, letting the seasons come. Warding off death, welcoming life.

That night I did not care.

I knelt behind a termite hill of the correct height, and trained my sights on the fire itself. I saw the sick comedy of what I was doing in the moments before I squeezed off the shot. The rifle shuddered and my ears numbed with the discharge. I lifted my head and saw the fire explode into millions of flying embers. The music stopped.

Figures scattered, howling like a banshees off their mounds. I

240

slipped away, and that night I slept soundly, knowing that they would be frightened of me and my rifle. That my power over them was re-established.

We took a short cut up to the Flora River, then followed the east bank of the Daly. Camping one night near the junction of a creek called Yuwaiyunn, I blazed a tree and swore to return one day, for it was some of the prettiest grazing land you'd ever see, with cascades in the river where the deep blue water hit beds of stone, throwing white spray and gurgling happily as it did so. Further down the Daly I met a raiding party of horsemen.

There were at least thirty altogether, returning from the rugged country to the west, blood spattered and tired.

The man in charge was that same corporal I had met at the Elsey months earlier – George Montagu. He told me how they had ridden out to avenge the murder of a white telegraph worker, and the brutal wounding of two more.

'We made them pay – every member of the Mangarrayi tribe we could find. Man, woman and child. When one white life is paid for with twenty, thirty miserable black ones they'll learn.'

We camped a night at Berry Springs, near the thriving outpost called Southport, and as we neared Palmerston we came across small camps of black men and women, members of the local Larrakeyah tribe. Some were anxious to trade for grog, sugar or flour, none of which I possessed, having baked the last Johnnycakes the day before.

Still, these exchanges were pleasant enough, and I was impressed by these handsome, well-built people.

'Pintpot and Pannikin both from alla same mob,' Whistler told me.

'Well if they're all as friendly as those two, we won't have any trouble around here.'

As we drew closer to Palmerston itself, with the occasional broken-down cart and some struggling market gardens, I started looking around for somewhere to stay.

I had no intention of spending any more of my cash on a hotel room,

241

and neither did I want to sleep in an itinerant town camp. With these thoughts in mind, Whistler and I settled into a clearing on the banks of a stream called Rapid Creek, a mile before we hit town. The bank was high enough to keep us safe from 'gators – pleasant and private, screened with the drooping branches of pandanus palms.

We dropped our swags, and after clearing a good fireplace and boiling the billy I left Whistler to hold the camp and watch the gear while I went to town. I left my rifle behind, but made sure I wore my revolver, all six chambers primed, but with the hammer safe.

Whistler was sitting cross-legged in front of a good blaze as I left, brewing more tea. 'You bringin' back more tucker?'

'Yeah, I will. Plenty tucker.'

But as I turned away food was the last thing on my mind – my belly hollow with fear at what I might find in town. I day-dreamed of finding Gracie and bringing her home to my camp, yet something told me that was unlikely.

Palmerston in 1885 was, to my eyes at least, a grand city, with real streets, botanic gardens, a hospital, a fine residence for the governor, a butcher shop and even a baker. The smell of fresh bread broke through my anxiety and made my digestive juices flow. I bought a knotted loaf to take back to camp. I don't believe that I had seen so many people since Sandhurst – proud unsmiling China-men, drovers, adventurers, gold prospectors, strolling gentlemen and their families.

From China-town I took the path known as 'Traveller's Walk' down past clumps of banana trees towards Fort Hill, with a dozen ships at anchor close inshore in Kitchener Bay. I noted Macassar prahus, ketches, a three-masted barque, a Burns and Philp steamer and an exotic looking craft that must have been a Chinese junk. Lighters were busy hauling cargo to and from the cluster of warehouses and offices on the isthmus between the hill and shore, and a steady stream of pedestrians – business types, labourers and strollers alike – hurried up and down the path.

Left and right I looked, half expecting to see the bearded face of Walter Oswald. Running into him casually was the best I could hope for.

242

In that happy circumstance I would be within my rights to hail him as a familiar face, and inquire of Gracie with seeming innocence.

Almost everybody greeted me with a tip of the hat and a kind word, but my first real conversation occurred when I stopped to admire an impressive but unusual two-storey building overlooking the bay. It had huge arches on the lower level, a seemingly continuous balcony on the upper, and must have had grand views.

'That's quite a house, wouldn't you say?'

I turned. The man who asked the question cut a neat figure in solar topee and whites. 'I've never seen anything quite like it.'

'They call it Knight's Folly, after the gentleman who built it. John Knight is his name, and he's a firm friend of mine. You're a drover, by the looks of you?'

I took off my stained hat and held it in my hands. 'That's right, my name's Charlie Gaunt. I was with the Duracks, all the way from Cooper's Creek to the Kimberley.' I said this last with a note of pride. Everywhere I went people were familiar with the family and the big drive. No one ever mentioned the poor bastards like me, who near starved to death to stock their stations.

'The Duracks, eh? Well I met Black Pat and Tom Hayes on this very spot as they filled a ketch with provisions for the Kimberley.' He thrust out a hand. 'My name is Alfred Searcy, Customs Inspector. Well met, and please let me know if there's anything you require. Where are you staying?'

'A little out of town. I've got my boy with me. But sir, you might be able to help me, I'm looking for a friend of mine. His name is Walter Oswald, a blacksmith with a dark bushy beard.'

'I've met him, yes. He's down in Pine Creek, last I heard. The Celestials have pretty much taken over the place now, and he's working down there.'

'What about his daughter Gracie, is she with him?'

Alfred Searcy was a wise man. He read me like a tracker reads the spoor of a thief. 'You'll have to ask him about that. Now if you'll excuse me—'

Pine Creek was a hundred miles to the south of Palmerston, and Whistler could not understand why I had to change from my usual pace, and push the horses on almost all night, with only a couple of hours in our swags past midnight.

'What for we hurry, hurry?' he asked me. 'Back alla same south like we just come.'

'Because the people I'm looking for are in Pine Creek.'

'What people?'

'Gracie, the one I told you about, and a piccaninny too.'

Whistler grinned, seemingly pleased. 'You gonna make her your wife prop'ly?'

'That,' I said, 'is the idea.'

Pine Creek was, like so many other mining towns, a termites' nest of hurrying people. The noise never ceased – of pick axes striking stone, raised voices and the stamp of ore batteries. Each of these machines had its own particular rhythm, depending on the number of stamps. Most were driven by steam engines and the puff and pant of these added to the racket.

The centre of town was a collection of shanties – gold buyers, banks, stores selling mining tools – shovels, pans, even cradles. China-town made up perhaps half the overall area, mostly flimsy buildings, some with walls of woven reeds. I hoped no fire ever ran through it for it would have burned like gunpowder.

Men stood around in groups, eyeing us off as we rode in. We passed a man in fancy duds, riding a magnificent bay stallion that must have been worth a fortune. Gold shone from his cufflinks and the rings on his fingers.

Everyone, from the sweepers outside the storefronts, to the barman serving customers on the verandah with beer at ten in the morning, wore revolvers in their belts. A guard outside the Bank of South Australia sat on a chair, half asleep, holding a fancy Winchester repeating rifle known as a 'yellow boy' over his ample belly.

The operator of a water cart, drawn by two Clydesdales, each at least eighteen hands high, was hosing water over the street in an effort to hold down the dust. After a long dry season it was everywhere, drifting over the town from the mines. Tribesmen of the Mangarrayi, tall and heavily muscled, stood at street corners, and Whistler pressed in close to me, like a shadow, almost touching, for as I've said, he feared his own people more than white men.

Everywhere people were talking loudly and shouting, competing with the machinery, and I kept walking through most of the business premises and into the industrial yards on the fringes. We passed one blacksmith, with a hand painted sign that read something like:

JOE KERSBROOK, SMITHY. I HAVE A REPPUTATION FOR QUOLITY WERK JUST ARSK AROUND.

Through an open doorway I could see glowing fires and a man sweating over his anvil. At a chair near the door sat a woman who I assumed to be his wife, with a cash box and ledger, a Webley revolver sitting on the table in front of her.

I told Whistler to wait with the horses while I walked in through the wrought iron gate. The woman brightened as I approached, 'Well good morning indeed. You're the handsomest visitor I've had in many a day.'

I was taken aback by this, not least because up close it was plain to see that she was no youngster, with crinkled skin and creased eyes. My eyes flicked worriedly to the man I assumed was Joe Kersbrook, pounding away at a rod of glowing metal.

'Oh don't worry about Joe. He aren't my husband, he's my son. Now how can I help you?'

'I'm looking for another blacksmith, a man by the name of Walter Oswald.'

'What's it worth to you?'

'What do you mean?'

'I mean if I tell you where to find Walter Oswald what are you going to give me in return?'

I felt in my change pocket. 'How about sixpence?'

She cackled, 'I was thinking of a kiss.'

I started to turn around. 'I'll ask someone else.'

'Now, hold on there lad, I was only joking around. No one has kissed these lips for many a year. Walter Oswald is working out near the Chink mine at Frances Creek. Six or seven miles from here.'

'Has he got his daughter with him?' I felt as if my whole life hinged on her answer.

She gave a knowing smile. 'Ah, so now I know why a young handsome thing like you might be looking for a bloke like Walter Oswald.'

'So is she with him?'

'I don't know. Never seen him with a daughter if that's true. What did she look like?'

I thought for a moment. 'Black hair, grey eyes. Always smiling, but she rides as good as any man.'

The blacksmith's mother rolled her eyes. 'You've got it bad, sonny. No wonder you don't wanna kiss an old hag like me.'

'You're no hag.' I said. 'But have you seen her?'

She smiled, showing yellow teeth with long ivory roots. 'No, not that I can think of. But he might be hiding her away. If I had a daughter I'd be keeping her under wraps around this place too. A lot of wild men here, let me tell you.'

'Thanks. I'll be seeing you then.'

I walked back out the gate, over to where Whistler was waiting with the horses, still looking unsettled.

'You find 'im boss?'

'Not yet, but we know where to look.'

Our journey to Frances Creek took us on a track that headed north over scrubby, stony hills, honeycombed with mine shafts; abandoned or working, along with mullock heaps and men sweating, straining and cursing. All the normal manners of the road seemed to have no place here, and donkey teams carrying ore to batteries did not pay the slightest heed to travellers. It was up to you to move off the track before you were trodden under.

Once we had passed the big Caledonian mine, the greater part of the populace were brown-skinned and slanted of eye. The ride took the best part of two hours, and finally, reaching the mine locality, a thick-set Celestial stood with a rifle at the boundary of a series of claims. After stating our business, we moved on towards some poppet heads down the creek. A narrow water channel, called a race, made its way along the contours of the hills.

The first shaft we came to was manned by dozens of workers. Some rough bough sheds and shanties were clustered around. As we walked the horses through I smelled opium, and saw dull faces through darkened doorways.

We passed a bunch of coolies in the process of putting up a new shanty, maybe a joss house or men's quarters I had no idea. My joints had started shaking with worry at what would happen when I found Walter Oswald, and for the first time I considered turning around and riding away from there.

Soon we passed a quarry-mine, with donkey teams hauling ore up and out, the whole affair conducted in a pall of dust. Men shouted in their foreign singsong tongue, accompanied by the braying of animals.

Up ahead we saw a kitchen of sorts where shift workers were being given their meals. They stared at us as we passed, but just a little further on we reached what surely must be Walter Oswald's blacksmith shop. It was built more strongly than nearby shanties, partially of stone. On an iron pole out the front hung a chain of old horseshoes, joined like lace by heat and hammer. This, I guessed, was as good an advertisement for a blacksmith as any.

'Wait here,' I said to Whistler, then dismounted and handed him the reins. My boots raised puffs in the dust and ash that surrounded the smithy as I advanced. Reaching the dark threshold, I peered inside, to where a furnace of coals was glowing like Hades.

'Hello,' I called, with my head half indoors, not wanting to surprise the man. I tried again, louder, then looked back at where Whistler waited patiently with the horses. He looked blankly back at me.

My heart thumping like a drum, I took my first step inside, feeling the heat from the coals on my face. On the anvil was a lump of iron, still glowing from the heat. It occurred to me that the blacksmith had been there just moments earlier.

'Mr Oswald,' I tried. 'Are you there?'

Still no sound from inside.

I moved on, tasting bile in my mouth, torn between fear and an overwhelming desire to see Gracie again. The floor of beaten earth, overlaid with ash and iron slag, crunched underneath my feet. I stopped at an opening leading into the back, fully dark now save for that glowing orange light from the furnace.

Through the opening I saw a bedroom, screened off from the rest of the space with woven rushes. I called again. No answer. I took one more step then heard a noise.

I snapped my head around and saw Walter Oswald coming for me from his hiding place around the wall. I recognised his black beard, and felt the strength of the arm that whipped around my neck, all but crushing my windpipe.

With the point of a knife pricking at my neck, his face up close to mine, he hissed, 'I knew the bastard who did my Gracie wrong would come looking – and it was you – I should have known, you feckless traitor.'

'We fell in love,' I said, choking for breath.

'Save me from your bullshit. A sixteen-year-old lass in a stock camp wouldn't know love if she tripped over it – but to be tricked into giving a young man his carnal desires – that's how it happens. You wanted her and you took her.'

He pushed me away from him, moved the knife to his left hand then punched me on the nose with his right. Blood ran down over my lips. The blow seemed to take no effort on his part – just a tap – yet it landed so hard that I was forced backwards against a rickety bush-made table.

I went down, pain streaking from my nose deep into my head, as if he had found multiple sources of agony with that one blow. I sat on my arse, looking up in the half-darkness at his blurred form, legs astride. He wore no shirt, showing the power of his physique.

But now it was all out in the open. He was, it seemed, the only thing standing between me and the girl I loved. My temper flared. Fear evaporated. I came to my feet, cocked my fists, then kicked a chair away so it splintered against the wall.

'Where is she?' I asked.

He threw the knife away so it clattered against the walls of the shanty. 'Where scum like you will never find her.'

I stepped in and fired my left at his chin. Walter used no footwork. He had no footwork. But his hands were like lightning. He took my fist in one huge paw then retaliated with a straight right that I only just managed to dodge.

'I love her. I want to marry her,' I said.

He showed his teeth. 'You think I would let my only daughter hitch up with a shiftless drover?'

I got a good punch in then, feinting with my left then launching a right hook that looked lazy, but swept in on his defences and took him fair on the cheek. His facial expression didn't change. Knowing I'd got in a good one, I waited to see how he'd react.

I didn't have to wait long. He came at me like a big old bull ready to charge to the death, swinging wild blows with left and right, landing many with the power of kicks from a stallion. All those hours spent training with Bob Perry, and all that talk about punches that will end a fight meant fuck-all. Nothing seemed to work on him.

The only thing that kept me on my feet was the wall of the shanty which I struck with the small of my back along a set of rough shelves. Down came plates and enamel mugs in a crazy rattle, a mess of porcelain and tin all over me and the floor.

Now I sank to my knees, and he started to kick me, boots thumping into my gut, and my face. One hard blow ground my ear against the side of my head and I could feel the skin tear as it struck.

Oswald staggered back, breathing hard, then bent down and picked up the knife. With the blade shining from reflected firelight he stepped towards me. Murder was in his eyes. He was going to kill me.

I plucked my revolver from the pouch at my side, and levelled it at him, levering back the hammer.

'Stop!' I yelled.

But he did not seem to hear me, just came towards me with the knife. I pulled the trigger. A sheet of flame came from the muzzle and the discharge made my ears ring.

I had never killed a white man. And I had never killed anyone up so close. In the half-light I scarcely saw where the bullet hit. But I saw the change in his face. He sat down, and started to laugh. Blood appeared in the corner of his mouth and dripped down into his beard.

He wiped it with the back of his hand, skin coming away crimson.

'She's already married,' he said. 'So you'll never have her.'

His voice had gone strangely quiet, almost friendly. But his words wounded me worse than a knife blade.

'Where is she?' I asked.

'With her husband, you blessed idiot.'

I got myself up to my feet, watching as he started to die. Whistler must have heard the shot, for he called to me from the main door.

'Hey boss. Yolabat in there?'

I leaned against the wall. Walter Oswald slumped over onto his back. A gurgling sound issued from his throat.

'You shouldn't have bloody well picked up that knife,' I said, glaring at him, then looked back down the passage to where Whistler had started making his way down towards me.

'Stop there,' I said, and he did so, but I could see his confusion, eyes shining orange from the forge. 'Now go back out and hold the horses like I told you.' My voice, I realised, was shaking, and Whistler didn't always jump when I told him to jump. He edged into the room and I did not have the energy to turn him away.

Whistler's eyes were white and huge, but he said nothing as the blacksmith's legs went into some strange final gallop, thrashing on the ground as if resisting the pull of the afterlife.

As I watched Walter Oswald die, I heard horses out the front, on the road. It was inevitable, of course, that the sound of a gunshot would bring people.

The policeman must have been close by, because he was first at the threshold, calling out in authoritative tones. I was still inside, next to the body of Walter Oswald, when I saw him walk through the door, dressed in the uniform of the South Australian police force. I recognised him straight away. It was George Montagu, the corporal, and behind him I could see an interested crowd of both whites and Chinese.

The policeman turned and roared at them. 'Get back you lot. Right away.' Then he walked past the forge and towards me. 'I've had reports that a gunshot came from these premises. What can you tell me?'

I was a grown man, but I felt like a stripling.

'It was an accident, I swear it was.'

'What was?'

The policeman was walking towards me, big and menacing, and I let him slip past me into the room where the blacksmith's corpse lay on the ground. Unmoving now.

'Jesus Christ,' the cop said. 'Is he dead?'

'Yes.'

He didn't ask me what happened, just said, 'I saw you down on the Roper months back, then again a week or so ago out on the Daly. You're the drover, Charlie Gaunt, aren't you?'

'Yes, that's me.'

'You don't want this kind of trouble do you?'

'No fear. He was coming at me with a knife. I swear he was going to kill me.'

'I have to tell you, Charlie, this could go either way with a judge. He might give you a couple of years in Fannie Bay, or he might hang you by the neck.' He pointed at Whistler, standing still as a post on the other side of the room. 'So who might this be?'

'My black boy. His name is Whistler. He doesn't talk much.'

'Perfect. There's our murderer then.'

I was so stunned I couldn't respond for a moment or two, but then opened my mouth to protest. I was forestalled by the policeman shouting through the opening at the people gathered outside. 'I told you gawkers to back off out of here and you'd better damned well do it or I'll arrest you for obstruction of justice.' This done he turned back to me. 'You really want to take the rap for this?'

'It was an accident.'

'How you going to prove that? You've only got one witness, and he's as murderous-looking as any nigger I've seen.' The policeman lowered his voice. 'I'll give you one chance. Lay your revolver down on the floor. I'll take a statement from you, then you walk out of here a free man, and we both forget every word we've exchanged in this place.'

I felt a heavy foreboding, but even that black cloud was not as forbidding as the thought of a noose around my neck.

'And what will happen to Whistler?'

'Justice will take its course.'

I stared at him. 'Why are you doing this?'

'How old are you, twenty-two, twenty-three?'

'Twenty.'

'I don't want to see a good young bloke like you, with his life over before it's begun.'

I laid my revolver gently down on the floor. 'Don't hurt him,' I said.

'No need for anything like that.' He marched across to poor Whistler, who was now cowering against the wall. 'Let's have your wrists, boy.'

Whistler started whimpering like a kitten, his eyes flicking pitifully between me and George Montagu. I could not look away, even as the big corporal lifted first one wrist and then the other, closing cuffs of iron over them.

The policeman pushed Whistler ahead of him down the passage, and I followed them towards the light, past the still-hot forge and out into the sunlight. An undertaker had arrived, and Montagu stopped to talk to him.

'This nigger did murder today. You'll find the poor blacksmith inside in a pool of blood. Keep the revolver – that'll be evidence.' He pointed at me. 'This is young Charlie Gaunt. He did his best to stop it from happening, but this here boy is a cold-blooded killer, like most of his kind.'

Whistler and I locked eyes, and he paddled as if through a river of

252

hands that restrained him, trying pathetically to get to me, desperate for my protection. I pushed him away, mindful of what the spectators would think if I showed him any kindness. I'll never forget the look on his face at the moment at which he realised the extent of my betrayal.

I think I knew then what was going to happen, but I was distracted by the sight of the undertaker carrying out Oswald's body. Seizing the moment, Whistler slipped down and out of Montagu's grip, barging his way through a couple of bystanders. Running a little awkwardly because of the manacles he took off towards a heap of mine tailings. I wanted to slow everything down. I wanted to stop that inevitable chain of events, but Montagu strode quickly to his horse and pulled his repeating rifle from the scabbard.

'Get out of the way you fools,' he roared, clearing a line of fire. Then, lifting the rifle to his shoulder he fired at Whistler's retreating back. The first shot missed, but the second took him down low, left of the spine, where it must have ripped out a kidney.

Whistler dropped to his knees and continued to crawl towards the bush. There was a grim smile on Montagu's lips as he flicked the lever without taking the butt from his shoulder and brought another cartridge into the chamber.

Again he fired, and this time Whistler went down face first.

Ah, good Christ, how the memory of that day rakes through the ashes of my soul, the day I killed not one man, but two. One who had never done anything but work hard and love his daughter. One who had trusted me completely, and asked nothing of me in return but to walk at my side.

The policeman turned to me and lowered the rifle. 'Sometimes,' he said, 'justice is swift.'

They dragged Whistler's body back along the track by his feet. Three men fetched shovels and set to work digging at the foot of a young woollybutt tree. As soon as the depth was near enough to adequate, they dragged the body in and filled it up. There was no undertakers cart for dead blacks, just a hole and enough dirt to keep the goannas from bringing up the remains.

I rode back to Pine Creek and the police station with Montagu. He took my statement at his desk. He wrote most of it himself.

Afterwards, alone and bereft of companionship, stripped by my own weakness of every vestige of humanity, I rode south into a deep scarlet sunset, Krakatoa's legacy.

My dreams of finding Gracie, of spending the rest of my life with her, were thrown to the wind. She was married to another man. And besides, how could I look her in the eye with the knowledge that I had killed her father, and let a loyal servant take the blame? For the first time in my life, I reckoned myself a coward.

I rode listlessly south and east. I passed familiar hills and creeks, and occasional parties of prospectors. I shared billy tea and a yarn or two, but tarried no more than a few hours with anyone.

I camped on Poolooarmee Billabong on my way down the Roper, just twenty-four hours after Constable Power, along with John Palmer, the manager of Elsey Station, and three Native Police, finally caught up with the 'big man' Charley and his surviving warriors.

The lawmen had tortured an old Yangman Elder known as Goggle-eye into leading them to Charley's camp. With the benefit of surprise, they had rushed the camp at day-break, preventing Charley and his men from reaching the spears they had stacked against the trunk of a banyan tree.

I saw the pyre where they burned the bodies, and I can still smell the reek of it. Brass cartridges littered the earth. They had not burned Charley's body, but were taking it back to the Elsey to prove his death and thus dispel the legend that had grown up of his invincibility.

Even in death he was a huge man, every muscle across his arms, chest and abdomen fully developed and unblurred by body fat. His beard was long and full. His eyes had rolled back in his head so only the whites showed, and no one had thought to close the lids.

I hawked in the back of my throat and spat on his dead chest.

Power looked up at me enquiringly.

'That bastard speared my horse,' I said.

I was good and evil all at once. Sorry and glad.

I needed time to think. I decided then and there, standing beside the corpse of a man, my spit dribbling down his chest, that I wanted to go home to my mother.

CHAPTER TWENTY-SEVEN

When 'Wanderlust' controls the man, he wanders like a rudderless ship at sea anywhere.

Three months after I rode off from Pine Creek I hit the outskirts of Melbourne, closed my nostrils to the unfamiliar smells and tipped my hat to the ladies, stopping once for a fortifying beer before reaching St Kilda. When I knocked on the door of my mother's house an attractive girl in her early teens answered. It took me several seconds before I recognised my sister Nellie.

She looked me up and down – at my moleskins and dust – the horse shit spattered on my boots and leggings from the road, then took a step back. I realised that, though I was only twenty, I had turned into the man I had always wanted to be.

I heard a noise from the other room. 'Who's there?'

Ma and Marion joined Nellie at the doorway. Ma recognised me in an instant.

'Oh dear God, Charlie,' she said.

For the first time in five years I held my mum in my arms. Let me tell you now. There is nothing like that. Nothing in life that can compare. Even now I miss her embrace so much I stop typing and blink tears from my eyes. Strength flowed into me. I started to cry like a boy. I hid it as well as I could, but when she gripped my shoulders and held me at arm's length so she could look at my face, she saw what I felt.

Marion was distant and bordering on unfriendly. I put up with it for a week or so then cornered her. I asked her the trouble.

'What do you think? How could you?' Rode off on your precious horse and left us. Can you imagine what it did to Ma?'

'I said I was sorry.' And so I had, on that first tear-streaked night at home.

'Sorry is just a word. It means nothing. You've changed Charlie. I don't even want to know what you've done up there. Something hard and horrible.'

Whistler settled back deeper into my memories, and I somehow rationalised what had happened as a sacrifice on his part rather than any conscious decision on mine. I started to walk taller again, and became an afternoon regular at the Esplanade Hotel overlooking the beach. I was no drunk, seeming to instinctively grasp the ability to seek and hold a certain warm tipsiness. My stories of the north, however, soon drew an attentive audience. I had ridden off as a boy, and come back a big, tanned, raw-boned man, who could handle a horse, stockwhip, and rifle like few other men on earth.

Yet Augusta, my mother, could surely see the shadows in my eyes from the things I had seen and done. She was middle-aged, and still lived by the values of her Church of England upbringing. I noticed, however, some strangeness in her habits, and the sherry decanter was getting a little too much attention.

I took a job at the Newmarket sale yards, and I loved to show off my flash riding. There wasn't a horse in that city I couldn't tame. The local try-hards lined the rails, no doubt hoping to see me fall. Occasionally one wanted to fight me, and I was able to add to my reputation by laying them out in the dust with a well-timed uppercut.

When I came home in the evening, after an hour or two at the pub, we settled down for a quiet time around the lounge room, while the women embroidered or played whist at the table. It wasn't like my other life – my real life.

Gracie was never far from my thoughts. Had the blacksmith told the truth? Was she at that moment languishing in some single mothers' home in Palmerston? Or was she back in Queensland. I had to know. I told myself that even if I could not have her, I needed to know where she was.

I day-dreamed of bringing her home to meet Ma, Nellie and Marion.

There was only one thing about that image that bothered me. It was true that Gracie had browner skin than any woman my eyes fell on in Melbourne. Would they reject her for that? I didn't know, and that feeling made me feel more out of place.

There were other reasons for my restlessness. I missed the north. I missed the space and the characters, and the danger. I missed the excitement. I was physically and mentally ready to leave, but several things were holding me back, partly the obvious love and pleasure Ma showed at me being home, and partly, I have to admit, my status as a local hero.

I swore not to slip away in the night this time. I announced a day, and I weathered mother's tears. Her desperate words I can still hear in my dreams, the soft love that even now I can feel around me like a shield. I gave notice at the yards.

'But you don't even have a job up there,' Marion said.

'Oh, I'll pick something up,' I said. I knew for a fact that good ringers don't exactly grow on trees, and that bosses were always looking for new men.

'Off you go then. It's just like you to come back for just long enough to raise Ma's hopes then leave again.'

'I've got my own life now, can't your see that?'

She folded her arms in front of her chest. 'I see quite enough, thank you.'

And so it was that I rode north once again. I knew the route now. I knew the waterholes, and the stations likely to give a traveller flour and beef on the road. I headed north through New South Wales then west to Boulia, threading my way up the Georgina to Urandangi.

Everything was going ahead; new streets, roads, towns and stores. Cobb and Co coaches dashed around the countryside with teams of fresh horses waiting at every turn. From Urandangi I cut across Lake Nash and up into the Barkly: those dead-flat grasslands, horizon to horizon, with herds of fat cattle around the brand-new bores.

It's always strange riding back to the Territory after an absence. You return with longing growing in your heart. Yet, when you first smell the honey-rich scent of the bush, and see the first glowing yellow-red sunsets on stone ridges, you are tentative, wondering if she will let you back in again.

It takes a while, but of course she does, and there's a euphoria in that moment, and from that time on it's as if you never left. I took a few weeks' work on Brunette Downs, helping sort cattle after the muster, but my destination was Palmerston, and as soon as I had the cash to finish my journey I took my cheque and went.

In Palmerston I headed for the offices of the Northern Territory News and Gazette, requesting and poring over their newspaper archive. I found a death notice for Walter Oswald, and an article destitute of fact but bursting with invention, about how a wild blackfellow from the Gulf Country had shot the blacksmith in an argument over tucker.

> '... Brave Corporal Montagu shot the murderous nigger when he attempted to escape, and the Gazette commends him for his attention to duty and excellent aim.'

My heart thumped in my chest in that reading room, and I caught the eyes of others in that room. Surely, I reasoned, they would see my guilt. What if Montagu talked? Even just to one or two people. Word would get around. I felt myself a fool for coming here.

Still I pored back through the editions. The paper was printed only once a week, on Saturdays, so it did not take me long to find, tucked away, a wedding notice:

> The Botanic Gardens was the venue for last Saturday's marriage between Grace Oswald, formerly of Toowoomba and Mr Joseph Newton, from California, United States of America. Mr Newton is the visiting captain of the clipper Ethel May, now such a spectacular sight in our
> harbour. Mr and Mrs Newton will spend their first months of married life on board, bound for such far shores as China, Burma,

I felt hollow in the chest. All that time I had been hoping that Water Oswald was lying, and that she wasn't really married.

I went to the Terminus Hotel in Smith Street, and for the first time in my life I set out to destroy myself with alcohol. That eighteen-year-old who delighted in cream soda was long gone, his innocence worn down by a hard world and bad choices.

Late that night, my veins pumping more rum than blood, I fought and beat two men on the street outside the bar, then mercifully fell asleep face down besides the adjoining stables. If I had not slept at that point I would almost certainly have been arrested, and the last thing I wanted was attention from the police.

Without any real plan, only an aching heart, I remembered my promise to the Randall brothers. Florida Station was a long way out: as remote as a man could be in Australia. That suited me perfectly.

CHAPTER TWENTY-EIGHT

I cannot describe the horrific condition of these poor unfortunates. Eighty per cent in that camp were afflicted with that dread disease that had overtaken the dead blacks we found outside the camp. Lubras were to be seen suckling babes with the eyes eaten out of their head, and with fingers only stumps; old men in the last stages of the disease crawled around the camp on all fours, jabbering incoherently; nearly everyone in that camp was afflicted.

FLORIDA STATION stretched from north of the Roper to the Arafura Sea, ten thousand square miles of coastal scrub. It had been originally taken up by pastoralist John Arthur Macartney and first managed by Wentworth Darcy Uhr, an ex-policeman who was so deadly with a stockwhip that he rarely bothered with carrying a gun.

I stopped at the Roper River, renewed my acquaintance with Matt Kirwan and drank a tot or three of his whisky. I crossed the bar and rode for several days through wild country.

This wilderness suited my state-of-mind perfectly. Evidence of Gracie's wedding had knocked me for six. Bitterness ran in my veins. Jealousy is not just a word, it's an ulcerated sore that starts in the heart and drips its poison throughout the body. You want the feeling to go away, yet there is no cure once it sets in. I felt it in my burning throat, through sleepless nights. It robbed the pleasure from every moment, even those that should have been a triumph. Jealousy changed me for the worse. After many days of riding I reached the homestead, a solid structure built of paperbark logs near a Goyder River waterhole. It was fortress-like, and well it might be, for it had come under determined attack several times.

There were eight stockmen in residence, and a number of Chinese growing vegetables, cooking, and performing menial work. I spent a few days at the station before being enticed off on a ride to explore the far reaches of the run.

Mick Pender, Alf Randall and I loaded three packs and, with a string of spare mounts, set off to the north. It was all new to me, and I could see quickly that this was not good cattle country, with spinifex, heat, mosquitoes, and rugged sandstone hills. In five days of riding we reached the Arafura Swamp, where the Goyder River broadens into a vast freshwater lake, alive with millions of sea birds, 'gators, reeds and lilies. The wet season, only recently departed, had left it brimming full.

Below the swamps we found fresh native tracks, and following them up we came upon a leprosy-ravaged village. This disease, I have been told, was brought into these parts by the Makassars visiting the coast, and it extracted a terrible price.

The sight shocked me deeply. It was pitiful, heartbreaking to see, but there was nothing we could do.

That was enough of Florida Station for me. I impressed on Alf Randall to turn back, and once we reached the homestead, I rode away south, heading down the Gulf Track, where fresh stations were still springing up. Many were marked out by rich men on maps, in drawing rooms as far away as Adelaide or even London. These rich men then hired stockmen and purchased cattle in order to stock the land within the required two years. Everywhere I rode were signs of the great takeover: the hoof prints of cattle and horses in the dust.

Over the Queensland border, in need of some company and funds, I arrived at Lawn Hill Station in time to meet up with a drover called Charlie Willis who was taking a mob of cattle back across the Territory border to McArthur River Station, near Borroloola.

At Skeleton Creek between the Calvert and Robinson Rivers, we were attacked by a mob of Garrwa warriors. The cattle rushed and some of the horses were taken. We followed the tracks to find three dead horses and one badly injured.

We linked up with the manager from Lawn Hill, Jack Watson, who heard the story and promised retribution. 'I'll stir the possum in them, and no mistake,' Jack said, and that he did, in two weeks of wholesale slaughter. More ghosts to wander the deep gullies and broad plains of the Gulf Rivers. We took what we wanted and killed those who stood in the way. Their songs fell silent, their brotherhood with the animals and the water diminished.

I started to wonder if God himself had intervened when, years later, Jack Watson was eaten by a 'gator at Knott's Crossing, Katherine. Tudor Shadforth, a handsome and dashing stockman who was also on that trip, was later speared to death at Ord River Station in the Kimberley.

CHAPTER TWENTY-NINE

The pool has no banks, the water being level with the surrounding land. Calm and uncanny this miniature lake seems, like an immense sheet of glass, at times a beautiful azure blue, at other times a deep emerald green according to the reflection of the sun. Although fish are in the small streams running in and out of it there are none in the pool. The reflection of those paperbark trees on the surface of the water, is very realistic and stands out as if on a looking glass.

Although this scene I have depicted is a beautiful one, the impression it gives one on first viewing it is, its uncanny stillness. Not a bird is to be seen. It strikes one that beneath that beautiful surface there is something deadly about the spot, and gives a weird uncanny feeling.

WHEN WE REACHED McArthur River Station, Tom Lynott, the manager, took possession of the cattle, and offered me a job. This was, at that time, the biggest cattle station in the world, stretching from the coast inland to the Barkly Tableland.

It should have made money, but Tom Lynott was a poor manager, who knew how to spend, but not earn. The owners, Amos and Broad of Sydney, were eventually sent to the wall after blowing more than a hundred thousand pounds on improving and stocking the run. At one stage they brought in fifty Chinese workers just for the purpose of building yards, but who spent their time prospecting instead.

Lynott sent me out to take charge of a stock camp called Doughboy Hollow on the Kilgour River. This was a tributary of the McArthur that flows down from the rugged Abner Range. My offsider was one of the refugees from the Queensland judiciary that I had met at Borroloola, Pigweed Harry.

Pigweed was an old-school ruffian, red-faced and running to fat around his middle. He had lost most of his teeth, one way or another, and he preferred offal or fish to beef steaks. If forced to eat the latter he'd tenderise it with the butt of his revolver for a few minutes, or stew it on a slow fire for hours.

We did not look for trouble, but the local Ngarnji people, hungry for meat and mischievous by nature, would drive the cattle up gorges, then roll rocks down on top of them. The resulting maimed and dying cattle infuriated us. Pigweed had compassion for the cattle, but none for the stone-age hunters.

'Shoot on sight,' became the rule.

Pigweed drank spirits from before sundown to bedtime each evening, and during the day if there was no work to be done. I took his lead, enjoying the way that liquor quieted my scruples, and gave those other beasts that festered inside me – jealousy and rage – free rein.

In late April '86 Pigweed Harry and I took cattle forty miles to a stock camp run by Ted Lenehan, an experienced cattleman who had, like me, started off with Nat Buchanan. Ted was a good bushman, but with a habit of taking chances no sane man would take. He could also best any man I'd ever met at swearing. If no blasphemy or crude word seemed right for the occasion, he'd make one up.

Lenehan had built a permanent camp, including bark huts, on the Parsons River at a waterhole called Broadmere, and sent a black boy to guide us in – a sly looking wretch by the name of Gobo, a born and bred Ngarnji man.

Pigweed, particularly, disliked Gobo on sight. 'I don't trust the crooked smile on that bastard,' he said. 'If he so much as looks sideways at me I'll knock him down and teach him a lesson.'

Not knowing what to expect, we walked the horses down a stretch of soft ochre-tinted sand, dotted with clumps of spinifex and silver box trees. It was only as we neared the waterhole that a range of strangely eroded cliffs came into view. The horses went quiet, as if they sensed that something was not to their taste ahead.

Nearing the waterhole, we saw smoke rising from Lenehan's camp on the other side. Yet, it seemed that we were no longer in a hurry. We were distracted by the unearthly beauty of the place, where the cliffs came down to meet the paperbark-lined water. These unusual stone faces were surmounted by rounded pillars, some with heads like hammers or chimney tops. All were composed of angled layers, and pock marked as if from the impact of countless rifle bullets.

Broadmere took our breath away, but even then I had a strange feeling that something wasn't right about it. The black boys were frightened of it, even Gobo, who kept well back from the banks and muttered to himself constantly.

Pigweed and I soon worked our way around the pool, running the cattle into holding yards Lenehan had set up. Scarcely a word was uttered until the work was done, but then with the stock secured, there were back slaps and tots of rum in tin mugs.

Not caring that we had seen a couple of big freshies out sunbaking on the banks, Pigweed Harry stripped off and was soon splashing and bellowing in the pool.

'How long can you stay, Charlie?' Ted asked me.

'A few days, maybe a week. As long as the rum holds out.' We laughed together.

Lenehan had a lubra called Ada and she came shyly over, slipped under his arm and snuggled against his chest. She was a nice little thing, and the pang of missing Gracie near bowled me over.

A week after we arrived at the camp, around midnight on a bright and moonlit night, I was fast asleep in my hut when a close and percussive gunshot broke the stillness. Reaching for the revolver I kept every night in my swag I ran outside to find Ted near the door of his hut, with his rifle in his arms and a dead black man at his feet.

'What's up?' Charlie asked.

'That black bastard nearly got me; only for Ada I'd be a box of cold meat.' Ted, it turned out, had been asleep in the hut with his woman. It was she who warned him that there was someone at the door. Silently reaching for his rifle he had fired right through the bark-clad door, striking the would-be intruder under the armpit. The huge .577 calibre shell fired by the Snider rifle made a quick death inevitable.

'The cheeky bastard,' I said. 'What made him think it was alright to come sniffing around a white man's hut?'

'Cheeky orright,' added Pigweed. 'We can't have that kind of thing going on.'

There would be trouble over this, and I knew it. I didn't want to be part of it, yet even then, I would not walk away.

Pigweed was keen to mix it up with them. 'We'll be back in a fortnight with another mob,' he said. 'Let's put the fear of God into this lot – make sure we don't have any more trouble.'

Lenehan thought for a moment, then shook his head. 'Nah. I'm going after these gazabos tomorrow or the next day when I get a bunch of fresh horses together. Alec and I will turn the trick, won't we Alec?'

Alec Amos was the son of Robert Amos, one of the station owners from Sydney; a raw jackaroo sent to toughen up and 'learn the ropes' on the station. I had doubts about how he would go in a mix-up with the local tribesmen.

Still, there was work to be done, and in the morning Pigweed Harry and I left Broadmere, riding off to our semi-permanent camp on the Kilgour.

Three days later Alec Amos and a black boy called Nim rode hell for leather into the camp. I could tell straight off that something momentous had happened. Young Amos was as white as a ghost.

'It's Ted,' he cried, bringing his horse to a standstill and swinging off his saddle. 'They've speared the poor bastard and I'm pretty sure he's dead.'

I poured him a pannikin of tea and waited while he drank it down.

'Tell us what happened.'

'Well Charlie, Me, Ted, Nim and Gobo rode out to teach the blacks a lesson. But that bastard Gobo was in cahoots with them and led us straight into an ambush. When Ted saw what had happened he dropped the treacherous dog with one shot in the back, but a whole crowd of blacks were on us. We shot a few of them, but then Ted said we had to run for it … that's when his horse got speared in the shoulder, and as he tried to pull it out he was struck – low down in his back – into his kidneys.

'We tried to get away, then … we stopped and I tried to pull the spear out, but it wouldn't come. We could hear the blacks coming up on us, dozens of them. There was no point staying with Ted … Nim and I got on our horses and …'

Pigweed's voice struck like a whip. 'You ran off and left our mate dying there.'

Alec Amos looked at that hard man's face and nodded slowly. 'He was as good as dead, I swear it.'

Pigweed's revolver appeared in his hand, as if by magic. 'You low coward. I should blow your fucking head off.'

Alec started to blubber. 'Please don't kill me. I wouldn't've left him if he hadn't been all but dead already …'

'Killing this miserable cur won't save Ted,' I said. 'Let's get over there and see if there's still a chance.'

So we sent Alec Amos in disgrace back to the homestead, while Pigweed and I galloped to Broadmere. Nim took us to the scene of the fight.

First thing I saw was the flies. Clouds of them surrounding a black object the size of a football. The smell hit me next, and I slowed my horse to a walk. Pigweed did likewise, and we were just a few paces away when he exclaimed loudly and swung off his horse.

'Damn the rotten bastards, the sick mongrel curs.'

It was then that I saw what that bloody dark thing was. It was Ted's dismembered head, sitting under a tree, patches of skull visible through tears in the flesh and tissue that surrounded it.

His body was nowhere to be seen, though we found some bones around nearby campfires, later on. Pigweed swore blind that they had eaten Ted's flesh.

Choking back bile and tears of rage we carried Ted's head in a saddlecloth, and bore it into Broadmere, burying the grisly remnant at the base of one of the grand paperbarks that line the water there. We carved his name in the trunk, and every time I think of that place, I shiver and remember how Ted Lenehan's head looked on that day.

I remember the rage I felt, that pure unadulterated rage. I wanted to wipe the Ngarnji people from the face of the earth. I forgot the lepers, Whistler, and my protesting conscience.

Make no mistake: this frontier war was one of hard, angry, uncompromising men meeting hard, angry, uncompromising men, but our weapons were better.

CHAPTER THIRTY

*Blacks were rushing to all points only to be driven back with a deadly
fire. One big fellow, over six feet, rushed towards the boy and I. I
dropped him in his tracks with a well-directed shot. Later on, when
we went through the camp to count the dead and despatch the wounded,
I walked over and was astonished to find, instead of a buck, that I'd
killed a splendidly built young lubra about, I should judge, sixteen or
eighteen years of age. The bullet had struck her on the bridge of the
nose and penetrated to the brain. She never knew what hit her.
When the melee was over we counted fifty-two dead and mortally
wounded. For mercy's sake we despatched the wounded. Twelve more
we found at the foot of the cliff, fearfully mangled.*

TO BORROW A LINE from the great poet Banjo Patterson, 'There was
movement at the station for the word had passed around.' That
observation held true in this case, only this was not a hunt for brumbies,
but for men. For blood to pay back blood, and the stakes were death.

There was no Man from Snowy River, but the 'cracks' who gathered
to the fray were hard men indeed: Pigweed Harry, M.C. Smith of
Borroloola, Lynott, Weldon, McLelland, Gallagher, Campbell, Mooney,
Lister and others. Seven reliable station black boys added to the total.
Twenty-two men in the party all up.

Every white man and woman in the Territory was baying for blood.
The NT Times reported that Ted Lenehan had been simply going about
his business on the station when he was ambushed and killed by blacks.
I knew that wasn't true, but I also knew what had to be done. I would
stand with my mates. That was all I had.

We set off on horseback, with our Snider rifles and Martini-Henry
carbines, on the trail of eighty men, women and children. We found the

main camp deserted and tried to cut them off from reaching the rugged fortress of the Abner Range. Too late! They were travelling fast and knew the land like the backs of their hands.

Some of the old lubras could not keep up. Ignoring them, we climbed the escarpment, leading our horses, no mean feat in gorge country. Every yard I rode I felt the murderers' eyes on me, the flaked stone heads of their spears aimed with deadly force.

Late in the day we came upon a couple of native children finishing off a wild honey 'sugar bag' in a tree. Knowing that the native camp must be close, we tied the two children together and sent them back to the station with a boy as escort.

After scouting out the Ngarnji encampment, we settled down for the night at a nearby spring, but saddled up as soon as we saw the morning star. We dismounted and crept closer on foot, surrounding our targets, who were sleeping near a precipice in that rugged country.

When one of them sat up and stretched, the act seemed so natural and innocent that I had to remind myself of how they had hacked my mate's head from his body with a stone knife. Smith and the police boy next to me fired, then we all joined in. The tribesmen woke quickly and tried to retaliate but ours was a deadly fusillade and their spears no match.

Afterwards, counting the dead, I hid my shaking hands, and swallowed down the sickly slime in the back of my throat. We drank rum around the camp with the smell of the bodies we were burning reeking like an abattoir.

I knew that this was an ending and a beginning. My thoughts extended no further. Some moments in life are like that. Nameless but overriding emotions, maybe an unconscious recognition that the way has been lost somehow, fighting their way out from the cloak of rum and mateship. I did not know what I would do but was smart enough to hear the bells of change.

The next day I rode to the station homestead and asked for my cheque.

CHAPTER THIRTY-ONE

What a tragic scene was being enacted around that waterhole! Maddened cattle, some blind with thirst, moaning and walking through the water, being too far gone to drink. Up the bank they went and wandered out on the downs. After the drought broke, we found that some of them had wandered six miles out from the river before dying.

THE TRACK TO HALL'S CREEK was an ants' trail of men pushing wheelbarrows, loaded-down Chinese coolies from the Palmer River Fields, and families in wagons. Few of

these wannabe gold-miners were prepared for the hard road they had chosen.

Malarial fever killed many of these gold-seekers. Outlaws and desperate men rode by alone or in gangs, raiding 'soft' targets if the opportunity presented itself. The lonely tracks were also watched by the remnants of the tribes: grieving, hurting, lashing out in pointless retaliation that only brought more men with guns.

I joined the flow of gold-hungry travellers across the Territory to the diggings. I was used to hard living, and enjoyed the company of larrikins and hard-nuts; at the Elsey, Katherine, and on the trail itself.

Something had changed inside me. I was tired of making money for powerful men in drawing rooms and offices across the southern states. Just as there was no share in the Durack family's fortunes for a hired hand like me, there was no share in the McArthur River Station that I had bloodied my hands to help clear. To Amos and Roberts my life was no more important than that of the Ngarnji people I had killed.

Never again would I see an employer in the same light. I was a free agent, a hand for hire. I was curious to see if, with a pick and shovel, I could strike it rich without too much hard work.

The Hall's Creek field centred on the junction of the Elvire River, Spring Creek and Hall's Creek, all tributaries of the Ord. It was rich in pockets, but with fifteen thousand prospectors arriving on the fields, it didn't last long; the real heyday persisted for only a matter of months.

I stayed for the peak, and in that time I learned enough about gold digging to assist me in my mining ventures later in life. I was no richer when I left than when I arrived.

Bored with dry-blowing gravel I went back to stock work. I made contact with my old mates from the Durack Trek, and soon renewed my acquaintance with some of them.

My first job in Western Australia was at Ord River Station, and there I heard the story of how Big Johnnie Durack had been speared and killed on his run. My mate Duncan McCauley had been speared also, but not fatally. Jerry was dead, and some of those original stations had already been abandoned or carved up.

I didn't stay in one place for long. For the next eight years, I worked short stints across the north, a few months here and there, with long breaks in between.

Most of the time I worked as a ringer, sometimes breaking horses or droving. I worked on Brunette Downs again, then Eva Downs and VRD. I did my job, but with the knowledge that the rich consortiums that owned these places were not my friends.

I wasn't above killing the odd bullock, or even stealing an occasional horse, provided they were station stock, and not the property of another ringer. The manager of Brunette at one stage, Ginger Roberts, gave me a job because he reckoned it was better than having me ride around the run pinching cleanskin horses!

I worked on one of the Territory's most picturesque stations, Auvergne Station on the Victoria River, originally a Durack holding. I remember that a stone spear head was embedded in the old homestead door from an attack, and that the ringers there were never safe. Next came a stint on Austral Downs Station as Head Stockman.

In 1889 I took a job as horse-breaker, then stockman at Lake Nash on the border between the Northern Territory and Queensland. The worst drought in history, however, saw us setting off with the surviving herd of 4000 head, for the last remaining waterhole on the Rankin River.

We reached it with cattle dying all the way, and then saw terrible scenes as the surviving beasts gorged themselves on water and then went down on all fours to die.

More death, more darkness.

Martin Costello, son of the owner, the Durack's relative John, lost his favourite horse, a beautiful thoroughbred that had borne him all the way from Goulburn, New South Wales. That expensive stallion was gored and killed by an enraged bullock before our eyes, and it was all I could do not to sit and weep along with him.

Dead cattle. Dead Men.

I was on Brunette Downs when a black boy called Cupid stabbed a stockman, Bob Hamilton, to death. Bob, it seemed, had defended himself with a butcher's steel. We arrived on the scene to find Bob dead in his bunk and Cupid spilling blood like a human sieve. Before our eyes he walked outside to drink from a puddle, and fell forward, having finally bled to death.

Soon afterwards my good mate Fred Jeffereys went missing at a waterhole near Tennant Creek. Usually known by the nickname 'Wonditta,' Fred was twenty-five years old, a grand horseman, bushman, and no feast or famine could change the cheerful smile he always wore.

We found his body beside a waterhole. The Wagai tribesmen had first speared Fred's boy, whose bloated carcass lay in the water. Then they had broken Wonditta's arms and legs, and left him in the sun to die slowly. This time it was personal.

For every bone in Wonditta's body a Wagai warrior bit the dust. I hated myself. But I did what my heart told me to do. And all the time I just wanted her back, but I did not know where she was.

CHAPTER THIRTY-TWO

On over big ironstone ridges; dark caverns, black and forbidding looking, then through a forest of coral cups from the size of a cabbage up to forty feet high, stems two feet through, like champagne glasses. The great feeding ground of fish of all species and the home of some of the best actors of the deep. In some places myriads of fish, red and silver schnapper, white fish and others will swarm around the diver, looking curiously in his face glass.

OVER TIME, the gold rushes that created an insatiable market for beef, moved elsewhere. Distance to markets was one great burden to the Territory station owner. Redwater Fever was another. The Northern cattle industry went down on three legs, then two. London speculators sold out. Stations closed. The strongest and best-funded survived, and I'm pleased to say that Tom Kilfoyle's Rosewood Station was one of the stayers. All, however, cut costs and reduced their workforces. The day of the black stockman: supreme horseman, hardy, and working for blankets and rations, was upon us.

Besides all that, I'd had enough of station work. With a small nest-egg, I shifted west to Broome. An hour after riding in, I visited the post office, where I found a letter from my sister Nellie. It had been redirected from Katherine, and the post mark was some eight months old when I sat at the Roebuck Hotel on that shady verandah to read, a glass of cool ale at my elbow.

My Dearest Brother Charlie

I have so much news I scarcely know where to start. You will have seen that I'm posting this letter from good old Yorkshire, far across the sea from you.

Marion and I sailed on the Royal Mail Steamship Ormuz, landing in London in a scarcely believable six weeks. With some help from Uncle Henry we were able to sail saloon class. The dining halls were the equal of any ball room. Not your style, dear brother!

Arriving in London, we took the train north to meet William, at Murton, where he is now the Colliery doctor. Murton is a grey town of drizzle and sleet, brown brick terraces in rows back from the coal pit. I don't think you'd like it. William lives in the doctor's residence, within earshot of the coal drops, where wagons are loaded with coal all day and night. The coal dust blends with the constant light rain to create a dark stain on everything from urchins to windows.

Each morning William walks down the Terrace to his surgery, where he treats not just miners but their families, catering to the usual illnesses as well as immunisations and childbirth. Accidents at the pit are common, and William is called upon to treat horrific injuries, many of which prove fatal.

As you can probably imagine, dear Charlie, William is still a passionate weekend cricketer, bowling and batting down the order for Murton Colliery in the North Durham League.

As for myself, do you ask? I'm now working as a probationer nurse at Bethnal Green Infirmary, London. I have to admit, dear brother, that it's a gruelling schedule of duty and instruction. I have also to report that a man is courting our sister Marion. John Bryden Hawthorne is a surgeon, a classmate of William's from Edinburgh University. I do suspect that they'll be married soon. Wouldn't it be grand if you could come over for the wedding!

I must close on a sour note. I am worried about Mother now that she's alone. I don't know how she is coping with the loneliness of life without a husband, or any of us. She's living in Brunswick, now. Do please write to her.

Be safe, dear brother. Marion will write soon, I am sure. Give her time, she still loves you, deep down.

Your loving sister Nellie

I winced at the suggestion of attending an English wedding. The idea of sitting in a church in a stiff collar did not appeal to me. Murton sounded dreary, into the bargain. Besides, it was far from certain that Marion would welcome me.

I wondered if I was jealous of William, and his important job. Perhaps just a little. Brotherly rivalries die hard but still I would not have swapped his coal town for my open-air life.

When I had finished reading, I borrowed paper, steel pen and ink from the bar and wrote a reply, before heading back to the post office to send it. It's strange how as a man gets older he thinks more and more of his childhood home and of those who shared it with him.

Living in Broome, I became fascinated by the pearling luggers that came and went from that peaceful bay. I spent many an evening at Guntheame Point gazing at the milky blue sea as the sun sank into the waters, the luggers returning, sails limp in the late afternoon calm.

Sometimes I fancied that I saw the tall ship Ethel May sail majestically into Roebuck Bay, Gracie standing at the rail. In those daydreams I imagined that her Californian husband was dead, and I invented hundreds of ways in which this might have happened. Mutiny was my favourite invention, with Gracie's husband shoved overboard on a dark night, preferably with multiple stab wounds so he would never come back.

One day I saw a beautiful half-caste girl who reminded me of Gracie. I saw her on the street and stopped mid-stride when I saw her. She was very young, only twelve or thirteen, and I did not attempt to talk to her. But that night, lying in my swag in a camp out of town, I thought back to Gracie and wondered if I had been naive about her ancestry.

Had Billy Higgins known immediately, what I refused to acknowledge, because I could not face the thought that the girl I loved had Aboriginal blood?

Long after midnight I had connected all the evidence. Her brown skin. The hair-straightening. Her rich brown eyes. Her mother must have been black. This realisation did not make me want her less, but it gave rise to a new flood of emotions. The blacksmith had worked hard to keep her heritage a secret, but it was true, and I guess I had always known it, deep inside.

Meanwhile I was busy pondering my next move. The idea of making money still appealed to me, and at that time the pearling business was a goldmine for smart skippers who knew their stuff. Fortunately, I had managed to save enough money to throw in with a partner, a local businessman called Stanley Piggott, to commission a lugger. The keel was laid by the firm of Chamberlain, down in Fremantle, currently overrun with orders for this fast-growing business.

My boat was called *Mona*, and she was a worthy vessel, almost fifty feet from stern to bow, with a stout cabin, diving platform, and davits for the tenders to hang. She had two sturdy jarrah masts, with a lug sail set on each.

I was no seaman back then. In order to become one, I set off on a shake-down cruise with a case of whisky, a skeleton crew, and an old Malay skipper who I found at the pub as my teacher. We sailed on the flood tide, bound for Cygnet Bay, King's Sound, in a golden dawn.

We reached the pearling grounds without too many mishaps. There I picked the brains of every skipper I met. After some practice dives that netted a few bags of shell, we sailed back to Broome.

By the time we dropped anchor in Roebuck Bay, I had made and learned from every mistake it was possible to make. I counted myself a competent beginner. Not only that, but I was learning to love the sea and the picturesque coast.

I engaged a Jap diver, provisioned the lugger, and headed north again. For six years we brought pearls up from the deep. Some years prices were good and we were lucky. Other years we scraped the last of our bank accounts to keep the *Mona* afloat. One day, my diver, Muchisuki, working in water twenty-three fathoms deep, stayed below for too long, and stopped responding to signal tugs on the lifeline.

It took an hour to bring up his lifeless body, and there was not a mark on him. A mystery that was never solved. Apart from the tragedy of losing a man I respected, his death put financial pressure on the enterprise.

With no cash to employ another diver I took on the role myself, and the man who once roamed the savannah and open woodland of Australia's north, now worked the bottom of the sea. Up to three miles a day I wandered underwater, collecting shell and placing it in a netting bag.

I had run-ins with eighteen-foot-long sharks and huge diamond fish that became entangled in the lines, dragging a helpless diver behind in their panic to be free. Despite the dangerous work, I soon proved that I could do the job profitably.

For three and a half years I carried on the dual roles as skipper and diver, but pearl theft by employees was a constant problem, and shell prices were tumbling. I had women in those years; some who stayed in my bed for months before they sailed away to ports unknown. One or two accompanied me on the lugger for weeks at a time. Yet, with Gracie I had found something so wildly delicious that nothing else would compare. I hungered for her, and the life I lived, it seemed to me, was just a shadow of what it could be.

When the Boer War broke out I was already washed up. I had started drinking more, and for the first time my gut was hanging over my belt. Mona spent more time at anchor in Roebuck Bay than chasing pearls.

Storm damage suffered off the Lacepede Islands in '99 was the final straw for both Mona and my partnership. Our London insurance company had, unbeknownst to us, gone belly up, and we decided on a cut-price sale rather than an expensive refit. Besides, I had to move on. The world was calling me.

CHAPTER THIRTY-THREE

As we turned to gallop off, a fusillade of bullets from the house greeted us. One of my boys was shot dead out of the saddle, the other boy's horse was dropped from under him, and my horse reared into the air, fell and rolled over on top of me. About a dozen Boers then rushed out of the house and surrounded us and marched us up to the farm. On a seat at the table was a young fellow about twenty, a veldt cornet (lieutenant) in charge of the party. He asked me several questions, which I answered evasively. Whilst we were talking the boy was taken out, stood against the wall of an outhouse and shot dead by a firing party. They then stripped me of all my clothes and boots and turned me adrift.

IN 1899, WAR BROKE OUT in South Africa. Jumping at the chance to try soldiering, I boarded a ship for Singapore, where I'd heard that a regiment of colonials was being formed. This fell through before I got there, so I continued on to Port Elizabeth, South Africa.

I caught a train to Bulawayo in Matabaleland, where a Captain Bull was recruiting men for the First Imperial Light Horse, a South African unit financed mainly by gold money from Johannesburg.

I and fourteen others were outfitted with horses and brand new Lee Enfield rifles, then marched for nine days through the veldt. When we arrived at Tiger's Kloof, a colonel by the name of Briggs lined us up and examined us one by one. In my mid-thirties then, I was older than most of the others, but many were more experienced in matters of organised warfare.

'Have you seen active service before?' Captain Bull asked the first man in line.

'Yes, the Zulu Wars, at Isandlwana and Rorke's Drift.'

'Jolly good show. Wounded?'

The man slung his rifle and lifted his right sleeve to show a caterpillar-like scar, white against his tanned skin. 'One of the fuzzy-wuzzies got me with his assegai, sir. Managed a lucky shot and took his black head off, or I would have been staring at my own guts sir.'

The others laughed, and the Colonel moved down the line. 'What's your name?'

'Henry Wilde sir.'

'Good name for a fighting man, where have you seen service?'

'The Matabale uprising sir.'

'Glad to have you with us.'

When he came to me, he looked me up and down curiously. 'So Gaunt, you're an Australian, they tell me?'

'That's right sir.'

'I don't imagine you've seen any action then?'

'I was a drover in Australia sir, we fought a frontier war with the blacks.'

'You'll find this a little different to plugging natives, Gaunt. The Boers are better shots than you, and they know this country like the backs of their hands.'

'I'll hold my own sir.'

'Will you? And what makes you think that?'

'Because I can ride a horse as good as any man, I can shoot, and I'm used to living rough.'

'Very good then, we'll see.'

Remounts were always a problem for the regiment, and when I and some others managed to surround and pen a herd of wild Boer ponies, I was one of the few who could tame them. Unofficially at first, I was soon the designated rough-rider for a battalion of mounted infantry.

Reaching the rank of sergeant, I lived the life of a soldier, fighting at the pivotal battle of Colenso. I was also, during the war, captured, and went close to being shot dead by my captors.

My sister Marion's brother in law, Bob Hawthorne, was at that time a businessman in Barberton, giving me a handy place to recuperate. I did re-join my regiment, but my heart had gone out of the fight.

When it was all over, I have to say, I had even less regard for brigadiers and generals than I did for wealthy men and their corporations.

I took a ship home to Melbourne, arriving at Ma's little rented house in Brunswick. She shed tears at the scar of a bullet graze I had copped at Colenso.

'You could have been killed. Promise me Charlie, no more war.'

Fifteen years had passed since I'd seen her, and the small signs of strangeness I had noticed back then were now more telling. She did not travel to my sisters' weddings, and never met her grandchildren, instead remaining at home in Melbourne.

While I was there, word reached us that Uncle James had died from a short illness in Queensland. He had for many years lived on Bierbank Station, working at the hotel there as bookkeeper and odd jobs man for the owner, Ridley Williams.

I was a beneficiary of my Uncle James's will, a goodly sum of money. Finally, I had the funds I needed to begin a search for Gracie in earnest. I had convinced myself that she would be alone somewhere, widowed and yearning for me.

Uncle James's money was the impetus for what would become two decades of international wandering. Two decades of trying to recapture how it felt to be fifteen-years old, riding north through Western Queensland and into the wilderness of the Northern Territory. Of how it felt before I had the blood of so many on my hands. Rum helped, as I have said, but I dealt with my demons by wandering first and foremost.

I was adventurous by nature, fearless and adaptable. I had learned the trick of humility, and was not above learning from anybody.

Those early and abortive forays into gold mining at Hall's Creek and also, a little later at the Wandi Goldfields, must have infected me with a dose of gold fever. I spent many of the following years sailing the seas and chasing the yellow metal.

In British Guiana, I made a rich strike on the Comawaruk River. I worked it for six months, took a good haul of gold, but then, abandoned by my labourers and with greedy men circling, I packed up and left.

I sailed into San Francisco for the first time, on the *Barracouta* from Panama. Given that the Ethel May was registered in that city, I knew that it was the most likely place to find Gracie. The clipper, I learned, was still sailing, but had not been home for years. Some suggested that the owner and his wife now lived abroad, perhaps the Far East.

After an unsuccessful search, I headed north to Alaska. There I became a prospector, horse dealer, and ran a team of huskies and malamutes. I rescued a camp of men on the frozen Skeena River, and I proved myself as capable a man on a frozen frontier as I had in Australia's tropics. Still, it wasn't enough, and I moved on.

I returned to America, living the life of a hobo, riding boxcars from the Texas panhandle to California, evading 'bulls' – the police – and outlaws. I still panned for gold when I got the inclination, and never missed a chance for making a buck: selling grog to Indians or trading horses. On winter days with no food or shelter I would sometimes knock on a respectable door to ask for help; cadging meals in return for tall stories. This was when I refined my yarns, remembering the detail for that far off day when I would write them down.

In Arizona I sat drinking in a bar while a gunfighter walked in and shot the bartender between the eyes, then a Mexican policeman, and finally the dealer of a card game. The gunman was killed, in turn, by an Arizona Ranger who just happened to be strolling by, while I examined the floor from a prone position under a table.

I would not hesitate to chop wood or cart hay for a lone woman with a tribe of brats, but avoided, like the plague, lifting a finger for the rich. Everywhere I went I saw the excesses of the 'owner class', and made it my business to extract what leavings I could from their fine tables.

It was for them that as a young man I had killed, clearing cattle stations that were often later abandoned. I relived each death in my nightmares, and saw plenty more grisly scenes to fuel these nocturnal horrors.

I rode into the Yaqui Valley of Mexico, armed with a .30-30 Winchester and a Colt .45, just in time to see the Yaqui Indian tribes embark on a spree of killing. The white governor of the state had confiscated their ancestral lands and sold them to Mormons from Utah, who arrived in their hundreds to settle on the purchased land.

I was caught in the middle like a filling on a sandwich while the Mormons were slaughtered in their hundreds, and the government Rurales rode in to retaliate. I watched from the safety of the hills while these soldiers, armed with modern weapons, all but wiped the Yacqui Indians from the earth. The only remnants of that proud and warlike race were locked away in prisons where they continued to die like flies.

I lived in Hawaii, for a time, sailing a small freighter in the choppy seas between the islands of Kalawao, Kauai, and Maui. Was this paradise on earth, a diet of fresh seafood, the company of exotic Polynesian women and salt air enough for me? Of course it wasn't.

After a year or two I quit the boat and travelled on, as if pushed from the memories behind me. The ghosts of the black men and women I had killed did not haunt the shadows overseas like they did on home soil, but I was always looking, never finding. In every port I scanned the silhouettes for that clipper ship, the *Ethel May*.

I pined for the love of my life. The sensual guide of my youth.

I received a letter from a nursing sister in Cheltenham, Melbourne. It was a hard thing to read. Ma had been charged with public drunkenness and fined two shillings and sixpence by the magistrate. She had been admitted to the first of several benevolent asylums – the institutions in which she would spend the last decade of her life.

CHAPTER THIRTY-FOUR

What a time we had, clawing canvas that was almost frozen stiff, fingernails bleeding, the wind howling furiously through the rigging, tearing the sails out of our numbed hands.

FOR THE FIRST TIME in many years, I shipped back to Australia on the *Euryalus*, visiting my mother in her room at the Cheltenham Benevolent Asylum. Her eyes shone as I told her of the things I had done and seen, but there was a vacancy in her gaze. It was the loneliness that got to her, I believe. Three weeks I stayed in Melbourne, living in a boarding house, drinking and entertaining front-bar tables of factory workers with my stories, strolling the streets of my youth and visiting my mother once or twice a day. I gave her a feather from an American bald eagle and a small nugget from the Yukon.

Both went in the glory-box that had adorned her dresser for as long as I could remember.

When I wasn't there, Ma wandered the corridors of the asylum like a ghost, with tiny shuffling steps and spectacles too large for her shrunken face. Sometimes, when other residents had visitors, occupying the common room in their Sunday clothes, talking and laughing, she would creep up and sit and listen. Just to be part of them for a while. Not to be lonely. To feel connected again.

I loved her, but could not stay there. I was getting older, but still felt youthful and impatient for adventure. That drive for the sensory pushed me out again. Within weeks I sailed from Sydney, bound for Singapore and the Far East.

In China I took on work as a customs official at Shanghai.

In Burma I voyaged on a steamship up the Irrawaddy to the city of gold, at Mandalay. One of my old mates from the pearl industry in Broome was running a fleet of divers on the islands off the river mouth, and I put in a month or so for old times' sake.

I sailed back to San Francisco; that beautiful city of streetcars and hills. I was in my late forties by then. I purchased a half share in a skiff, and took to hunting Dungeness crab in San Francisco Bay.

Like most of the other boats, each morning when the harvest was done, we moored at Fisherman's Wharf, and there set up a fire under a cauldron, boiling the day's catch and selling the cooked crabs in paper cups to the people of the city who wandered down to buy.

After the hard labour of hauling in pots, selling the catch was both social and fun; standing in the sunshine looking down along the piers or out to Alcatraz Island. It was on that wharf that I met a man whose books had given me much pleasure, over the years: Jack London, the novelist.

'You want to write?' he asked, squeezing a cylinder of crab flesh out from a spindly red leg. 'Then start at the beginning and don't stop until it's finished.'

'I've done so many different things,' I told him. 'I don't know what to leave in, and what to leave out.'

'Simple,' the great man said. 'Write about the things that changed you. Ignore the rest.'

I enjoyed San Francisco. I made friends and lost them, but there on the wharf, even while I was talking to mayors and liars, hard-bitten old seamen and lads off on their first adventures, I gazed out to sea, scanning for the sails that might belong to the *Ethel May*.

I never did see that clipper, for they were becoming rare by then, but one day on the San Francisco waterfront, my hands running with crab juices, I did see Gracie one last time.

Down below the docks each day, on the shore and some pontoons set up by the city, a hundred or more sea lions would loll around in the sun and shallows, chase each other, and entertain the tourists who came in from the mid-west. Farmers with their wives and children gaped at these huge creatures.

Over several months I had trained one huge old bull to come up on to the wharf, at which point he would take crabs from my hand. I called him Nero, and sometimes he let me pat his head after he'd finished the first crab, always angling for a second. The sight of my fingers, inches away from his befanged jaws, had the crowd clapping and whistling with delight.

'You think he's scary,' I told the crowd, 'then you should see the 'gators back home in the Territory.'

The feeding became a tradition, carried out at noon each day, just as the crab-hungry tourists and locals started to arrive in numbers. The trick made my partner and I the most popular crab-sellers on the wharf, and after a while we were selling for other skippers as well, and had a thriving little business.

The strange thing was that when I saw Gracie I didn't recognise her at first. Always with my eye on the crowd, I noticed a party of four come strolling down from Nob Hill. There was a young woman, arm in arm with her beau, a well-dressed young cove with all the confidence of youth and wealth. Behind them walked a lady on the cusp of middle age, and a silver-haired gentleman with a patch on one eye. I was busy clapping to get Nero's attention at the time, so didn't let them distract me for long. The crowd was gathering, to watch the big sea-lion eat.

It didn't take long for Nero to waddle and flip his way up, and I climbed atop a barrel with my crab hand outstretched so the crowd would see how big Nero was, his body rippling with blubber, as powerful as any bull.

After the second crab, with Nero stubbornly resisting my efforts to pat him, I looked into the crowd, at which time I noticed the silver-haired gent walking on past with the older woman. The young woman stopped to watch the fun, and she looked up at me, with the morning sun making red highlights on the jet-black hair that fell from her bonnet.

I saw her face then, and it stopped my heart. She looked the same as she had on the day she had first ridden up to me on the cattle drive. By some magic she had not aged by one day.

'Gracie!' I shouted, then dropped the crab I was holding above Nero's head. He caught it in mid-air, swallowed it down, then roared so loud the crowd squealed with delight and backed away. For my part I had forgotten crowd and sea lion alike, stepping down from my barrel and onto the wharf.

'Gracie?' I hurried up close, looking through the rouge and eye-liner to the light brown, perfect skin of her face. She wore clothes that would have been worth my half share in that crab boat.

It was her! Exactly as I remembered, as beautiful as breath. Youthful and sweet.

She gave me a look of distaste. 'My name is Elizabeth,' she said.

I knew I had moved up too close to her. But I couldn't be wrong. How could I mistake those lips, that skin? I reached out to touch her and she pulled back.

'Steady on there, buddy,' said her beau.

'Gracie?' I shook my head as if to wake myself from a daydream. 'I'm sorry. But I'm so sure that I know you.'

'My mother is called Grace,' the young woman said. 'She's over there. Is it she that you're thinking of?'

As I followed the direction of her eyes, the older woman turned to look at me. She was eating crab from a paper cup. Then it hit me in the guts like a kick from a horse. It was her.

I walked over, as if in a dream.

'Gracie?'

Her eyes widened. 'Charlie?'

Who did this to you? I thought. For thirty years her image had been frozen in my mind. Who stole the youth from your eyes? Your vital skin. Who robbed us of the best years, and brought us together like this, where everything is impossible?

'Charlie?'

For a long time we looked at each other. The familiar. The new lines. The changes time had wrought. Her family stood back. They and the rest of the world receded.

I understood her thoughts as she looked at me. I was not the same. I had lost teeth, others had yellowed. I limped a little from old injuries. Those small incapacities that don't slow a young man down much, had started to accrue with interest – a crook hip from when a stallion called Black Ned threw me in the yards at Auvergne in '91 – a bad back from a falling spar on the schooner *Matterhorn*, sailing downwind in the roaring forties with a cargo of phosphates in '07.

Twenty-eight years had passed since we made love on a horse under the moonlight. It felt like a century. Tears formed in the corners of her eyes, and fell slowly down her cheeks. 'How can it be?' she asked. 'How can you be here?'

'I've thought about you … every day,' I said.

'Me too,' she said. The tears, one after another, reached the edge of her chin and fell to the dock.

I nodded towards the beautiful young adult who was so much like Gracie at the same age. 'Is she … my daughter?' I asked.

Gracie nodded her head. 'Does she know that?'

'No, Charlie. She doesn't know.'

I choked up. 'Why didn't you wait for me?'

Gracie's face hardened. 'Do you think I had a choice? Besides, what kind of life was there for me in the Territory?' She nodded towards our daughter. 'They would have taken her away from me, into some home for half-castes in Pine Creek or Alice Springs.'

I shook my head. 'I didn't care … didn't even know. You were just the girl I loved. It was years before I even realised that you …'

Her eyes met mine as she finished the sentence. '… were black. That's what you mean isn't it?'

I nodded, unable to speak while she went on. 'Dad tried everything he could think of so I could grow up as a white girl. But some things are just – inside you. My mother was a Yirrganydji woman from Cairns. Why do you think I had to straighten my hair every day? At school I had to pretend that I had Javanese blood just so no one knew the truth.'

'You never told me.'

'I never told anyone.'

'I didn't care. I still loved you, and I would have married you.'

'Sure, Charlie, and I would have lived alone in a tiny house in Camooweal or Katherine while you droved your cattle and popped your head in once or twice a year.'

'Your father died,' I said.

'I know.' She crossed her arms in front of her chest.

There was nothing more to say. No way back through the years. No point to anything more than that momentary reconnection.

When she had collected her family and left I sat down on my barrel and wept like a child. The next day I found passage on the first ship to sail from that place. The cruelty I had dealt out was returning to me in the harshest form.

The Great War had recently broken out. I pictured the Light Horse in action on the desert sands, but I was too old to join, and war no longer attracted me.

On April 17, 1916, at forty-eight years of age, I boarded the SS *Persia* in Honolulu, heading back to Australia, after receiving a letter from William saying that Ma's health had deteriorated.

She died five days after my ship sailed, of heart failure and pneumonia. Her death certificate stated that she was seventy-two years old, a widow, with two sons … *nothing further known*.

My brother William, after twenty-five years of breathing colliery air and treating the sick, died in 1919. Nellie and Marion were both widows by then, living together in York Avenue, Hunstanton, in Norfolk. It was a desirable location, just back from the sea, both women helping to raise Nellie's two children, Wilfred and Nellie.

I too, was finally running out of steam.

Returning to Australia, I tried unsuccessfully to revive my mining skills in Kalgoorlie, Western Australia. I lived in Cloncurry, Queensland for a year. I loved the landscape there, but my true home was the Territory.

I settled in Pine Creek, handy to Darwin but still wild enough for my taste, where a man could live rough without too much attention from the government.

I wanted to be as close to my country's heart as I could. For if there was anything, apart from Gracie, that I had truly loved in my life, it was the Australian bush.

CHAPTER THIRTY-FIVE

I sowed my seed and reaped a crop of wanderlust, leaving a legacy of world-wide experience and empty pockets.

BUT WHAT OF THAT BLACK MAN, Bismarck, who slipped a garrotte around my neck? Well I fought him for a long time, so close I could smell the opium on his skin, and the drying sweat of withdrawal. Finally I managed to push him to the floor, my neck bleeding badly, but I was able to fetch my rifle from the wall and train it on him.

I aimed the foresight at his chest. I knew that no one would blame me if I pulled the trigger. Self-defence. There would be no charges or trouble. After all, what was one more black life?

I found myself in a cold sweat, my hands shaking with rage and confusion.

'Why did you try to kill me?' I shouted. 'What have I ever done to you?'

'Why did you come alonga here?' he asked.

'I live here.'

'No. Why you come alonga blackfeller's land?'

'It's my country too,' I said. I was born here. I wanted to understand it, to be part of it.

'You put a gun alonga my country, a bullet in it. Killim' blackfellers, all gone.'

It was true. I could not argue. I let that old black man stand up, then put the rifle on the table, barrel facing towards me. 'I don't care if you kill me,' I said to him. 'But I can't undo what I have done.'

That drug-crazed old man must have thought I was insane, for he backed away and left. Later he was sentenced to eighteen months at hard labour for robbing my shack, and would have copped more if I had pressed charges for his attack on me that night.

But it was that murderous old thief who brought the words to my fingers and saw me tapping away, night after night. The pages piled up, and slowly the story came to be told. Working at my kitchen table in Pine Creek, I have poured my memories forth into words. I have written, along with this personal account, twenty or thirty articles that have been published in the Northern Standard newspaper, edited by Fred Thompson, bringing me a touch of notoriety.

I live on the Two-mile Creek, outside of Pine Creek, in a one-roomed hut, with corrugated iron walls and roof. Here I drink rum, dream, and occasionally yarn with the few old mates from the track who have survived spears, old age and hard living. Most of the time I am alone.

Pine Creek isn't a bad town, with Jimmy Ah Toy's store and the Playford Hotel. Just down the road lives my cruel and wild old mate from Borroloola, the skipper of the *Good Intent*, Maori Jack Reid.

The blacks who have managed to avoid both missionaries and rifles, live in humpies along the railroad track. The locomotive, 'Leaping Lena', arrives twice weekly on churning iron wheels with a blast of steam, bringing mail, stores and news. Every week the leper truck passes by, taking afflicted Aboriginals from the missions, communities and stations up to the leper colony on Channel Island.

Everything made sense before I started this writing business. It has changed me in ways I never would have expected.

Today I do a very surprising thing.

I leave the hut before sunrise, taking special care as always to secure the lashings and lock up the place. First I walk into Pine Creek, to the little cemetery. I find the grave of Walter Oswald. I know exactly where it is, but I have never been close to it. I bring no flowers, I just stand and stare. After fifty years it is unkempt, the headstone sinking wonkily into the ground.

When I turn away, I know what I have to do.

Frances Creek is a long way, but old buggers like me, all bone and skin, can walk all day under a hot sun. I reckon on eight or nine miles, and arrive not long after noon. Old mines are ghostly, lonely places, and this one is worse than most. The Chinese are long gone, and even the poppet heads have been cannibalised for heavy timber.

Iron junk remains in quantity, and partially ruined stone walls lie here and there, with rusted sheets of roofing iron. Clearings where nothing grows surround old shafts, and the wind moans in the she-oaks along the creeks.

Fifty years have passed since I walked this track with Whistler, searching for the blacksmith. The day I killed two men. I walk up the hill, remembering how I felt.

The ruins of the forge are better preserved than most of the rest. I feel like a fifteen-year-old boy, a youthful heart, and relive the parade of passions that pursue a man. These tides that push him to eat, to love, to kill, and all the petty jealousies that drive him on to deeds that he must eventually regret.

I walk into the threshold of the forge, though the bough shed that stood behind it is gone. I must have my mouth wide open, for I swallow a fly, and try to cough it out until my lungs feel like they might burst.

Lost in a daze, I wander back out and stare across to a leafless woollybutt tree. It must have once been grand, but now it is grey and purged of colour, like me.

I walk across, and kneel, looking up at the sun and the shadow. I know that this must be the place where they buried him. On my hands and knees I start to dig. When the going gets hard I use a stick to chip my way down

It takes nearly an hour to reach the first of Whistler's bones. I dredge up half-century old tears from the ducts in the corners of my eyes. This rush of emotion surprises me. I bring out the bones and stack them up beside the hole. There are many more than I expected, but I sift through the soil with my fingers so as not to miss even one tiny finger bone.

I take off my shirt and use it as a sling to carry Whistler's remains. They are light and I am still strong, and on that endless night-walk the tears do not cease to flow, as if I have somehow tapped a spring deep inside that will never run dry.

I walk on through the dark hours of night, but I am a bushman, one of the best. Finding my way is second nature to me.

Walking east to a creek I know, the country gets uneven under my feet. Dawn is breaking when I find myself in gorge country, a narrow waterway in limpid pools between steep walls of stone. I use my penknife to cut a sheet of paperbark from the trees along the water's edge. Reverently I place Whistler's bones inside and wrap them into a parcel.

Then, just as I once saw a group of Whistler's people lay one of their own to rest, I climb those cliffs until I find a deep niche, where I push that precious package into the recess. I drink freely of the water of that little creek before, unburdened in more ways than one, I turn my head for home.

It's the strangest thing, but somehow, laying Whistler to rest in the way of his people helps to fend off the loneliness. The aching, biting, gnawing loneliness of my final years.

EPILOGUE

We are nearing the summit of the Great Divide and when we cross
down into the Valley of the Unknown, you'll wear a silk shirt with
a brass band in your wake, and I, perhaps following, wear a sack
cloth, a dingo as chief mourner, and the crows in their funeral garb sit
on the branches comparing notes as to when the feast begins.

BY 1936, I am having trouble writing my stories. Cataracts have made one of my eyes all but useless, and the other is failing fast. An operation in Katherine hospital doesn't help much. After also suffering chest pains, I move to Darwin to access medical treatment. Doctors diagnose an inflammation of the heart, and I sail for Brisbane on the next steamer.

My sister Nellie, by now a woman of some sixty-four years, arrives from England on the *Thermistocles* to see me. This is a kindness I don't expect. After all, she was only a child when I first left home. Still, blood is blood, and she sits on the starched white sheets of my bed, listening to my stories, and filling me in on the twists and turns of her own life.

Marion, it seems, has still not forgiven me. I don't blame her. She was perhaps the only one to see me as I really was.

Nellie has her children to go back to. They need her more than I. So finally, with no living family in Australia, I find myself discharged from hospital, a broken old man with nowhere to go.

On the dazzling shores of Southeast Queensland, North Stradbroke Island hems in Moreton Bay, her rocky headlands protecting that waterway from the rolling blue Pacific swells. This island is the site of an institution built for the unfortunate, the lonely, and the mad.

In early 1937, being just the twentieth inmate recorded for that year, I am admitted to the Dunwich Benevolent Asylum on North Stradbroke Island's west coast. They take me across Moreton Bay in an iron ferry. I share a smoke with the deckhand, watching the low, grey-green hills, studded with trees, grow in stature, as my new home draws slowly closer.

The institution itself is a series of elevated dormitories spread over a grassy slope. By the time they issue me with my grey pyjamas, the facility is already some seventy years old, with ten thousand graves deep under her sands.

There are dormitories for women, the insane, and the decrepit. The most capable of the men live in a tent city further up the hill, for the facility is overcrowded. There are black men here too. Strange wanderers of the plains. The invaded, the lost, and the empty. In their eyes I can see that they know what I have done. I hear the dead in the sea breeze on the high bars, and their spirits roam the cells.

What a joke on a man who once rode the grasslands and roamed the oceans! Who could shoot and fight, hold his own on any horse that ever breathed, and sail downwind in a gale without fear. Here, at night, there is the lonely howl of the lunatic, and the chuckling drunks brew their devil's mixtures with raisins and water, delight on their faces as they gather in their undead, unliving circles.

I live in a dormitory with forty cots, each white and identical. The walls of horizontal planks are also painted white. A window lets in the sun and air every third bed or so, and feeble globes hang from the ceilings. The boat comes twice a week with supplies. We limp, we forgotten people, to the dining hall for porridge, stews and rice, with sago pudding on Sundays. A Sister of Mercy called Sister Tuesley visits every day. A black spot appears on my face, and within weeks it has grown to the size of a coin. The doctors call it a rodent ulcer – but to me it is just a cruel trick of time and my old body – my skin is turning black.

My heart condition worsens, but there is no return to Brisbane hospital, just a transfer to the infirmary. I am smart enough to know that the end is close.

Every morning after tea, I hear voices raised in song from out on the lawns. One of the Sisters of Mercy has started a singing group, made up of geriatrics and lunatics. The women have voices like scratched glass and the men sound like growling old dogs. They sing songs that remind me of home, of childhood. Songs of the bush and the Church, and they remind of the night I dug up Whistler's Bones.

My story ends in this island prison. The nib of my pen moves urgently on the paper, for Death draws near. I feel his sickly breath on my cheek. I've never run from a fight, and I won't do so now.

My final visions are clear. I see Whistler driving Death's wagon, with Big Charley up there with him. Tall spearmen lope alongside, vengeance in their eyes.

I close my eyes and let them come.

Annotation from Sister Tuesley (handwritten in pencil):
When I entered Dormitory Three on my rounds on January the 29th,
1938, Charles Edward Gaunt had passed away. I took these pages
from his hands after he died.

Reference List

Note: Charlie Gaunt's original articles can be found at the National Library of Australia collection on Trove. They were published in the Northern Standard Newspaper between 1931 and 1936.

Books

Barker, HM. 1994. *Droving Days*. Perth: Hesperian Press.

Buchanan, Bobbie. 1997. *In the Tracks of Old Bluey*. Brisbane: Central Queensland University Press.

Byrne, Geraldine. 2003. *Tom and Jack: A Frontier Story*. Fremantle: Fremantle Arts Centre Press.

Cole, Tom. 2013. *Hell West and Crooked*. Sydney: HarperCollins Australia.

Cooper, John Butler. 1931. *The History of St Kilda: From its First Settlement to a City*. Melbourne: St Kilda City Council.

Corfield, WH. *Reminisces of Queensland 1862-1899*. Brisbane: H Pole and Company Ltd.

Durack, Mary. 1959. *Kings in Grass Castles*. Sydney: Vintage Classics.

Forrest, Peter and Sheila. 2005. *Vision Splendid: A History of the Winton District of Western Queensland*. Winton: Winton Shire Council.

Fox, Matt J. 1919-1923. *The history of Queensland, its people and industries: a historical and commercial review, descriptive and biographical facts figures and illustrations, an epitome of progress*. Brisbane: States Publishing.

Frazer, James George. 1986. *Marriage and Worship in Early Societies*, Volume 2. Mittal Publications.

Gaunt, Charles Edward. 1934. *Old Time Memories and Adventures*, by Charles Edward Gaunt. Carlisle WA: Hesperian Press. (Collected articles)

Gunn, Jeannie. 1962. *We of the Never Never*. London: Hutchinson.

Guthrie, Tom. 2014. *The Longest Drive*. Victoria: Tom Guthrie and Grampians Estate Wine Company.

Hothouse, Hector. 1970. *Up Rode the Squatter*. Adelaide: Rigby Limited.

McLaren, Glenn. 2000. *Big Mobs: The Story of Australian Cattlemen*. Fremantle: Fremantle Arts Centre Press.

Moffat, Angela G.I. 1987. *The Longreach Story: A History of Longreach and Shire*. Milton: The Jacaranda Press.

Pike, Glenville. 1972. *Frontier Territory, The Colourful Story of the Pioneering of North Australia*. Glenville Pike.

Raynes, Cameron. 2000. *Very Hard, That Day. The Moral Sub-Text of Aboriginal Oral History from the Western Victoria River Region*, Northern Territory. Darwin: CDU.

Roberts, Tony. 2005. *Frontier Justice, A History of the Gulf Country to 1900*. St Lucia: University of Queensland Press.

Newspapers

Brisbane Courier, The Queenslander (Brisbane), The Sydney Mail and New South Wales Examiner, Geelong Advertiser and Intelligencer, Ovens and Murray Advertiser, Powlett Express and Victorian State Coalfields Advertiser, Sunderland Daily Echo (Northern England), The Adelaide Observer, The Age (Melbourne), The Bendigo Advertiser, The Durham Advertiser (Northern England), The Geelong Advertiser, The Melbourne Argus, The Northern Territory News and Gazette, The Northern Territory Standard, The Prahran Telegraph, The South Australian Register, The Western Champion (Blackall), The Longreach Leader, The Mount Barker Courier and Onkaparinga and Gumeracha Advertiser

More books by Greg Barron, all available at
ozbookstore.com, good bookshops, and Amazon's Kindle store.

The Time of Thunder
Two men from across the world, linked by history, converge on Arnhem Land
in a bid to solve the fifty-year-old disappearance of a man, and to uncover a
Korean War mystery that will have global ramifications.

Camp Leichhardt
Ben Mulligan went down to the Roper River fishing camp to fish for
barramundi and find peace. Instead, he found himself caught in a cruel
conspiracy, and ultimately fighting for his life.

Outlaw: The Story of Joe Flick
Born in the battleground between two races, Joe Flick is a promising youth. A
series of incidents lead him on a path that ends in a bloody tragedy in one of
the most beautiful environments on earth.

Red Jack and the Ragged Thirteen
The Ragged Thirteen were a band of thirteen larrikins who put their stamp on
Australian folklore with their devil-may-care journey across the wild Northern
Australian frontier.

The Last Days of Dom Sebastian
Archaeologists Francis da Costa & Nicolá Massane follow a trail of relics &
myth, uncovering a tragic love story, and a voyage past the edge of the known
world to Australia's Kimberley.

Galloping Jones and other True Stories from Australia's History
Galloping Jones was a bare-knuckle-fighting larrikin who could tame any
horse. Moondyne Joe escaped prison using an ingenious plan that made a
whole colony laugh. Based on the popular Stories of Oz history posts, these
sketches of Australia's past will inform and entertain you. Above all, they will
remind you of what life was like, in the days before highways and smart
phones.

Scan to visit ozbookstore.com

www.ingramcontent.com/pod-product-compliance
Lightning Source LLC
Chambersburg PA
CBHW030629110726
47901CB00002B/378